Fate Cannot Stay:

Book Two of the Mage Saga

By D. Art & Kay McKinney

Chapter 1

The fall day was bright but blustery. From time to time, a particularly strong gust of wind could be heard whistling through the exterior parts of Hona Castle, as though the castle itself were lamenting the passage of summer and the coming of winter.

It was a strange place to be sure. Built nearly a millennium and a half ago, it was intended to be a military hard point to defend the interests of a fledgling kingdom, Empleheim. The city that grew around the castle, Niado, would eventually become the capital city of Empleheim. As the nation prospered, the castle was renovated to hold more of a governmental role.

The barracks were subdivided into regal quarters for reigning monarchs and their esteemed guests. A large, elaborate library was added in place of the internal training yard to signify Empleheim's commitment to recovering the lost knowledge of the golden age, a time of unparalleled prosperity under the guidance of the great mages. The castle still retained its massive underground storage vaults that were designed to allow the soldiers and adjoining civilians to weather a lengthy siege. It was genuinely a place that afforded a great sense of security, with its high walls, fortified gatehouse, and singular, conical tower that provided a spectacular view of the surrounding city, of which it was the tallest point.

At its peak, Empleheim had rediscovered the power mages, whose first members established the Order of White Mages. Prior to this, most, at least in Empleheim, thought that the mages were simply icons of fiction, entities created to entertain the fancy of the simple and the uninformed. Yet the white mages demonstrated convincingly that reality was indeed stranger than fiction.

In the early days of the Order, one young mage rose rapidly to prominence. He was substantially more gifted than any that had come before him, and soon he became the order's representative figure. White mages served dual roles as healers and banishers of darker entities.

With the rise of the white mages in Empleheim, there also arose black mages in the western neighboring kingdom of Daninamy. Being diametrically opposed to one another from a philosophical perspective, fighting between the Order and the Black Dragon, as the black mages called themselves, became regular along the kingdoms' borders. Neither kingdom want to become involved politically, and while supporting their respective mages financially, no proper soldiers were ever fielded in the altercations between the two groups.

It was the gifted young white mage of Empleheim who ultimately prevailed against the Black Dragon, sending them into hiding, and it was for this act that he was awarded the honorary title of the White Lion of Empleheim. Adderil Windslo, by mundane name, was not enthusiastic about such pomp, and even less so when the Order of White Mages changed its name to the Order of the White Lion. He was given personal quarters in Castle Hona, and a special chamber was carved from the castle's storerooms for the purpose of his personal study.

This was all, of course, ancient history, and only a few years later, in a single ill-fated moment, the entire nation of Empleheim vanished. Or more accurately, the infrastructure of Empleheim vanished, leaving its populace dispossessed of material goods, roads, buildings, fences, and the like. The empty country became the center of ill will, and if there was a curse to be uttered, it would invoke the vanishing of Empleheim as the cruelest of fates.

Fearing for worse to occur, the people became refugees among their neighbors, and no one strayed again into the obviously cursed land of Empleheim. It remained a wilderness for nearly a millennium, until it returned as suddenly as it had disappeared, not aged a day more than the day it was lost. Every town and city positioned where it had been so long ago, but without any population to be seen.

Niado's streets were now overgrown, and its once lively markets slowly crumbling. No customers visited its businesses, though many still had non-perishable goods on their shelves. The farms at the periphery of the city grew wild things, and animals were now the sole inhabitants of the city's outer residences and estates.

Castle Hona was a beautiful exception. Small children ran and played in her courtyard, while older children and teenagers sat in the library learning from the sigil mage Iekaruga. Of the library's three floors, the first one had been converted to a sort of open schoolroom, where the more scholarly of Hona's denizens took turns teaching the younger ones the basics of knowledge, whether reading, writing, history, or as was a recent addition, the principles of mage power.

Keena wasn't so sure she felt comfortable with her children learning about how to become mages, but her husband had assured her that it would be better that they understand it earlier, than for them to make some grave mistake later while stumbling through it.

A humored smile came to her face as she looked over at the White Lion of Empleheim, the only person alive to have known Empleheim when it was populated. He was now pretending to be the creature he was named for, chasing their youngest children around the bedroom they had converted to a nursery. It was counterintuitive to her why he might have been given such a fierce title among his people. He was a healer, a gentle, reasonable, and humble man. He was nothing like a lion at all, with the exception that he was incredibly courageous. Achron, as he was currently known, had to be courageous in the face of helping her raise the twenty-four children she had born him, plus the two they had adopted.

At the moment, the delighted sounds of their eight youngest children laughing and running from the "lion" made it obvious that he wasn't really suffering with this particular burden. Dorra, Iekaruga's rather recent wife, had marveled that Keena's six-month-olds were already up and toddling about. Of course, it was only fair that Dorra was impressed; she was human, and the beautiful gift she now carried for Iekaruga, his first child, would also be human.

Achron was human as well. Keena and their children were not. They were Fearian. Like all Fearians, the tips of their ears were pointed, and as they were from the forest caste, they bore silky, long-haired manes that started at the top of their heads and flowed down the center of their backs to their other distinctive Fearian feature: their tails. Their tails were roughly the same length as their arms, and uniformly fluffy in a two-toned brown, lighter at the base, with darker discreet bands near the tips.

Outward physical features were, of course, not

4

the only things that separated Fearians from humans. Keena and Achron's children took a whole year to be born, compared to a human's nine months, and they were born in litters—hence, the eight identically aged little ones that played excitedly with their father.

In some ways, they developed much faster than human children, though they started out life much smaller. However, unlike humans, the girls would not be of childbearing age until around age twenty, and would remain fertile for no more than fifteen years. Practically, this meant that their physical drives would be mostly dormant until they became of age, at which point, for a female Fearian, life was nearly unbearable without the company of a male.

Humans differed in these respects, being slower to develop things like walking and independence, but their girls being faster to reach maturity, and retaining fertility for more than twice the number of years. A Fearian might have twelve children in two litters in a short window of time, while a human might have twelve children over thirty years. But the result was the differences didn't really amount to a significant variation between their population structures. Humans didn't typically have twelve children, and neither did Fearians, as their fertility was substantially lower than that of their human counterparts.

Keena was one of the few people who understood the differences between the two, as she was one of the few people to have inhabited both worlds. The Fearian side and the human side looked remarkably similar in terms of geography, flora, and fauna, but the culture, cities, and manner of life of the Fearians and the humans were markedly different. There were still human conventions and ways of thinking that confused her.

Despite Castle Hona's presence on the human side, there were more Fearians there than there were humans. Partially because, through a mechanism she did not fully comprehend, Keena had given birth to an unprecedented four litters, with the last being the largest. She was still trying to grasp the idea of being a mother of twenty-four children by birth.

Keena knew a small sense of worry about the future of her children. They lived in practical isolation in the abandoned city of Niado, surrounded by the ruins of Empleheim. For good or ill, practically no one knew of their existence. This was concerning, because it meant that there weren't many prospects for her children to have families of their own.

There were some, of course. Mekki, the older of the two sea caste Fearians that her mother had volunteered to aid them when Keena was expecting her second litter, had born her own six children to Viwy, the peculiar mist mage who had been conflicted about whether he wanted a Fearian a full head shorter than himself as a wife. The man was clearly no longer conflicted about the issue. But this was only sort of helpful, given that Mekki's children were only about a year older than her own youngest.

Keena's eldest were now fifteen, and she feared for the difficulty the girls would face in a few years without being properly spoken for. It certainly wasn't an insurmountable challenge, but it was an unnecessary one among her own kind. She supposed that perhaps things were not entirely without recourse. Her daughter Sheena was more than a little taken with the odd Fearian boy they had found in the ruins of the great mage's tower, Creed by name.

He wasn't the best fit for Sheena, in her opinion. As desert caste, Creed had a tail as long as he was tall, a fine, thin affair with a tuft of black fur at the end. He was also of a much darker complexion than the rest of them. He, of course, did not have an obvious mane, as it was the practice of male Fearians to keep their manes shaved from the neck down.

However, these superficial exterior features were not what made him unsuitable in her mind, but rather that Creed was melancholy, and often brooding. He was also a powerful energy mage, and something that he had called a prodigy. Despite his youthfulness, he had been trapped in the mage tower outside Niado for some three millennia. Unlike modern Fearians, he was a rather rude and surprisingly uncivilized person. Despite her reservations, there was a subtle sweetness in the way Sheena was able to bring out of his own dark reflections by boldly asserting his involvement in what could almost be a normal life. Yet Keena had trouble shaking the feeling that he would subvert her precious, bubbling daughter with his constant negativism.

Sheena's littermate brothers, Dane and Kraysin, spent a fair amount of time with the two young apprentices that Iekaruga had brought with him. They were sisters, Fearians of the mountain caste with stouter tails, short manes, and tufts of fluffy hair at the tips of the ears. While Prinial was a model child to be envied, her sister Ahnya, on the other hand, was such a wild and flamboyant person that Keena didn't really want to see Kraysin around her.

It didn't help her confidence that both girls had accidentally found a way around the normal reality that Fearians of the female persuasion had no access to their power until after they reached maturity, and this was not until after their wedding night for reasons Keena chose not to entertain. Prinial was a good girl, but Ahnya was the one who was the impressive mage. As a grand water mage, Ahnya could do some rather incredible things with water, most of which ended up more troublesome than helpful.

Not that she didn't have her own esoteric

children. Addie, who was the same age, had always been a troublemaker, but one particularly badly executed joke had caused the girl such grief that she was now much more reserved. This centered on Mekki's younger brother Pyx. The boy, or rather man now, was an indispensable aid to them, and though he was Addie's senior by some seven years, she would not deny him her hand in marriage if he sought it. Given the constancy of their company since the ill-fated altercation that almost left them without him, she assumed that was not too far off.

The other two among her oldest litter were of much more concern in light of the reality of their isolation. Rin was a beautiful redheaded girl with a darker red mane and soft brown eyes. However, unlike the boldness of her hair color, she was incredibly shy. Keena and Achron had tried to encourage her to become more outgoing by assigning her a room with the other person they discovered at the ruined tower: Hanni.

Hanni was human, yet also Creed's cousin, though he seemed to dislike this notion since she did not recognize him as such. Keena didn't know the details, but Hanni had had almost no memory at all when she came to Castle Hona, not even knowing how to speak. Yet, she was a wonderfully sweet child, and she had regained proficiency in matters of everyday life in a rather short period of time.

Even with a roommate less social than herself, Rin remained shy, though she had formed a close kinship with Hanni. Still, it seemed that Rin would simply not overcome her shyness no matter what they did. Given the paucity of suitors vying for her attention, it was likely that Rin's life would be would lonely and difficult. It almost pained Keena to think about it, but it was strangely less painful than the last of the oldest litter.

Emeril was a good and obedient daughter, but she was also incredibly strong-willed. She wasn't interested in families or children; no, she just wanted to be like her father. She pined after becoming a white mage, and it was mostly out of concern for what she might do if ill-prepared that the children now received instruction on such matters.

The earth mage Seifer, an orphaned human young man who had adapted quite well to living with them in Hona, had made the mistake of showing interest in Emeril. She had told him to his face that he was wasting his time, because she had better things to do than entertain his company. Keena groaned that her own daughter could be so rude, but she felt a little vindication in that it was probably Achron's influence and not her own.

Emeril was willful, but she feared that the girl was not prepared for the powerful driving forces that she would experience when reaching fertility. It could be overwhelming, which was precisely why Fearians as a people did not allow their daughters to go unwed any longer than necessary. And this was again Keena's concern for her own. Achron seemed less concerned, but then again, he wasn't so familiar with Fearian life, or even women in general.

Keena chuckled at the thought, but watched him fondly, as she could not think of anyone she would rather be with. She didn't know how they would help Rin, much less Emeril, and that still left their eighteen other children, but Keena felt some relief in knowing that Achron would not leave his children in need. He was faithful to care for them, regardless of the circumstance, and regardless of their needs, just as he cared for her.

She reached up and gently brushed the beautiful carved opal flower that hung at her neck. All these years into their marriage, it still seemed impossibly wonderful that someone such as herself, a lowly Fearian woman, could find herself bound to someone as incredible as Achron.

Chapter 2

"I don't know if I really want to do this." Rin glanced with concern at the spiral staircase before looking back at the others. Creed didn't seem to want to be there either, but then again, he often didn't look like he wanted to be there.

Sheena attempted to placate her. "Oh, come on, Rin. You can't just spend all your time cooped up in your room or the library with Fishy! You need to get out and do new and exciting things!"

Sheena gestured to the tabby cat that sat on the floor next to Rin. They had found the animal as a stray, and Rin had made it her duty to care for it. She was also the one who had dubbed it "Fishy" based on its interest in dried fish. The animal had responded to her care by following her about the few places she went beyond her room. Rin didn't really like to socialize, and often she found that the others just got in trouble by doing "new and exciting things."

Rin looked to Dane and Prinial for support, but found none as Dane asserted, "I want to see the inside of the tower, and maybe we will even catch a sight of the high queen's entourage."

Prinial nodded, adding, "There might be some old tomes up there. It's worth at least looking."

11

They were expecting a visit any day from the high queen of Fearia, or as they would have called her had they had opportunity to know her, Grandmother. Rin didn't know how the high queen and her attendants would be able to visit them without the gate between the human side and the Fearian side being activated, but the queen's messenger hadn't seemed to consider this a problem.

While it was true that some Fearians possessed the power to slip between the two sides of the one world, this was normally an individual exercise, not a shared one. The only instance of a shared movement between the sides was that of their parents, who still shared the unusual bond that had formed between them shortly after they first met.

Rin thought the stories she had heard of her parents' adventure that led to their union were wonderfully romantic, but only a wistful dream for a timid girl like herself. Her timidity was part of the reason she was tagging along on this trip to the top of the only tower in Castle Hona. Naturally she was not entirely without moral support, and she looked to Hanni, who merely nodded for her to proceed with their daring, if quasi-permissible, venture.

Technically they were prohibited from the tower because it was not maintained. The timbers that supported the upper loft and the wooden walls that formed the apex of the tower were in questionable condition. With the many other things going on about the castle, no one had been up into the tower to repair it or even check what was up there, for as long as any of them had been at Hona. Or at least, that was the rumor circulating among the children.

Sheena led a less than enthusiastic Creed up the long, wooden, spiral staircase. Rin followed, trying not to wince at each step that creaked as she ascended, with

Dane and Prinial close behind. The stairs were anchored between the outer wall and a central wooden beam made out of a series of securely connected poles.

It was a long climb to the top of the tower. The wooden decking of the floor was quite dusty, with enough cobwebs to weave a fine silken gown. The disturbingly thin boards that formed the wall paneling of the tower were starting to separate from one another, and narrow bands of sunlight illuminated the inside of the room.

Rin was both relieved and disappointed that there wasn't much of anything in the tower. There was an upholstered chair whose stuffing was shredded, a badly weathered desk, and a mostly empty bookshelf with only a few odds and ends on its dust-coated shelves. Dane stepped tenderly, as though he feared falling through a weak spot. "It's pretty obvious no one has been up here in a while, but too bad there aren't any books here."

Prinial nodded. "True. But what is that over there against the wall?" She pointed at an oblong object, wrapped in tattered cloth and tied with a decayed cord.

Creed looked at it warily. "I don't know, but maybe it's a bow or something for defending the tower?"

Sheena moved to the window on the far side of the tower. "You have got to see the view from here. It's amazing!"

The others joined her slowly, not immediately forgetting the dilapidated state of the structure. Though Rin was hesitant to leave the security of the heavy wooden landing, she really did want to take a look. Even Fishy sauntered over, his nose twitching at the air. Rin sighed and gingerly made her way to the window.

The view was indeed breathtaking. The tower was the tallest point in the city of Niado, and at least in the direction the window faced, nearly the entire city was visible from the high vantage point. After a couple moments of hushed excitement, Dane and Prinial wandered off toward the mysterious object on the other wall, while Hanni, followed casually by Creed, moved toward the desk to investigate it.

Sheena started to follow, but only took a few steps before stopping to look curiously at an upturned crate that sat on the floor near the wall. Rin approached her as she said, "What do you think is in it, Sheena?" The crate was inverted, but there was some kind of cloth and maybe wool wadding that was visible through the slats. Fishy sniffed at it suspiciously.

Without any warning, Sheena tipped the small crate over on its side, and half a dozen dark rats scurried out from it in a panic. They weren't the only ones who panicked. Rin screamed in fear and jumped back sharply—an ill-advised maneuver. She landed on the weathered planking next to the window and broke cleanly through it, falling backwards from the tower.

The others froze in shock. Fishy, ignoring the scampering rodents, whirled and leapt through the opening in the wall. Rin had little time to think as air raced past her, but she saw Fishy come flying out of the tower and fall toward her. Midflight, the cat's body shimmered, and it took on the form of a horse-sized gryphon. The creature was two parts majestic, and three parts terrifying.

It compressed its body into a sleek profile and dove at an incredible speed. Rin would have screamed when it caught her firmly in its talons, but she was winded by the sudden deceleration as it spread out its wings, turning its dive into a swooping glide seconds before they would have struck the castle roof. Powerful wing strokes brought them back up into the air and carried them rapidly away from Castle Hona and Niado.

The others stared out the window as the gryphon and Rin flew off into the distance toward the sharp-tipped mountains known as the Dagger Peaks. Dane spoke first. "W-what just happened?"

Prinial muttered with resignation, "We are in big trouble, that's what just happened."

Sheena expressed a slightly less focused opinion. "Um, am I the only one that thought gryphons weren't real?"

Creed shook his head. "They aren't. They don't exist at all."

Amid expressions that suggested that he was less than intelligent, Creed stood his ground, waving his hands defensively. "No, seriously, they don't. That wasn't a gryphon, or a cat. That was a metamorphic mage."

Hanni turned toward the stairs as she spoke softly but calmly. "Rin needs our help. We must inform Father of what has transpired."

The others appeared reticent to admit to their disobedience in being up in the tower, but they also knew that the only person among them who could reliably track Rin was Viwy, and they could not tell him without telling Achron.

* * *

Achron scratched his head with mild consternation as he looked blankly at the guilty teenagers before him. He repeated their story in summary, because he wasn't sure if he followed it accurately, or even had all the pertinent details. "So, you were in the tower you're strictly forbidden from being in."

They nodded with some reluctance, and he

continued. "And while you were up there, some rats startled Rin, and she fell from the tower."

More nods. "And then her cat jumped out after her, turned into a gryphon which Creed claims means it's a mage, saved her from falling, but then carried her off?"

Sheena spoke nervously for the rest of them. "Yes, Father, that would be an accurate description of what happened."

Achron sighed. "All right, you are all in a bunch of trouble for sure, but that is going to have to wait until we rescue Rin from an uncertain fate. In the meantime, stay out of the tower. It's obviously not safe." His command was greeted with whimpers and murmurs that could easily have been interpreted as "yes, sir."

Achron dismissed them, saying, "I am going to retrieve your sister now, but don't think this means you're off the hook." They dispersed from where they had been standing more or less at attention in front of him, and he added, "Creed, you're coming with me."

The young Fearian stopped midstride a few steps behind Sheena, and turned as he exclaimed, "What! Why?"

Achron ignored his bluntness to the point of rudeness. "Because you're the only one who has extensive knowledge about metamorphic mages."

Creed said nothing, but merely nodded. Sheena, who had paused to learn what would become of Creed, turned and touched his shoulder as she spoke softly. "Be careful, ciega." Creed gave her a nonchalant shrug, but she smiled as she returned to vacating the room. Achron wasn't sure what to make of Sheena's predilection for referring to Creed with a Fearian word normally reserved for a very close, affectionate relationship between siblings. Technically he was a brother by adoption, but there really wasn't any warrant for the word, as far as he could tell.

Hanni waited outside the door as he left the room, her expression serious. "I want to help Rin, too."

Achron put a reassuring hand on her shoulder. "Thank you, Hanni, for your concern. I am glad you want to help, but this is a task best accomplished by as few people as possible. Please, just wait here until we return."

Hanni looked disappointed, but she replied without any deviation in vocal tone. "Yes, Father."

Achron smiled kindly at his adopted daughter. "Don't worry, Hanni. We will be back with Rin before you know it . . . and hopefully before your grandmother gets here."

She nodded and left. Hanni was a sweet girl, and it pained him that she still bore the hideous band of runes down one side of her otherwise lovely face. It was like a brand or scar that spoke of her previous condition as a type of experimental slave. As a consequence, she had no memory of who she was in the past prior to Achron's delivering her from runic enslavement. Along with Creed, she was from the era of the war of mages that took place immediately after the end of the golden era, some three millennia ago. Also like Creed, who was an energy mage, she was a very powerful mage. Strangely, though she had forgotten her identity, she had not forgotten how to wield her mage power.

This was something that few other than Achron knew about. Even Creed, her cousin, was under the impression that she had lost her ability to perform as a prodigy red mage. The prodigy, as he was still coming to understand, was the result of a rare occurrence that permitted humans, and to a lesser extent Fearians, to tap into their power at an incredibly young age. As a consequence, they developed into powerful mages rather early in life. In hindsight, Achron thought that he had also probably been a prodigy, though without any initial guidance he did not come into his own power until he was a late teenager.

Still, as far as skill was concerned, Achron was among the best of those who lived in Hona Castle. But that wasn't going to make a huge difference in his current problem, as being a white mage, he was forbidden by oath from taking human or Fearian life. This was his secondary motive in bringing Creed along. The young man had been a commander and combatant in the mage war, and if push came to shove, he might need his aid to rescue Rin. Not that he wanted things to get ugly, but that rescuing his daughter wasn't an optional outcome.

Entering the kitchen to find supper preparations underway, Achron found Viwy dutifully toting a basket of potatoes. Seeing Achron's expression, Viwy set the basket down and turned to him. "Achron, what's with the stern face?"

Achron admitted begrudgingly, "We have a problem, an emergency of sorts, but we should talk about it in private."

Viwy nodded and followed him as he continued on toward the nursery where Mekki and Keena would be watching the youngest children. It was going to be hard to tell them of Rin's odd abduction without inducing at least some sense of panic, unwarranted fear of domestic animals, and possibly just a little bit of annoyance, as he could be reminded that he was the one that gave permission for the keeping of said stray cat-turned-gryphon. Despite this, Achron felt a mild urgency, unsure as he was about what exactly was going on.

Chapter 3

Rin's shock and terror faded to a numb fear in the course of the long flight to the mountains. The creature's mighty wing strokes brought them to a soft landing on a steep cliff ledge that bore a deadly vertical face on the one side, and an enormous gaping cave on the other. The gryphon released her from its large talons, and Rin scrambled away from it and to her feet.

Uncertain whether Fishy was a gryphon disguised as a cat, or a cat disguised as a gryphon, she backed up slowly, wary of the ledge. Rin spoke with a tremble in her voice. "F-Fishy! Take it easy—"

She stopped abruptly, flinching as she realized two other large, menacing gryphons loomed just inside the shadow of the cave opening. They emerged into the light, eyeing her, but mostly glaring at the other gryphon. They let out a low warning growl.

Unlike the gryphon that had abducted her, they were both a drab brown-black color. Fishy, as a gryphon, was marvelously patterned, with the feathers of his neck and incredible wings bearing stark black striping against a brilliant white background. Iridescent gold spots were centered in dark circles near the ends of the feathers.

The air around him was distorted as his form shifted again. Much to Rin's dismay, Fishy was now neither a cat nor a gryphon. The young man that stood in the gryphon's stead appeared to be a few years older than she was. He looked somber, and his plain clothes seemed strange by her standards. His shoulder-length blond hair was tied back from his face with a black braided cord, and he returned the two gryphons' stare with his own brown eyes. He raised his hand off to his side, making a fist at eye level.

The two gryphons mimicked his example, and shimmering momentarily, they took on human forms. Both were older, a man and a woman, of ordinary appearance. Though they looked a little doubtful, they both dropped slowly to their knees, paying homage to Fishy.

He turned partially toward her, his eyes fixed on the cave entrance, as he said in a distinct accent, "'Twould be best if you stay close to me. Most have never seen an outsider." Rin was speechless, unsure what to think at this point, but followed his suggestion.

Entering the cave, she saw it quickly became non-cavelike. The space was a complex series of large caverns, with rooms and corridors cut into the rock. Traveling through the place, she could not comprehend if it was some kind of enclave, or a large fortress built into a cave, or even a city. People plainly made great effort not to stare at her, and a few of them managed to succeed. It made her feel uncomfortable, which in turn made her suddenly realize something shocking.

As they were passing through a large tunnel, with dozens of humans coming and going, Rin gasped aloud, causing her guide to stop and look toward her with concern. She covered her mouth with her hand, her face flushing brightly, as she blurted out more loudly than she meant to, "Y-you slept in my bed!?"

Fishy turned his eyes away from her as people around them stared in shock, before realizing that it was inappropriate and hurrying along with their business. His own face reddening slightly, Fishy muttered, "Can we talk about that later?"

Rin felt horribly self-conscious, and ever so slightly violated, but simply nodded weakly. She couldn't exactly leave the place without some assistance, and as irrational as it sounded, she felt safer with Fishy than she did by herself. It seemed that not everyone's gaze was directed at her, however; a number of people practically glared at Fishy, as though he were more of an invader than she was.

In a quieter part of the confusing complex of caves and chambers, he stopped before an ornate wooden door. He reached out and knocked with a light tap. There was a scrambling sound on the other side, and then the door was thrown open, and a girl somewhat younger than Rin practically jumped at Fishy with a joyful shout, embracing him with the same fervor her voice carried. "Harku! I feared I would never see you again!"

Rin tried to be as small as possible. There was a certain unwanted sense of jealousy that even her former pet cat had someone.

They held each other in silence for a moment before the girl reluctantly let go of him. Harku inquired, "Arru, how are you? Is all well?"

She smiled meekly. "It's fine. Nothing changes here, Harku. He is still adamant that the traditions be kept at any cost." Harku grimaced, but said nothing.

Arru seemed to notice Rin out of the corner of her eye and turned to greet her boldly. "Oh, hello! I am Arru. What's your name?"

Rin looked at Harku, but he deliberately avoided her gaze, so she stated her introduction for herself, a little more crisply than was normal for her. "I am Rin."

Harku sighed. "I . . . I had to bring her here.

21

Please keep her safe. I have to go plead my case . . . again."

Arru looked at him with concern, and then back at Rin, before speaking with uncertainty. "He won't listen to you. And, well, you know . . . ."

Harku shuddered as he turned and walked away from them. "I-it just isn't that simple, Arru. Please keep her safe."

Arru nodded firmly. "I will, Harku. You have my word!"

He disappeared down the hallway, and Arru focused her attention on Rin. "Please, come in!"

Rin glared after her former domestic companion until he rounded a corner, and then nodded before following the younger girl through the door. The room beyond was a simple but pleasantly decorated sitting room, with two wide, open archways that led into other rooms. The one straight ahead was clearly a dining room, and the one to the right was a bedroom where the bed itself was cordoned off from sight by a wooden screen.

Arru led her to a large flat cushion on the floor next to a low table and gestured for her to sit. "Please have a seat. Would you like some tea?"

Rin spoke softly while her mind whirled about all that had happened. "Um, sure, that would be fine. Thanks."

Rin watched the young girl as she busied herself with preparing them tea. Arru seemed far too young to be having anything to do with Harku. She had long, lovely, red hair, not unlike Rin's, and lively brown eyes. It seemed odd to Rin, but Arru's skin was incredibly pale. She supposed living in a cave would have that effect on anyone, but it looked almost unhealthy.

As the girl returned with a wooden tray that had both teacups and a freshly steeping pot of tea, Rin asked,

"So you are also a gryphon?"

The girl laughed genuinely as she said with pride, "Yes, I too am a member of the gryphon clan, so I am a metamorphic mage. I am the only red gryphon among our clan right now." She poured some tea and handed it to Rin from across the table, and then poured her own before sitting down.

Biting her lip as if embarrassed, Arru admitted, "Of course, I am not nearly so powerful as my brother."

Rin tilted her head slightly. "Your brother?"

Arru looked a little surprised that the matter needed clarification, but she added, "Yes, Harku." Rin stared down into her tea intently, feeling especially sheepish about misinterpreting Arru's connection to Harku. Arru caught on to her change in demeanor and inquired, "Is there something wrong with that?"

Rin looked up, trying not to sound guilty. "What? Oh, uh, no, not at all."

Arru studied her for a moment and then sighed as she spoke apologetically. "I . . . I am sorry, Rin, for what my brother has done to you. I can make you normal again if you'd like."

Rin felt lost. "Uh, normal?"

Arru looked at her, incredulous. "Yes. You know, not having a tail, or pointy ears, or whatever that color difference is in your hair?"

Rin attempted not to be rude as she stated flatly, "What are you talking about? This IS normal. Your brother didn't do anything to me." She added in a low mumble with a sense of annoyance, "Other than infiltrate my private life as a homeless fish-eating hairball."

Arru missed the second part of Rin's comments, and shook her head uncertainly. "Are you sure? I have never heard of such things being normal for people."

Rin nodded as she explained. "It's normal for my people. I am Fearian." Arru still looked a little unconvinced, but Rin opted to change the subject. "What was your brother doing, leaving his family here to be off somewhere out in the middle of nowhere?"

The younger girl dropped her gaze to the table, a blush of the sort that showed deep personal shame creeping across her face. She opened her mouth, yet she said nothing for several moments, but then spoke without further provocation. "It's not something I want to talk about, but I think you have to know, since—well, since you might be able to help.

"My brother is the golden gryphon, the leader-to-be of our clan. But the clan's traditions mandate that he marry a red gryphon to assume his role as our rightful leader, and I am the only red gryphon left among our people. When our mother passed away from the sickness, he swore that he would protect me from any harm, but our father would not permit there to be an exception to the traditions. When it became obvious that he would have to marry me, he fled to spare me the shame of such a relationship. It is considered vile among my people for siblings to marry."

Arru sighed sadly. "Everything is so twisted, and I just don't think there is a good solution."

Rin was stuck on something else, and she mused, "Your brother just abandoned you here?"

Arru looked up to meet her gaze boldly, her face honest as she spoke in defense of her brother's honor. "He had no choice, for like my mother, I suffer from the sickness, too. Just a few hours' exposure to the sun is debilitating to me, no matter what form I take, and it seems that a single day in the sun could very well claim my life. I had to stay, and it's probably why the others are not keeping me under guard. I couldn't really find anywhere else to live in the darkness. Harku's power is exceeded only by his kindness and devotion. I don't deserve to have such a noble brother."

There was a brief lull in their conversation as both girls grappled with a reality so foreign that it was hard to even begin to comprehend it. After several sips of tea, Arru returned to the former topic. "Fearian, hmm. Where are you from?"

Rin started, "Oh, I am not from Fearia. I am from around here. Hona Castle in Niado."

Based on Arru's expression of confusion, she gave directional information. "It's not too far from here, south I think, in the center of a large, ruined city."

Arru looked more than a little concerned. "What? You mean you live in the cursed wilderness?"

Rin wasn't sure if they were thinking of the same place at first, but then she remembered her father's explanation that the entire land of Empleheim was gone for a millennium, and that some people interpreted that as meaning the land was under a curse. He had assured them that that was not true, and if anything, it was now a special place, because it was their home.

Rin replied simply. "Well, cursed isn't how I would describe it. It's where me, my family, and my friends make our home."

Arru looked away as she spoke to herself. "But . . . that place is forbidden, even to my people." Arru met her eyes again. "Rin, are you a mage?"

Rin tried not to sound disappointed. "No, unfortunately not. Father says it's best for now that we be content without mage power since we don't know . . . ."

Rin came to a stop, recalling she wasn't supposed to talk about it to other people. Only Father and their adopted brother Creed knew the details of it, but generally, she and her siblings possessed some immense power that had been sealed away since the golden age millennia ago. It was unclear what the power they contained could do, or even if it were accessible to them personally.

Shrugging, Rin finished a little awkwardly. "It doesn't matter anyway. I am Fearian, and Fearian girls don't come into their power until they are mature."

Arru appeared bewildered. "I am sorry, but I don't understand."

Rin felt embarrassed talking about such things with a younger girl who was a total stranger, and a human. She shook her head, focusing intently at her nearly empty teacup as she tried to dismiss Arru's confusion. "Oh, it doesn't really matter. I am just not a mage, that's all."

In the following awkward silence, the door to Arru's chamber was thrown open violently, and a regally dressed middle-aged man entered the room, along with two armed men, announcing bluntly, "Ah, this is where that worthless gold gryphon is stashing his ruse."

Arru rose to her feet. "Leave, Turric! You are not permitted in my room without permission."

He ignored her as he glared at Rin, who stood as well, trembling under the man's baleful gaze. Turric spoke with sharp contempt. "That sneaky little Harku will not play games with our sacred traditions. This metamorphized freak cannot be allowed to replace the rightful way of our people."

Defiantly, Arru approached Turric, putting herself physically between him and Rin as she spoke. "I said you are to leave my room! Don't make me tell Father about your poor behavior. Unless, of course, you think you can challenge my brother."

The man sneered. "Don't take me for a fool, Arru, and don't stand in my way." Arru didn't budge, and Turric struck her sharply across the face with the back of his hand, knocking her to the side. She staggered to her feet, and he gestured for her to be detained by one of the men with him. "It's a shame the only thing you inherited from your mother was her weakness. Some thought you could actually be more powerful than she was."

Blood ran from her nose as she strained against her captor, shouting, "You can't do this, Turric! Harku won't let you get away with it!"

Her words were ineffectual. Turric approached Rin, drawing a long, thin blade from his belt as he commented darkly, "It's a shame that Harku chose to adorn such a pretty face with those odd features—not that it will matter in a moment."

Rin backed away slowly, raising her trembling hands as though they might prevent him from doing what her imagination suggested would be her undoing. Rin couldn't really make her mouth utter anything more than, "Please . . . don't."

He didn't appear particularly concerned about her plea. "Don't worry. Whatever he said to you was a lie anyway. He has to marry someone else, especially now."

Rin longed to be home, in the comforting presence of family. She wanted desperately for her father to be there to help her. Her mind went to her closest confidante, perhaps the only other person she trusted with her life. Rin's back bumped into the wall, and she whispered, "Hanni!"

Chapter 4

Hanni sat on the edge of her bed, swinging her feet idly. She trusted Achron, trusted that he knew what was best, but she really wanted to go and help her sister. She missed Rin's ever-present quietness. Rin was a pleasant person, always eager to listen, and shared only things of value. It was Rin's general demeanor that gave Hanni encouragement when she struggled the most with her lack of any real identity. While it had been some time since Rin was the one leading the conversations, Hanni loved her sister for her longsuffering patience, and her willingness to just be there while she was regaining a working vocabulary.

It felt unfair that she could not join the group involved in Rin's rescue, but she also recognized that there wasn't that much she could add. Creed was a powerful energy mage, Viwy could find Rin as a mist mage, and Achron's abilities as a white mage were quite respectable. Hanni wasn't much use to them.

She knew now, having presumably learned it again, that she was a red mage. Fire was her second nature, her companion, and the most immediate outflowing of her power. It could be very destructive, which was her main reasoning in thinking that she had little to add to the rescue mission.

Though she could not remember her surname, even now, her power had never left her. It functioned like a reflex, and whatever she had done in the past, it was honed to a razor's edge. Hanni was a force to be reckoned with, even if she often felt like a nameless soul, purposelessly adrift.

Suddenly, Hanni felt her mage focus rise, that state of mind that permitted mages to use their power accurately, and with it, her perceptions of her surroundings. She slipped off her bed and took several steps forward as her power surged within her, which was odd, as it seemed to come unbidden of her will. It had never been outside her direct control any time prior, or at least any time she could remember. Fire embraced her out of thin air, blocking her vision of anything else, but then it faded, though the wealth of power within her only grew.

When the fire was gone, she found herself in a dimly lit room cut out of solid stone, nothing like her and Rin's bedroom in Hona Castle. A man carrying a weapon stood not far from her, and though he looked surprised, she immediately sensed that he was a serious threat.

Hanni wasted no time, and with a calm, cold, and calculated expression, she swept her hand through the air in front of her, leaving a floating trail of fire. The levitating flames rapidly condensed down to a metal shaft that bore six brilliant rubies in its head. Behemoth, the raging flame. A relic from the ancient time of the great mages, and her personal staff.

She reached out and took it from the air, the white-hot metal having no effect on her. She was, after all, a red mage, and her skin glowed with a red cast. It was gone from her mind that being able to summon her staff at will was the mark of a grand mage. Yet the short-lived classification system for mages was lost to all but

Creed, it seemed.

The armed man and his cronies backed away fearfully. In what would have been an authoritative voice were it not for its wavering tone, the man demanded, "Who are you?!"

Hanni had no need to answer the question, as a voice exclaimed, "Hanni? HANNI!"

She turned to see her sister Rin, and felt confused. Not just because Rin had been abducted, but because the fair red-haired Fearian was also aglow with a bright red luminescence.

Someone behind her cried urgently. "Look out!"

Hanni didn't even flinch. This warning was followed by a shriek of pain. Undetectable in the pale light of the room, the air around Hanni was hotter than that of any furnace, and for an attempt on her life to stand a chance, it would require mage work.

Hanni noted the red-hot dagger that lay slowly cooling on the floor before she spoke solemnly to the frightened man who clutched his burned hand. "I am Hanni Windslo of Hona Castle. Leave my sister alone, or your hand will be just the beginning."

The man backed toward the door, hissing, "You're trapped in here. You can't escape, little scarred witch!"

Hanni answered with a deadly calm. "You underestimate my abilities. I could melt the top off this place in the blink of an eye, and unless you and yours are magma proof, I don't think I am the one who is trapped." The man wasted no more words and bolted out the door, along with the two other men who were with him.

Hanni looked around the room thoughtfully. It was obviously someone's living quarters, presumably those of the young girl who wiped blood from her face while standing and staring at the floor, as though hoping not seeing Hanni would somehow make her own self unseen. Hanni relaxed and let go of her staff. It vanished much like it came, in a burst of flame.

She turned to Rin as the steady red glow faded from both of them. "Rin, I don't understand. How did I come to be here so suddenly?"

Rin shrugged, looking a little sheepish. "I-I don't know, either." Hanni nodded, and thought that they would probably need to ask Creed about it. He was the one that knew all the secrets of mage power.

She approached the other girl, taking a napkin from the low table as she passed and offering it to her. "I am Hanni, and you are?"

The girl gingerly took the napkin from her and held it to her nose. "Um, I'm Arru. Y-you're not going to hurt my brother, are you?"

Hanni looked at Rin with uncertainty. Rin grimaced, but then sat at the table, motioning to the tea pot as she said, "It's . . . complicated. Would you like some tea, Hanni?"

Hanni shrugged and took a seat next to her sister. "Sure. Father and the others will not be here until tomorrow sometime, if I don't miss my guess."

Arru joined them and spoke wistfully, more to herself than to them. "Your father is actually coming to rescue you? But how will they ascend the cliff, or get past the guards?"

Hanni dismissed her concerns. "Viwy is a mist mage, and can move across distances through the mist, and Father is a white mage who carries Tianna, the silver star, which bears the Aegeis."

Arru shook her head slightly, her eyes widening. "Just who are you people?"

Rin and Hanni smiled at each other and replied in unison, "Family." They both chuckled at the silliness of it.

Achron wanted to satisfy his curiosity as they rode swiftly along the overgrown main street of Niado. "Creed, tell me of the metamorphic mages of the mage war." Viwy inclined his head in their direction, eager to learn more of the lost past.

They were traveling north, on the few horses that they had acquired from previous trips for supplies. They were far more self-sufficient than they had been even a few years before, but there were still things that were not available around Hona Castle. Simple things, like salt and sugar and other sundries. Most of their food they grew themselves. It would have been a lot of work were it not for the efforts of Iekaruga and his apprentices. They had developed, with the aid of the reluctant earth mage-in-training Seifer, automated irrigation systems for their crops.

Creed frowned. "The metamorphic mages were cowards. Most of them fled to remote places to form secret enclaves. The few that became engaged in the war served as spies, since they could look like anyone or any animal at will, if they were skilled enough. They were sort of a necessary evil from everyone else's perspective, kind of the lowest denominator, regardless of how you looked at it."

Achron considered that before asking, "So, why would that particular metamorphic mage infiltrate us at Castle Hona? And for that matter, how come you didn't detect him?"

Viwy shrugged. "Well, I detected a cat, but I suppose if I had been suspicious of said cat, I could have properly identified him by looking at him through Arbik."

Achron knew that the man had no more reason

than the rest of them to suspect that Rin's cat Fishy was anything more than a standard feline. The relic staff that Viwy carried, Arbik, the yellow eye, gave him the ability to conceal and reveal truth in much the same way that Achron's own staff gave him command of the Aegeis, a perfect ward against any and all assault.

Creed responded to Achron's first question. "Eh, it's hard to say. Given how long ago the war was, it must mean that there is an enclave not far from here, and that things are not well at home. Frankly, it's shocking to think that one of those groups is actually still in existence."

Viwy arced an eyebrow. "Why is that?"

Creed glanced at him with a dour expression before he replied. "Well, let's say you and some hundred of your buddies hole up in a cave somewhere, and life's great for a couple of generations, but because of the hardships of being isolated from all the conveniences of life, you keep a fairly steady population. Now, who do you marry after a millennium of that? Because unless you bring in people from the outside, you're all going to be related after a while . . . and not distantly related, either."

Viwy grimaced as he muttered, "Yeah, that's pretty gross."

Achron thought that it was more than gross. It was an invariable recipe for reaching a kind of inherited disease collapse that could wipe out an entire population. Creed was right; it was nearly impossible that they could have lasted so long without the introduction of fresh blood.

It never failed to impress him how mature Creed's thinking was, despite the young man's age. As a father many times over, it made him sad. Creed had never really had a childhood. He was trained to kill and served as a commander of an assault squad before he was even a teenager. He was an instrument of war, practically deprived of anything of value. Achron contemplated how he might have been viewed by his family at the time. Someone with great power, born on the cusp of a great war, and conformed to a role in that war, never to have a genuine choice in the matter. Like anyone growing up in such conditions, he didn't question his role or his place, but embraced them without reservation.

Probably the only reason Creed was still with them at Castle Hona was the consistency with which his oldest daughter, Sheena, attempted to make him, sometimes forcefully, a part of their family. Creed seemed to be slowly accepting this new reality.

However, Achron worried that it might not be enough. Creed had improved, but then halted, as though Sheena had reached the limit of what could be done from the exterior. Creed himself would have to want to choose a new life and let go of his past. Right now, he was not ready to do that. Achron couldn't tell if it was fear of the mundane, the burden of having taken countless lives in war, or some other reason, but whatever it was, Creed was not interested in embracing life at Castle Hona. It was more like he tolerated life at Hona, and he was waiting for some other life to catch him up and take him away.

Achron was slightly biased against his potential departure, because he was not blind to Sheena's growing fondness for the brooding Fearian boy. Sheena's interest in Creed may or may not have been intentional, but at this point he genuinely worried for what would happen to her should Creed choose to leave. Sheena would be heartbroken, and he didn't want to see her go through that. He could try to direct her attentions elsewhere, but he doubted that would do anything. Practically, then, his only hope for her was to encourage Creed to stay at

Hona, and he wasn't entirely sure how to go about that. Their current efforts were for Rin's sake, but Achron hoped that perhaps he could learn a little something more about Creed while they were at it.

He started by digging into Creed's expansive knowledge of the past. "Creed, how did the mage war start?"

Creed looked thoughtful for a moment before beginning his tale. "It wasn't something that people talked about much, but as far as I could tell, it centered around who would ascend to the positions of the great mages, and who would receive their power. No matter how skilled the rest of us are, the great mages of the golden era were powerful beyond us all. So the first person to gain their power could rule both sides of the world without any resistance. Tensions were high, and people were on edge as everyone searched for the power gems of the great mages. Then she took them all, before anyone could obtain them."

Creed clenched his fist, and anger was plain on his face as he continued. "After they vanished, distrust and brewing dissension boiled over into all-out conflict. I was very young, so I don't remember who took the first strike, but the golden age ended dramatically. Various groups of mages formed coalitions quickly, and as far as I know, the conflict continued long after I was caught up in whatever that was that took me out of the action."

Viwy looked puzzled. "So, who was 'she'?"

Creed sneered, as though even the memory disgusted him. "Seleen Kiusonna, the great silver mage. Unlike the others, she never had any descendants, or even trainees. She never taught anyone her secrets or formed any base of operations for the preparation of other mages. When the others passed away, leaving behind their legacy and the gemstones imbued with their power, she stole all the stones and cast them out of time, where no one else could ever hope to reach them."

Achron had heard this part before, but he asked about what he had not heard. "What happened to Seleen?"

Creed grimaced. "A blue mage caught her unprepared and incinerated her with a bolt of lightning. I guess even great mages lose their edge when they are old and decrepit."

Achron wondered if that were true. It made sense that as the last great mage, Seleen would have been fairly old, but he doubted that meant she was decrepit. Instead, given her foresight to remove the greatest sources of power from the hands of the greedy and proud, she was unlikely to have fallen to such a fate. Rather, to him the story sounded like the bitter, wishful thinking of the displeased, not something that had actual weight.

Could Seleen ever have anticipated that those limitless sources of power would be returned to the world in the form of his children? Achron still wasn't sure how he should respond to the reality that each of the children born to him were imbued with one of the twenty-four mage powers, making them incredibly rare and powerful relics. It was difficult to even think about it, mostly because he never looked at his children as objects, but as young and developing people whom he loved deeply. Reconciling the two realities was not something that he relished, but it was something that, sooner or later, he was going to have to deal with.

That thought reminded him that they had an urgent mission to rescue Rin, and he spoke his concerns. "Creed, Rin isn't the metamorphic gem, is she?" He didn't think so, but in all honesty, he couldn't exactly remember what Creed had said about Rin back when he had first expressed that they were more than ordinary Fearian children.

Creed shook his head. "No, she is Sublimis Rubis estis Ulurtis, or the majestic ruby of the great red mage, Ulurt." Creed looked contemplative, and then added for their benefit, "The bright red mage, since there is more than one kind of red mage."

Creed knew more about the ancient past than the rest of them put together, but sometimes it only added to their confusion instead of clarifying anything. Achron didn't really want to know what the other red mage was, if the first was fire. Whatever it was, that meant Rin was not in danger of being exploited by the metamorphic mages, as her power was not something they could make use of.

Just how much had the interloper had learned from them? Did he understand that Rin wasn't ordinary? Surely, he at least knew that she wasn't human. What could his motives be? It was beyond frustrating that he had probably learned a fair amount about them, but they knew essentially nothing about him. At least, Achron assumed it was a him, since he hadn't paid much attention to Rin's pet, and Fishy wasn't exactly a gender-specific name.

Chapter 5

Rin stared wordlessly at the empty bowl on the table in Arru's living quarters. It was late in the evening now, and they—that being Rin, Arru, and Hanni—had finished their evening meal, and still awaited the return of Harku.

The meal wasn't much really. Some kind of thin soup, and small loafs of simple bread. Rin wondered if this were normal fare, and if so, how the people of the gryphon clan could survive on such a meager diet. She didn't complain though, as it was clearly meant to be a kind gesture of hospitality.

Arru broke the silence hesitantly. "Um, Hanni, was it?"

Hanni nodded, and Arru continued. "I-I don't want to be rude, but what happened to your face?" Hanni merely shrugged, unconcerned with the ugly line of sharp, angular, raised scars that ran from the middle of her neck up around her chin, and along the side of her face to disappear into her hair.

Arru turned her gaze back to the table to avoid looking at Hanni's disfigurement. "Well, I can't do anything about it myself, but I am sure that Harku could make the scar invisible. He is really skilled." Hanni eyed her curiously, but made no other indication of what she thought of the idea.

Rin speculated on what it would be like to have the ability to look like any person or animal. She thought about what kind of animal she would want to be, but nothing really stood out to her. She thought ruefully that she would really like to look like Sheena, if she could look different, since Sheena was very beautiful. Yet there was some sense in which she realized that Sheena's beauty was as much from the boldness that she envied intensely as from her appearance, which reflected their mother's own beauty.

It felt a little shameful to want to look like someone else when she knew that none of her siblings bore the same bright red hair and darker red mane that she did. Her mother had assured her that she was beautiful in her own right, but she didn't feel that way. She couldn't decide on what she would rather look like, because in reality, most of what she preferred in others was not appearance, but deeper traits that she knew she lacked. Sheena's boldness, Hanni's resolve, Kraysin's ability to take charge of any situation, and many more. To her, it seemed as though she were the only one who struggled with self-confidence and shyness.

As Rin mused about her place in life, a knock sounded at the door. Before Arru could reach it, the door opened, and Harku entered. He looked haggard, like he had been engaged in fight to the death, and barely escaped alive.

Arru approached him swiftly, but slowed to a stop a few paces from him. "What did Father say?"

Harku sighed. His drawn-out answer communicated both his disappointment and a sense of deep reflection. "I . . . well, he wasn't very interested in listening to me, nor was he willing to permit a break in our traditions."

Arru's face fell. "I am sorry, brother."

Harku continued. "I was given an ultimatum. Either we marry, or the right of high clansman will pass to another."

Arru looked stunned and interrupted him. "But who?!"

Harku's expression hardened. "That schemer, Turric, who has been filling Father's head with nonsense, of course."

Arru gently touched her face. "He was here earlier."

Harku shifted his sober gaze toward the table, but his concern quickly transitioned to confusion. "Hanni?! What are you doing here?"

Hanni looked at him calmly as she replied. "I do not know how I came here, only that I am here for Rin's sake . . . Fishy."

Harku winced. "Please don't call me that. I am Harku Loon of the gryphon clan."

Hanni tossed her head lightly. "What you want to call yourself is your business."

He studied her suspiciously but said nothing. His sister interrupted their exchange and asked urgently, "What are we going to do, brother?"

Rin stood and spoke more boldly than she felt, and with an embarrassed flush on her face. "Harku, I— well, I will help you in whatever way I can." She only vaguely understood what that might mean, but she was tired of feeling useless, and being the last person to play a role in important matters. And she still felt a strange sense of responsibility for her pet Fishy, even if he had been pretending the whole time.

There was a moment where everyone stared at her, but Rin held her ground, still standing, still blushing, but now looking at the wall rather than meeting anyone's gaze. Harku replied solemnly, "Thank you, Rin. You are the sweetest person I have ever known, but I don't deserve your help. Quite the opposite, actually. I never intended to embroil you in the madness that is the gryphon clan politics and traditions run amok. I just . . . ."

His shoulders drooped as he studied the floor. "I didn't know what to do when I had broken my guise. After living for more than a year among your people, I still couldn't say what they would do to me for my subterfuge."

Hanni commented, "Well, you certainly wouldn't be sleeping in her bed any longer." Rin felt her face grow hot, and she fixed her eyes on the table with intensity.

Harku, unable to fend off his own embarrassment, attempted to defend himself. "Hey, it's not my fault your castle is so drafty."

Arru's eyes conveyed her shock at this announcement. "Um, so, brother, is there something you're not telling me about what happened while you were away?"

He glared at her briefly, and then shook his head. "It's not what it sounds like." Hanni appeared to differ on the matter, but to Rin's relief, she kept her opinion to herself.

Harku cleared his throat loudly and returned to the previous discussion. "I am grateful for your willingness, but it will not resolve the problem at hand. I have no audience with my father. He has no interest in considering any alternative." After a thoughtful pause, he added, "I would return you to your home this very moment, but I fear that you will not be permitted to leave peaceably."

Gazing toward the wall as though she could see them already, Hanni informed him, "That does not matter. Father will be here very soon, and he will take us home."

Harku looked doubtful. "I don't want to disappoint you, but we are far above the ground at the top of a mountain, and most of my people are capable of fighting entire groups of armed men, let alone a solitary healer mage."

Hanni fixed her eyes on him and shook her head. "You should not underestimate our father, and he does not travel alone. Viwy and Creed are with him." Harku understood something about Achron, but he knew less about Viwy, and practically nothing about Creed. Partially because Rin's ability to interact with Viwy and Creed were unsurprisingly similar to Harku's knowledge. Hanni's tone softened. "We will be leaving, but given your current circumstances, you could come with us if you like. I am sure Father would be willing to entreat your family for you."

* * *

It was well into the night, and Achron watched patiently as Viwy held his hand to the bright yellow cat's eye stone on his staff. The mist mage dropped his hand to his side as he said, "Well, no doubt about it. Rin is up there." He pointed to the sheer cliff that stood before them.

Creed spoke flatly. "No doubt a sure way to isolate those who can fly from those who cannot."

Achron craned his neck back to look up the immense rock face. "Is it too far for you, Viwy?"

Viwy shook his head. "No, we can reach the top in an instant, but there are guards."

Achron turned to Creed with his instructions. "Remember, show them we are serious, but don't kill anyone. Rin's life is at stake." Creed nodded soberly. Despite his past, he had no delight in taking life.

Achron ordered, "Okay, we are going to the top.

I will protect us as needed, and Creed will get their attention. Got it?" Creed took his staff from his side and brushed the citrine stone embedded in its shaft to extend it to its full length. Viwy began to glow, having recently obtained to the level of higher mage, in preparation for taking them through the mist.

In the blink of an eye, they were transported to the top of the cliff in a puff of misty vapor. Their sudden appearance must have been shocking, but the two sentry gryphons emerged from the dark interior of the cavern, growling menacingly. Achron reached out and grabbed a hold of his staff. It rapidly materialized outward from the center, and the numerous opal stones that ran the length of the staff gleamed in the darkness, matching Achron's skin that glowed faintly with white light.

The gryphons approached slowly, their large bodies low to the ground as though prepared to pounce on the would-be invaders. Whatever apprehension they should have inspired, Creed was not so impressed, and sharply tapped his staff on the rocky surface. The yellow-green stone at the top of his staff, as well as Creed's own skin, grew bright as mage power flowed through him. An intense beam of yellow-green light lanced out at the peak of the mountain above them, and Achron was especially grateful that he was not facing Creed in combat during the great mage war. The pointed tip of the mountain, well deserving of its designation as part of the Dagger Peaks, was severed, and with a loud rumble, it slid free and fell, barely missing the ledge and falling below with a deafening crash.

The three visitors were obviously in a class all their own, and the gryphons backed slowly into the gaping cavern. Several others joined them at the entrance, keeping a wary distance. Another light source appeared as a man carrying a torch exited a side tunnel and hurried toward them.

Viwy shot Creed a wry expression as he asked rhetorically, "Don't you think that was a little bit much?"

Creed shrugged nonchalantly. "Achron said to show them we are serious."

Achron motioned them to silence as the man emerged from the shadows of the cave and greeted them hesitantly. "Ah, welcome to the home of the gryphon clan, fellow mages. What brings about your visit?"

The man hesitated and tilted his head slightly as he stared at Achron. "Say, now. Have we not met prior to this?"

Achron thought the man seemed familiar, and despite the dim torchlight mingled with the illumination of mage power flowing through the three of them, he slowly came to recognize him. "Yes, in Wythwood, southeast of Empleheim. You were looking for someone at the time."

The man nodded slowly and glanced at Creed as he spoke. "It seems you always keep odd company."

Two of the gryphons reemerged from the cavern, returning to human form but taking up watchful positions just behind the man, who continued to speak. "I am Moneck, the gryphon clan outrider. I am the mediator between the clan and those of the outside. I assume you are here for matters of more import than an exchange of pleasantries?"

Achron nodded calmly. "That is correct. I am Achron of Hona Castle to the southeast. One of your clansmen has kidnapped my daughter."

Achron was surprised to see that the man's expression suggested that he was very confused. Moneck replied a little defensively, like Achron were accusing him personally of the crime. "Are you certain of this? It isn't likely that any sane person would be in the cursed land, let alone one of our own."

Achron was about to correct the man bluntly, but one of the other clan members spoke in a low but respectful voice. "Moneck, this man speaks the truth. He returned with a strange girl, sort of like that one." The fellow bobbed his head toward Creed. Achron could tell Creed was agitated by the lack of respect for his personhood, but he had confidence that the young Fearian would keep his cool despite the blatant affront. Creed wasn't typically a ray of happy sunshine, but he was disciplined even without the mage focus.

Moneck wheeled toward the man, his displeasure clear on his face. "What?! And no one thought to inform me? I should have you cleaning latrines for the next twenty years!" The man cowered slightly as he apologized repeatedly, but Moneck ignored him, turning back to Achron. "Very well, I am mistaken. Please, come with me. You shall have your daughter back shortly." He gestured for them to follow him. "We shall speak with the clan lord, and he will enforce her return."

As Achron and the others fell in behind Moneck, the light from their skin fading, the man asked, "How is it that mages of your kinds still exist? Were you not all wiped out in the wake of the great mage war?"

Achron replied knowledgably. "Most were, but there has been a reawakening of the mages, though there are not many of us at this time."

Viwy elbowed him as he commented, "Yeah, sorry, Achron. You can't do everything yourself." Achron narrowed his eyes at him before returning to his conversation with Moneck.

The gryphon clansman looked confused for a moment, but changed the subject as they continued through an entire underground city cut into the mountain. "Last we met I was looking for the heir of our clan. He deserted us, and I was tasked with his retrieval.

I never found him, but now he arrives without my knowledge, and apparently a kidnapper."

Creed interjected, "Why did he run away?"

Moneck looked at him thoughtfully before he spoke to Achron. "Was it born that way?"

Achron warned him, "Creed is Fearian. Do not presume the difference in his features means he is lacking in anything." Moneck looked back at Creed for a moment. The young Fearian continued to be outwardly calm, but Achron knew he really wanted to tell the gryphon outrider that he was daft.

Moneck returned to the standing question. "Harku fled because he was unwilling to reconcile his personal preferences with the longstanding traditions of our people."

Viwy and Achron nodded. Creed, however, was not the least bit swayed by this response. "What a bunch of gibberish! You just said something without saying anything at all. I don't suppose you are actually going to answer me?"

Moneck's expression hardened. "You're awfully impertinent for someone scarcely out of childhood."

Creed's eyes flashed with anger, though he spoke calmly. "My sister was kidnapped by a runaway metamorphic mage from a secluded enclave, and I want to know why. You can tell me, or I can ask someone else."

Achron was tempted to tell him to ease up a little, but there was a deeper reality that Creed was concerned about, something that Achron had simply presumed. Moneck's answer painted a negative picture of this Harku character, but without actually addressing the point of Creed's question. Was Harku a threat, or was something very off about the gryphon clan?

Moneck hesitated, but chose to explain. "A golden gryphon must propagate the clan's line through a red gryphon. Harku refused to marry the only red gryphon currently among us. It is the way of our people, yet he refused to obey even his own father, and fled to avoid his responsibility. His return is odd, given that nothing has changed here, and indeed, the general disposition concerning his actions has been quite poor."

Viwy wanted to satisfy his own curiosity. "What is a red gryphon?"

Moneck told him, "Well, in essence, it's a member of the clan who has red hair."

Achron was curious as to the significance of this for the clan, though he now knew the significance of it for Rin. "Why is that so important?"

Moneck spoke with pride. "Our people have followed the ways of our ancestors since we fled the carnage of the great mage war. It has always been true that the heir of the clan should be united to a red gryphon. We have never had another practice, nor such a shortage of those qualified."

Chapter 6

Something was still missing from this equation with Harku and gryphon clan traditions, but Achron was really more interested in reobtaining his daughter than dealing with other people's problems. Moneck seemed satisfied with his own explanation and hurried them along through tunnels and chambers.

They drew a fair amount of attention from those they passed, in part because of Creed's appearance, but also because of their atypical manner of dress. Achron would never have suspected that such a large population could live in such a place. He wondered why his people in times past had never noticed their interesting neighbors. He supposed that the entrance to the clan's cave was far above the ground, but it was still odd that there hadn't been any reports of gryphons circulating in the palace back before Empleheim was lost.

They were ushered into a large room with a central low table surrounded by dense cushions that served as seats. Apparently the gryphon clan had no formal throne room. An old but spry-looking man wearing more elaborate clothing than the others stood with his back to them, engaged in a heated conversation with another man, who had fresh strips of white cloth wrapped around one hand.

Moneck glanced at the other man with disdain, but then ignored him as he made his presence known. "Lord Kanant, there is a matter that demands your immediate attention."

Kanant, the older, more regal man, replied angrily before turning around. "Moneck, what further trouble could you possibly bring me?! The mountain shakes like a fearful child, my son has lost any sense of clan pride, and now dangerous vile fiends from another world have invaded our sacred halls?!" He swiveled to glare at Moneck, like he blamed the outrider personally for bringing these ills upon them.

Moneck was unaffected, and tilted his head slightly in a subtle gesture toward the people standing to his right while he remained mostly expressionless. The gryphon clan lord looked at Achron and his friends and flinched before rapidly politicizing his own expression.

Before Achron could say anything, Viwy stepped forward and gave a lavish bow as he announced loudly, "May I present to you King Achron of Empleheim, ruler of all of the northland from the edge of the Dagger Peaks to the river Rylet!"

Achron shot Viwy a withering gaze, but a verbal rebuke would have to wait until they were home. Creed unhelpfully confirmed the facade by bowing low himself. Moneck eyed them suspiciously, clearly attempting to fit this new information into his previous perception of them.

Lord Kanant spoke briskly but respectfully. "Welcome, King Achron, to the halls of the gryphon clan. I am Kanant, clan lord. What is it you seek from us?"

Achron muttered and cleared his throat before continuing in a conversational tone. "Would you morons get up already! Ahem, I am here to retrieve my daughter, who was abducted by one of your clansmen, Lord

Kanant."

Kanant scowled. "What?! Preposterous!" Moneck tried to get Lord Kanant's attention, his hands flapping in a calming manner, but the other man either didn't notice or just ignored him. "Such a crime deserves nothing less than permanent banishment!"

Moneck interrupted his pronouncement. "Lord Kanant, do not be so swift in judgment. The culprit is none other than your own son, Harku."

The third gryphon clan member there, the man with the bandaged hand, smiled unpleasantly as he commented, "How . . . unfortunate."

Kanant stared down the man momentarily, but then sighed as he steeled himself. "Harku is beyond help. He has violated our traditions, broken our laws, and refuses to listen to reason. Another heir must be chosen, and Harku must be expelled." Moneck grimaced but made no answer.

Achron repeated Moneck's caution. "You should not be so rash with your own child."

The old gryphon restrained his speech for the sake of their company, but it was obvious that he was not of a mind for a conversation on the topic. "King Achron, your advice is respectable, but you know nothing of our ways, or of the situation at hand. Therefore, you should keep your thoughts to yourself."

Achron sighed as he conceded. "Fine. I am just here for my daughter."

The man that remained unintroduced leaned forward eagerly, staring at Creed, and requested, "Please tell me you are going to take the fiery one with you, too?" Achron maintained his calm demeanor, but his mind began to race. The "fiery one"? As far as he knew, Rin was the only abductee, and she didn't have access to the power that she carried in herself.

Lord Kanant rebuked the man. "Silence, Turric!

It is not yours to speak to outsiders!" The man lowered his gaze and nodded in what was probably supposed to be a respectful gesture, but it looked more simpering from Achron's perspective. Kanant commanded Moneck, "Outrider, take King Achron to his daughter in Arru's chambers, and then send them on their way with an appropriate gift."

He turned back to Achron. "I have much to accomplish, King Achron. I trust that our peoples will live in harmony, but in case you need our support, you should know that I can field more than one thousand combat-ready gryphons."

Achron smiled politely, but he had not missed Lord Kanant's scarcely veiled threat. He reached out and gripped nothing, and the gryphon clan members took a step back as Tianna materialized out of the air. "It can be hard to say what the future holds, but there is not a person in my kingdom who does not have familiarity or capacity with the power of the mages. It is unlikely that there is an enemy we cannot face if united." Achron chose to retain his staff and turned to Moneck. "Please, lead the way."

The man nodded, and they followed him from the room as Kanant and Turric watched them intensely. Achron didn't want the gryphon clan to presume that they were without recourse, or worse, some kind of easy prey.

Moneck led them on another winding and confusing journey through tunnels and chambers, past many other gryphon clan members, to arrive at a door along a nondescript hallway. Achron marveled that any of them could find anything in the place. Nothing was labeled, and it all looked the same after traversing it as quickly as they had. Moneck reached for the door, but seeming to think better of his actions, knocked loudly instead of opening it.

A young female voice called for their admittance, and Achron presumed this was the said "Arru," who was apparently younger than he had expected for someone who had their own chambers. Moneck opened the door, entering first. He stepped to one side as Achron and the others came in behind him. The room was pleasant, if sparsely decorated. Like the meeting room they had just come from, there was a low table in its center.

Rin jumped up from where she had been sitting at the table and ran to him with a happy shout. "Father!"

Achron caught her up in his arms and held her close as he sighed with relief. "Rin, are you okay?"

He set her down and she nodded. "Yes, Father, I am fine." Her expression shifted to some mixture of sheepishness and guilt as she looked at the floor, muttering, "Um, so, I, uh, I am sorry . . . about the tower . . . uh . . . ."

Achron's voice was gentle as he ruffled her hair affectionately. "We will talk about that later, Rin."

He looked up as Creed expressed the same uncertainty that rapidly hit Achron when he saw who else was in the room. "Hanni? How did you get here? I thought you stayed at Hona!"

Hanni shook her head slightly as she answered. "I don't know really. Rin needed my help, so in an instant, I found myself here."

Achron could see that Creed had some idea of what might have transpired, but he kept it to himself. Based on the gryphon clansman's description of "fiery one," he guessed Hanni's presence was accompanied by her power. But they could work on understanding the matter later. "Well, regardless of what happened, it's time to go home."

Achron noticed with some surprise the young girl who remained at the table, watching them closely.

She couldn't be more than ten years old, but her age wasn't what was surprising. Her thick red hair immediately brought Moneck's story back to mind. She had to be the only red gryphon of the clan.

Achron observed that Moneck was fixated on the person he hadn't noticed yet, because he stood on the far side of the room, leaning on the wall, his gaze glued to the floor. His words confirmed Achron's presumption about his identity. "Forgive me, Achron. I did not intend you or yours any harm. I . . . I just wasn't sure what to do when I could no longer conceal myself. Please, go. Return to your home. My place is here, difficult or otherwise."

Moneck cleared his throat loudly. "Actually, young Lord Harku, you have been formally banished by your father. Your place is somewhere, but it is not here." Harku looked up at him, but no shock registered on his face. Rather, he seemed to have anticipated Moneck's proclamation and returned to his sober study of the room's floor.

"NO!"

Achron thought he would fall over when he realized that it was Rin who had spoken. Everyone looked at her, and despite the flush on her face at becoming the center of attention, she continued with unusual ardor. "Father, we can't leave Fish—er, Harku homeless! We have to take him back with us."

Viwy leaned close to Achron and whispered, "Maybe one of the metamorphic mages is imitating Rin?"

Achron stalled at the real, but doubtful, possibility. "Uh . . . ."

Creed interrupted the lengthening silence by turning to Moneck and stating, "You can wait outside."

Moneck blinked a couple times, but then shrugged as he turned to the door, saying, "I guess it doesn't matter, if that's what you want."

After he left, Creed walked up to the girl at the table. She rose, her expression as uncertain as her words were obvious. "You have a really long tail."

Creed crossed his arms. "You are Arru?" She gave a hesitant nod. He turned toward Harku as he asked for direct confirmation. "And you're Harku?" Harku nodded without looking up. Creed addressed them both. "And you are brother and sister?" More nods.

Viwy asked in concern, "Creed, what are you doing?"

Creed broadened his gaze to the others and explained. "The metamorphic mages had their own cultures, and they were often stupidly complex. No doubt they carried this with them when they fled the war."

Harku raised his head slowly. "What war?" It was rare for anyone to speak of Creed's origins, so it made sense to Achron that Harku would not know about Creed.

Creed did not answer him, and instead looked intently at Arru. There was a disturbing silence before he asked bluntly, "Arru, what will become of you in your brother's absence?"

Arru looked surprised, but then hung her head. "I-I will be given as wife to whomever is appointed as the next heir, likely Turric."

Creed observed pointedly, "You mean the weasel?" Arru flushed with shame, and merely stared at her lap.

Viwy stuttered with disbelief, still stuck on the earlier revelation. "B-but—but he's your brother!"

As Achron's understanding of the situation came together, he objected to something else. "But you're just a child! Turric must be at least twenty years older than you."

54

Arru shrugged weakly as she replied. "I-it's our way." She didn't sound particularly convinced, but rather was repeating what she had been taught.

Rin looked at him imploringly. "Please, Father." Achron sighed as he recalled Lord Kanant's words. Was one person worth risking war?

Arru was the picture of youthful innocence. A lovely child sheltered from the harsh world beyond her clan. Inexperienced, naïve, and probably not fully understanding just how horrific her situation actually was.

He looked at Harku, who remained silent in solemn contemplation. The young man, only a few years older than his own children, had sacrificed everything to protect his sister. A king living as a homeless vagabond, with nothing more than a vain hope that he might find some solution to his fate. Achron wasn't sure he would even know how to function in such circumstances.

It wasn't really a choice. "Well, I guess they can stay at Hona Castle, if that's what they want."

Viwy whispered urgently, "Achron, is that really a good idea?" Achron shook his head slightly to indicate his own uncertainty, but said nothing.

Harku didn't look up as he lamented, "I don't deserve your hospitality after I infiltrated your home and lived among you as an enemy."

Rin objected to his view of the situation. "Harku, you're not an enemy."

Harku lifted his eyes toward her, his expression pained. "Yes, Rin, I am. I came to Hona Castle because I observed a young redheaded girl and determined that she might serve as a substitute for my sister. You were my prey, to be captured, and used in exchange for the sake of my sister. I was biding my time until the opportune moment would come. But you were so rarely alone that days turned into weeks, and weeks into months."

Rin lowered her gaze to the ground, looking somewhat defeated as she murmured, "O-oh."

It was Achron's turn to recognize that there was more to the story than had been told. He came to the defense of his daughter's tender heart. "Sure, but what happened? Months does not explain years."

Harku paused before he admitted, "I . . . ." He stopped and swallowed, avoiding his own sister's gaze, as naturally she didn't exactly know the whole of it either. His frustration was evident when he began again. "How could I harm such a kind-hearted person? How could I treat the one who lavished tender affection on me as something to be used? Would I not be worse off having betrayed the gentlest of souls for my own sake? I don't think I could have lived with myself if I had gone through with my initial plans."

He took a deep breath and let it out slowly. "Rin, you are not so different from my sister. Soft-spoken, gentle, lovely, innocent. It was as though I had traded one terrible circumstance for another. I was, I am, afraid of what you think of my long-standing deception. But what could I do? There is nothing left but to face the unavoidable reality. I am sorry, Rin. Please do not hold it against my people."

Rin contemplated his words for a moment, but then she reiterated her offer. "Please, come with us to Castle Hona."

Arru smiled politely, but her voice was sad. "Thank you, Rin, you are truly a kind person. But you know that I cannot leave this place. I would not survive the first day."

Achron thought this was a dramatic exaggeration, and he queried, "What? Why is that?"

Arru explained in her own simple way. "The sunlight makes me very sick, as it did my mother, and my grandmother before her."

His daughter turned imploring eyes on him. "Father, you can help her, can't you? You are the White Lion of Empleheim!"

Achron kept his reply as calm as he could. "I can try." He didn't want to give Rin false hope, but he really didn't want to disappoint his shy daughter when she was demonstrating that she could see beyond her own fear enough to care about others. He was also mildly annoyed that she knew his former title, since he hadn't exactly spread it around after settling down at Hona, but apparently it was something that his children were aware of, regardless of his preference.

Rin did not understand enough of white mages to know that his skills lay in saving life and fighting darkness, not in correcting inborn issues. However, something seemed wrong to him about the notion being sickened by sunlight. That did not make sense, nor would it be expected to cause such a rapid death as she seemed to suggest.

Achron tried not to feel anxious as the others watched him approaching Arru. The girl trembled slightly as she spoke in awe. "The White Lion? I have heard of you! But, um, aren't you supposed to be a thousand years old or something?"

Achron deflected the question. "It's complicated. Now give me your hand."

She held out her hand, and he took it in his as he looked thoughtfully at her skin. She was pale, though that was to be expected for a red-haired girl living her life underground. It struck him as odd that they had so many people here, but only one with red hair, when presumably there were more in past generations. He let go of her hand and gestured to the other.

Creed complained aloud, "White mages are so weird."

Achron ignored him. It was probably hard for

Creed to conceive of, but unlike the young Fearian who was a mage of mages, Achron was trained as a healer who was also a mage. He knew much about illness, and the body, and the various things related to his craft. Being a white mage was additional for him.

Taking the girl's other hand, he stopped short. Of course that was the problem. He felt slightly dumb that he was looking for a sign of malady. Achron pointed to her upper arm as he asked calmly, "So, what is that?"

Though Arru seemed confused by the question, she smiled proudly as she replied. "That is the gryphon's mark, a symbol of high status among our people. There used to be more, but most were lost when one of our storerooms collapsed." Achron looked the woven silver bracelet that fit snugly on her arm, a consequence of the elastic weave. The silver band was attached to either side of a simple open metal triangle. Achron didn't have to see the reverse side of the triangle to know that it had sharp, angular, black lettering on it.

Achron spoke softly. "Let me guess. It was your mother's?"

Her eyes widened. "Y-yes, it was. But how did you know?"

Offering no explanation, Achron merely held out his hand.

"May I?" Arru hunched her shoulders, a little embarrassed. "Well, I am not really supposed to take it off." Achron waited patiently, and she continued. "But if you wish." She took it off and handed it to him. Achron smiled at her reassuringly and looked at the inverse side of the triangle.

Viwy muttered, "You're being awfully cryptic, Achron."

Achron soberly announced his findings. "It's cursed. You are affected by sunlight because this confines you to darkness. It also causes you to have red hair and fair skin. Without it, you should have looked like your brother. I can solve the former problem, but I can't undo the latter."

Harku looked more than a little upset by this information and demanded, "But why?"

Creed responded thoughtfully. "The metamorphic mage clans were always in conflict. They did not engage in warfare, but they often tried to undermine one another. The gryphon clan must have had these made, in connection with their traditions, to ensure that the leadership would never include people who lacked allegiance to the clan. By this point, there probably isn't anyone who knows that none of your so-called red gryphons were born that way."

Achron recalled what had happened last time he acted rashly about such an object, and he told Arru, "To break the curse, I must also destroy this bracelet. There is no other way to release you."

Arru looked at it sadly, but she nodded as she said, "I . . . I understand."

The room was bathed in soft white light as Achron's skin began to glow. He reached out and touched the bracelet, and it was consumed in a bright flash, leaving only a fine metal powder. There was a moment of silence, and then Achron, the light fading from his skin, brought everyone back to their immediate concerns. "We are returning to Ilona Castle. Whether you come with us is your own decision, but you are welcome to stay with us, if that is what you decide."

Harku stared at the wall, clearly uncertain that he could, or even should, accept such an invitation. Rin spoke to him, her tone nearly pleading. "Please, Harku, do come with us. What's past is past. We can begin again."

There was this odd feeling that Achron had concerning Rin's interaction with Harku. It was almost as though there was no distinction in her mind between Harku and Fishy, like Rin was using her emotional attachment to her former pet to permit herself the necessary motive to openly beseech a young man who, truth be told, she didn't actually know. Obviously, he was not altogether eager to be coming with them, but Harku looked at his sister for a moment, and then ordered, "Arru, gather what is most important to you. We must go." She nodded and darted off to one of the side rooms.

Viwy gestured to the door as he said in a lower voice, "What about that Moneck character?"

Harku retrieved an ink pot, quill, and scrap of parchment from Arru's belongings. "Moneck is a good man, and though he holds tightly to the traditions, he is not beyond reason. I will write him a letter and explain what you have revealed, and perhaps he will make the best out of a bad situation." Achron wasn't so sure that would be effective, but it was better than nothing.

But Viwy had another concern. "Aren't they going to object to us just waltzing out with your sister?"

Harku smiled slightly. "Not if someone carries her with them."

Viwy seemed unconvinced. "Like it won't be obvious with your sister riding on someone's back."

Arru emerged from her room with a simple knapsack with various odds and ends tied up in it. Harku studied the group thoughtfully before he announced, "Since only one of you had the presence of mind to bring a traveler's cloak, Creed, you will have to carry my sister."

Creed flinched visibly as he objected. "Wh-wh-what!? No, not happening . . . ever!"

Hanni and Rin both laughed at his overreaction, and he stiffened defiantly before he sighed and muttered, "Okay, fine. Let's just get this over with."

Arru looked at Harku uncertainly. "Brother, I don't think I am powerful enough to do that."

He put his hand on her arm, saying, "Don't worry, Arru. I am."

In an odd motion, Harku pulled a single hair free from his head and dropped it. As it fell, the hair formed into a long wooden staff, shaped from a soft yellow wood with a fine grain. The head of the staff curved into a vertical spiral, like that of a freshly emerged fern, that made two complete turns, ending with a cherry-sized topaz in a diamond cut. Harku started to glow with a yellow-orange light, matching the topaz in color, and reached out to tap his sister on the forehead. She was immediately transformed into a soft, red-furred mouse.

Harku scooped her up off the floor and cradled her in his hands. Creed sighed and stepped forward, gingerly holding his own hands out. Harku set Arru the mouse down carefully and cautioned, "Do be gentle with my sister."

The mouse turned in circles in Creed's hands as it sniffed nervously at the air. Creed muttered, "Sure, but you should know that this is not my normal skill set."

There was an awkward moment where Creed and the mouse stared at one another, and then he jolted, as though realizing he was supposed to do something, and after some hesitation and shuffling, he tucked the mouse into an inner pocket in his cloak. They left Arru's quarters, where they were greeted by a patient but bored Moneck. He looked at Harku first, who merely nodded, and then turning, he led them back to the entrance.

Along the way, Moneck had given instructions for their parting "gift." The gryphon clan were mostly hunters and gathers, operating in gryphon form much of their time beyond the clan stronghold. Hence, the gift amounted to copious amounts of dried meat. Creed was

61

spared from participating as the rest of them shouldered coarse fabric bags of cured venison.

Moneck clasped Harku's shoulder as he spoke soberly. "Clansman, friend, may you find what you seek beyond the Dagger Peaks."

Harku replied with equal sobriety. "Moneck, you have always been good to me. Please do not let the clan fall into tyranny or disarray." Harku held out his letter, finishing simply, "And please promise me you will give this to my sister."

Moneck took the folded paper. "I will. May you never surrender to the encroaching darkness."

Harku swept a look across the ledge that was the gateway of the home he had known since birth. "That is easier said than done." His gaze stopped, catching sight of Rin out of the corner of his eye as she watched him intently. She looked away quickly, but a faint smile played at her mouth, and he added, "Though I do not face it alone."

Moneck turned and disappeared into the cave. Achron nodded to Viwy, and they vanished from the cliff ledge in a pulse of mist. Reaching where their horses were tethered and mounting up, in doubles this time, Achron commented, "I don't know how long it will be before they find that their precious red gryphon is missing, but I want to get home before that happens. So if you please, Viwy?"

From horseback, Viwy reached out and smacked his staff sharply on the ground. The lightly wooded montane forest was rapidly filled with a thick, fog-like mist, and with his skin and staff still glowing, Viwy led them through it back toward Hona Castle.

Achron hoped that he hadn't missed his mother-in-law's arrival. It would look rather bad to be absent during the arrival of the high queen of all Fearia. Especially if he were absent for some task that might make it appear he could not protect his own.

Chapter 7

Keena smiled apologetically at her mother. She had not offered many details on her husband's absence, simply stating that he would be back soon with the older daughter her mother had yet to meet.

Entertaining her mother Yanna, the high queen of Fearia, made her slightly uncomfortable. Beyond this, the queen's entourage, some fifty Fearians of occupations ranging from guards to cooks to personal advisors, were now staying in their relatively meager castle. Hona was far more functional than it was aesthetic, quite homely compared to the splendor of the castle at Ravenloc, from where her mother ruled their entire race. Apprehension at Achron's sustained absence only made matters worse.

Her mother waited patiently for her to introduce the remaining children. Seeing her again after so many years apart felt odd, even nerve-wracking, as though her mother would be passing judgment on her success in the intervening time. But Keena knew that her mother was a kind and reflective person. She was slow to be direct, and often spoke in a roundabout way. Her mannerisms were ideal for her position as high queen, which demanded solutions to a never-ending string of diplomatic and interpersonal problems.

Keena's youngest litter scuffled and twittered as

they waited for their introduction to their grandmother. She tried not to wince at how badly that struck Fearian sentiment on proper decorum as she started with the best behaved of the eight. "This is Gray."

The little boy nodded politely, his bleach-blond hair and white mane only slightly unkempt. His eyes were the same color as his name, and he bore a solemn expression that, with imaginative prowess, could be interpreted as polite reserve. Keena unconsciously let out a small sigh. There was little point to pretending they were more formal than they really were. Her young children revealed it readily, more so than she wanted to admit.

Keena maintained a veneer of calm and moved on to her next son, whose piercing bright green eyes could not distract from the scruffy state of his dark brown hair and darker mane. He made his brother appear well-groomed by contrast. "This is Weth, and this . . ."

Keena gestured to the next child quickly, as Weth was often rather distracted, and had a bad habit of interrupting. Combined, these traits meant she had a very narrow window before he would interject something disturbingly random.

". . . is Krysi," she finished.

The little girl seemed to oscillate between excitement and nervousness, bouncing from side to side with an energy that caused her white-gold hair and mane to dance. She had clearly forgotten she was supposed to nod respectfully. Her dark blue eyes were fixed on her grandmother, which regrettably only added to her rudeness. Yanna appeared unperturbed by the child's lack of manners and smiled kindly.

Continuing the introductions, Keena declared, "This is Yirrum, and this is Rhesa." Yirrum was not remarkable by Fearian standards, having amber eyes, blond hair, and a slightly darker mane, but he did seem

65

to be fairly intelligent for his age.

In contrast, his sister was quite dramatic, even for a Fearian, with her bright pink hair and dark red mane. Her light blue eyes made her hard to redress, because not even in her most frustrated moments did Keena wanted to see the lovely little girl cry. As though ever seeking an equal, Rhesa was infatuated with anything remotely beautiful, whether flowers, precious stones, or butterflies.

Keena moved onto the next pair of children. "This is Onni and Inno, who we think are twins." The little boy and little girl had black hair and manes and the same two colors of eyes. However, while Onni's right eye was blue and his left eye green, Inno's were reversed, with the right eye green and the left blue. Yanna studied them for a moment. "Very interesting."

One more. Keena finished with a sense of relief as she began to say, "Lastly, this is . . . ."

She trailed off as she glanced around for her last-born son. Her relief gave way to irritation; he was nowhere to be seen. Her eye caught movement by the doorway, and she saw Pyx usher the wayward child into the room. Keena continued in as calm a tone as the situation permitted, while the child in question darted to the place he had been assigned, looking about as guilty as one would expect. "Ahem, lastly, this is Adderil."

Adderil stood still, his light green eyes downcast with the knowledge he was in some measure of trouble. His blond hair and brown mane were as badly kept as Weth's.

Keena's mother knelt before the little crowd with a welcoming smile. "It's very nice to meet you all. Now, come here and tell me something about yourselves."

The children's reluctance about the ordeal turned to eagerness as they crowded around their grandmother to share whatever came to mind first. Their mother was decidedly relieved that Yanna was content to skip further formalities, though some of her attendants appeared a little disturbed by this departure from their cultural norms.

Keena didn't care to admit it, but despite her best efforts, her children's mannerisms were as much human as they were Fearian. While she still entertained notions of returning to Fearia for their sakes, her mother's visit was teaching her that that would be a difficult transition for them. Her hopes for their brighter futures in her native land might not be able to be realized. But if not, she could not see any alternative to the current life in Hona.

She shook her head as if to clear it, and determined not to focus on the negative while watching her mother play with the children.

* * *

Achron stopped abruptly at a distance from Hona Castle around midday. The people he could see near the castle were not familiar, and thus had to be connected to the high queen's visit. He gave an exaggerated sigh. "Rats. Of course she came while we were gone."

Creed quickly dismounted before fishing in his cloak for a moment, producing the red-furred mouse that he had carried the whole way from the Dagger Peaks. As Viwy's concealing fog faded away, the mouse squinted in the bright light and sniffed at the air. Harku also got off his horse, and Creed set the mouse down on the ground as the other man approached, summoning his staff. Harku knelt and gently touched his sister, causing her to resume her normal form.

Arru glanced down at herself, as though making

sure she was normal again, and then briefly scanned the skies. She stepped toward Creed as she spoke. "Thank you, sir Creed, for providing me with safe and warm transport."

Creed looked embarrassed, then a little nervous at her deliberate approach, his tail twitching from side to side. "Yeah, sure, glad to help."

Arru reached him, holding her hands behind her back and looking up at him, as he was a head taller than she was. "I really want to show you my gratitude, but I possess nothing to give you. Well, nothing apart from the common gestures of a young lady." Achron thought that "lady" was a stretch, given Arru's age, but predicting what was about to come, he still found the situation amusing.

Creed, on the other hand, looked apprehensive by this point. Arru began to close the small distance between them by standing on her tippy-toes, and he stammered out, "Wha-what gesture?"

He was not so distracted as to be short on reflexes, and suddenly realizing what was occurring, half-shouted in a panic as he jerked away, knocking himself to the ground. "WHAT! No, don't kiss me!" Creed scrambled backwards before jumping to his feet, dusting himself off.

Looking genuinely hurt, Arru tried to apologize, her tone much like her expression. "I-I am sorry. I just wanted to say thank you. I didn't mean anything else by it." Harku watched Creed with concern.

Achron took pity on the confused pair and explained. "He is Fearian, and for a Fearian, a kiss before witnesses completes a marriage."

Arru's face turned bright red as she clapped her hand to her mouth in shock. "I-I-I am so, so sorry." Harku merely looked contemplative.

Creed shook his head and attempted to reassure

68

the girl. "It's fine, Arru. There is no way you would have known that anyway. Your gratitude is fully accepted without any tangible display. Now, it would be great if we could finish our trek home. I am exhausted."

Achron nodded his agreement, and they remounted, with Arru riding behind her brother, and continued toward the stables outside Hona Castle. Achron hoped that they would have time to freshen up before meeting with his mother-in-law, but word of their arrival must have preceded them. After getting the horses situated at the stable, they encountered High Queen Yanna and her entourage waiting to meet them in Hona's courtyard.

Achron attempted to maintain an air of nobility as he, and the ramshackle group with him, approached the regally dressed and demeanored assemblage that was the high queen and her attendants. He was particularly interested in knowing how the queen had arrived with so many people apart from the sigil gate, but he resigned himself to the fact that his curiosity would likely not be satiated until later. Keena was with them, but quickly came to Achron's side, hugging Rin tightly, whispering her relief.

Achron addressed the group formally. "Your majesty, high queen of Fearia, welcome to our humble home here in Hona Castle." He nodded politely, but he recognized from the attendants' expressions that he was doing it wrong again.

In ironic contrast, Queen Yanna greeted him casually. "My dear Adderil, your attempt at Fearian formality is appreciated but unnecessary. We are family, and this is not the Fearian side of the world. Therefore, neither you nor we are required to operate by the dictums of Fearian culture. Please, call me Yanna." Achron felt a little relieved. "Ah, okay."

The other denizens of Hona Castle gathered as

they realized that Achron had returned home. Keena, still holding Rin's hand, introduced her final daughter. "And, last, but not least, this is Rin." She then looked down at Rin as she said, "And this, Rin, is your grandmother." Rin nodded politely, apparently more correctly than her father had, and Yanna smiled at her.

Keena elbowed Achron discreetly, and he cleared his throat before introducing the others. "These are newcomers from the gryphon clan of the Dagger Peaks, Harku and his sister Arru. This is Creed, and next to him is Viwy."

Yanna stared at Creed intensely with an expression that was hard to discern, but not one Achron had seen on her face before, though her voice remained controlled. "Creed? Where do you hail from, young Fearian?"

Creed replied honestly. "I was born here, near Niado in Empleheim."

Unsatisfied, Yanna asked a further question, seeming momentarily oblivious to everyone else there. "And where was your mother born?"

Creed was clearly growing suspicious, but answered anyway. "My mother was born in Iekkonim."

There were a series of gasps from the queens' attendants, and Keena grew pale. Achron was lost at the significance of this, but Yanna brought it to light. "Your caste has been extinct for millennia. If you have any respect at all for your heritage, then you must marry a Fearian, for you are the last of your kind."

Skepticism lined Creed's face. "Are you sure? The night caste of Iekkonim are the most resourceful of all the Fearians. I find it unlikely that I am the last."

Yanna explained succinctly. "When the ancient war shifted along racial lines, Iekkonim was the first place to succumb. It is now nothing more than a faint memory. Even the land where Iekkonim once sat is gone."

Creed remained stoic, but his eyes betrayed that this revelation had shaken him. Yanna calmly transitioned back to a more ordinary topic. "I apologize for my abruptness, but surely you understand that your caste has always held a special place among Fearians, and its absence has been felt for a long time. Now, I presume you are weary from your travels. Let us reconvene later for a more familial conversation."

Achron concurred. "Yes, thank you. Come, everyone. We will meet over supper later today. Pyx, please show our new friends to their rooms."

Pyx stepped quickly from the sidelines. "Yes, sir." He indicated that the gryphon clan members should follow him. "This way, please."

Arru and Harku complied, and Achron could hear Arru asking, "Are you a servant? You're too young to be a servant, aren't you?"

Harku chided her gently. "Arru, don't pester Pyx. He is several years older than you."

Arru spoke defensively. "But, but he is so small!"

Achron just shook his head. Arru would have to grow accustomed to the Fearian menagerie that made up most of the population of Castle Hona. But at the moment, he was more concerned for Creed than he was Arru. The young man had enough to worry about without being burdened by some revelation about his being personally responsible for the continuance of an entire Fearian caste.

It was odd. Achron would never have expected Yanna to be so blunt, but perhaps it was the sudden shock of seeing someone who was not supposed to exist that inhibited her usual political approach to things. And Achron clearly wasn't the only one who was worried for Creed's sake. Sheena watched Creed with deep concern, furrowing her brow, playing idly with her hands, staring at the young Fearian with an earnest sympathy.

Achron took Keena's hand and walked toward their room, intending to inform her on what had transpired among the gryphon clan, as well as to be informed himself of how the visit from his mother-in-law was to go in terms of schedule. Somewhere in there he also planned to sleep, but he wasn't going to get his hopes up just yet.

* * *

He moved in complete silence through the hallways of the castle, his dark skin and hair affording him a near perfect blend with the night's shadows. Not that it mattered. Everyone else was sound asleep, and the distinctives of his caste were kind of pointless around his new home. Creed's long tail gave him an incredibly flexible balance, and even without his mage power he was a formidable combatant.

Combat was not part of his consciousness now. He was pondering what he was supposed to do with his life considering what he had learned earlier that day. In a sense, he thought of himself as human, since that was the side of the world that he had grown up on. His mannerisms, his thinking, and many of his friends were human. But there was something particularly depressing in knowing that he would never meet another night caste beyond his mother. He was alone in ways that almost no one could experience.

Creed stopped at the base of the stairs that led to the tower. The same tower they had been in trouble for visiting so recently, the same tower that Rin had fallen from, and the same tower where his investigation into the strange object in the corner had been halted prematurely. He would not bother to brave the tower a second time, but he couldn't sleep, and aside from that, he was fairly confident that the object he was interested in was a relic from the golden age.

He hesitated, and then sighed heavily. Did he even care anymore? Did it matter if he violated Achron's stern command not to ascend the tower? Did it matter if the object was a relic? Did anything matter anymore?

Someone spoke into the darkness. "Creed?"

Creed turned sharply to face the other person who stood behind him in the hallway, somewhat successful in covering his surprise. "Sheena? Aren't you supposed to be sleeping?"

She looked serious compared to her normal happy, yet ever-so-slightly domineering self. She smiled slightly as she replied. "Aren't you?"

Creed glanced to one side as he commented dismissively, "I couldn't sleep."

Sheena stepped closer, moonlight caressing her face from the window, though she was still partially concealed by the shadows. "Yes, I couldn't either."

Creed fixed his eyes on the staircase thoughtfully as he asked, "And just why is that?"

Sheena sounded a little distant, as if she couldn't, or perhaps didn't want to, tell him her reasoning. "Oh, well, you know, there has been so much excitement these last couple days, what with Rin being abducted, and Grandmother visiting. What are you doing here, Creed?"

Creed attempted to not look suspicious. "I, uh, I am out for a stroll to help me sleep."

Sheena laughed. "You liar. You're going back up to the tower again, aren't you?" She stepped completely into the soft moonlight. Her simple, off-white nightgown seemed to glow faintly, and with her long blond hair draped loosely over one shoulder, she looked almost otherworldly.

Creed turned back toward the stairs, muttering, "Yeah, okay, but you should go back to bed."

She came to stand beside him and took his hand in hers. "Hah. And let you have all the fun?"

Creed sighed and let go of her hand. "Sheena, thank you for your friendship, but sometimes I just want to be alone . . . ."

He trailed off for lack of what to say. Sheena's efforts to give him purpose and life beyond his own dark ruminations were heroic, and largely efficacious, so he had no desire to be unkind to her. However, he feared what was transpiring was ill-fated, whether she knew it or not.

Sheena was unperturbed, grabbing his hand again, this time in both of hers. "Creed, I know you want to be alone, but I don't want you to be alone, not now, not ever! Even if I am the only one who prevents you from dark solitude, then I will still be here to help you."

Creed looked at her with mild annoyance, but refrained from trying to retrieve his hand. "Come on, Sheena. That sounds sappy. Besides, the only way that would work in the long run is if we . . ."

Creed stopped abruptly as Sheena flushed lightly and studied him with what he found to be an alluring-yet-disturbing expression. "Uh . . . we . . . ."

Pulling gently on his arm, she leaned toward him intently. Creed managed to conclude limply, "Um . . . what are you doing, Sheena?"

She blinked innocently as she replied. "Well, nothing really. But Grandmother did say you have a marry a Fearian."

Creed groaned. "Yeah, don't remind me."

Creed knew something of Sheena's interest in him, but apparently it was more than the passing fancy he had presumed it to be. His tone became flat. "Besides, she didn't specify which Fearian."

Sheena tilted her head slightly with a sly smile. "Oh, as if you had another Fearian to choose from."

Creed opened his mouth to suggest that he had plenty of other options, but for some reason, the only person that came to mind was Rin, and it was laughable to mention her, given that in the years they had lived in Hona together, she had spoken to him maybe twice.

Creed pulled his hand from hers and turned to climb the staircase, telling her bluntly, "I am not getting married, Sheena. Not to you, nor to anyone. Now go back to bed."

Naturally she wasn't interested in complying with his command, and bounded up the stairs after him as he ascended. Her words were edged with her own annoyance. "Come on, Creed. That doesn't even make sense. Didn't you hear what Grandmother said?"

He waved his hand at her dismissively. "Yes, I heard what she said, and it doesn't matter. I can't have children anyway, so it just doesn't matter."

Sheena spoke sarcastically. "Oh, and why is that? Because you won't have any time to be moody if you have half a dozen children?"

Creed spun around and pinned Sheena tightly to the tower wall as he spoke sternly and directly in her face. "No! It's because I am a prodigy, and one of the wonderful things about being a prodigy is infertility! I literally cannot have children. So Grandmother can say everything she wants, but it won't change anything!"

Sheena was obviously startled by his directness, but she spoke bravely, despite his fierceness. "That doesn't explain why you said you won't marry me!"

Creed clenched his teeth, but then sighed as he released her from the wall and placed his foot on the next step, reluctantly disclosing his reasoning. "It's because . . . because I could never willingly deprive my dearest friend of the joy of being a mother."

Creed continued to the top of the tower, but this time, Sheena remained behind. He reached the last stair and wondered why he bothered. Tears came to his eyes, and he considered going back down, because strangely he didn't want to be alone in that moment.

He scoured the tears from his eyes. He was a soldier, a battalion mage of rank. There was no place for emotional sentimentalism. Yet he felt especially vulnerable and weak as he reminded himself that there was no place for such a person in the current world.

The oblong object wrapped in tattered cloth rested in the corner. He could feel it as he neared, which was why he suspected that it was a relic. He picked it up and ripped the decayed fabric from it. The frail stuff fell away quickly, and he held a long metal staff in his hands. The end of the staff formed two tines, and wedged between them was a respectable block of amber about the size of his fist. The shaft had repeating bands of angular shapes running its length.

Creed had to dig through his memory, but the identity of the staff came to him. It was Ferrilin, the etcher's point, the relic staff created by Hemn Corralin, the great rune mage. It was a finely crafted staff, though useless in his hands. In the hands of the rune mage Dorra, it would be invaluable.

Now Creed's curiosity was satisfied, but it did little to make him feel any better. He hesitated. What did he want out of life? What he was he supposed to do, or where was he supposed to go? Nothing made sense. Did he really want to be alone, or was it that he afraid of what would become of Sheena if he let her into his life?

Creed shook his head slightly. Who was he kidding? Sheena already was part of his life. He just hadn't been willing to admit it to himself. Despite his best efforts, she had managed to become one of its center points, by winsomeness and sheer force of will. But he could not undo what he had done. He had spoken to her in full honesty, but in so doing, he had changed the course of their relationship. Tears sprang to his eyes again as he wished there had been some better way, some other place that he could have told her more appropriately.

He turned and descended the stairs slowly, his mind wandering as he tried to decide what he should, or even could, say to Sheena. He cherished her friendship, and hurting her was the last thing he wanted to do.

Creed made his way toward Sheena's room, but he paused at the door, since he knew that she, like all of Achron's children, shared it with at least one of her siblings. He needed to talk to her, but he didn't want to wake her sister, or worse, be misunderstood. Creed lamented that he had to leave things as they were for the night. He seriously doubted that she would sleep well for it, and he felt considerably guilty about that.

He let his hand fall limply to his side from where it had been raised to knock on the door and returned to his room, contemplating just how alone he was. Estranged in time, culture, and really everything. There was so little that gave him any continuity with his present surroundings that he wondered why he stayed.

Creed propped the rune staff against the wall by Dorra and Iekaruga's quarters before making his way to his own. He put his hand to his door and murmured to himself, "I guess I just need to accept that I am alone."

Creed thought he would have a heart attack on the spot when someone beside him disagreed emphatically.

"NO! You are not alone, Creed! Not even if you want to be! Because I am not going to leave you alone!"

He jerked back, staring in the direction of the voice for a second before he sighed with relief upon seeing Sheena. How long had she been waiting? She looked defiant, her arms crossed, her gaze firm.

He stared at her for a moment before he felt the weight of his thoughts that day, and with his eyes feeling very wet, he embraced her tightly, much to her surprise. Pointlessly trying to blink back his tears, he offered a broken apology. "I am sorry, Sheena. I . . . ."

Rapidly regaining her composure, Sheena slipped her arms around him and whispered to him, holding him close. "It's okay, Creed. But I am not giving up on you. No matter what it means for me."

Creed murmured softly, "I don't deserve a friend like you, Sheena." She answered with a gentle hug. He added, "I know how to trust someone else with my life, but you are teaching me how to trust someone else with my heart."

Sheena responded with a kind of suppressed excitement. "Oh, Creed, there is so much more to you than can be seen on the surface."

By impulse he wanted to tell her that she was mistaken, but perhaps it was just a matter of perception. Creed was often content to let the world slide past him without saying a word.

They held each other for longer than Creed could gauge, an hour or more. Creed released her slowly, and Sheena sighed as she let go of him in return, albeit reluctantly. He ordered quietly, "Go to bed, Sheena."

She smiled that silly smile that she gave him from time to time, and tossing her head, she turned and left her soft voice hanging in the late-night air. "You, too, Creed."

Creed stood there and watched her disappear into the shadows of the hallway that would lead her back to the other wing of Castle Hona. He whispered as though she were still right there. "My dear Sheena, what I am I to do with you?"

He paused, listening to the empty hall, as if by

some strange chance there would be an answer, but naturally nothing came. Creed turned in for the night and slept surprisingly well, for all the things whirling through his mind. Despite the distance between them, Sheena seemed to hold him, even in sleep.

Chapter 8

Achron sat across the table from his mother-in-law during breakfast. It was anything but fancy for sure. Hot porridge, with a generous helping of fresh, sweet apples diced and mixed in. Their Fearian guests didn't seem to object to this sort of simple fare, given their taste for all things fruity.

He only passingly pondered how his own hospitality would fit into their strange approach to commerce. The Fearian side lacked a monetary system, but instead was a balancing act, split along caste lines, between services and goods rendered, and services and goods utilized. Obviously they were not going to be rendering his family any services or goods that he knew of.

Three long tables in the dining hall were filled by the population of Hona Castle and the queen's entourage. There was a low hum of reserved conversation and tableware sounds in the air. Despite their general lack of strict ceremony, the family ate at regular intervals. It was a bonding experience, as well as a time to assess how things were going for each person.

Achron's focus was elsewhere as he applied to Yanna for the information he had yet to acquire. "So, Yanna, I must admit that I was wondering about how you all arrived here from Fearia without the use of something like a sigil gate?"

Yanna smiled. "While you may not have observed it when last you visited Fearia, we have not lost as much of the knowledge of mage power as you humans have. We still have some of our own who practice the various caster arts. I could certainly never say that we have lost nothing, but that while you and your people have found a few of your so-called mages, we have many kinds of casters among our people."

Achron remembered the casters he had encountered, primarily that they were scarcely worthy of the label. Sure, there seemed to be a good number of them, but other than Iekaruga, most were novices in terms of ability. Still, he chose to refrain from pointing out that the Fearian casters were meager compared to the mages and casters now living at Hona.

As she gestured to a middle-aged Fearian man sitting nearby, Yanna added, "This is Ankid, a caster who is skilled in the manipulation of space. It is he who brought us to this side."

Though the man's expression indicated how summarily unimpressed he was with anything in Niado, he nodded stiffly, as though his introduction demanded that he at least acknowledge his surroundings. Achron brushed off the chill of the man's coldness and told himself that he probably just always looked like that.

Opting to change the subject, he asked, "On another matter, what can you tell me about the golden chronicle?"

Yanna regarded him suspiciously as she returned his question with her own. "Oh, and why would you ask about our sacred record of history?"

The other Fearians that sat with her eyed him darkly, but Achron's answer was only partially defensive. "I have to teach my children about their people's history. They are Fearian, after all."

Yanna interrupted politely. "Well, half-Fearian."

Achron contradicted her. "No, they are fully Fearian. There is no such thing as a half-Fearian."

She tilted her head with a sense of curiosity. "And how do you know that?"

Achron glanced down the table toward Creed. The young night caste Fearian looked strangely lost in thought. Those around him were in animated conversation, but his distraction was evident. Achron turned back toward Yanna. "Creed told me that."

She mused, "And how would he know such things, I wonder."

Clearing his throat lightly, Achron continued irrespective of her comment. Creed's background was not something he wanted widely known, for Creed's benefit, if for not for issues it might cause should his own children take unhealthy interest in the secrets that Creed knew about them. "So, about the golden chronicle. Why are there three perspectives that change to two?"

Yanna shrugged and offered her explanation. "The first perspective is Fearian, from the Fearian side. The other two are not, as is apparent by the attitude they reflect toward things that Fearians hold in high regard or view as base. There was an ancient and violent war that resulted in the separation of the human and Fearian sides of the world. After the separation, there were only two chroniclers to write in the golden chronicle, not three."

Achron mulled over the ramifications of Yanna's words. He had already come to the conclusion that the change in perspective was a consequence of the great mage war. He could also have guessed that one perspective was Fearian, but who was the other? It sounded like Yanna was saying that the chronicler was immortal, and Achron asked along those lines. "But how could the chronicler live so long?"

Yanna laughed and shook her head, saying, "What?! The chronicler is a job that is passed from one Fearian to another in a line of succession, just as the chronicle keeper is."

He was mildly annoyed that she didn't at least recognize that his confusion on the matter was not a sign of his intelligence, but of his minimal knowledge of Fearians. He posited bluntly, "Yes, but humans don't have such a tradition, so what of this other recorder?"

Yanna looked thoughtful for a moment, but simply admitted, "I am not sure. Presumably it is the interpretation of events by various people to afford a broader perspective than would be possible with just one account. But I have no doubt that it reflects that of a number of individuals. Some who were present at the time, some investigating the past from later times. Regardless, the golden chronicle only addresses our ancient history, and other tomes are available in Ravenloc that cover more recent things."

Achron nodded. "Thank you." The conversation was clearly over; however, he wasn't entirely convinced about the matter. The central perspective possessed such a uniform style that it made him doubt there could be more than one author. Logically, the only reasoning for that was if it were added last, at a single time toward the end of when the golden chronicle was completed. The notion struck him as problematic, though, to have such a large portion of the book written in place after the fact, and between the other two accounts of Fearian history.

Keena took up his slack, broaching more familial topics, and Yanna seemed eager to move away from discussing the golden chronicle in detail. Achron was about to return his attention to the chatter at hand when someone shouted.

"Die, betrayer!"

83

By the time Achron turned toward the threat, it was far too late to respond. One of the high queen's attendants leapt skillfully over the table, with a long, razor-sharp blade aimed unwaveringly at Yanna. A second before the blade would have pierced her chest, it became water that splashed onto the table. Without the resistance of his sword, the would-be assassin fell over a startled Yanna and crashed onto the floor. Scrambling to his feet, the man bolted, but he had scarcely advanced two steps before he was transformed into a tortoise.

For a confused moment, nearly everyone in the dining hall stared at one another, trying to determine if what they had just seen was even real. Achron turned sharply toward Harku. The metamorphic mage was already standing, his skin aglow with a faint yellow-orange light, his staff in his hand, and his gaze focused. However, he was not looking at the tortoise that was doing its best to vacate the premise quickly; instead, he was looking at the first mage to have acted.

Seifer dropped his outstretched hand from where he had intercepted the assassin's weapon. He looked terribly embarrassed, apologizing awkwardly, like a child caught doing something forbidden. "Er, uh, sorry about the water there. It was just the first thing that came to mind."

Achron could hardly believe that the mage-in-training could operate with such daftness. Creed asked the obvious. "How did you end up there in time to stop him?"

Seifer looked a little reticent to answer and dropped his gaze, muttering, "Uh, you know, he acted like a bad guy, so I just watched him . . . closely."

Partially recovering from her shock, Yanna stood and demanded, "Speak, human! Where did you learn of the casters' arts?"

Seifer stammered wordlessly at this sudden

accusation, but Harku answered the question for him. "Human? I don't think that is the inner reality." Every eye turned toward him, including a stare of complete bewilderment from Seifer. "You are under the distortion effects of a metamorphic mage. Your appearance has been altered."

Seifer's mouth fell open. "Uh, what? W-wait, that can't be true!"

Creed interjected forcefully. "It has to be true. The power of the mages is cleanly divided. Just as only a human can be a white mage or a rune mage, only a Fearian can be a water caster, or in your case, an earth caster."

Yanna turned her penetrating gaze onto Creed, but he ignored her, and she said nothing.

Seifer's complexion grew pale as he fearfully asked no one, "S-so . . . I-I-I have a t-tail?!"

Harku's reply was flat, as though he had little vested interest in the matter. "Apparently so, but I have no intention of reverting you if you do not wish it." Seifer turned and made his way back to his chair at another table, clearly not in a mental state to assent to the novelty of knowing he wasn't actually human.

As the intensity of the moment passed, everyone resumed eating. One of the queen's personal guards detained the tortoise, which did not constitute much of a challenge, but Yanna seemed intent on interrogating the traitor. She explained the situation to Achron and Keena with an almost disturbing calm.

"There has been quite a stir since you last visited. Some Fearians are calling for a formal reestablishment of political relations with humans, while others are arguing that I, and the other queens, have betrayed the basic ethos of our people. They claim we are opening ourselves to the abuses and savagery that has colored our past. Tensions are rather high, and I can only guess that opposition runs deeper than just one person's attempt on my life. I suppose your talk of the golden chronicle so incensed him that he could not wait any longer for an opportunity."

Keena bit her lip. "But what are you going to do, Mother? The very fabric of our society is dependent on the functioning of the caste system. If enough people resist the system, everything would be chaos!"

Yanna looked serious, but she spoke in a lighthearted manner that made Achron wonder if she knew some important piece of information that he was lacking. "Perhaps, but there is not enough heart in those who are angry to change the way things are."

He wasn't sure what she meant by "heart," but Keena seemed to understand, and he deemed it a wiser course of action to ask his wife later rather than his mother-in-law now.

* * *

Creed was in a mild daze. He was walking in the courtyard that evening by himself, or as close to it as he could muster. Exhaustion slowed both his body and his mind from having been up most of the night, and then having to socialize in some pointless obligation that he would have been happy to live without. Still, it was a small thing compared to what Achron and Keena had given him.

He was relieved to know that the impossibility of Seifer's being a human earth mage was not connected to some maleficent motive. It was anyone's guess how the man had come to be metamorphosed into the appearance of a human, but he could easily imagine a metamorphic mage discovering a lone Fearian and recognizing that there was no future for such a creature among humans. Still, the whole situation left more questions that his normally analytical mind preferred.

Achron's voice sounded behind him. Creed felt a sudden flush of anxiety. He would have to talk about Sheena with her father before too much longer, but he did not relish any thought of the conversation. He had numerous concerns about how well he fit, or rather, didn't fit, into the Windslo family.

Creed turned, trying to appear casual. "Yes?"

Achron slowed as he approached, watching the young Fearian closely. "Hey, are you all right? You look a little worn out."

Creed half-smiled, knowing Achron wouldn't understand the full depth of his answer. "Family has that effect on me."

Achron chuckled as he glanced over his shoulder before commenting, "Yeah, you are not the only one who feels that way."

Achron cleared his throat and informed him, "I wanted to ask you about the golden chronicle."

Creed arched one eyebrow as he spoke. "Just what is this golden chronicle thing anyway?"

Achron looked a little disappointed. "Oh, it's the record of ancient Fearian history, from prior to the mage war through some time after it, but I guess if you haven't heard of it, you probably don't know anything more about it."

Creed thought for a second, and then spoke slowly as he tried to be certain about what he said. "It wasn't called that in my time. The great mage Heket was the Fearian chronicler, and the great mage Ferir was the human chronicler. It was recognized at the time that the golden age was unnatural, and that it must be recorded, or those who came after would never believe that it occurred. The right of chronicler was passed on to those whom they trained."

Achron prodded him for more. "What about the

third chronicler? Who was that?"

Creed blinked and tried not to be abrasive as he stated plainly, "There was no other chronicler."

Achron's brow furrowed. "But why is there another perspective on the history that falls between the human and the Fearian?"

Creed narrowed his eyes, considering that new information. "No ordinary person would have such a perspective . . . unless they knew both the chroniclers."

Achron frowned. "Yet it's that perspective that continues after the other one, the human one, stops."

Creed was silent for a moment. The whole thing had not interested him deeply; after all, what did it matter who wrote what about history in the past? However, the notion that there was someone else recording what had happened who was not one of the designated chroniclers, and whose legacy exceeded that of those so designated, made Creed uncomfortable. The great mages held secrets that they had not shared with anyone, even their own followers. If this person knew the chroniclers well enough to write along the same lines of history, then they, and possibly their descendants, might know some of those secrets.

He speculated nonchalantly. "I suppose a friend of the chroniclers would have some record of visiting their towers. I know where Heket's tower was located in Fearia."

Achron looked at him long and hard before he finally said, "You do realize this practically means we HAVE to go investigate what remains of his tower."

Creed corrected him with a smile. "*Her* tower, and, yes, we must investigate it."

Creed was more than ready for something a little less mundane, though he also recognized that Heket's tower could be in worse shape than Grypni's. Achron mused, "I suppose we will have to wait until Yanna returns to Fearia, but perhaps that could be the excuse we need to travel there."

Creed nodded, but his mind traveled back to the last time he had been to the land of his ancestors. It wasn't a pretty memory. It had been a violent battle, the same one that had removed him from the war, and resulted in his being trapped for millennia. Creed tried to put it from his mind as Achron left him to his thoughts in the courtyard.

Chapter 9

A sunny, breezy fall day offered the perfect weather for kite-flying. Pyx found it a bit of an odd thing, the brightly colored, patchwork geometric shapes stretched over light wood frames and held aloft by a stiff breeze.

He sat on the top of the shallow hill that ran down to the river. In the open, grassy area before him, several Windslo children were taking turns flying the worn kites that had been rescued from abandoned buildings around the city. The youngest were in the courtyard with their grandmother and parents, but here, the older children played with their siblings and friends.

Addie sat next to Pyx and leaned on him rather heavily. She said nothing, content to enjoy his company. Addie could be very frustrating with her antics, yet she was also a sweet and sensitive person most of the time. There was some point in the past where Pyx had crossed over from finding her annoying when she was a child, to finding her endearing when she was older. From a little sister, to a maturing young woman he wanted to be with.

It was a strange and almost embarrassing transition. Given the trouble she had gotten him several years ago, he was a bit concerned about what response he would get from her father when he asked for her hand in marriage.

He had been an assistant of sorts to the Windslo family, along with his older sister Mekki, helping with routine tasks, repairing things around the castle, and spending many hours watching over the children, as he did now. For most of this time, Addie had been adamant she was going to marry him, and she said as much far too frequently. As it happened, their union was now something of certainty to them both, but Pyx wasn't so certain when that time should be. Addie was sixteen now, and more a woman than a girl.

Pyx's confusion came from contemplating what cultural norms he should pursue. Addie's father was human, and humans did things differently than Fearians. Most Fearians were spoken for prior to age fifteen and married several years later. Humans were more erratic in their practices and sometimes did not marry until much later in life, occasionally with little or no betrothal period. Pyx was sea caste Fearian, and Addie was forest caste. However, they lived on the human side of the world. All these factors jumbled together complicated the scenario for him.

He reflected on how best to proceed while keeping a watchful eye on the kite fliers. Kraysin was trying to help his younger sister Thiesa keep her kite in the air, while Ahnya gave a string of contradictory suggestions on how he should accomplish this.

Ahnya was a mountain caste Fearian who had joined them shortly after Creed and Hanni. She was Iekaruga's least promising pupil, though it hardly mattered, because she was already a very competent water caster. Her sister, Prinial, was her opposite in terms of discipline and scholarship. Prinial was training under Iekaruga to be a sigilist. Despite her discipline, however, she was not as powerful a mage as Ahyna.

Nearby, Prinial and Dane helped Byrn, Marral,

and their newcomer, the red-haired girl named Arru. Their success with keeping the kite aloft was far superior to that of Kraysin and Ahnya, thanks to Prinial's precise, calculated instructions and Dane's careful efforts to follow them. Pyx was not unaware of the peculiar pairing between the sisters and the brothers.

Kraysin's latest attempt afforded him a fleeting victory as his kite soared upward on a sharp gust. But the breeze shifted, and the kite plummeted toward the ground as its twisted strings made it catch the air wrong. A subtle glow enveloped Ahnya as a column of water shot out of the ground and caught the kite, preventing it from smashing.

Most of them were unperturbed by Ahnya's actions. If she was around, someone or something was going to get wet spontaneously, and that was just how it was. Pyx smiled at Arru's expression. She would have to get used to such things if she was going to live here.

Emeril helped Harto and Zollen with their kite by herself. They didn't seem to need as much help anyway, but Pyx still felt sorry for her. It was partially her own fault for being so stubborn and self-sufficient, but Emeril operated as a law unto herself. She was independent, and her principle desire was to be a white mage as her father was. While it wasn't widely known, Emeril studied the mage's craft in her free time, and had gone so far as to beg Iekaruga's wife Dorra, a rune mage, for a fertility rune-engraved amulet.

Emeril had a dilemma. Female Fearians did not come unto their own power until they reached physical maturity, and that did not occur until after they were married, if the woman in question were of noble character. But Emeril wasn't interested in getting married. There was one exception, however, accidentally stumbled upon by Ahyna and Prinial. A fertility rune seemed to enable a female Fearian's power apart from age or physical relationships. But Achron had requested that no such objects be crafted.

This was where Pyx had speculate. He didn't know why Achron was concerned about his children developing their skills early in life. It seemed reasonable that it would be better for them to become skilled in the use of their power as early as possible, but then again, as someone who was not a caster, or mage as the humans called it, perhaps he was just missing something.

Either way, practically it meant that Emeril wasn't ever going to get what she wanted until she swallowed her pride and found a husband. Pyx shook his head slightly. Somehow, he couldn't imagine anyone they currently knew being a willing party.

He glanced about the field and wondered where Rin was. She was often on the periphery, keeping mostly to herself. Right now, she was nowhere to be seen. Pyx thought this peculiar, but not peculiar enough to warrant looking for her. She was probably back at Hona, playing with her cat.

Pyx realized that he hadn't seen the cat in a couple of days. Not that he saw it every day, but the feline's absence was a bit strange. Rin had pampered the cat, to be honest, and it seemed inseparable from her. It was a little disconcerting that the shy Rin would become attached to some stray cat as though it were a member of the family. Pyx didn't want to be the one to tell her, but she would have to work on a real relationship eventually. The cat just wasn't going to cut it.

The thought made him a little sad. Rin had always been a sweetheart, but she was far too shy to form relationships, even with people with whom she lived for years. Pyx felt for her, but he had no idea what could be done about it. Her father had already talked to her about the problem, and it clearly wasn't helping.

His mind refocused on the moment when Addie

asked with a lighthearted voice, "Pyx, when are you going to marry me?"

Pyx cleared his throat as he replied wryly, "Oh, you know, sooner or later."

She gave him a smug grin. "Well, I do hope it is sooner and not later."

Pyx merely smiled, watching her warmly. Addie's curious orange-blond hair was beautiful in the sunlight. Her light brown eyes bespoke the mischief she was often engaged in, yet they also belonged to someone who cared deeply for those around her. Pyx had no doubt at all that Addie was worth waiting for. He just wasn't sure how long he was supposed to wait. He resolved to broach the matter with Achron in a manner consistent with her desires, that being sooner instead of later.

* * *

The wind was refreshing, and the sun was quite warm for the time of year. But Rin felt empty as her hair was blown back from her face. She leaned against the ramparts of Castle Hona, resting her head on her arms as she stared vacantly over the large field beyond the castle, where bright kites danced in the distant air.

With the excitement of the gryphon clan ordeal fading, she sensed the return of her own self-induced isolation. She no longer had a furry companion to keep her company at night, and it made for a strange sort of sleeplessness. At the height of a bad situation, she had been willing to be committed to a relationship with a man she didn't know, but had lived with for more than a year. Now, she couldn't even muster enough courage to talk to him.

Rin sighed wistfully. She really did want to be anyone but herself. She could see the others out in the

94

grass, playing or watching, each a person or personality she would rather be.

She looked up in surprise when she heard someone approaching. It was Harku. She whipped her head back around, facing the field, trying to calm herself down. What was she going to say to him? How should she even feel about him? What if he asked her how her day was? Or if she wanted to eat lunch with him?

Her mind raced for answers, but came up blank. Harku stopped beside her and turned to look out toward the field. Rin simultaneously wished he would leave, and stay. He opted for the latter, but continued to say nothing. After several minutes Rin spoke tentatively. "Um, aren't you going to say something?"

His reply was soft. "No, not really."

She stared at him incredulously before looking toward the kites once more.

His words were not vain. He remained silent for some time longer. Rin finally broke the silence as she sighed and said, "I guess you have better things to do than keep me company. You are not a cat anymore."

She waited for him to respond, or leave, and after a few moments, he spoke softly. "I miss you, Rin."

Harku's strange statement only added to her consternation, and she met his gaze as he clarified. "I miss sleeping snuggled against your back, nestled in your soft mane . . ."

Rin flushed brightly and turned quickly away from him as she muttered, "Oh, that."

He continued with sincerity. ". . . that sweet and gentle smell, like a physical manifestation of your character." He stared at the kites again, finishing simply, "I haven't slept well since we returned from the Dagger Peaks."

There was another period of silence before Rin spoke her thoughts. "Y-you flatter me needlessly,

Harku."

He didn't look at her, but his face was serious. "No, Rin. Rather, you think far too little of yourself. You think you are of no account, but I know otherwise. You are as beautiful inside as you are outside. Your failure to recognize it is both a part of your beauty, and a part of your weakness."

Rin couldn't think of anything to say to such a direct statement. She just stared and wondered if he were going to leave soon. For his part, Harku didn't move at all, but watched the kites in a frustratingly unhurried manner. Rin finally asked with a little annoyance, "Why did you come up here? I was happy by myself." It wasn't true, of course, but he was acting so far outside her expectations that it bothered her.

Harku smiled. "I wanted to speak with you. To ask you something."

Rin found this simple revelation odd. "Well, why didn't you just say so?"

Harku turned toward her, his smile broadening. "Because that is not how someone interacts with you."

Rin blinked. What was he even saying?

Harku spoke again, giving her a fond look. "I have the pleasure of having lived within your inner circle. You let me in, and I came to know you. You confided in me your hopes and your dreams, your fears and your desires. When you were lonely, I was there. When you were afraid, I offered you courage, and when you cried, I gave you comfort. I know you well, Rin."

It wasn't that she hadn't passively observed that this would be true, but she hadn't actively thought about the implications. Rin felt extremely vulnerable, perhaps even slightly violated. Harku turned back to the rampart's vista and added mournfully, "But you never knew anything of me. I learned everything, but you learned nothing. A one-sided relationship."

An unsettling mixture of emotions welled up in her heart as she suddenly realized what that had to mean from Harku's perspective. His initial motives were suspect, to be sure, but beyond that early time together, he had given her everything . . . and received from her practically nothing. A one-sided relationship where he had given her everything she needed—a friend, a comfort, a companion—but she had scarcely given him anything more than a place to sleep and table scraps. She had doted on her pet cat, but that was hardly even the minimum for a real relationship.

She hunched her shoulders. "I-I am sorry, Harku." Rin couldn't think of anything else to say, but the more she thought about it, the more unworthy of him she perceived herself to be. What could have so motivated him during that time that he would continue to meet her needs, even though he did not benefit from it? This was the same man who had sacrificed everything for the sake of his kid sister. What kind of person lay beneath the surface of this man she barely knew?

The silence drew on, and Rin forgot she was nervous about talking to people she didn't know. She took the initiative and inquired, "Harku, what did you want to ask me?"

His only answer was silence, and Rin stepped toward him in curiosity. Harku looked worried, and didn't budge from contemplating the distant sky. Rin told him earnestly, "Harku, there is nothing to be afraid of. What did you need of me?"

He spoke in a low voice. "That isn't true, Rin, for I could lose you, and that I do fear."

Rin murmured the phrase as she pondered its implications. "Um, 'lose me'?"

Harku seemed a little surprised, but then knelt in front of her, taking her hand. His words were measured, coming from an honest and sober heart. "Rin, would you be willing to continue together what I began alone? Not to live in an unequal relationship, but to develop an equal relationship. I still want to be your courage, your comfort, your friend. But would you be mine?"

Rin said nothing for a moment. While a portion of what he had said before was lost on her, what he said now was not. He was serious, and it was plain that he had thought about this far longer than just the last few days. For her, however, it was rather sudden.

Her initial reaction was to say thanks, but no thanks. She didn't know him that well, and she didn't feel comfortable around him. Yet she vividly recalled Arru's statement that Harku was kind, devoted, and noble. His sister's boldness to stand in defense of her brother was a strong testimony to his character, confirmed by his actions, even if they were sometimes misguided.

Her first words came scarcely above a whisper. "I am afraid . . . because I don't know you . . . ." Harku looked down at the stonework of the top of the wall, as though he did not want to see in her eyes what she would say before she said it aloud. Rin continued in a small voice. "But I want to. I just don't know how. I-I don't know if I can . . . ."

He turned his eyes up at her again. "Rin, you're not alone anymore, and you don't have to be. I will help you, and I will not give up just because it is difficult."

Rin took a deep breath and let it out, asserting her decision more boldly than she expected she could. "Yes, Harku. Yes, I will be yours, if you will be mine." She added hastily to her answer, as she realized there was at least one complicating factor. "A-and if my father permits it."

He was technically her kidnapper, after all. There might be some issue there. Yet Rin believed she could convince him otherwise if she needed to.

Harku rose slowly and embraced her, his voice thick with emotion. "Rin, I love you so much! It's hard to even tell you how long I have wanted to hold you in my arms, to tell you . . . ."

He gave up trying to say anything and held her tightly. Rin's concern about checking with her father became rather unimportant to her, and she returned his embrace, glad tears running down her face. Was it really the lonely, fearful girl who had found a faithful friend, a reliable companion? Someone who loved her despite her shortcomings, who loved her without reservation and without condition? It was overwhelming, and Rin didn't want the moment to end.

She did not see where Achron and Keena stood, misty-eyed, in the courtyard below, watching a little longer before entering the castle to afford Rin and Harku some privacy. She would learn later that Harku had already secured permission for her hand in marriage, albeit with Achron's expressing substantial doubt concerning the young gryphon clansman's success. It was difficult for them to account for Rin's own heart.

They knew her as their daughter, but she was not the same person they had categorized as shy and unwilling to reach out to others. She had learned, among other things, that she could reach beyond herself if she had sufficient motivation, and Harku had presented such a motivation.

Chapter 10

Keena hesitated. "I don't know, Achron. I'm worried about what you might find. Last time there were traps, demons, and enslaved mages. Are you sure this is such a good idea? I mean, what will be gained by it?"

Achron tried to reassure her, avoiding correcting her on the matter of there being only one enslaved mage. "Well, yes, there are some unknowns here, but it shouldn't be as dangerous as the last mage tower. And there is a lot to be learned, especially about the great mages. We don't know where they came from, or how they got their power, or even who was recording some of the history at the time."

Keena nodded but tilted her head slightly as she spoke with a great deal of practicality. "But, Achron, why does this matter for us? For our family?"

It was a good question. He had to admit that personally, he was more driven by curiosity than by any real need. Still, there was a secondary reason that it mattered. He cleared his throat before answering. "It's partially because of the children that I want to know. Rin demonstrated that she isn't just some passive energy source to be used by a mage, but that she can, given a need, invoke the power concealed within herself. If we are to help the children deal wisely with what they contain, then we must know more about it."

They had both hoped that their children could lead ordinary lives despite their extraordinary natures. That they could marry, have families of their own, and live at peace with those around them. However, Rin's invoking of Hanni proved that this was a tenuous dream.

Based on the girls' descriptions, her action was frighteningly similar to what happened when the skilled mages among them invoked their staves. The frightening part was not the similarity, but the fact that Rin had acted by accident, without any training, and with little knowledge of how mages operate. If she, a female Fearian not yet of age, could act this way, what terrible things could be done intentionally by someone trained in the mage arts? What mistakes could a novice make while still learning the craft?

Keena sighed, looking discouraged. "I fear for Emeril for that very reason. She is so headstrong, and I just can't think of what to tell her anymore. No matter what I say, I can't get through to her."

Achron put a comforting arm gently around his wife. "I know, my dear. It's hard to not know. She isn't a little girl any longer, but she still listens. You have to talk to her like the woman she is becoming, rather than the little girl she was."

Keena leaned into him, and he held her close as she muttered ruefully, "How do you know stuff like this anyway?"

Achron merely chuckled. He certainly wasn't an expert on parenting, but he did have a millennium more of experience in general life than she did. Well, sort of. A lot of that time he had skipped through.

He retained some measure of his ability to slip through time, but he was careful not to use it. He didn't want to repeat what had happened when he first received that ability. His loss of Emeril, his daughter's namesake, was but a distant memory, yet still a painful one.

Keena's resigned but calm voice broke into his thoughts. "I presume you are not going alone into this endeavor?"

Achron smiled and shook his head. "Of course not. I need Viwy to find the place, and Creed to identify and deal with threats."

Probing further, Keena asked, "How will you get there, and for that matter, get back?"

Achron grinned with satisfaction at his own cleverness. "It's only fitting that we offer our services to your mother as an honor guard, what with crazy Fearians running loose everywhere. It just wouldn't be safe."

Keena pushed him away playfully as she glowered at him. "That's a terrible plan! Do you really think my mother will believe that's what you are doing?"

He laughed a little sheepishly. "No, not really, but I don't think she will ask either."

Keena tried to give him a rebuking glance, but couldn't hide her smile. "I suppose not. But do try to keep from embarrassing me any more than you have to."

Achron placed his hand gently on her face and kissed her with tender affection. "Of course, my dear, of course."

She sighed with some humor, "You're hopeless, Achron."

He smiled slyly, but it was true. There was no way he would ever grasp the subtleties of Fearian mannerisms. He was forever going to be that awkward rude stranger in Fearia. Thus far it hadn't really been a hindrance, just an annoyance.

* * *

Creed entered the room and dipped his head in a

102

courteous nod to the high queen of Fearia before taking up a position next to Viwy, who stood behind Achron. Creed didn't like the way the high queen watched him. Her careful regard made him feel uncomfortably important.

Achron was explaining to his mother-in-law his intention to show his respect for her by offering himself and others as an honor guard to escort her back to her palace in a place called Ravenloc. Creed had not heard of a place with such a name in Fearia. He supposed that many of the places had different names from the time he had last been there.

While he was pondering this change, Sheena darted into the room and came to a stop immediately beside him. He glanced at her with mild annoyance as he murmured out of the side of his mouth, "Sorry, Sheena. We are about to escort Grandmother back to her home. You will have to stay here."

She grinned at him with infuriating cheekiness as she replied in a smug whisper, "Oh, I know. I am going with you!"

He replied impulsively, and not so quietly as before. "What?! Ridiculous! You're not fit for the type of thing we are attempting to accomplish."

She frowned and crossed her arms defiantly. "Fit or not, and whether you like it or not, I am coming." Creed grimaced, thinking that her stubbornness could be as annoying as it could be sweet.

At that moment, Achron, speaking of their plans, stated succinctly, "I will lead the front of the honor guard along with Viwy, and Creed and Sheena will bring up the rear."

Creed stifled an exclamation of disagreement with a spontaneous coughing episode. This drew only a few glances, and if the high queen noticed, she ignored it. "If it is your desire, then I will not stop you. However,

I assure you that it is neither necessary nor expected by my people."

Achron nodded politely. "Yes, as you have said, but I must insist on this gesture of gratitude and respect for your willingness to visit us here at Hona Castle."

Sheena elbowed Creed. "Ha, see, I told you!"

Creed gave her an annoyed glance, but held his peace. He was of the mind that this was a bad idea, and as soon as the high queen was out of the room, he was going to let Achron know his complete lack of approval about the issue. It wasn't that Creed didn't enjoy Sheena's company, but that he viewed this as a mission, and only a fool brought loved ones on a mission.

Yanna looked at each of them in turn before she spoke. "Thank you for this kind gesture. Now please prepare yourselves for the journey. We leave in an hour." With that said, she turned and exited with the attendants that never seemed to leave her side.

Creed promptly blurted out, "Sheena can't go with us."

Achron looked surprised. "I am sorry, but why is that?"

Creed could see her suppressing her humor, which irked him more than he cared for. "Look, the great mage towers are not museums full of neatly encased baubles. They are dangerous, trap-ridden. Protected by things that are difficult to deal with."

Viwy gestured casually from him to her as he interjected, "Yeah, but wouldn't that make this your opportunity to be the knight in shining armor?"

Creed was only vaguely aware of what that phrase meant, and asked, "Why would I want to do that?"

Sheena giggled, and Achron smiled, answering in a practical manner. "For the honor guard to be accurate to human customs, we have to have four people.

104

Sheena is the most flexible person available at the moment, and a willing party who can help us."

Creed shook his head. "What? That's crazy. What about that metamorphic mage, Harku?"

Achron evaded the question. "He is, uh, kind of preoccupied at the moment."

But Creed wasn't out of alternatives. "What about Hanni?"

Achron shook his head. "Hanni stays as someone who can protect our families, should something happen while we are away."

Creed tried again. "What about Pyx?"

Achron replied smoothly. "No, Pyx is too integral to keeping the little ones from killing themselves."

Creed tried to get his mind to present other options, but none came. Viwy waved his hand dismissively. "Stop stalling already. You heard the queen's orders."

Creed glared at him, his face turning red, and his voice overly loud. "And just what does that have to do with anything!"

Viwy looked a little surprised, and he glanced at Achron, who shrugged before saying, "Everything, because her orders were that we be ready to leave in an hour, unless I missed something."

Sheena burst into laughter, and he turned away, hoping the burning flush he could feel was perceived as anger. "Yeah, right. Let's . . . do that."

Sheena grabbed his arm and practically pulled him along as she spoke with cheerful excitement. "Come on, ciega! We only have a short amount of time to pack before we have to leave for Fearia!"

Creed stumbled, but managed not to fall as he hurried after her, doing his best to sound persuasive.

"This isn't some kind of vacation, Sheena."

She gave him a winsome grin. "If I am traveling with you, ciega, then I shall be delighted enough in that!"

Creed rolled his eyes but decided that there was no changing the situation. He would just have to operate with an extra level of care, but frankly, he really hated trying to complete a mission and simultaneously protect an asset.

* * *

Achron reflected on how smoothly the whole honor guard exercise had progressed. As expected, nothing had occurred. Well, that was to say that they had not been attacked. Creed seemed strangely nervous, and unsurprisingly Sheena seemed rather giddy. The poor girl had never been to the country of her people, or really that far from Castle Hona, so everything was new and interesting to her. In addition, she got to share this experience with Creed.

Emeril had been less than happy to learn that her sister was going on some grand adventure without her, but she kept the details of this disappointment to herself. Achron loved his daughters, and he wanted to see Sheena happy, but he had another motivation for choosing her. He wasn't sure what they would face in Heket's tower, but he did know that Creed's power was in synchrony to the power within Sheena. Achron didn't want to be in a place where they needed more power than Creed could manage on his own.

There was some reciprocal link between a skilled mage and the majestic gems, almost as though the mage were functioning as the gem's staff. Achron was rather curious about how this relationship worked, but there wasn't anyone to ask about it, and he seriously doubted the capacity of his random musing to arrive at any kind of coherent understanding, at least not without more examples. Regardless, Sheena would not be in any real danger, even if they faced very real enemies in Fearia.

In some ways, Achron was relieved that after the years that had passed, no one seemed to recognize him. But with this naturally came the consequence of not having a crowd of Fearians to come to his aid.

They were on a major road that ran from Ravenloc to the heart of the fertile plains of Fearia. The rolling hills, scattered clusters of forest, and numerous patches of farmland were markedly picturesque. Achron could almost believe that this place was peaceful and happy, safe from the troubles that plagued the rest of the world. However, he had not forgotten about the dark malicious creatures he had confronted the last time he was here.

Ankid had not been pleased when Achron told him that were going to see something before they returned. The man told them that when they were ready to return to their home, they needed only to ask a gold caster to return them to the other side. He had given them a passage crest, a mark symbolic of their right to travel to the human side of the world. He could sense the disdain in the way Ankid refused to consider coming with them, and even implied that if they asked him to send them home, he may or may not have the time to bother with it.

Achron had no reason to doubt the man's loyalty to the high queen, but he seemed particularly unhappy with humans being on the Fearian side. Regardless, his reticence was their advantage: Achron didn't have to explain his actions to the man.

As they walked, Achron and Viwy attempted to keep their identities concealed by their cloaks. Being human in a place without humans made them stand out for sure. Fortunately, the differences between them and the Fearians were subtle enough that, so long as no one stopped to have an extended conversation with them, they could pass as locals.

Sheena practically was a local, though the Fearians in this area were field caste. They had cat-like tails and short manes, differing from Sheena's forest caste features. However, the fertile plains were close enough to the great forest that seeing a forest caste Fearian was not all that unusual. It was Creed that drew several curious glances. He was out of his element on multiple levels. Not only was his own caste gone, and the next nearest caste rare, but his mannerisms were very obviously human and not Fearian.

Viwy and Sheena were in the lead, and Achron walked alongside Creed, taking up the rear. They traveled along the main road at Creed's behest, though the young man seemed uncertain that they were in the right place.

Achron determined to make the most of his opportunity with Creed, and he opened the conversation casually. "Sheena spends a lot of time with you, Creed."

Creed glanced at him warily and kept his reply guarded. "Yeah, that's true, but I can't seem to convince her that she doesn't have to be at my side every moment."

Achron chuckled lightly. "Sure, but you do realize that she thinks the world of you."

Achron was a little surprised when Creed sighed and admitted, "I wish she wouldn't. There is a brighter future for her elsewhere."

Achron hesitated, trying to evaluate Creed's statement. It sounded oddly like something Keena might say. He aimed to gather more information. "Oh, and how do you figure that?"

Creed answered directly this time. "Prodigies don't have children, Achron. None of the ones I knew of ever had any offspring. What kind of brother would I be to subject my sister to that fate? She deserves to be a mother. I . . . I just can't knowingly subject her to that."

Achron marveled at Creed's maturity. Then again, he had always been sober and careful in his thinking. Achron mused aloud, "You know, the journey of life is more than procreation. And that journey is best taken with one's closest friend. Perhaps the cost is uneven from your perspective, but it would be silly to make such a decision alone, as though you were the only one who had any say in the situation."

Creed studied Achron, his expression mysterious, before returning to staring down the road. They walked on for a time before Achron asked, "You do like Sheena, right?"

Creed only muttered, "Sheena deserves better."

In a way, his response didn't answer Achron's question, but it told him that Creed didn't just like Sheena. He genuinely cared for her. Like any man who had come to truly love someone, he would rather lose her than see her suffer loss. And, like many, he failed to correctly value himself in light of this reality. Their situation left Achron in a quandary. There really wasn't anything he could say to Creed that would help him see that his dilemma was overstated.

Creed stopped to glance at his surroundings before looking back at the map he was carrying and complaining, "What is this? Everything is so different from when I was here last."

Sheena smirked a little. "Please tell me we haven't been walking in the wrong direction for the last couple hours."

Creed frowned slightly at her, but simply returned to analyzing the map. "Why did they have to go and change all the names?"

Several travelers strolled by them, chatting excitedly about something called the "festival of the star harvest." Achron looked to Viwy after the Fearians had passed and inquired, "Well, I don't suppose you could locate the ruin then?"

Viwy shook his head. "Eh, not so much. I didn't detect any unusual swells of power, and without knowing what I am looking for, I can't get much more direction on its location unless it's in view."

Achron sighed and turned back to Creed. "So are you sure that it's in this area?"

Creed lowered the map and squinted toward a clump of trees, saying, "Yes, it's somewhere out here. But Heket wasn't one to flaunt herself, so it probably isn't a grand rising spire like my grandfather's was."

Sheena looked curiously at a way marker indicating a fork in the road ahead. She offered, "Well, maybe we should ask someone if they know about any ruins in the area?"

Viwy spoke with some sense of humor. "Now little Sheena, that is far too practical and logical. It's just not how we do things out away from Hona. First, we have to wander hopelessly, lost for days before we even entertain such notions, and next . . . ."

Achron cleared his throat loudly, interrupting Viwy's attempt at comedy. "Yes, dear, that is an excellent idea." Glancing toward the sky, he added, "It's getting on toward evening, so it wouldn't hurt to stop somewhere anyway."

Achron wasn't particularly sold on the notion of the Fearian caste system, or the lack of a currency, but he did appreciate the fact that it made traveling in Fearia quite easy. Sheena did the talking, and they all were able to eat or stay the night without the need to carry money or worry about cost. They could also travel with no

110

concern of being robbed. Not that robbers stood a chance against three skilled mages.

Achron gestured that they continue down the road. Sheena happily led the way as they turned off toward a charming little Fearian field caste community. The cluster of several hundred small, white stone houses with thatched roofs nestled among the low hills and open fields was the definition of quaint. In the evening sunlight, children played in the dirt streets, and people milled about, returning from a day's work in the fields. The atmosphere was one of lively excitement.

They approached a large building at the edge of town that was obviously a hostel. The rest of them waited while Sheena conversed politely with the manager to arrange for their stay. Viwy and Achron stood off to one side, conversing lightly. Achron caught something from the corner of his eye and motioned the other man to silence, smiling as he watched Creed.

The young Fearian was staring blankly at the map that refused to reveal its secrets to him. A bright-eyed and cheery-faced girl approached him and spoke pleasantly. "Hello, traveler!"

Creed startled a little, and looked up at her as he replied limply. "Uh . . . hi."

She wore a simple, long-sleeved red blouse and a dull gray skirt. The clothes of a commoner. Her tail flicked back and forth with some measure of excitement as she said, "We don't often have travelers in our little town who come from so far away! Please tell me you will be staying for the festival."

Creed blinked, not mentally caught up to his unanticipated conversation. "F-festival?"

The girl pivoted from side to side idly, but her voice was welcoming. "Yes! The festival of the star harvest is tonight! You and your companions are most certainly invited to join us."

Creed seemed to grow a little nervous and responded noncommittally. "Thanks, but we are kind of busy. I don't know if we have time for festivals."

A grin lit the girl's face as she pleaded for him to embrace the enthusiasm she clearly felt. "Oh, come on, it will be fun! There will be great food, music, dancing!"

Creed pulled back slightly as he echoed, "D-dancing?"

The girl seemed to realize something and casually mentioned, "Oh, um, I am Eida, by the way." An awkward silence ensued, and then she said, "So, what's your name?"

Creed didn't reply, partly because he didn't have to. Sheena returned from her business and, seeing him in conversation, joined him. "Ciega! Who is this?"

Creed just looked at the field caste Fearian for a moment, fumbling about for the answer. "Uh . . . Reda, was it?"

She laughed as she corrected him. "No, it was Eida, and you still haven't told me your name."

Sheena chuckled as she patted his shoulder and spoke fondly. "You will have to forgive Creed here, Eida. He is socially reluctant. My name is Sheena."

Sheena nodded politely, and Eida responded in kind. "Well, a pleasure for sure. We have little to offer guests here in Tomin's Knoll, but you are here at the perfect time. Tonight is the festival of the star harvest, and you are all welcome to participate with us in food, dancing, and other festivities." She paused and batted her eyes at Creed as she said with a strange emphasis on the pronouns. "I do hope you will be joining us."

She didn't wait for an answer, but giggled and turned to sprint happily down the packed dirt pathway that wound through her little village. Creed just stared after her as Sheena commented, "Wow, she sure was chipper. A festival does sound fun, though."

Creed was of a different opinion. "We have way more important things to do than some silly dancing."

Sheena grinned teasingly at him. "Ciega, I didn't know you couldn't dance?"

Creed flinched, in part because of her words, and in part because Achron had approached him and put his hand on the young man's shoulder, saying, "I think we have an important mission, but it may be that this festival is our best opportunity to ask discreetly about our quarry."

Creed sighed, reluctant to admit Achron was probably right. "Okay, fine, but I am NOT dancing."

His face flushed only slightly at his companions' mirth regarding his conditions about the festival. Sheena gave an exaggerated sigh. "Oh, that is too bad. I guess I will just have to dance by myself."

Chapter 11

Creed hung back from the festivities, watching the energetic dancers in a large open meadow. He sat on one of several bundles of straw that served as impromptu seating. As the name of the festival suggested, the stars shone brightly on that moonless night. Tall poles topped with torches illuminated the meadow, and the sounds of stringed instruments playing in harmony mingled in the air with joyful and excited conversation.

He had no desire to be there; he wanted to be out looking for Heket's tower. Viwy appeared to be more interested in sampling the local menu, and Sheena was doing far more dancing than talking. Only Achron seemed to be gathering intelligence. Creed knew some guilt for not engaging in the task that he felt like everyone else should, but it was plain that the other Fearians kept him at a distance. Perhaps it was his rare form, or his dark coloring, or maybe his atypical mannerisms. Whatever the cause, they were polite, but unwilling to open up to him.

Not that he was much of a conversationalist himself. He muttered under his breath, "'Socially reluctant,' hmm? I'm respectfully reserved, thank you very much."

Without warning, someone grabbed his arm and

pulled him to his feet. "Come on! Dance with me, Creed!" He staggered into a trot as Eida forced him to accompany her.

He thought about resisting her efforts and telling her to leave him alone. She was, after all, being a pest as far as he was concerned. But just then he caught sight of something around her neck that glinted in the firelight. It was a leather-wrapped stone on a simple chain, nothing more than what one would expect of a peasant—except that the modest stone bore rune marks on its surface. It was a chrysoprase, the stone of a mind mage, the stone of Heket.

Eida giggled freely at Creed's poor attempts to dance with her, as he focused on inquiring indirectly about the stone. "Uh, whoops, sorry. So, uh, that's a nice pendant you have."

She misled him as they, or rather, she, moved through the simple traditional footwork. "Thank you, Creed. It's sweet of you to say so, but I suspect you have seen far more marvelous things than my mother's pendant."

Creed tried another direction. "Tell me about your mother."

He stumbled over his own feet, but Eida only laughed. "Oh, you are an odd one, aren't you? My mother was slain by a shade beast some years ago, but me and my brothers continue without her, and I have this pendant to remember her by."

Creed apologized as he tried to come up with some other approach. "Err, I am sorry for your loss."

Eida looked a little more serious, but she shrugged and said, "It isn't good, but it isn't abnormal, either. Tell me about your home, Creed. It must be wonderful!"

Creed wasn't following her logic. "And what makes you think that?"

She smiled broadly. "Aren't your people the ones who work with precious stones, gold, and silver?"

He wasn't sure what she meant, but apparently there was some tie between his supposed caste, doubtless misidentified, and his role in society. He veered the conversation back toward his own curiosity. "Oh, uh, right. So where did your mother get such an interesting pendant?"

She brought their motion to a slow but certain stop and tilted her head slightly, observing him in a manner that made him uncomfortable. She thought aloud, "You are so different from anyone I have ever known."

There wasn't an obvious appropriate answer to her statement. He wasn't sure if he was even supposed to answer her, and instead all he managed was a verbal pause. "Uhhhh . . . ."

Her face broke into a clever smile, and she began pulling him away from the dance. "Come. You danced with me, so let me show you my secret!"

Creed was thankful that the darkness concealed his embarrassment as they quickly distanced themselves from the commotion of the festival. What could she mean by such an invitation?

Once she had led him out of the village, she spoke in a low voice, as though she were afraid someone might hear them. "You have to be quiet, because it's dangerous to go beyond the village at night."

As they crested a small hill, she paused and turned to look at him. "You have to promise me that you won't tell anyone about what I am going to show you, Creed. My father forbade it be known to any, lest the evil humans come and try to hurt us for it."

Creed stammered back, "O-oh right, of course, nothing for evil humans!" She nodded firmly, and a chill ran down Creed's spine. What would she say if he told her that his adoptive father was human? Worse, it meant that the people with whom she had to do were heavily influenced by the anti-human contingent. The same group of Fearians who felt strongly enough about the issue that they were not afraid of attempting to kill their own high queen. He decided to keep the matter to himself for now.

She led him further than he thought she would, but eventually they reached the edge of a wooded thicket. Eida glanced carefully about, then they headed into the small clump of trees. From the outside, it looked like any other of the wooded patches that dotted the rolling hills of the Fearian plains. But as they entered, he caught a glimpse of an ancient ruin.

Eida retrieved a long, soft brown staff with a simple ribbed haft, and a crown with a fist-sized cabochon chrysoprase. Creed recoiled slightly at the sudden sight of Yindil, the infinite sum. She confided in him sarcastically, "Of course, we can't get in without a magic stick!"

Creed felt and sounded breathless. "R-right."

Walking deeper into the woods, Eida stopped at an overgrown stone platform that had a staircase in its center. At the base of the stairs, he could see a solid stone door inlaid with an elaborate chrysoprase crest. Eida stopped and gripped the staff in both hands as she hunched her shoulders a little sheepishly. "Creed . . . I just want to say . . . well, I am not spoken for yet, you know, and I, um, I would love to travel . . . ."

Creed wiped his sweaty palms on his tunic as he desperately wished he was not alone in the dark with this forward peasant girl. It wasn't fair to her that he was keeping things to himself, things that would change her entire outlook concerning him. Creed sighed and looked at her soberly. "Eida, this place is very special to you, but I must admit that I am not from Fearia."

117

She took a sharp step back away from him, fear edging her voice. "W-what?! Where else is there!?"

Creed replied softly. "I am from the human side of the world."

Her eyes wide with her mortification, she took a second step back from him, and then a third, and stated with far too much emotion, "Y-you lied to me!"

She hurled the staff at him, and he reached to catch it out of the air as she turned and fled from the woods, sobbing. Creed stretched his hand out after her, but then let it fall to his side. Somehow it didn't really feel like a success to him, despite the fact that he stood on the threshold of untold secrets.

Heket was a mind mage. The great mind mage. She had known things that few others could, and she had held a revered role as the designated historian of the Fearian mages. Her tower would likely be well protected. Creed hesitated as he debated about waiting for the others. He sat down in the stairwell and leaned against the wall. Viwy would be able to find him, and he didn't want to blunder into any traps. Without the mist mage's ability to see the unseen, Creed probably wouldn't stand a chance inside Heket's tower.

He scrunched his face with concern, as this was at odds with Eida's notions of showing him her secrets. Surely if the place were genuinely dangerous, the girl would not have been so glib about entering. The more he thought about it, the more uncertain he became. Creed remained there, trying to arrive at some conclusion about what course of action he should take.

* * *

Sheena had rarely been so exasperated. It was bad enough that Creed wouldn't participate in the wonderful festivities that any sane person would delight

118

in, but it was downright infuriating that he was so easily duped by the trampish wiles of that sneaky cat of a Fearian, Eida. The girl was polite, but obviously had some kind of ulterior motives. Sheena felt a little undervalued that Creed was so taken by a girl substantially younger than herself.

She rationalized that she was not jealous, but objectively weighing a potentially dangerous situation. Dangerous for Creed, that was. Despite the seeming lack of danger surrounding her own person, Sheena had trouble motivating herself to enter the dark and overgrown woods before her. Yet she was not about to allow that little cat take her Creed away . . . even if he was completely incompetent. She told herself that dark forests on moonless nights were not scary, but before she could attempt to step forward, something shot out of the woods and ran smack into her. They crashed to the ground with a mutual cry.

There was a brief failing of limbs, and they both scrambled away from the point of impact, jumping to their feet and facing their foe like a frightened rabbit ready to bolt. Sheena let out an audible sigh of relief when she saw it was just Eida. "Whoa, don't scare me like that."

It was hard to see Eida's expression in the dark, but she sounded especially unhappy. "W-what are you doing out here! Are you going to betray your people, too? Like your worthless adopted brother?" Sheena knew that she and Creed were so different in appearance that they practically had to have different parents, so it was not surprising that Eida recognized at least one of them had to be adopted.

She tried to sound reasonable, but her voice was not as steady as she would have liked. "What? I don't know what you're talking about. Creed is the last person who would betray anyone!"

119

Eida crossed her arms as she stated disdainfully, "Oh yeah? Well, he has sided with the evil humans! He is going to desecrate the secret treasure of my people. He will even hurt us if we don't stop him!"

Sheena's voice grew louder as her ire was stoked. "You are wrong! Creed isn't like that, and neither are all humans!"

Eida shook her head in disgust, anger in every word, as though she had been personally hurt by the supposed betrayal. "Fine! You sacrifice everything that is good and right, but I won't. I am going to tell my father, and he and our people will stop you liars!" She whirled and took a couple rapid steps before suddenly halting. Sheena glared after her, but then let out a frightened gasp as she saw what had arrested the girl.

A stone's throw beyond the field caste Fearian stood a monstrous, four-legged beast twice as tall as they. Its body was covered with short, dark fur, and its long, ugly, rat-like head was a wicked display of huge, dagger-like teeth. Its sleek form suggested that it was fast, dangerous, and always ready to eat the unsuspecting. Its eyes gleamed with an unnatural green light. It let out a low growl as it stalked toward them slowly. More pairs of floating green orbs flickered in the darkness. The beasts circled, hedging them in against the forest. Sheena counted five, no, ten, or maybe even more of the things.

She dropped her voice to a whisper. "Eida, we have to run into the woods. It's our only hope. Creed . . . ."

Eida interrupted her with a sob. "Creed must be dead by now, and they want us to run into the woods. It's where they overpower their prey, where everyone dies if they draw attention to themselves. I-I was . . . I was a fool to come here at night."

Sheena felt a sense of terror at the thought of

losing Creed, but she had to believe he was okay. He was a warrior, after all. A soldier of the highest caliber. His reluctance to use his power was only fuel to her imagination of what he was truly capable of.

Sheena clenched her fists and muttered to herself, "If Rin can accidentally summon Hanni, then surely I can call my brother." Eida turned to look at her, but the other girl's expression was lost in the darkness. Sheena closed her eyes and whispered as she focused her mind on and heart on her closest friend. It wasn't difficult, since she did it nearly all the time anyway. She spoke boldly. "Creed, I need you!"

There was a strange stirring in her mind, and the wooded hillock became brilliantly illuminated as a column of yellow-green light flashed from sky to ground, materializing Creed on the spot. Creed looked a little confused, but he snapped to the moment rapidly. Eida screamed as one of the impatient beasts lunged at her, but it was incinerated in an instant, cut down by a beam from the tip of Orion, Creed's relic staff. His skin glowed brightly with the light of an energy mage. Twirling the staff, he brought the end of it down firmly on the ground. Dozens of spheres of light jumped up to the level of his eyes.

The creatures shrieked angrily, attacking from every direction, and in the light of Creed's power, it became obvious that their numbers were well above a dozen. Creed flicked his hand sharply, and high energy rays shot out of the spheres in rapid sequence. In the blink of an eye, not one of the monsters remained.

Sheena was extremely grateful Creed was normally such a mild-mannered person, because he was oddly more frightening than the things he had just removed from existence. She looked down at her hands, and saw that they glowed faintly with the same light that enveloped Creed. Creed remained at attention, eyeing the trees, and then with a wave of his hand dismissed the energy spheres.

Eida spoke fearfully, and Sheena jerked her head up, recognizing the same concern. "W-what if there are more of them?"

The glow faded from Creed, and he returned his staff to its collapsed form. "Morkrats hunt in packs. If the pack is gone, then all those in this area are as well. But how did they get here?"

Eida darted her gaze across the clearing several times, clearly not certain she believed him. "They have always been here, and no matter how many we kill, there are always more."

Creed's face knit in confusion, and Sheena asked, "Have you fought them before?"

He nodded. "Yes, the mage league I was part of was in bitter conflict with the one led by the summoners. They often used morkrats, since they are easy to summon, but effective against the unprepared."

Sheena felt surprised. "So there are summoners doing bad things here in Fearia?" Creed eyed her with mild disapproval, and she put her hands on her hips as she defended herself. "Hey, not all of us know . . . like . . . everything!"

Creed rolled his eyes as he looked suspiciously toward the forest before asking Eida, "Are there any humans in Fearia?"

She glared at him, sounding more confident than she had been moments before. "Well, there weren't before you got here. Now I think that only you can answer that question."

Creed muttered, "Surely they didn't. It's forbidden!"

Sheena spoke a little testily. "Come on, Creed. Stop being so cryptic!"

Creed sighed slowly and explained. "Only

humans can be summoners, and during the war, they fought indirectly by drawing dark creatures from another place. However, these creatures, which for lack of a better word were called demons, were unpredictable, and often killed anyone they came across. Therefore, it was universally agreed upon that no summoner was to invoke a permanent structure to draw them continually. A demon gate. If you have no humans, but demons persist, then you have a demon gate problem."

Eida spoke with a measure of triumph, but glanced around again, like she was still not sure they were really safe. "I knew it! Humans ARE evil."

Creed shook his head. "Yeah, you can think that if you want, but that gate isn't going anywhere without the aid of a human." Sheena looked questioningly at him, but then put her hand to her mouth as she realized who it was he spoke of.

Creed stepped toward the woods, but stopped when Eida grabbed his hand. "Wait! If you . . . if you are going to see my secret treasure, then I want to be the one to show it to you."

Creed arced an eyebrow at her, but then shrugged. "Fine. Lead the way." Sheena quickly grabbed his other hand, not wanting to be outdone by the sly and seemingly fickle cat.

As they headed into the woods, Eida asked, "So, um, how is you know so much about these creatures?" Her casual air only succeeded in making her sound awkward.

However, Creed was mostly scouting their surroundings and responded anyway, distracted from the conversation. "I fought in the mage war three thousand years ago."

Understandably, Eida looked surprised. "What!? How does that work? You're hardly even an adult!"

Creed paused his forward stride and, in an

annoyed tone, informed her, "It's complicated, and I am an adult, thank you very much."

She glanced at Sheena, who simply nodded. Eida spoke apologetically. "Sorry, it just sounded ridiculous." Creed had no interest in pursuing the matter further, it seemed, since he said nothing more.

Returning to the sunken stairwell and the stone door, Eida picked up the staff from where it lay resting against the door. She smiled at them proudly and placed her hand on the chrysoprase crest. The staff glimmered with a faint blue light, and the door shifted and opened. She motioned for them and entered first. They followed her into the subterranean structure. Sheena marveled at what she saw.

The large circular antechamber was lit by a dim blue illumination, and rows of books lined the walls. Pleasant wood furniture was scattered about the room. It was a respectable receiving room, and Sheena was relieved that it was not some kind of awful dungeon, crypt, or some such as she had half-expected. There was a sense of reverence about the place, as though great effort had been made to keep it pristine.

Eida stepped to the middle of the room. "This place is my treasure, my sanctuary from the hard darkness that is in my life. The loss of my mother, my father's preoccupation with the threat of humans. My brothers' inability to understand their only sister." She hesitated, a touch of fear in her tone. "I-I . . . . it is strange that I would show it to someone who is in league with the enemy. But you saved my life, and if you are going to come here anyway, let it be as my friend, not my enemy."

Creed nodded as he said, "Thank you, Eida. We are not here to ruin your treasure, but to learn of the ancients."

Sheena felt a warm sense of pride that Creed

was her closest friend. He could be remarkably elegant when he wanted to be.

Eida started slightly. "So . . . you're not here to loot this place?" Creed shook his head. Giving him a puzzled expression, she asked, "But what else is there that could cause you to come all the way from the other world?"

Creed looked around with obvious apprehension. "A long time ago, this was the tower of Heket the great mind mage. She was charged with recording part of the ancient history written in the golden chronicle."

Eida stifled a gasp with her hand. Creed continued. "It was here that she worked, it was here that that she knew things no one else could, and it was here that she would have met with the others responsible for recording the histories. I know of Ferir, among the humans, who wrote another aspect of the history in the ancient chronicle."

Eida interrupted him with a desperate denial. "NO! Humans cannot have written part of our sacred history!"

Sheena tried to soothe her. "Eida, there was a time when there was no avarice between humans and Fearians."

Eida turned to face a bookcase as she muttered sullenly, "T-that just can't be possible."

Sheena opened her mouth to respond, but Creed shook his head, and she reluctantly refrained from correcting Eida. Creed pulled a book off the nearest shelf and thumbed through it casually. Sheena approached him and inquired, "So, what is in these books?"

Creed closed the volume and returned it as he answered with a single word. "Data."

Eyeing the numerous crowded shelves lining the room, she echoed, "Data?"

Creed ambled along the wall, explaining as he went. "Yes. Mind mages lack brute force like I possess, or practical power like that of Father. Instead, they have abilities related to numbers and information. They can calculate trajectories, weights, distances, velocities, and so forth in their minds instantly. In the mage war, they often served as tacticians and engineers, and calculated the likelihood of victory in a conflict. They could also be deadeye archers, but such a task was a waste of their skills under most circumstances."

Creed gestured to a wall uninhabited by books. It was covered with odd whorls, citrine stones, and symbols cut out of chrysoprase. "Eida, what is beyond this antechamber?"

Eida jerked slightly, giving him a startled look. "B-beyond this room?"

Creed turned back to the wall and walked toward it cautiously. "Yes, this is just the front of the tower complex."

Creed slowed and then stopped as he approached the wall. Sheena could not comprehend the source of his hesitation, and finally asked, "Creed, what are you so nervous about?"

Creed sighed and told them, "It's . . . just that the watcher is still intact, and I really don't want to find out the hard way what it is capable of."

Eida studied the wall curiously. "What's a watcher?" Sheena felt a similar question rise in her mind and looked at Creed.

He replied flatly. "Every great mage tower was supervised, or perhaps better, protected, by a watcher. A construct of sorts that could identify threats and deal with them appropriately. After the war broke out, some of these were modified in ways that made them especially dangerous for the unwary."

As though the watcher realized that its existence

was known, the wall seemed to shimmer, and a translucent apparition of a young woman appeared. She was clearly Fearian, field caste Fearian at that, and she spoke in a soft monotone, addressing them politely but coldly. "Welcome to Heket's tower. Lady Heket is not here at the moment, but I, her shadow, will assist you in her stead. What is it that you require?"

Creed stared at the watcher, transfixed by its phantom appearance. Eida was too confused to be so frozen, and she blurted out, "Why does it look so much like me?"

Chapter 12

Sheena blinked rapidly. The resemblance, apart from the apparent difference in age, was incredible.

The watcher attempted to answer Eida's question. "I was formulated off Lady Heket's form. Are you her daughter?"

Creed coughed and replied, "Yes! Ahem, I mean, yes, Eida is a daughter of Heket. May we gain admittance to the primary complex?" Eida looked uncertain but nodded, extending the staff for the watcher's perusal.

The watcher announced, "You bear Lady Heket's staff, and her genuine likeness. Please, enter."

The image flickered and vanished, and the wall slid smoothly out of the way, revealing a large corridor. Unlike the room where they stood, the corridor was dusty, and its air stale. The watcher flickered back into place on the wall. "Be wary. The upper levels of the tower have been destroyed, and I have sealed off these levels from the threat above. Do not attempt to access the upper levels, young master."

Unnerved by the talking apparition that could be her twin, Eida stuttered, "Um, y-yes, w-we won't."

Eida grabbed Creed's arm and clung tightly to him, paying no heed to his annoyed look. Sheena felt a slight pang of jealousy and took Creed's other arm. He switched his gaze to her, but she simply tossed her head. If Creed was too dense to understand that not dancing with her in lieu of dancing with a stranger was deeply troubling, then he didn't deserve to understand her current behavior.

Creed complained as they continued down the hall. "You do realize that if a threat appears, I won't be able to respond as quickly if you're both holding on to my arms."

Eida's tone sounded sheepish. "I-I . . . um, I am just a little scared."

Sheena tried to dismiss his concerns by pointing out, "I don't think anything has moved in this place for a long time." Neither one of them let go of Creed.

The corridor led to a large circular junction of a room, also well populated with bookshelves crammed full of tomes of numerical information. Several hallways branched out from the hub.

Creed paused in the dim light and peered down the hallways that vanished into darkness. "Watcher, is the sigil illumination system still in place?"

The translucent woman responded in her emotionless voice. "Negative. The system was impaired by upper level structural damage."

Creed followed up with another question. "Watcher, which one of these hallways leads to Heket's personal chambers?"

The watcher gestured to one of the doorways. "The master's personal quarters were lost along with the upper levels of the tower, but her private record room remains down the northeast hallway."

Creed's body tensed as he invoked his mage power. A luminescent yellow-green ball of light rose from the ground to levitate in front of him. It maintained its relative position as they started down the hallway.

Eida's curiosity had not been at rest, and she asked, "How could you possibly know how to talk to that thing? Or what might be inside a place no one has been in for generations?"

Sheena gave her an amused smile. "What? Didn't you believe him that he is three thousand years old?"

Eida dropped her gaze, appearing a bit embarrassed. "Well . . . not really . . . but I guess there isn't another explanation."

She contemplated this for a moment. "Does that mean Creed is immortal?"

Sheena chuckled. "Naw, we've grown up together for several years now, and he has gotten older."

Creed rolled his eyes. "Would you two stop talking about me like I wasn't right here!" he huffed.

Sheena just laughed, but Eida bit her lip and apologized. "S-s-sorry, Creed."

The trio passed a number of doors before reaching the end of the long, curving hallway. The final door was ornately patterned, but lacked any visible mechanism for opening it. Creed spoke to the apparition that followed them along the wall. "Watcher, can you open this door?"

It told him, "Negative. It is sealed by the master. Only she can open it."

Creed nodded at Eida. "All right. It's time to test your bloodline. If you would be so kind as to put your hand on the center of the door?"

Eida reached out, but then hesitated, and asked fearfully, "W-what's behind this door? What if . . . what if my resemblance is incidental? I-I am just an ordinary girl." There was a sense of bitter resignation to her voice, as though fate had chosen poorly, and naught could be done about it. She would always be nothing in a caste that was already of little account.

Creed responded with a bluntness that Sheena was used to, but that troubled Eida. "Don't be silly. You're obviously a direct descendent of Heket, and the room beyond that door is possibly the most boring place you will ever go."

Sheena spoke with greater care. "It's okay, Eida. I am sure your heritage is far more grand than you realized. What matters is what you do with it."

Eida took a deep breath and hesitated a moment longer before reaching out and placing her palm on the door. A pulse of light rippled through the elaborate swirled lines, and the small citrine stones embedded in the door began to glow. A cloud of dust rose as the door shifted and opened. Creed sauntered into the room, chased by the girls, who did not want to be without a light source.

Sheena believed Creed knew what he was talking about, but she was still a little impressed with how accurate his description of the room had been. Shelves lined the walls of the modest room, and while highly organized, they mostly contained stacks of unbound paper and blank volumes waiting to be filled. A plain writing desk sat against one wall, neatly decorated with writing implements, long-dry ink wells, and bottles of ink.

Sheena took a step toward the desk out of curiosity, but Creed caught her arm. "It's possible that the last person to stand in this place was Heket herself. I think we should show some respect for her wishes that this room not be entered. She sealed it, and we are here for a purpose, not for rifling through her personal possessions aimlessly."

Eida stared at him wide-eyed, as though stunned by his words. Sheena nodded her agreement and waited by his side while he took in their surroundings.

Creed gestured to a strange metal stand on the

desk. "That's where she imbued the Sublimis Chrysoprasis estis Hekesis."

Eida studied the object, her brow furrowed in uncertainty. "What is that?" she inquired.

Sheena replied for him. "The majestic chrysoprase, a legendary gemstone imbued with the fullness of her power. But Creed, who is it?"

Still intent on the desk, Creed answered distractedly. "Oh, uh, Adderil is the majestic chrysoprase."

Eida shook her head. "What do you mean, 'who'?"

Creed coughed, remembering he was in the company of someone apart from his family, and muttered, "Ah, don't worry about it. It's not immediately important." He approached the desk cautiously and examined its contents.

Eida had another question. "Creed, how did Heket die?"

He replied, "Like all of the great mages, she died peacefully in her old age. Well, almost all of them, anyway."

Sheena was curious about the exception. "Just 'almost'?"

Frustration was clear in Creed's face and voice. "Yes. Seleen the traitor! She stole all the majestic gems, and arguably singlehandedly started the war. She met a violent end, in part for her crimes."

Creed reached for the strange metal stand and gasped, yanking his hand back. Eida and Sheena flashed their eyes toward the stand with apprehension, but there was nothing obviously wrong with it. Creed whispered, "I don't understand. How? And why?" He reached out and lifted a smooth sliver of metal from the stand. It was about the length of his hand, but narrow and cylindrical. It glimmered in the yellow-green light. He continued his self-focused monologue. "Was she mocking her?"

With a slight shake of her head, Sheena quipped, "So, Creed, I don't suppose you could actually talk someone other than yourself?"

He gave her a rebuking glance that was completely ruined by his half-smile. "This is one of Seleen's silver shards. Obviously left in place of where the majestic gem was, but why? Surely no one would ever enter this room to see it? At least, not any time on the same scale that Seleen lived. It's . . . just confusing."

Eida glanced around the room nervously as though she feared the person of whom Creed spoke might jump out at them from the shadows. "So, uh, if it was sealed, then how did she get in?"

Creed stared blankly at the silver shard in his hand, and then replied limply, "I don't know. And I probably don't want to know."

He tucked the shard into the pouch that hung from his belt as he surveyed the desk further. He reached out and retrieved the only unordinary volume that sat on the desk. It was elaborately decorated, and the cover was made of metal. It bore a secured locking mechanism opposite the spine.

Eida spoke with almost breathless excitement, "I-it looks like the golden chronicle!"

Creed shook his head. "It's similar in structure, but it's not the same. Regardless, if this does not have the answers we seek, then nothing here will. Let's go."

Sheena was surprised at his abruptness, and swept her hand toward the rest of the room. "But Creed, we have scarcely looked at what's in here!"

Creed turned toward the door as he spoke. "No, this is Heket's journal. Nothing else here warrants being disturbed. And I really don't want to find out if Seleen left some kind of trap behind. That woman was devious in ways that shouldn't be true of anyone."

Eida spoke cautiously as they left the room. "Um, Creed, isn't it a bit much to feel such animosity for someone who hasn't been alive for many years?"

Creed's expression hardened at the memories. "She threw an unstable world into utter conflict by her selfish actions. I lost family, friends, and most of my current lifetime to a bloody conflict that she instigated. I have no need for another explanation of my continued anger toward her."

Sheena put her hand on his shoulder sympathetically. She agreed with Eida, but she knew Creed well enough not to attempt to talk to him about it. Eida said nothing more, but took his hand and held firmly to it.

They had just reached the hub when the watcher announced calmly, "Warning. Intruders detected. Master, what action should be taken?"

Eida looked fearful, but Creed told her, "Just tell the watcher to hold action until further notice."

Eida nodded and stammered, "H-hold action, please!"

The watcher spoke flatly. "Affirmative. Action withheld."

Sheena shot Creed a concerned look, so he explained. "The only person who could reliably find us is Viwy, so I am pretty sure it's just Viwy and Achron."

Eida stated, "Those are the other people with you."

Creed just nodded. Sheena wondered what Eida would think of her father and her friend not being Fearian. At the end of the main connecting corridor, they stopped where the door had been resealed. The watcher opened it wordlessly as they approached, and indeed, it was Achron and Viwy who turned to look at them with surprise as they emerged from the hidden entrance.

Sheena let go of Creed's hand and ran to

134

embrace Achron, calling out, "Father! You missed out on the rest of the complex!"

Achron dryly observed, "Yes, and you missed out on the utter turmoil caused by someone's distant light display."

Creed opted to stare at the wall as he muttered an apology. "Eh, sorry, Father."

Viwy glanced nervously behind him, urging, "Come on, we have to get out of here before they descend on this place."

Creed grabbed his staff from his belt. "They?"

Achron looked intently at Eida as he said, "Yes, the local Fearians presumed the worst of the event, and have mustered no small force of their casters to deal with it."

Creed lowered his staff with a sigh. "Great. Then I am not going to be much help."

Eida recovered her voice enough to blurt out what could have been an accusation, but was probably more of a recognition of a previously underappreciated reality. "You're humans!"

Viwy hesitated, staring at where she clasped Creed's hand tightly. Achron spoke for them both. "Yes, and we are merely looking for some information. We do not intend to be in Fearia any longer than necessary." He turned back toward the door, motioning to them. "Come. We have outworn our welcome here, and I don't want to give the radical Fearians any place for conflict."

But Creed stopped him. "Wait, Achron. There is a demon gate here. You have to close it!"

Achron fixed his attention on Creed, awaiting further explanation. Creed quickly provided it. "The summoners must have given up on abiding by the provisions set forth, and committed a forbidden act. It's not presumptuous to assume that it is the reason that Heket's tower is no longer standing."

Achron grimaced. "I am not sure the four of us are qualified to stop something that destroyed an entire tower of mages."

Creed replied with confidence. "Not at all! They didn't have a white mage, the only mage that can close a demon gate. We have the greatest white mage alive with us!"

Achron gave him a dour expression. "Yeah, thanks, but given the dearth of white mages, I am not so sure that is saying much."

Eida's eyes were darting back and forth between them, but Sheena resolved her unspoken question by adding, "But Father! You really are a great white mage!"

He looked at her for a moment, and resigned himself to the change in course. "Okay. Let's get rid of this demon gate, but quickly, or we are going to have other problems." Achron turned to the field caste Fearian girl. "Uh, Eida, was it?" She nodded, and he continued. "This is going to be pretty dangerous, so I hate to say this, but the safest thing is for you to stay near us until we can deal with the gate." Eida edged closer to Creed and bobbed her head wordlessly.

They left the lower complex of Heket's tower and emerged into the starlit night. Achron reached out to his side and gripped nothing. In a blaze of white light, his staff materialized outward from his grip. He glanced at his long-time friend. "Viwy, gate, please." Viwy's staff formed out of a sudden burst of mist, and he brought his hand to the cymophane stone in the center of its curious latticework head.

Viwy dropped his hand and gestured on into the woods. "It's not too far that way, but you're going to need some firepower. There are dark things milling about it."

Creed spoke softly to Eida and Sheena. "Stay close." Liberating himself of them, he drew his own staff. Under Achron's direction, they burst from the brushy growth into a modestly clear area that was strewn with the remnants of the tower. Brilliant beams of yellow-green light ripped through dozens of dark creatures, leaving little more than the two large black stone columns that made up the physical frame of the demon gate. Between them shimmered a strange kind of darkness, otherworldly, that distorted the light around it, like the hot air rising from molten metal.

Viwy whispered, as if he feared that the gate would overhear him. "Creed, what's beyond the demon gate?"

Creed's reply sounded a little doubtful. "Well, I can't say for sure, since they are unidirectional passages. Nothing can enter from this side. The other side is dark, filled with every imaginable horror. It's not something that should exist in this world." Creed looked toward Achron as he directed, "Banish it, like you would one of the horrors that comes from it!"

Achron dipped his head in acknowledgement, and his skin began to glow brightly as he gripped his staff in both hands. For several moments, he focused intensely on the structure before them. As they waited for the purge, an enormous lizard-shaped horror, dark as the night, with bright red eyes, stepped halfway through the gate, bearing a mouth loaded with interlocking, needle-sharp teeth. Sheena shivered, and Eida grabbed onto her with a frightened squawk.

Creed made no move, even when Viwy urged, "Uh, Creed!"

Creed replied coolly. "It's too late."

Scarcely were the words past his lips when there was a radiant flash from Achron, and a wave of white light swept over them, purging both the demon and the gate. Achron dropped to one knee, panting as sweat ran down his face from the effort.

The entire area was suddenly illuminated by another source, and Fearians began to emerge from the woods around them. They were mostly field caste Fearians, and they carried a variety of weapons. Sheena saw that some of them were makeshift things that were not really battleworthy, while others were rudimentary staves, put to shame by the relic staves carried by her father and friends. Brilliant colors of light streamed from dozens of casters. Sheena was no expert in mages, but what she had been taught by Iekaruga told her that probably none of them were more than novices.

One of them stepped forward, a well-dressed man she recognized as officiating the festival they had been enjoying not so long ago. He spoke sternly. "You have desecrated a sacred Fearian site, humans. We invited you to participate in our festivities, and you betrayed us. For that you will make an accounting . . . with your lives!"

Eida stepped away from Sheena as she spoke loudly, with no small measure of exasperation. "NO! You can't do this to them, Father!" The man flinched sharply at hearing her, staring speechless in incredulity. The girl begged him, "They destroyed the demon gate, the cause of the monsters who hunt us at night. They have helped us, not harmed us!"

Brandishing their staves, the mages summoned hundreds of the same kinds of light orbs that Creed used as preparation for combat. The man looked dejectedly at the ground, and his words were grave. "The enemies of the Fearians are in our midst. Eida, if they have brainwashed you, then you must be counted among them. Please, show your Fearian loyalty, and step away from them."

Eida remained where she was, stunned that her pleas had fallen on deaf ears. Sheena whispered apologetically, "I am sorry, Eida. You had better go."

Eida shook herself, and her face grew severe. "No! I am not going anywhere! Father, surely you see that they have done us no harm! Where are the injured? Where is the loss? Have we become so insecure that we condemn the innocent without evidence?"

Facing away from his daughter, Eida's father shouted out, "Fire!" Eida gasped, and Sheena threw them both to the ground, partially shielding Eida with her own body.

They lay huddled on the ground for a moment as light flashed around them. They heard Viwy comment, "Oh, great. So how are we supposed to get out of this one?"

Sheena jumped back to her feet, flushed with embarrassment, as she quickly realized that they were safe within the translucent sphere projected from Achron's staff. The Aegeis was impenetrable by force, and the hundreds of light beams aimed at them sheared off it harmlessly.

Achron stood slowly, leaning on his staff, his fatigue obvious. Sheena helped Eida back to her feet, listening to his answer. "I am not sure, but killing them is not an option. It would only justify their claim against us." Creed and Viwy nodded.

Eida studied the Aegeis around them and asked in a trembling voice, "H-how long will it hold up?"

Achron sighed. "Well, it's hard to know for certain, but as far as I can tell, forever."

The barrage stopped abruptly, and Eida's father spoke angrily, his voice muted, but not silenced, by the Aegeis. "If we cannot destroy you, then we will remove you from Fearia! G-goodbye, Eida."

Viwy looked toward Achron, but he just shrugged. Sheena wasn't sure what kind of threat that was, or even if they could make good on it.

Eida met her father's eyes for a second before he

turned his back on the scene. Still under the effects of her shock, she just shook her head slowly, whispering, "No . . . no . . . why won't you listen?"

Several casters, working in tandem, enacted their power. There were bright flashes of faintly yellow light, and the Aegeis simply vanished. Sheena recoiled sharply. Creed was also surprised and exclaimed with concern, "What?! Where did the Aegeis go?"

Achron sighed and lifted his eyes toward the sky. "It didn't go anywhere. It's exactly where I put it." He tapped the staff on the ground, and the swirly white sphere recondensed onto the top of the staff. Viwy looked at him like he was out of his mind. Achron explained away their confusion. "They sent us back to the human side, where we will remain without a gold mage."

Eida hugged her arms to herself, admitting in a small voice, "I-I . . . I am so sorry. I . . . ."

Creed offered her some consolation. "It wasn't your fault, Eida. You cannot control other people."

Achron requested, "Lead us back to Hona, Viwy."

The mist mage nodded, and after checking his orientation, he pointed in the right direction. "Come on, everyone. Let's go home."

Sheena felt excited to be returning home, yet she knew sadness for Eida's sudden estrangement from her own home and family. She took the younger girl's hand and sought to comfort her. "Don't worry, Eida. You will find more than just a place to stay at Hona Castle."

Eida blinked at her. "Me? Live among humans?"

Sheena laughed lightly as she thought of how few of Hona's members fit that description. "Actually, you might be surprised." Eida only appeared confused. Sheena smiled. "Oh, you will just have to see for yourself."

Eida hunched her shoulders slightly. "B-but . . . so when can I go home?"

Sheena grimaced. Not just because what she asked was impossible, but because she seriously doubted that Eida would receive anything close to a warm welcome after the events of a few moments ago. Creed volunteered himself to tell her. "I am sorry, Eida, but at the moment there is no way for those of us on the human side to traverse to the Fearian side."

With a sharp intake of breath, Eida stared, first at Creed, then at the ground. As the group started forward, she stumbled after them, lost in shock over her rapid change in circumstance. For her, it would be a long and dark walk to Hona Castle as she struggled through being forcefully removed from everything she knew into something completely foreign.

Chapter 13

They trudged through the remainder of the night and most of the morning to get back to Hona Castle. Once they reached the edge of Empleheim, they traveled much faster on the old roads, though even these were starting to become flat, weedy paths through ever encroaching forests. Achron knew it would be only a matter of time before Hona was little more than a long-lost ruin in a long-lost land.

He wasn't sure how much that actually mattered. The deteriorating roads did make supply runs much harder, so there was a practical problem with it. The last trip had required only mild detours to evade fallen trees and new saplings, but with uninhibited plant growth, soon enough the cart wouldn't even fit down the road. Such a mundane thing, but rather important for their continued existence. They had no shortage of daily food, thanks to a cooperative unity of manual labor coupled with sigil-automated tasks, yet other things still had purchased from their nearest neighbor, Wythwood.

As they made their way through the crumbling remains of Niado, and Castle Hona came into sight, Achron discreetly observed Eida. What had begun as an exciting prospect for a simple village girl had ended in heart-wrenching loss. He wondered how she would grapple with the sudden change. She was no older than his twelve-year-old Thiesa, which ignited his fatherly instinct toward her. However, she was not exactly a confirmed friend. Her father had left no doubt that she was taking the wrong side of the issue when it came to humans. He knew a measure of relief that she would be surrounded mostly by her own people.

A piercing cry echoed through the air, and Creed crossed his arms as he warned, "Brace yourselves." Viwy looked up and flinched with a gasp of a yelp. Eida jerked her head upward and let out a scream. Sheena took hold of the girl as though she feared Eida would run. Standing firm in the rush of wind and dust that blew over them, Creed muttered, "Show-off."

The regal gold-tipped gryphon watched them intently without blinking. Rin slid off his back and ran to Achron, embracing him tightly. He returned her hug as he asked, "Well, did I miss anything exciting?" She smiled at him warmly, but merely shook her head.

Achron seriously doubted that her engagement to Harku would remain a secret for very long. He had no real objections to the young metamorphic mage, but out of concern for Rin's inexperience in such matters, he had dictated a period of waiting before they could be formally married.

The gryphon flickered, and Harku stood where it had been. He approached them calmly and hailed them. "Welcome home. I assume your escort of the queen was uneventful?"

He hesitated when he saw Eida, but held his peace. Achron replied, "Yes, thank you, Harku. Everything was fine."

Creed scowled slightly and added, "Yeah, minus not actually finding any real answer to our questions."

Achron cleared his throat and gestured to Eida. "Anyway, this is Eida. She will be joining us at Hona for the time being."

Harku gave her a polite bow. It was a form of respectful greeting among his people. It was also meaningless to a native-born Fearian. "A pleasure, Eida," he intoned.

She apparently felt less amiable, as she stated bluntly, "Y-you were just an animal!"

Sheena told her, "Um, he is a metamorphic mage. That's normal for him."

Harku turned toward Rin and held his hand out. She took it, and the two of them joined in what remained of the journey back to Hona. Viwy chatted emphatically of their brief visit to Fearia. Achron, on the other hand, observed Sheena closely as she made idle conversation with Eida about life in Hona Castle. Though Sheena spoke easily, she was, to his eyes, more focused on Rin and Harku. Sheena was perceptive, and her sister was the last person she would expect to walk hand in hand with anyone, let alone a male stranger. She would know about the change in relationship between them before nightfall. Creed was about to have other problems than figuring out who else might have been involved in writing the golden chronicle.

Sheena was bold, and could be forceful. There was no doubt that a level of sibling rivalry might put pressure on Creed to join the ranks of the betrothed. Of course, this was not something Creed personally believed was appropriate.

Achron realized he couldn't predict how Creed would respond to this scenario. He tried to think of some way to encourage Creed to abandon his inaccurate view of his self-worth. He had come upon no real ideas by the time they reached the castle gate, where the others greeted them. Turning to Sheena, he ordered gently, "Sheena dear, could you introduce Eida to your mother, and the two of you find a room suitable for her?"

Sheena acquiesced with a nod. "Yes, Father!"

Creed headed toward the castle, presumably toward his own room, but Achron stopped him with a word. "Creed?"

The Fearian's tail flicked with a sense of nervous anticipation as he watched Rin and Harku enter the castle proper. "Yes, sir?"

Achron motioned that Creed accompany him. "Come with me. I want to hear about what you found in Heket's tower."

Creed relaxed visibly as he fell in step with Achron. "Yes, let's do that."

* * *

The library was quiet just after midday. Light diffused through the glass rotunda, and those who stood around the table held their collective breath as Creed retrieved the metal-clad book that had once been the personal journal of the great mind mage Heket. He placed it in the center of the table.

Iekaruga was there, curious to see what they had found, as well as his wife Dorra, who was there in official capacity. As the only rune mage among them, she was the most likely person to be able to open the sealed journal, or at least to know what would be required to open it. Viwy and Achron watched eagerly. Keena, as keeper of a similarly bound tome, was also there. Creed momentarily wondered who was watching the youngest children, but given there were other qualified adults in Hona, he presumed that things were under control elsewhere.

Dorra slid the book toward herself and traced her fingers over the delicate metal relief on the cover. The intricate pattern resembled intertwining leaves and stems of vining plants. A smooth flat area, devoid of filigree, ran parallel to the spine. Here, a long vertical series of small runes were etched into the metal. Like the golden chronicle, this tome bore a snug locking mechanism that prevented it from being opened by force. Also like the golden chronicle, the mechanism was tied to the runes, rather than having a physical key.

Dorra examined the runes carefully before she shook her head and observed, "These are not runes I have ever seen before. There is a basic letter set from which meaningful sentences, of a sort, are normally constructed. But these runes are not even lettering I know. I would need something else that uses them in context to come to any conclusion about what this might even say, let alone how it could be opened by manipulating them."

Achron's attention swung to Creed, but he admitted, "Sorry, I don't know what those runes are, either."

Creed addressed the crowd before him. "Heket's tower was more confusing than informative, so I say we investigate the tower of the other designated chronicler, Ferir. His followers were part of the storm league after the war started, but that league's base of operations was in Fearia at Akira Soldino's tower."

Viwy chimed in with his usual sarcasm. "Right! Now as soon as you explain why that particular detail is important, then we can proceed to talk about whether such a venture is practical at this time."

Creed reminded himself that some things he considered common knowledge were completely foreign to anyone born after the great war. He clarified. "It means that Ferir's tower shouldn't be any more dangerous than Heket's tower. The storm league was one of the mage coalitions that fought in the war, and I would not want to attempt entry into Akira's tower. Her followers were a force to be reckoned with."

"What kind of mages were they?" Achron asked him.

Creed looked down at the sealed book, recalling the past. "They were Fearians in the kinesis mage category."

Glancing up, he saw the general lack of understanding and added, "The more powerful among them could manipulate large-scale weather phenomena, but more commonly one was accosted with smaller things like tornados, flash floods, or fist-sized hail."

Dorra's eyes widened. "I don't know of anyone who thinks of tornados as 'smaller things.'"

Achron resumed discussion of the practical. "So, as best as you can remember, where was Ferir's tower?"

Creed mulled over the question as he picked up a map from the table and rolled it open. He scanned the map before he gestured to a place northeast of Niado, saying, "It was somewhere out here, nestled within a large crevasse that we called the 'earth scar.'"

Viwy frowned a little. "That would take a week to get there on horseback, and I don't think we have that kind of time right now."

Keena spoke pointedly. "Achron, Viwy, your children need you. You can't just run after every little treasure that piques your interests."

Achron met his wife's gaze and assented. "Yes, this isn't exactly just down the way. I am only vaguely familiar with what was called the Bugillow when Empleheim was a thriving kingdom. It is outside our borders, and somewhat of a wilderness area. There just wasn't much out there. And with it in the low mountains like that, and sparsely forested, fall would not be a pleasant time to visit. Winter would be unwise at best, so, even if we go, we would have to wait until summer." Viwy just nodded sagely, though he did look slightly disappointed.

Creed spoke up confidently. "Well, maybe it would just be best if I go alone then."

His adoptive mother left no room for doubts about her feelings on the matter. "Absolutely not, Creed. That would be too dangerous, and this isn't a place where you could fit in. You would be beyond Empleheim, and anyone you encounter will not be familiar with our kind."

Creed spread his hands, objecting to her concerns. "But I'm not a defenseless child!"

Keena stayed calm, but her firm tone allowed for no further discussion. "Creed, I forbid you from taking off on some treasure hunt by yourself. Now promise me you won't try to sneak off and do this."

Creed's eyes snapped to Achron, but the older man merely nodded. It was infuriating to him that they were treating him like some naïve child. Did his years on the battlefield mean nothing to them? Or perhaps they simply could not grasp the realities of his past. Creed sighed and met their gazes with his own. "Yes, as you wish. I promise not to leave by myself."

Keena gave a curt nod. "Good. Now, we will investigate this matter when we have better weather and more time." To Creed, her compromise felt the same as saying they would get around to it some year, maybe.

As those gathered in the library dispersed, Achron picked up the sealed volume from the table. "Well, I guess I should put this out of reach of the little ones. We will find a way to open it in time, and then we should have answers to our mysterious chronicler." Creed said nothing, looking blankly off into the dimness of the library as he contemplated some alternative to waiting.

Achron paused as he walked past Creed and put his hand on the Fearian's shoulder. "Don't worry Creed. I am sure there will be an opportunity to resume our

148

pursuit of the mysterious soon enough."

Creed glanced at him as he replied. "Sure, soon enough." Achron nodded with a reassuring smile and left the library, and Creed in it, empty and alone.

In the silence, Creed absently looked about the library, wondering whom he could dupe into coming with him so that he would not technically be violating his promise. The difficulty would be in asking the right person the first time so that word of his ploy would not reach the wrong people before he could put some distance between Castle Hona and himself. Naturally, Viwy would know where he was, but if they were as occupied as they claimed, then they shouldn't be able to pursue him fast enough to catch him.

It was possible that Harku could catch him on the wing, but surely he couldn't technically force him to return home—unless he morphed him into some diminutive form. Creed sincerely hoped that would not occur.

Still plotting his escape, he stood to leave just as Sheena burst into the library. Her agitation was apparent, and Creed paused, disconcerted by her inexplicable perturbation. Sheena was rarely ever perturbed, and when she was, the cause was typically obvious.

She did not keep him waiting long. "Creed! Rin and Harku are engaged! Can you believe it?"

This outburst only added to his confusion. Rin was a quiet girl, for sure, but it wasn't entirely ridiculous, in light of Harku's strange relationship with her, and it certainly wasn't a matter of desperation in his mind. A little mystified, he replied, "Uh, that's nice."

Sheena half-exclaimed, half-shouted with exasperation. "Creed!"

Her forcefulness made him recoil. "Hey, what? I know Harku is kind of sheltered, but that's normal around here, so . . . ." Her displeased expression grew darker, so he finished limply, "Shouldn't you be happy for her?"

Sheena opened her mouth, her face reddening, presumably with anger, but rather than rail on him, she simply muttered, "Hmph! You are such a dense, senseless . . . ." She sighed. "Of course I am happy for my sister, fair or not."

She made no sense to him, and regardless of what she said, she most certainly did not sound happy. What was worse was the reality that if anyone would join him on his venture without reservation, it was Sheena. Creed tried to be subtle. "You know, we didn't really solve the mystery of the third chronicler. We could probably find what we need in the old tower of Ferir."

His attempt to change the subject fell flat. Sheena glared at him, her tone sullen and accusing. "Oh? So you can dance with the first pretty girl you meet?"

Creed blinked, trying to identify why that was relevant. "Uh, say what?"

She faced him again, dropping her arms to her sides as she spoke with more glumness than anger. "You do realize that there is more to life than mysteries, mages, and power, right?"

He replied seriously. "Of course I know that, Sheena. There is also food, and sleep, and honest work."

It was hard to describe the expression on her face, but he concluded it was not a positive thing, since she pivoted on one heel and stormed out of the library, talking to herself about how she must be cursed. Creed scratched his head, certain he was missing something, but uncertain as to what that might be. He shrugged, and decided that he would probe some people casually about the matter of potentially investigating Ferir's tower while he waited for Sheena to calm down.

Chapter 14

Eida lay on the bed of the room that Sheena had shown her. Tears rolled down her cheeks and silent sobs shook her shoulders as she tried to process her sudden abandonment by her own father. It was so unfair, so unkind. Had any other Fearian been thus deserted?

The horrible scene played through her mind again and again. Why did she even bother anymore? Eida felt anew all the sharpness of the pain of losing her mother, as though it were only yesterday that the dark creatures that haunted their existence had taken her from them.

There was an energetic knock on her door. Eida sniffed, working to compose herself. She waited, hoping whoever was on the other side of the door would just leave. But instead, a second knock came a few moments later. Eida chose to ignore it again, wanting to be alone, to hide in the darkness, and not have to talk to anyone.

The persistent person knocked a third time, and then simply entered. Eida wiped her face hurriedly, addressing the intruder with a slightly broken voice, covered by a thin veneer of composure. "Y-yes? What do you want?"

The young forest caste girl greeted her in a happy sort of sing-song. "Hello! I just wanted to ask if you would like to come with us for apple picking!" She had dark brown hair with a long, lighter brown mane. Her eyes were an intense purple color—a rare enough color among Fearians already, but its vividness was something Eida had never seen before.

The girl paused at Eida's hesitation, and gestured to herself with a flourish. "Oh! Sorry for not introducing myself first, but I am Thiesa! What's your name?"

Despite her lack of interest in socializing, Eida smiled slightly at the enthusiastic girl. "I'm Eida." Who was this other Fearian who wanted her to participate in something without even knowing her name? Her sorrow was momentarily displaced by curiosity. What were apples?

Thiesa pointed to the door, informing her, "Come on, Eida! The others are waiting!"

She slipped from the bed as she asked, "Others?"

With a bright smile, Thiesa nodded and turned, moving to exit the room. "Yes, so let's go!"

Eida followed her, thinking that Thiesa was probably about her own age, which meant she was too young to be Sheena's litter mate. The older Fearian girl had told her that their whole family lived in the castle, but she had not said just how many people this family might include. Being that they were in the human lands, Eida presumed that most of the castle's residents would be human.

When they came out into the hallway, no fewer than seven people were waiting for them. Three were indeed human girls, but the other four were male Fearians, and all of them were around Eida's age. Thiesa gestured rapidly to each in turn. "These are my brothers Byrn, Marral, Harto, and Zollen, and these are Dorra's children Brea and Cilla, and this is Arru, Harku's sister!"

Thiesa made a sweeping motion toward Eida as she completed the introductions. "And this is Eida, everyone!"

Several of them nodded or waved in welcome, but Zollen spoke with a neutral tone. "Thiesa, I don't think Eida has a context from which to understand half of what you said."

Thiesa merely shrugged. "Oh, it doesn't matter. Come on! Let's go pick APPLES!" Marral joined in her excitement by giving a small cheer, but it ended up strangely comic, since no one else was sharing in Thiesa's dramatic approach to life.

The group left the castle and entered the orchard that was immediately off to its side. A variety of yellow and red fruit hung in large, carefully pruned trees. The air was crisp but not cold. Eida briefly wondered why the human side was also in the autumn season, if their worlds were different.

Several of them picked up burlap bags that had been modified by adding a shoulder strap. Thiesa placed one over Eida's shoulder and said, "Here, just follow our lead." The others began to climb the trees in order to reach the ripe fruit.

Eida still felt uncertain about this whole venture. "Um . . . are you sure?"

Zollen spoke up, in what almost sounded like an apology. "We are happy you have joined us, Eida, but please don't feel obligated to participate in something that might be outside your normal activity."

She came to her own defense. "I can climb trees, thank you very much."

Thiesa joined her as she walked toward a tree, conversing casually. "Don't mind Zollen. He just thinks too much about everything, that's all."

There was a sense in which the other young Fearian was perceptive. Eida's village did not have many

153

trees, and where there were trees, she wasn't really supposed to go. So, her tree climbing experience was minimal. Still, it wasn't like she had never climbed a tree, and she wasn't about to be outdone by a bunch of sheltered forest caste who lived in a castle.

It was a perfect day for such an activity, and the gentle breeze that rustled leaves as she ascended the large apple tree was fresh and cool. It bore the promise of a coming winter, and of the harvest season. Melancholy set in as she thought of a home she would not see again, at least not anytime soon. Eida made the mistake of remembering the many happy times she had experienced in the harvest festivals, and knowing she wouldn't experience them this year was crushing. She picked an apple or two, but her heart wasn't in it. Her mind wandered back through a morass of pain and loss.

She stretched out onto a branch to reach for a lovely red apple. Without warning, the branch she held to steady herself snapped, and she fell from near the top of the tree toward the ground. Someone shouted, but Eida had no time to say anything. She hit something strange, and air rushed past her with a deafening roar.

Eida landed with so little force that she wondered if she had fallen at all, though the spreading branches above her, visible from where she lay on her back in the soft grass, were certain confirmation that she had in fact fallen from the tree. She sat up, confused but unhurt, and her breath caught when she saw Zollen, his arm outstretched, unnatural orange-pink light illuminating his skin.

While she blinked and attempted to understand what had happened, the light around Zollen began to fade. Marral commented with concern, "Uh-oh. Father is not going to like this."

Thiesa added her thoughts, just shy of a rebuke. "Zollen! You're not supposed to . . . well, you know!"

Zollen dropped his arm and shot Marral a stern glare. "I know, but he doesn't have to find out, now does he?"

Harto pointed out, "What kind of person would allow someone to fall to their death if they could stop it? I don't think Father intended us to withhold from doing good, just from acting thoughtlessly."

Cilla, who was a little younger than the rest of them, stated emphatically, "Oh, so that means Zollen is safe from making Achron angry—ever!"

Zollen gave her an annoyed look as some of the others smothered laughter. He walked up to where Eida sat and offered her his hand. "Are you all right, Eida?" She took his hand hesitantly, and he helped her to her feet.

Brushing herself off, Eida sought some understanding of what had just occurred. "W-what was that?"

Zollen knelt and retrieved the apple she had attempted to pick. "Well, I am a mage of some sort. I can control air. But you cannot tell anyone about this, because we aren't supposed to . . ." He grimaced as he ended, muttering, ". . . do stuff."

Eida was at a loss. Clearly Zollen had abilities that exceeded any she knew of among her own people, but he was forbidden from using them? Still a little shaken from the fall that wasn't, she asked, "But why not?"

Thiesa answered in her typical chatty manner. "That's easy. You see, none of us born to Achron are normal. We all have something special about us."

Harto chided her. "Thiesa! We're not supposed to say anything about it!"

Thiesa clapped her hand to her mouth. "Oops!"

Arru interrupted with her own logic. "It's okay. She is one of us now, and it would only be a matter of time before she learned about it. I mean, I know, and I have only been here a little while."

Eida echoed with curiosity, "Special?"

Zollen explained simply. "Well, it's hard to tell you much, because we don't actually know much about it personally. Creed is the only one who understands it. However, what we do know is that each of us bears a great power within, and we have been warned that we should not exercise that power. It is beyond our control, and it could cause great harm. Most of us have no sense of how to even access our power, so it's rather unlikely, but still, Father speaks for our best interests."

Eida didn't follow most of what he had said, but she nodded, trying not to think that she was causing trouble for them. Having grown up as the only girl in her field caste family, she was often more of a burden than a help. Girls weren't allowed to work the fields, so that left little for her to do that felt meaningful.

Zollen held the apple out to her, suggesting, "Maybe you should pick apples from the lower branches of the trees."

She took the apple, but her mind was elsewhere. The answer to her question was probably obvious to them, but it wasn't to her. "Why did you invite me to pick fruit anyway? Isn't that just a forest caste thing?" She looked up, flicking her tail emphatically. "I am field caste."

Brea tilted her head at the unfamiliar word. "What's a caste?"

Zollen cleared his throat and tried to offer her a reasonable explanation to something he knew only conceptually. "So, in Fearia there is something called castes, where different groups of Fearians have different societal tasks. We are forest caste, and in Fearia, the forest caste provides other Fearians with wood and fruit and so forth."

Marral muttered to no one in particular, "That sounds weird."

The interruption did not deter Zollen's monologue. "Eida, we don't have such a system here. We are collecting apples because we need to, if we want to continue to have a variety of things to eat for the winter." He smiled as he looked toward the sky. "Plus, it's a fun thing to do on such a wonderful day." He looked back at her with a slightly more sober expression, adding, "Thiesa didn't want you to be left out of what we enjoy doing, but if you would rather, you can go do something else."

The bright sunlight reflected off the shiny apple in Eida's hand. After a moment's silence, she tucked it into her bag and moved back toward the tree trunk as she spoke over her shoulder. "No, I will help you. I hope you're ready to catch me again, though. This isn't something I have ever done before."

Zollen turned a little pale, but she began climbing the tree again as several of the others chuckled. He remained fixed in place for a time, apparently trying to decide if she were serious or teasing.

* * *

The wind blew through the upper parts of Castle Hona with a low moan that an active imagination could easily construe as an apparition or horror. It didn't help the illusion that it was a moonless night, and the third level of the library was rather poorly illuminated.

Creed sat in a chair near the wall of books that lined the periphery of the upper library. If he had wanted to, he could have reached up and touched the low ceiling. He wasn't thinking about that, however, but instead turned the oblong silver shard over in his hands. In the one day since their forced return from Fearia, he had yet to find anyone motivated enough to even suggest to them that they sneak away to complete their investigation of the mysterious chronicler.

Viwy was caught up in taking care of his family and supervising the canning, drying, salting, and storage of the fall crops so they would last through the winter. Iekaruga was engaged in teaching the children, something he shared with Achron, Viwy, and their wives, and also directed the organization and accounting of the contents of the stores in the castle. Iekaruga had expressed interest in the matter, but with all that was going on, and with Dorra expecting, the man was certainly not remotely interested in traipsing beyond the borders of Empleheim.

Achron was the most likely candidate to go, but he, too, was occupied with winterizing the castle, from sealing windows with fresh plaster, to checking the timbers of the roof to ensure they would tolerate the regular snowfalls of the north woods, to staking straw around the outer walls to help decrease draftiness before the first snowfall.

None were activities with a lot of pressure, but there was never a shortage of things that needed to be done. Achron had stated bluntly that he could not leave until everything was ready for winter, and by that time, Creed was certain that it would be far too cold to venture to the northeast.

So here he sat. Creed looked blankly at the hand-length silver shard. It was heavy, like metal, but it wasn't any kind of metal he was familiar with. It was harder than true silver and had a dull luster. The shard has widest at its center, and the ends tapered to points that were sharp enough to stab with. The function of the silver shard was lost on him. He was fairly sure it bore no intrinsic energy. But he also knew that the shard didn't have a normal origin. It was created by Seleen, likely for some nefarious purpose.

The object was as perplexing as it was frustrating. Seleen's operations were generally presumed to be the eccentricates of an aging, demented mind. However, there was no doubt that the shard had been left behind intentionally, precisely where he had found it. It was a message, one lost to time, but certainly not one produced by a feeble mind. It was something clever, something insidious, something that said, "I am operating off a larger master plan."

Few in his time spoke of Seleen with anything other than derision. It was rare to hear her name and not also hear her called insane, crazy, or even diabolical. Creed hoped that last comment was just commentary and not a reality. His own experience with such things was frightening enough.

But regardless of her reasoning, insane or intentional, there were plenty of witnesses to her public execution. The only great mage to die such an ignoble death, but then again, Creed had to wonder if perhaps she might have murdered some of the other great mages. Indeed, would Heket really have willingly let Seleen into her private chamber to take her majestic gem and leave one of her own silver shards in its place? It seemed unlikely, but there simply wasn't any information about it.

He sighed, lamenting his inability to understand what happened. Just then, he heard someone climbing the nearby stairs, and he looked up from his contemplations. He watched as Sheena appeared, rising from the stairwell as she stepped up to the third level of the library. She seemed far calmer than the day before.

She walked up to him, glancing curiously at the shard before she spoke. "Ciega, I figured you would be up here." She clasped her hands behind her back and shifted her weight from side to side nervously. He suspected that she had not come to see what he was doing, but rather, that there was something personal that she wanted to say that was important to her.

He gave her his full attention, putting thoughts of unresolved mysteries out of his head. In the dim torchlight, Sheena's soft blond hair seemed to glow slightly. To be sure, it was an optical illusion, but it made it nearly impossible not to stare. He knew she was incredibly beautiful, but he rarely studied her long enough for it to affect him. Unfortunately, this became one of those times, and it took substantially longer than he cared to admit to actually listen to her.

"I . . . well, I just wanted to say that I am sorry. I shouldn't have been so upset with you, and it was wrong of me to avoid you today. Will you please forgive me?"

Creed was silent as he tried to get his brain to process what she had said and develop some kind of appropriate response. He didn't understand why she had been upset, but he was happy to put the scene behind him. He cleared his throat, replying, "Uh, yes, I forgive you."

Sheena sighed with relief, though she still looked a little nervous. She brought her hands to her chest, clasping them again, as she asked in a soft, uncertain voice, "Ciega, does this mean you will take me?"

Creed suddenly felt his palms sweat, and his pulse seemed to double in an instant. His voice sounded unnatural as he forced the words out, while trying to suppress his unhelpful imagination. "T-take you?"

She shrugged innocently. "Yes, you know . . ."

Creed was completely befuddled. This was arguably a different question than the one she had asked him before, and while she could be quite brazen, it was more than a little out of character for her.

Fortunately for him, she continued by saying,

". . . on this slightly unlawful adventure you are planning. Um, are you okay? You look flushed."

Creed shook his head and redirected the conversation away from his awkward state of mind. "Er, yes, I am fine. How did you know I was planning to investigate the other tower?" He also wanted to know how she knew it was unlawful, but he presumed that would come out with the former answer.

A small smile came to Sheena's face. "Well, it was obvious you were disappointed with how little we found at Heket's tower, and I was talking to Father, and he mentioned how you promised not to take off on your own. I know you, ciega. I know what you think, and so I knew you would be concocting some way to get there."

After the emotional turmoil of the last few minutes, Creed was unbelievably thankful that she didn't really know everything he thought. He looked back at the silver shard before commenting, "Well, I hate to disappoint you, but if you're going, then that still only makes two people. No one else seemed interested, or at least not free." Creed also wanted to ask why she was talking to Achron about him, but he decided that he would probably be better off not knowing.

Sheena seemed surprised. Her voice had a slight off-tone to it, though he missed its meaning. "Really? So you're not bringing Eida with you?"

Creed wrinkled his brow in his confusion. "Why would I bring Eida? She hasn't a clue how life in this world even works. Besides, she's just a little girl, and probably emotionally distraught at the moment."

Sheena chuckled as she waved her hand dismissively. "Oh, never mind. When do we leave?"

Creed stood slowly, examining her with a degree of suspicion. "You seem awfully eager about this."

Sheena smiled brightly at him, and he thought his timing on standing was especially poor, though he did manage not to fall over. Her excitement flowed through her words. "I am about to go on another incredible adventure with my closest friend, so of course I am eager. I mean, anything could happen!"

Creed coughed as he spoke dryly. "Uh, not 'anything' exactly. You know, we will only be gone a couple weeks, hopefully."

She laughed with delight at his expense. "Oh, ciega, you're far too serious."

Creed sighed and muttered, "Maybe." He raised his voice to a normal tone. "Let's plan on leaving two days from now, after the evening meal."

He walked toward the stairs, and Sheena fell in beside him, listening attentively as he quietly provided her with a list of things she would need to pack for their journey. Creed knew that their travels would be longer than their normal forays to the nearest town, but even more, that it would be a lot of walking along what scarcely qualified as roads, and sleeping through chilly nights with little or no shelter.

He felt confident they could make the journey without trouble, yet Creed also knew a slight pang of concern for Sheena's safety. He wasn't so concerned about his own, but he had taken on singular oversight for her life. It was a strange burden. Were his skills up to the task of protecting her? They were unlikely to encounter anything dangerous, given that there weren't things like demon gates sitting on top of the tower site on the human side of the world. At least, Creed hoped there weren't.

Chapter 15

It had been a swift ride from evening far into the night. The adrenaline from stealing away had faded, replaced by the dull fatigue of a long ride well past the time when he would normally be sleeping. By now Niado was a good distance behind them, though it would still be a couple of days before they reached the edge of Empleheim. Creed slowed his tired horse to a walk as he glanced around the long-overgrown countryside for some place of shelter.

The wind was brisk, and it whistled and rustled through the bright leaves of the trees. Some trees were already losing their leaves to the cool weather, while others were still changing into their fall colors.

He looked at his traveling companion to gauge her opinion on their current circumstances. It was dark, of course, but from what he could see of her face, she seemed content to let him lead. He kept the horse at a walk until he saw the looming form of a building just off the road. Being Empleheim, it was some long-abandoned structure. He turned off to investigate it.

The solid stonework walls remained in fairly good condition, but its roof had been gone for some time. Creed dismounted and led his horse cautiously through the old doorway. The large, empty inner space was divided into two compartments by a single wall. Both rooms had a cobblestone floor littered with the remnants of the roof. Creed tied his horse to a metal hook that stuck out of the wall of the first room. Sheena entered, leading her own horse, and followed his example, and then the two of them removed the saddles and travel bags from their horses before entering the other side of the abandoned structure.

Creed glanced about before he began to gather timber once part of the collapsed roof. Sheena shivered slightly and pulled her cloak tightly about herself. "What are you doing, Creed?"

He replied a little bluntly, surprised it wasn't obvious. "I am making a fire, of course."

She gave an uncertain look at their surroundings. "Inside?"

Creed continued to arrange the timbers into a neat pile. "Ah, you know, this isn't really inside because it lacks a roof. It will keep the wind off of us, but it's still going to be cold in the morning." Sheena rubbed her arms vigorously and then yawned. Though she made no comment, it was pretty clear to him that she thought it was already cold.

Sheena startled with concern. "Creed, I don't think we brought anything to start a fire with!" There was a flicker of light, and a yellow-green orb rose from the ground beside Creed. An intense beam lanced across the wood pile, and it burst into flames as the orb faded, illuminating his sly grin. "You know, I didn't even think to pack such things."

For a second she glared at him, but then chuckled. "I am going to blame how tired I am for that mild disconnect."

Creed rested with his back against the wall and faced the fire. Sheena sat down next to him, just beyond arm's reach, giving a bit of a sigh. He turned his

164

attention toward her, pausing before he asked, "What's wrong?"

Sheena looked a little sheepish as she admitted, "I am sorry, ciega. It's just that I feel like some kind of criminal, sneaking away from my home without my parents' permission."

Sheena was a sweet and sensitive girl, so Creed was not surprised that this bothered her. He spoke reassuringly as he watched the flames dance across the old chunks of rafters. "It's okay, Sheena. Feelings are rarely accurate. Just ignore them and they will go away quickly enough, or at least that's what works for me."

Her silence made him curious, and he looked up from the fire to see her studying him intently. She said wryly, "Well, that does explain a whole lot of things."

Creed blinked, and added for clarity, "Uh, so, since we're siblings, and since I only promised not to go alone, we are not doing anything forbidden. We aren't violating any laws, so feeling like a criminal just isn't accurate."

His confusion was compounded when Sheena gave a delighted laugh. "You can be so funny sometimes, ciega."

He shook his head and glared indignantly at the fire. "I am being serious here, Sheena."

He tried to analyze what was amiss with his previous statements, but couldn't think how they could be misconstrued as humorous. Clearly this was another one of those times when he just didn't understand Sheena. It shouldn't have bothered him, but it did. He was certain that having spent as much time together as they had that he should understand her. It was like the more he came to know her, the less he understood her.

Sheena broke into his contemplation of his personal paradox. "Creed . . . um . . . have you ever considered that ignoring your feelings isn't the only

165

approach to life?"

He thought it was a little odd she was still concerned about the whole criminal thing, but he would be a poor friend if he didn't try to help her. Much to his chagrin, when he stated solemnly, "Of course not," she burst into open laughter.

He scowled at her for the rude interruption, and she managed to control her humor enough to ask, "S-so you're serious then?"

He glared at her, but kept a level tone. "Yes. Apparently the only one at the moment."

Sheena apologized, though a curious smile still played at the edges of her lips. "I am really sorry, Creed. I wasn't trying to mock you." She looked thoughtfully at the fire, and her eyes seemed to glow mysteriously in its light. It was certainly his imagination, but the glow accented her beautiful face so aptly that he had to force himself to resume watching the flames before he became lost in staring at her.

Unaware of his struggle, Sheena spoke up softly. "When I am sad, hurt, or lonely, I don't want to continue feeling that way. I would happily ignore my feelings then. But when I know something delightful, something joyful, something comforting, surely those things are not to be cast aside as though they were worthless? Should I . . . should I forget my feelings even when they are accurate? Rather, shouldn't I cultivate those that are good and proper, those that exist in their right place?"

Creed snapped at her. "Don't be so ridiculous, Sheena!"

She looked a little hurt, but merely shrugged as she muttered, "I-it was just a question."

Creed shook his head and glared angrily into the blaze. It was an absolutely infuriating question. Primarily, because he had never thought to ask it himself, and secondarily, because the most honest answer he could come up with was directly in conflict with his normal mode of operation. For a mage in training, feelings and emotions were only hindrances. It took a clear mind to manipulate the mage power. After a mage became adept at invoking focus, it was much less of an issue, since a mage in focus was not bothered by such things so long as the focus lasted.

Nevertheless, Creed wondered if perhaps he were missing something. Did Sheena really deserve his ire? After all, she had volunteered for this long trek in the cold night of her own accord. He didn't want her to return now and leave him on his own. Technically, he would still be keeping his promise, as he had not left alone, but more importantly, he had come to treasure Sheena as a precious and reliable friend.

Creed swallowed his pride and opened his mouth. "I am sorry, Sheena. I shouldn't have yelled at you."

She wiped her face on her sleeve as she replied unconvincingly, "Don't worry about it."

Creed realized his sharp words had cut deeper than he had ever wanted. It was so easy to cut people down in a moment, both metaphorically and literally, but it was so hard to repair the damage that was done. Creed would never admit it publicly, but he often envied Achron's abilities as a white mage to restore what was broken.

Sheena deserved better. Creed moved over to where she sat and put his arm around her shoulders. She leaned against him gratefully and sniffed back unwanted tears. He remained silent, not sure there was anything else he could say that would make a difference. Her soft voice reached him. "I am committed to you, Creed, but that makes me vulnerable to you, especially since . . . since you are not committed to me. I could, well, I could lose you in a moment."

Creed tried to rapidly interpret precisely what she meant, but he wasn't even close to successfully. His ego assured him that it was only due to his fatigue. She sighed whimsically, adding, "You must think me a shallow fool for living in such a one-sided world."

If he were brutally honest, he might suggest that she was a little naïve, but certainly not foolish or shallow. After a brief silence, Creed answered her gently. "Sheena, your world isn't one-sided." She remained silent, and so he continued. "I-I care about you. Deeply, honestly, more than just as my sister, but as my closest friend. I ignore my feelings most of the time, but my feelings for you are too strong to be ignored. I guess—I guess the problem I face is that you are someone so special, and I am not. You should have some wonderful person who understands you, not an incompetent loner who still can't decide what to do with himself. Maybe, if one of us must be a fool, it's me, not you."

He sighed a little, saddened by the depth of the reality of just how poorly suited he was to be her companion in life. Her silence was unnerving, and quite uncharacteristic, so he glanced at her, a little fearful of what expression she would have. Would she approve of his own assessment, or perhaps she would vehemently disagree with him?

It was neither. Sheena was fast asleep. Creed shook his head and looked into the fire once more. "Of course you're asleep. I guess that means I am at least an idiot, if not a fool."

* * *

"It isn't funny, Achron!"

Achron coughed as he tried to suppress external displays of the humor he saw in the situation. Keena

168

crossed her arms and frowned. "Your eldest daughter ran off to who knows what dangers with an adopted gloomy vagabond!"

Viwy noted aloud, "Huh, he does kind of have that wanderer hygiene thing going on."

They were discussing the sudden disappearance of Creed and Sheena, made obvious after their absence from breakfast and the following investigation that revealed they were gone. There was no doubt where they were headed, so the matter at hand was determining what to do with the delinquents. Keena was certain that they should be retrieved promptly, but Achron was of the mind that this would be good for the two of them. Certainly he had some concerns about what they might find in the great Ferir's tower, but he had come to trust Creed. The young man could be a little gloomy at times, but he had the situational awareness and discipline of an excellent soldier.

The only other person who remained in the dining hall vented her frustration. "Seriously, that worthless scoundrel! I mean, he didn't even ask me if I wanted to go!"

Achron rolled his eyes, but Keena spoke reprovingly. "Emeril! Don't envy your sister's bad behavior, and certainly not Creed's."

Emeril rose from her seat at the table and left, replying dutifully, "Yes, Mother."

In Achron's estimation, Emeril and Creed traveling together to explore some great ruins was highly unlikely. They didn't fight, but they had very contrasting personalities.

Keena eyed Achron intently, so he smiled and sighed as he turned to Viwy, asking, "Okay, how far did they get?"

Viwy touched the large cat's eye stone in the top of his staff. He grunted as he let his hand fall from the stone. "Well, they seem to have gotten pretty far already. Couldn't catch them in one day, that's for sure."

Achron thought immediately of a young metamorphic mage that could make a complete mockery of any horse's ability to traverse the land. However, he chose not to mention it. Keena dropped her arms to her sides and gave her husband a sober look. "Achron, I know you aren't as concerned as I am, but what if something happens to them? Is this really worth such a risk?"

Achron put his hands on her shoulders with a loving touch. "Keena, Sheena faces an impossible task. She seeks the love of someone who doesn't seem to think he can return her affections. We both know that she can't imagine any other outcome in life, and hasn't thought of anything else for years. If Creed can't come to terms with his own issues, then he isn't liable to stick around long enough for her to get through to him. This is the opportunity they both need to see one another without the trappings of their family life."

Keena huffed a little, then relented. "I suppose it could be for the best, even if I am not so fond of her undue affection for him. He has been remarkably reserved. At first I feared he would take advantage of her, but I was wrong. Creed may be badly mannered, but he is a noble soul."

Turning back toward Viwy, Achron ended up staring at the mist mage. His face had gone pale, and his expression was conflicted. Achron prodded. "So, you have an opinion on this matter?"

Viwy responded through clear distraction. "Uh, oh, man. I just realized that I am going to have to go through this kind of stuff too in a few years."

Keena and Achron laughed heartily, and Viwy muttered ruefully, "You guys are so encouraging."

Chapter 16

Passing beyond the edge of Empleheim took several days, but doing so lifted a weight of concern off Creed's shoulders. Creed had half-expected someone to show up at any point and demand that they return, and that would be it. It was one thing to evade enemies, but with family, resistance wasn't really an option.

He was still unsure what to do with the fact that the Windslo family felt like his own, perhaps more than his biological family ever had. As a prodigy, he was viewed more as a tool than a person, but Achron and the rest had not treated him that way. Even knowing that Creed had knowledge they did not, none of them had pressed him for information on how to access the power of the majestic gems, or even who represented what gems. Occasionally someone would ask a question about it, but it was always an honest question driven by curiosity.

As they traveled, the cloudy sky gave way to a light, but cold, rain. They suddenly emerged from some trees onto a surprisingly well-worn road. Creed regretted not having any kind of accurate map. Presumably this was a major thoroughfare, but it was not marked on the old map he had with them. Of course, his map was more than a thousand years out of date.

Checking his surroundings, he surmised that traveling along the road, as long as it didn't change from its northward direction, would take them where they wanted to go. Navigating on such a dreary day was a challenge, but Creed felt confident they were going the right way. Sheena merely watched him, silently following his lead. Given how their conversations had gone early in their journey, he didn't blame her for being a little hesitant to say anything.

Guilt nibbled at him that he hadn't worked up enough nerve to broach the topic of their relationship again. He really did want to explain it to her while she was conscious, but it was so hard to express it without an appropriate context.

"Creed!"

Sheena caught his attention with her soft warning, and Creed jerked his head up to see a man approaching them. He wore strange flowing clothes that were an odd mixture of bright, light colors and darker earth tones. He waved at them heartily and spoke with equal exuberance. "Hail! Travelers!"

Creed hesitated as he tried to decide just exactly what the man was, keenly aware that his own dull cloak and the cloth bandana wrapped around his head were the only things concealing his Fearian heritage. "Uh . . . hail, or something."

The man smiled, nodding approvingly. "Ah, 'tis a cold and dreary evening, ain't it?"

Sheena nodded, but Creed stated a little bluntly, "So, did you need something?"

The man gestured in some odd manner that Creed presumed was a form of introduction, as that was what followed. "Travelers, I am Beker, of the Cartise! Please, if you would consider it, let me show you the hospitality of the Cartise!"

Creed's hand dropped to his staff, which hung

loosely at his side. Almost imperceptibly, Sheena shook her head at him. Creed didn't know what the man's "hospitality" looked like, but it sounded suspiciously like a weak trap for the unwary. Regardless, how could he take someone with such bizarre clothes seriously?

The man tilted his head slightly and blinked as he eyed Creed's staff. "Oh, good, we don't allow weapons within our camp. Please, share our fire, and the tales of your travels."

Sheena accepted for them both. "Sure, that would be nice!" She turned toward him, motioning with her hand. "Come on, Creed, let's join them." He had serious doubts about this whole thing, but he relented with a nod, and their threesome went a short distance before they left the road.

Creed whispered in as low an audible voice as he could manage. "You do realize that this could be some kind of horrible trap, right?" Sheena merely shook her head again, this time in disagreement. Creed sighed and braced himself for what might be a desperate, but brief, skirmish.

They traveled through a thick stand of pine trees before emerging into a surprisingly large field, where numerous brightly colored wagons were arrayed in a loose circle. Tent-like structures also dotted the area, and in the center, several stone-lined fire pits glowed warmly. Despite the drizzle, women washed clothes and cookware in the small creek that bordered the camp. Children played within the circle of wagons. To Creed, the display before him looked like a surreal dream, with the pointlessly gaudy colors randomly assigned to just about everything. Creed was the last person to be terribly concerned about what he wore, but the Cartise seemed extreme.

As they made their way into the camp, Creed murmured under his breath, "Okay, so I was only half-right. It's not a trap, but it IS horrendous." Sheena smiled at his comment, but he wasn't sure if that was the effect he wanted. He was, after all, trying to be serious. The dramatic colors really were horrible as far as he was concerned.

They stopped just inside the camp, and Beker spoke with another man, who approached them and offered, "Let me take care of your horses."

Sheena dismounted, and Creed reluctantly imitated her. While he felt a little better about the whole situation, he was still highly skeptical about seeing their horses again, though the Cartise obviously had plenty of their own horses for pulling their floral-colored wagons. Beker led them to one of the fire pits, where he motioned them toward the ground. "Sit and warm yourselves. I will have some food brought for you."

Creed took a seat on the ground as instructed, as close to Sheena as he thought he could without looking unseemly. Glancing around the fire at the half-dozen other people of varied ages, he leaned over and spoke cautiously. "I am not sure what's going on here, but I am very skeptical that they are just randomly the friendliest people in the world. Be ready for anything."

Sheena gave him a warm grin. "Creed, I think sometimes you are a little too skeptical, but I will be prepared for whatever you think is best."

* * *

Beker returned with two young girls, each carefully carrying a bowl of thick brown soup. Kneeling on either side of Creed and Sheena, they offered them the bowls wordlessly. Creed took his hesitantly, muttering his gratitude while pondering the probability that it might be tainted with something.

The Cartise girl near him wore a highly

174

contrasting bright green and purple dress. Most of her black hair was in a thick side braid that hung down to her waist, while the rest of it was tied up at the back of her head. Her soft brown eyes and olive skin were akin to his own. He was unsure of her age, but it seemed that she was still a child.

Sheena took her bowl readily, and tasting its contents, she exclaimed her pleasure to Beker, who, having taken a seat near them, waited anxiously for their verdict. "This is delicious! Thank you so much for your hospitality. Do you always greet strangers this way?"

Beker nodded. "Yes, it is the way of our people to give hospitality freely, and to trade stories with strangers."

Sheena was intrigued. "Stories?"

Beker expounded for her. "Yes, legends of your homeland, myths of your people, tales of your travels. Stories of any kind that are your own."

The girls who had brought them food dutifully took seats next to them around the fire. It dawned on Creed that this was an exchange. They, as outsiders, were treated with excellent hospitality in exchange for what they could give that the Cartise did not possess themselves. Though, stories for food seemed like a poor exchange in his opinion.

His opinion, however, did not halt Sheena from dragging him into their part of the trade. "Come on, ciega. Tell them a story!"

Creed stared at her with concealed alarm. "What! Why me?"

She shrugged innocently. "Because you know so much more than I do." She flushed a little and added, "And I would love to hear you tell a story."

Creed groaned inwardly as he looked around the fire pit, increasingly nervous as each person there turned to watch him. Creed tasted his soup, and decided that its

175

bold meaty flavor was probably worth the risk of any embarrassment he might suffer from telling a story to a bunch of strangers.

Creed cleared his throat and began. "Uh, so a very long time ago, there were two different groups of people who lived ordinary lives. One was the humans, and the other a people called the Fearians. They were separated from one another, and went about life like you do today. Then one day, people on both sides were awakened to great power. In total there were twelve people from each of the two groups that received power. They joined together in unity and connected the two differing groups. A new era dawned, and they brought unity and great prosperity to all. They were known as the twenty-four great mages, and they trained others to follow in their ways. Power was awakened in many, and so the golden age was born. That age is long gone today, and the great mages are but a memory, as are the Fearians."

Creed wasn't sure what else to say, so he simply stopped and ate another bite of soup. The wide-eyed Cartise girl next to him asked, "What are Fearians?!"

Creed really didn't want to answer that question, and he was blissfully spared from doing so by the old woman across the fire pit. "Moku, don't you remember the story of the shattering? It is from there that the Fearians came."

The girl nodded as she deferred to the older woman. "Yes, Miss Uonya, I do remember the story of the great calamity. I had just forgotten that it included the Fearians."

The two Fearians present shared a glance and silently concurred that the woman's answer was evasive. It didn't actually tell Moku what Fearians were as much as that they should not be unfamiliar to her.

Sheena spoke up with curiosity. "What is the

story of the shattering?"

Uonya smiled. "It too is an old story, but one I am happy to share with you.

"There was a time when the world was whole. There were people, but they were not like us. They developed a great society, with marvels that words cannot explain. They traveled the breadth of the land in the blink of an eye. They could soar in the skies and delve deep into the oceans. They bore power, and used it to rule over the world with complete supremacy. They changed themselves to increase their power, but when they did so, they began to tear the fabric of reality.

"As the world unraveled, they became desperate, and in an effort to prevent their own demise, they shattered the world into pieces. In so doing, they became isolated and altered. They lost all their power, and most of their history. They are the Fearians and the humans, two altered forms of one original. One merged with the raw powers of one aspect of the world, like water and fire, while the other merged with the raw power of different aspects of the world, such as plants and animals."

* * *

Having never heard such an explanation for the origin of the world and its peoples, Creed thought aloud, "Who were the first people if they were neither human nor Fearian?"

The old woman shrugged. "I know nothing more than that, traveler. It is for me to repeat the stories, not to understand them. A traveler from generations ago told that tale to my people, and it has stayed within our repertoire ever since."

Creed nodded his understanding, but he was rather disappointed that she could not tell him anything

177

more. He hadn't considered the idea that perhaps the way things were now was not the way they had been originally. He supposed it didn't matter. If his story was about the golden age, something so far removed that it was scarcely imaginable, then hers was about some archaic pre-history that was prior to that.

Of course, he was assuming that her story had any bearing in reality. It was quite possible that the story was completely fictional. Yet he could not shake a nagging sense that it was more accurate than it should be, given she spoke accurately of a people that neither she nor her ancestors for generations would have ever heard of.

The woman inquired politely, "What are your names, travelers, and where do you come from?"

Creed responded hastily, so as not to allow Sheena time to say something that would be difficult to explain. "We are from far to the southwest. I am Creed, and this is my sister Sheena."

Uonya inclined her head toward him. "Southwest of here? There isn't anything immediately southwest but the long-cursed lands of Empleheim. You must be from a long way away indeed. Please, now that the rain has ceased, join us for our evening festivities."

Creed passed his now empty bowl to Moku with a rising sense of concern about what was going to happen next. Sheena volunteered their answer to the woman's invitation for some unknown activity. "Certainly! We would love to join you!"

The woman looked to Beker, and the man stood, clapping his hands sharply, apparently a signal for something many were waiting for. People quickly rose and set about clearing the area around the fire pits of anything that might hinder them. Several began to play instruments made out of simple things, like empty water barrels, or metal wire strung across hollow boxes. A few had clay instruments with holes in them that served to provide an airy, lighthearted sound.

Creed groaned under his breath as he lamented, "Oh, come on, not again!"

The Cartise began to dance, and Sheena stood before him with a surprising level of bashfulness. She clasped her hands behind her back and looked down as she spoke in a small voice. "Creed . . . um . . . w-would you be willing to dance with me?"

Creed knew some frustration at this turn of events and started by saying, "Uh, I don't really know how . . . ." He could see the clear disappointment on her face, though she tried to hide it, and Creed finished his thought awkwardly. "But I guess I can try."

Sheena glanced up to meet his gaze, her eyes reflecting the firelight, and Creed was hit with the sudden realization that he was in really big trouble. She smiled a strange smile and held her hands out for him. He took them, and she led him in a series of motions that he assumed were appropriate for the occasion. The Cartise people danced in their own patterns that were surprisingly similar to hers. It was a type of folk dance, high energy, and completed in pairs. It was slightly disorganized, but less awkward than he expected it to be.

He could not help wondering what their hosts were thinking. He had told them Sheena was his sister, but the way she looked at him as they danced communicated something entirely different. He might also only be excessively self-conscious about the matter, since he didn't see anyone outright staring at them. As a means of breaking the strange feelings he was experiencing, Creed blurted out, "Hey, where did you learn to dance, Sheena?"

She seemed lost in the moment, but she did answer his question. "Mother taught me. It's part of the culture of being forest caste."

179

Creed wasn't sure how long the dance lasted, nor was he certain if it lasted too long, or not long enough. Regardless, it ended about as abruptly and spontaneously as it had begun. Sheena reluctantly let go of his hands and turned as Beker approached them with a satisfied sigh. "Nothing like a good dance to help settle in for the evening, don't you think?"

Creed's expression and tone were unreadable. "Right."

Beker cleared his throat and gestured broadly to the camp. "Well, ahem, if you would like to, you can stay tonight here in our camp. We have extra tents set aside for guests."

Creed admitted, "Yes, we would appreciate that." Sheena nodded her own agreement. Neither one of them wanted to sleep out on the cold green with there being a good chance of more rainfall in the night.

For the remainder of the evening, they stayed by the fire pit and conversed with the Cartise people. Sheena said little to him, mostly listening to stories, and even telling some of her own. He didn't have much opportunity to hear what she said, though, as the young girl who had served him supper had apparently decided that he was the source of all wisdom. She pelted him with a steady stream of questions, and this time Uonya was nowhere to be seen. Creed tried to be vague and cold in his responses, but either Moku was too young to understand he was suggesting that she leave him alone, or she didn't care that he was trying to put her off.

As people moved to retire for the night, Creed was relieved to tell her he was heading to bed as well. Sheena joined him as they walked toward the two tents that Beker had so graciously offered them. The tents were made out of wooden posts with cross beams lashed to them. The walls and ceilings were heavy canvas, and the floors were covered with a thick rug atop a dense layer of dry straw.

Creed heaved an exaggerated sigh. "That girl could have asked questions for days!"

Sheena chuckled at his exasperation. "Oh, Creed, you have no idea how likable you are, do you?"

He grimaced. "You're just biased. Literally no one has ever said that about me before this moment." She laughed again as they came to a stop outside their respective tents.

Sheena touched his arm. He turned to face her, and she addressed him softly. "Creed, I-I want to thank you for dancing with me. It was delightful."

Creed felt like that wasn't the best word to describe the situation, but he mumbled, "You're welcome, Sheena." Without any warning she leaned forward and kissed him on the cheek. Sheena giggled lightheartedly and then vanished into her tent, leaving Creed paralyzed by shock.

After shaking himself a little, Creed entered his tent and removed his heavy traveling boots. He laid down on the relatively soft floor, using his cloak as a blanket. His staff at his side, he stretched and stared up into the darkness as he pondered the trouble he was in.

He could no longer pretend like he could control his feelings for Sheena. She had genuine power over him, and it was only a matter of time before he was powerless to resist her whims. Not that Sheena was petty, or that he didn't want her to have power over him, but he knew now that he was at a very serious crossroads. He would either have to leave her, for good, or he would have to become one with her for life. There was no intermediate solution, and he had realized in that moment when they were dancing that he was fooling himself if he thought there could be some stable middle ground.

It was far from easy to make such a decision. He

cared about her more than he wanted to admit, but he was also starting to notice the intrusion of a persistent physical desire for her. At first, he merely dismissed it, but it was becoming less dismissible, and that worried him. He didn't want to disgrace her or treat her shamefully, but he was certain this could not end well if nothing changed. In a way, he hoped that what they might find in the remnants of Ferir's tower would give him some direction in life. Some grand revelation that would lead him far from Hona Castle, and far from the precious flower that Sheena was.

He felt like an ugly stain by comparison. Sheena was pure, and sweet, and delicate. Creed was a man of violence and blood. The battlefield was his home, and too often he woke in the night to the nightmarish echoes of the dying cries of his enemies, their lives cut short by the raw power of a destruction mage.

He muttered bitterly to himself in the darkness. "Likeable, my tail! It's like she has confused me for some completely different person. Why doesn't she make sense!"

With confusion and frustration weighing on his heart, it took far longer for him to fall asleep than it should have.

Chapter 17

Creed came to full awareness just in time to intercept the hand of someone about to touch his shoulder. In the dim oil-lamp light, he blinked at the frightened face of Moku. He released her quickly, seeing tear streaks on her cheeks. She spoke urgently, even desperately. "P-please, sir Creed, you have to save my father! He's trying to reason with the soldiers, b-but I know they won't listen to him. Please, we can't fight soldiers!"

Moku didn't wait for an answer, and she darted from the tent without another word. Creed, snatching his staff, shot after her. It was still very dark out, and the fire pits were little more than glowing embers. Drizzle fell from the black sky, and Creed barely caught a glimpse of the bobbing lantern light that was the swift-footed Moku moving in the direction of the road that lay beyond the camp. She had a head start, but he was far faster and nimbler than she was.

He caught up with her in the wooded area just before the road. She crouched in the protective darkness of the trees, and Creed crawled up beside her, keeping low as he observed the scene before them.

A battalion of some fifty soldiers, moderately armored and carrying double-edged knight's swords, faced off with Beker. The Cartise leader seemed less jovial than normal as he attempted to persuade the battalion commander of something. The man was listening but did not appear inclined to change his mind. About half of the soldiers carried lit torches, and the others had additional torches at their sides. Creed knew what that meant. They planned to burn the camp to the ground.

Moku's little voice quivered with fear. "They think we are nothing but thieves and bandits because we don't live like they do. But we are not! Just because some people are dishonest doesn't mean that everyone is! Please, sir Creed, please . . . um . . . ."

Moku fell silent. He glanced at her to see that she stared at him wide-eyed and slack-jawed, but before he could figure out her hesitation, there was a loud smacking sound. Moku gasped, and Creed turned and saw Beker hit the ground. He struggled to stand, having been struck across the face with the flat of the commander's sword. Moku bolted from the woods to her father's side with a panicked cry.

Creed clenched his teeth and darted from the woods himself. He slid in the mud of the road, coming to a stop between the soldiers and Moku and Beker. There was an unsettled murmur among the soldiers, and before Creed could demand of them just what they thought they were doing, the commander of the battalion blurted out loudly, "What on earth are you!"

Creed abruptly realized that that in his haste he had left his headband, cloak, and boots back in his tent. The light clothes he wore now did nothing to obscure his Fearian features, and to them he must have looked like some crazed demon. There was the sound of swords coming free from their scabbards, and the clinking of uneasy men in armor shifting their weight.

Taking advantage of their uncertainty, Creed

proclaimed boldly, "I am the destruction mage of Empleheim, and the protector of the Cartise! Go home! Bother someone else."

The commander held his sword low in anticipation of striking. "We did not march halfway across the kingdom to be thwarted by some myth-spouting . . . thing . . . from a long-dead, cursed nation." He called loudly. "Men, you have your orders! Burn the camp to the ground and kill any opposition. Now—"

The commander cut off his orders to stare at Creed, who had cracked his tail sharply like a whip. The popping sound was much louder than the unsuspecting would guess. It served its purpose of catching their attention. Creed brushed the citrine stone embedded in his staff, and it extended to its full length. Open-mouthed gasps escaped from numerous soldiers as he began to emanate the yellow-green glow of his mage power.

The commander took a step back as Creed planted his staff firmly and dozens of orbs of light rose out of the ground, circling him in erratic orbits. Creed's voice was deathly calm. "You would be badly mistaken to think that you can stand against a mage. I tell you, go home."

While his confidence had obviously flagged, the commander still managed to shout, "He is just one man-thing. Charge him!"

Compliance was partial at best, and only six soldiers charged at Creed. He threw his free hand forward sharply. Beams of concentrated energy blasted out from seven of the spheres. Creed wasn't interested in carnage if he could avoid it, so he went easy on them. The pained cries of the soldiers who had rushed him filled the air. Two clutched their arms, one stumbled and fell face first into the mud, and the others were visibly shaken.

The commander raised his sword with a yell. "What's the matter with you cowards!" Three-quarters of the blade of his sword slid from the hilt to the ground, from the place where Creed's energy beam had sliced cleanly through it.

Such a stubborn fellow needed a demonstration. Creed spun his staff in his hand and whirled it through a sharp arc before halting its motion with his free hand. The darkness of the night fled as beams of pure energy raced down from far above them, forming a symmetrical cage of narrow columns around Creed. With frightening speed, the columns shot out from where he stood along an unseen path. The mud hissed and popped as it was nearly instantly fused into something akin to ceramic under the intense heat. The columns stopped about a dozen paces away from him, and he brushed his hand through the air, casually dismissing them. Steam rose from the ground around Creed, and the commander, and his men, began to back away.

Creed stood in the center of a perfectly circular ceramic plate that was nearly thirty paces across. Its surface was as smooth as glass, like fine porcelain. It bore an elaborate pattern of a wagon wheel. Creed repeated his warning a third time. "Go home, or I will reduce you to heaps of ash."

The commander wiped sweat off his brow, as indeed the temperature of the air was easily twice what it had been, though it was cooling quickly. He looked at the severed stub of his sword, and without a word, he motioned for his men to form rank. Scurrying away like scared rabbits, they moved in formation back the way they had come, a couple of them limping a little. Creed stood his ground until their torchlight faded from sight.

He sighed, and the glow left his skin as he dismissed the remaining orbs of light. Creed walked carefully across the slick ceramic disk and came to a halt before Beker and Moku. The man touched his face gingerly. "Well, uh, thank you, Creed. It is uncommon for us to have aid from a traveler. Most would have fled for sure."

Moku gasped sharply, putting her hand to her mouth as she exclaimed, "Y-you must be Fearian!"

Her father put his hand on her head gently as he motioned back toward the camp. "Ah, come now, Moku. The hour is late. Don't pester the man with any more questions."

They returned to the camp together without any further conversation. Creed entered his tent and used the water bucket by the entrance to clean the mud off his feet before laying down to sleep. He supposed that he could have just vaporized the soldiers, but then again, he was thankful he hadn't, since he had a rather young witness. It wasn't proper for a child to be exposed to such horrors.

Creed felt a deep sadness fill his heart, and he blinked back tears. Those precise horrors defined his experience growing up. Was there any future for someone like himself? Someone who had taken life at even a very young age? When he had told Achron that Sheena deserved better, he had not uttered an empty phrase, but an objective reality. Drifting off to sleep was easier this time, but no more pleasant.

* * *

Someone whispered near his ear. "Creeeed. Creeeeeeed. Creed!"

He raised his head groggily off the desk and peered at her with annoyance. Hanni spoke with playful exaggeration. "You can't sleep on your books, Creed! They won't just absorb into your brain, you know."

Creed blinked sleepily at the tome he had been

reading on the control and invocation of mage power. "Yeah, yeah, they could make this stuff more interesting. I just want to be able to blast people, not put them to sleep with a litany of big words."

Hanni frowned. "Grandfather would not approve of such a mentality. He told me that life is precious, and that we shouldn't use our power to kill."

Creed shook his head. "Hanni, things are not good now, Grandfather isn't alive any longer, and there is already rising dissension among the mages. It's going to be war, and there won't be another solution other than blasting people."

Hanni straightened resolutely. "I promised him I would never take a life, and I won't, no matter what happens!"

Creed rolled his eyes. "Oh, come on, Hanni! That's just crazy talk. You're way more powerful than I am, and your power is about as destructive as it comes!"

She looked pained, and muttered defensively, "But . . . but . . . it doesn't have to be . . . does it?"

Creed glared at her, and then leaned back in his chair, putting his feet up on the desk. "Whatever, Hanni. It's power, it's for blasting things, end of story. Or, in your case, it's for burning things. What else would you do with it?"

Hanni squirmed uncomfortably as she tried to sound persuasive, but failed miserably. "Well . . . uh . . . it can make it warm when it's winter . . . and . . . it provides light . . . and, well, there is cooking."

Creed burst into raucous laughter, and Hanni flinched slightly at his sudden outpouring of humor. "Cooking? Cooking!? You're the most powerful prodigy in Grandfather's tower, and you're thinking about cooking? That's a terrible waste of your abilities, Hanni. Unless, of course, you're cooking whole armies."

Hanni shuddered at the gruesome thought. She

spoke softly, but seriously. "Creed, don't you think we were given such precious gifts for something better? Some grand purpose that is for good, not destruction?"

Creed waved his hand dismissively. "What? You're nuts. Nobody thinks being a prodigy is a 'gift,' given the price one has to pay. Not that I want to have a family, but it's much more like a curse than a 'gift.'"

Hanni looked down sadly, muttering, "I wish you weren't so stubborn, cousin. But I am fairly certain it's a gift, not a curse."

She glanced up questioningly, as though something had dawned on her, and she asked, "Have you ever thought about what you could do with your gift that isn't destructive?"

Creed was caught off guard by the question, and responded a little too hastily. "Uh, what? Of course I have. And it ain't cooking, that's for sure."

She prodded him further. 'Well, what is it then?"

Creed tried to glare her down, but it failed, and he replied haltingly, "Err, well . . . I can help . . . with . . . stuff, you know . . . like . . . uh . . . cremations!"

Hanni looked appalled. She shook her head in wonder. "I thought Fearian boys were supposed to mature faster than girls. Clearly that doesn't apply to everyone."

Creed tried to jump down from his position on his desk as he objected to her suggestion. "Hey, I am very mature for my—"

Missing his footing, Creed slipped and crashed to the floor, taking books and the small desk with him. The chief librarian shouted angrily from the adjacent room. "Just what is going on over there!"

Hanni and Creed shared a momentary fearful look, and then they both bolted from the room. The head librarian was not someone either of them wanted to face when he was angry, not because he was violent, but

189

because he would lecture them for an hour if he caught them, which for a child was akin to torture.

* * *

"Creeeed. Creed?"

Creed jerked awake and spoke the first thing that came to his mind. "I-I am sorry. I was very wrong!"

For a moment, Sheena watched him curiously, and then grinned. "Creed, don't you think it's a little early in the day to be wrong?"

Creed sighed as he shook his head. The dream faded quickly from his memory, but still left him feeling a bit disoriented.

Sheena tossed him his cloak. "Come on, sleepyhead. You have to get dressed so we can go figure out the mysteries of the past!" He nodded, and she left his tent. Creed readied himself for their departure, positioning his headband to obscure the pointed tips of his ears and pulling his cloak about him to hide his long tail.

Creed went out into the morning. The new day promised to be much brighter than the one before, though not substantially warmer. Clouds were loosely scattered across the sky. Beker seemed to materialize out of nowhere. He was leading their horses behind him, and he greeted Creed with what must have been a standard Cartise salutation. "Hail, traveler."

Creed winced at the nasty bruise on the man's face, but nodded politely as he cast about for Sheena. She was walking toward them from behind one of the larger wagons, chatting happily with Moku. Creed thanked Beker for the hospitality of his people and took the horses' reins in his hand.

Moku kept her eyes fixated on him as he helped

190

Sheena mount her horse and turned to his own. She practically bounced to where he stood. "Sir Creed, I just wanted to thank you, so . . . here!" She thrust one fist toward him. Creed held out his hand. She placed a wad of fabric into it, and then closed his fingers around it with her other hand, as though she feared it would escape if she didn't. Her enthusiasm bubbled over into her gratitude. "Thank you again, sir Creed. I will NEVER forget your story!"

Creed bobbed his head, but he wasn't sure if that was a good thing or not. He mounted up, and waving farewells to the people who stirred about the camp, they rode quickly back to the road. Creed turned sharply before they left the woods, causing them to come out of the woods down the road from his display of power for the sake of convincing the soldiers to beat it. He didn't want to have to explain the new road decoration to Sheena. She said nothing about the slightly odd path he took.

Sheena reflected on their experience as they traveled northward. "See, Creed? It wasn't a trap. Those people were really nice, and you obviously made quite an impression on that little girl."

He smiled cheekily as he mused, "Yep, they were pretty weird." Sheena gave him a mock disapproving look, and then laughed.

Her comment reminded him of the gift the girl had given him. The fabric was a very brightly colored bandana. He unwadded it out of curiosity. Inside was a simple, thumb-sized spinal crystal wrapped in silver wire. The natural eight-sided crystal was a dark opaque red. It was not a precious stone, but it was pretty. Creed didn't see a piece of jewelry as much as he saw an honest memento of thanks.

Sheena came alongside him as close as she could on horseback and peered at what he held. "What did she give you?"

Creed smiled. "Oh, nothing really, just a brightly colored strip of cloth, and a crystal pendant." His smile faded, and he examined it more closely.

Sheena tilted her head, expressing her concern at the sudden shift in his expression. "What's wrong?"

Creed spoke slowly, as though he wasn't sure himself. "It's spinel. The gem of power for a sonic mage . . . just like Ferir."

Sheena looked intrigued. "Well, that's a curious coincidence, I guess."

Creed didn't answer her. It could be a coincidence, or it could be that the Cartise were in part descendants of the sonic mages. He thought that sounded like a stretch, but then again, perhaps not. Creed couldn't remember if the sonic mages descended from Ferir had darker features like those of the Cartise. He dismissed the notion as something indeterminate as he wadded the object back up and tucked it into the pouch hanging from his belt.

They were a few days' travel from the earth scar. Getting down to the bottom of the great canyon was a very real problem. The sonic mages had had several complex, sigil-driven lifts that allowed them to rapidly, and safely, move between the canyon floor and the upper edge. It was unlikely that these were still operational.

Sheena must have been pondering the sonic mages. "What can you even do with something like sound?"

He smiled as he replied. "Yeah, it doesn't seem impressive at first, that's for sure. However, sound travels very quickly, and condensed, it can be terribly destructive. Its concussive force can stun an army, and its sudden absence can drive a person mad. In the narrow canyons and crevasses of the earth scar, it could cause landslides, blocking off entire areas. That is why Ferir's tower was never assaulted. It was practically impregnable, tucked behind a maze of unstable canyons. Because it is sheltered by the earth scar, I suspect that it will be in much better condition than the other towers have been."

Eagerness played over Sheena's face. "Oh, well, that's good!"

Creed shook his head. "No, it's probably not. It will make getting in without setting off the security system rather challenging."

Sheena sheepishly mumbled, "Oh. Figures." Creed found an odd delight at her embarrassment over her misplaced excitement.

They spoke of what they might face once they reached the canyons, and how they could overcome such things. It was the sort of informal planning Creed hoped would make their journey to and from the tower painless and uneventful. Everything seemed so clear and straightforward that he was substantially disappointed when his nice plans were marred by the realities at the earth scar.

Chapter 18

Sheena had kept to herself most of the morning. Though the sky was clear and blue, a chill wind blew against them. The terrain had become increasingly mountainous, and snow-capped peaks were visible in the far distance. Most of the trees were pines, and the ground they were anchored in was rocky, not suitable for anything like the farming they did at Castle Hona. They had left the main road late the day before, and now followed a narrow path that Creed said would take them to the earth scar.

The beauty of the cold northlands surrounded her as her horse trudged behind Creed's, but she was lost in her own thoughts. Creed was clearly under a lot of pressure, but the cause of his trouble was less clear to her. Perhaps it was partially her fault, but she struggled to believe that, because it sounded both vain and guilt-inducing. Perhaps it was due to the concern he had for her safety, but that also seemed vain.

It was odd how much she both longed to be central to his life, and simultaneously did not want to be, for what trouble it might cause him. She had not cast aside her commitment to him. Sheena was resolved that she would be Creed's light in a dark place; she would be the stay that held him back from despair and gloom.

However, during their journey together, she had begun to reflect on how close she should be to such a reluctant person. What if her very proximity was a cause of Creed's sorrow? She sighed quietly as she looked over at him, riding down the road with a casual yet cautious air.

If she were completely honest, her quest to save the heart of Creed was no longer as charitable as it had been in the beginning. She longed for him to hold her, to caress and kiss her. She shifted her gaze to the path as they continued in silence. Where did the edge of selflessness overlap with selfishness? Was it wrong to do something selfless for selfish reasons? Or what if she operated in a selfish manner for selfless motivations?

Sheena didn't know how to answer her own questions, but at least their time alone together gave her opportunity to be more thoughtful about the matter. Away from the life of family and friends at Hona, she had much more quiet for contemplation.

She smiled to herself. This was partially because Creed was a terrible conversationalist, and most of her attempts at small talk ended quickly. Not that that prevented her from trying again and again. She found it fun at times to see Creed struggle to say anything about nothing. His extensive knowledge about all things mage did little to help him have a conversation about the weather, or the season, or the scenery. The only time he really got talking was if she asked him about the past. It made her want to hug him. He was so cute, but also so clueless that she wanted to hold him and tell him that she would always try to be there for him—whether he liked it or not.

Creed brought his horse to an abrupt stop. "Oh, this is just great!"

Sheena stopped a little less abruptly and tried to see what he saw. "What is it?"

Creed straightened and frowned, pointing stiff-armed. "Some idiot is living practically on top of the old lift system. It could take another day to find a different place to access the floor of the earth scar!"

Sheena looked at the large, wooden, barn-like building that had an adorable little cottage attached to one side of it. A steady stream of smoke rose from the chimney before it was whisked away by the breeze. She wasn't really sure why this meant they would have to divert their course. "Well, maybe they are friendly?"

Creed sighed and grimaced. "Yeah, that's actually what I am afraid of."

Sheena laughed and continued forward, shaking her head as she commanded, "Let's go, Creed. Meeting new people is good for you!"

She heard him gripe under his breath, but not much of it was intelligible. "Ugh . . . if . . . have to."

Tying their horses to a post outside the cottage, they dismounted and approached the door. Creed knocked loudly and stepped back to wait. The door opened after a moment, and a clean-shaven older man with salt-and-pepper hair looked at them with some measure of surprise. He hesitated, clearly unaccustomed to having visitors. "Uh, hello. Can I help you . . . with . . . something?"

Sheena could tell that Creed viewed the man with suspicion, so she spoke up in response to the man's question. "Sir, we are travelers from far to the south, come to see the earth scar."

The man blinked, a little dumbfounded, and then glanced over his shoulder in the direction of the great crevasse that ran for days' worth of travel just beyond the cottage, as though he had never heard of such a thing. He seemed to relax, putting one hand on his hip and saying, "Well, you know, the Bugillow really does look like some kind of scar, doesn't it. Um, are you here for the ruins?"

Sheena nodded. "Yes, we are—"

Creed cut her off bluntly. "We are investigating the history surrounding this place."

The man raised his eyebrows before looking back and forth between them. "You hardly look old enough to be out on your own, let alone scholars of history."

Sheena was impressed by Creed's cool response. "I am a prodigy. It's what I do."

The man scratched his head, a little bemused, and then shrugged. "Ah, well then. Welcome, fellow scholars, to the kingdom of Anidar's northeastern research post! I am scholar Herin."

Sheena filled in where she doubted Creed would. "Thank you, Herin. I am Sheena, and this is my brother Creed."

Someone spoke from the other side of the door. "Who is it, Herin?" The man cleared his throat and opened the door all the way as he said, "Come in, and I will introduce you to the other scholars at the post." Creed looked skeptical still, but Sheena gave him a reassuring smile and took his hand to lead him inside.

The cottage was quaint. It had a cute little fireplace and all the bare essentials. Small as it was, it felt cozy, and there was a sense of a happy home within the walls. Herin swept his hand toward the two people at the table. "This is my research assistant, and my wife, Colleen, and this is our associate, and son, Neamin." He gestured to Sheena and Creed. "And these are fellow scholars here to study the ruins, Sheena and Creed." Sheena smiled politely, and Creed nodded wordlessly.

The woman, who herself was graying, but with the beauty of her youth still clinging tightly to her face, addressed them warmly. "Welcome! Can I get you some tea? We were just sitting down for tea and biscuits before we return to the dig site."

Sheena shivered slightly from the blustery chill of their ride and replied eagerly. "Why, yes, that would be delightful! Thank you." She took a seat at the table, and Creed joined her.

Herin offered, "I would be happy to take your cloaks."

Creed waved his polite gesture away. "We have come far, and we are eager to reach the dig site, so I must decline." Herin shrugged and took a seat across from them, taking his cup in his hand. Sheena noticed that Neamin, who had yet to say anything, was staring at her in something like disbelief, and tried not to feel self-conscious.

As Collen poured them cups of a hot aromatic tea, Herin expressed his curiosity in their purposes. "So tell me, what is your interest in the ruins here?"

Creed answered him noncommittally. "We are interested in the ruins of an ancient tower down on the canyon floor. Something from the golden age."

The man's eyes widened, and he laughed a little. "S-say what? The golden age? The ruins here are old enough for sure, but is there anything left from the golden age?"

It was probably imperceptible to the others, but Sheena could see Creed stiffen at the man's comment. She knew all too well how sensitive he was about the reality that he was just about the only thing left largely the same from the golden age.

Sheena replied calmly in his stead. "Oh, well, we have reason to believe that there is. Have you encountered any large structures in your exploration of the ruins in the canyons?"

The man shook his head soberly, but then his face brightened, and he turned to Neamin. "Hey, tell them what you found yesterday, son!"

There was an awkward moment as the young man, perhaps a few years older than Creed and Sheena, started as he realized he was now going to have to speak. He started off poorly but caught up quickly enough. "I-I found, uh, things, err—I mean, there were the ruins of some kind of obelisk. It was scribbled on, like the ruins here on the cliff."

Creed scarcely contained his incredulity as he repeated, "Scribbled on?"

Herin nodded, and pulled a smooth chunk of rock off a shelf and set it on the table about the same time the woman set their cups down. The rock was flat on two sides, but the rest of it was rough, as though it had broken from a larger structure. On the flat surface, there were elaborate sigils that coalesced and separated several times. Creed looked at it, and then looked at them, and then muttered as he sniffed at his tea. "Scribbles indeed."

Sheena reached out and touched the sigils as more of a gesture of interest than anything else. As her fingers brushed the stone, visions of a terrible conflict flashed before her eyes, and Sheena jerked her hand back sharply with a gasp. Creed reached out reflexively and took her hand under the table, all without twitching as he committed to drinking his tea.

Sheena flushed slightly as the three other people watched her with concern. Sheena cleared her throat. "Ahem, sorry, it's just cold."

Herin reached out and took the fragment from the table. "Of course." He didn't sound like he believed her, but he wasn't about to challenge her either.

Sheena clung to Creed's hand, afraid of the strange event, and the frightening nature of what had so briefly entered her consciousness. Creed observed to no one in particular, "That fragment was destroyed by something pretty powerful. You should be careful what you bring back to your home. Something that destructive might leave a lasting effect."

Neamin chuckled a little uneasily. "Oh, now, please don't tell me you're superstitious about that whole mage mythology!?"

Herin rebuked his son gently. "Neamin, we don't insult the beliefs of guests."

Neamin apologized without conviction. "Sorry. I just thought you were scholars." Colleen shot him a look that could have stopped anyone dead in their tracks. The young man jerked and looked down at the table submissively.

She smiled kindly at them and held out a basket full of biscuits. "Have some biscuits before we face the cold again."

Sheena offered generous thanks as she took one, and then nudged Creed, saying, "Eat a biscuit, Creed." He shot her an annoyed glance but complied. Sheena wondered if someone had tried to poison him in a past life, given how skeptical he was of taking food from strangers.

* * *

Finishing their brief break, the scholars led them out into the large barn-like building. Passing through the door that connected it to the cottage, Sheena exclaimed, "This is incredible!"

The floor was part of the excavation site. It sat atop an ancient stone structure that was mostly concealed by a series of wooden frames lashed together with heavy rope. A platform connected to a complex of cables and weights hung over a torch-lit shaft that dropped straight down from the center of the open building.

Creed eyed the lift uncertainly, but Herin spoke

his pride as he explained. "The biggest challenge was designing a way to reach the canyon floor. The ancients left this stone passageway, but there is no telling how they actually traveled up and down it."

Creed muttered, "Scribbling."

Sheena elbowed him discreetly before stating, "It's really amazing that you built this all by yourself!" Herin nodded his thanks and motioned that they stand on the platform as he shouldered his bag of supplies.

Creed and Sheena joined Neamin and Colleen. Sheena took his hand as he eyed the sigil-encrusted stone scarcely visible behind the large frames that made up the bulk of the lift's structure. Herin checked several ropes and released the safety on the lift before taking his place on the platform. He turned a crank, and they descended . . . slowly.

Neamin explained excitedly. "Before my father built this lift, the only way to access the ruins in the canyon was at the shallow end of the Bugillow, where the bandits are entrenched."

Sheena felt a measure of concern well up in her mind. "Um, is it safe to be down on the canyon floor if there are bandits at the other end?"

Neamin blinked with surprise, as though he hadn't really thought about the danger that might be involved. "They have never bothered us before."

Creed appeared to be calmly watching their incremental descent, but Sheena had no doubt he was calculating possible problems and adjusting his approach to exploring the tower ruins in light of the bandit presence. She marveled at his ability to passively account for every situation. She was in a strange place, surrounded by strange people, and soon to face unknown dangers, but she felt safe with Creed nearby. She knew that he needed her, whether he was willing to admit it or not, but now she was starting to realize that she needed him as well.

The realization scared her, because she feared that he would just up and vanish from her life. She wanted to know what drove him at a deeper level, but despite their years together, Creed was often enigmatic to her. She wanted to understand him better, to be part of all of his life, not on the periphery.

Herin interrupted her thoughts by adding to the conversation about the bandits. "That lot of vagabonds has no interest in history, and there is nothing on this end of the canyon to draw them. We have worked here for years without the slightest sight of them. Though I wouldn't go poking around too far down into the canyons, just to be safe."

Creed's hand drifted to his staff as he commented, "Sure, who wants to deal with bandits anyway."

Sheena caught Colleen's intense interest in Creed's staff, which bore its own set of "scribbles." Collen looked away casually, but Sheena suspected that it wouldn't be long before they could no longer conceal who they were. She stated, more than asked, "The lift works."

Creed understood what she was saying and glanced beyond the ropes and the creaking wood platform. "Yes, it does, even after all these years." Neamin appeared confused at their exchange, but his father just shrugged at his questioning look.

Sheena was relieved when the platform came to rest on a large, flat stone square that bore numerous sigils. It was a stark reminder that what passed as ingenuity for the current people of the world was only a shadow of what once had been.

They followed a brief passageway that exited onto the canyon floor through an elaborate stone arch that was cut out of the solid rock face. Sheena could hardly take her eyes off the massive canyon walls towering high above her head. Dust and stones fallen from the upper edges of the canyon littered the ground. In some places, enormous piles of rubble had formed from where parts of the walls had collapsed and slid into the canyon.

The floor was strangely smooth aside from all the rocky debris. Numerous side branches splintered off in every direction from where they stood, and the whole of it was mesmerizing. Herin seemed to enjoy their expressions. "It's really something to see, isn't it?"

Sheena spoke softly, as though she were afraid that the answer might diminish her sense of wonder. "How did the Bugillow form?"

Herin laughed lightly. "Oh, that's an easy one. Over there toward the center is a river, and it cut out this canyon over millennia, long before the ancients built things in it."

Sheena noted a smirk on Creed's face that suggested he had an entirely different answer to the question, but she knew that she would have to wait for another time to hear about its actual history. Sheena glanced back at the beautiful stone archway they had just left and gasped with surprise. She could scarcely believe what she saw, and she grabbed Creed's arm and pointed. "Creed! Look!" Creed looked as surprised as she felt.

An elaborate carving of an eagle watched them from the rock. Its details were worn from ages of weathering, but it remained mesmerizing. Its eyes were a set of polished idocrase gemstones. She wasn't sure what it meant to Creed, but it told her that his kind of power was used for art and beauty prior to its application as a tool of war.

Neamin contributed less than he thought when he commented, "Yes, the ancients must have been some incredible stone masons."

Creed redirected their focus. "Where is this dig site you spoke of earlier?" Herin nodded, and they walked the length of the relatively small canyon they were in and entered the main canyon of the earth scar.

Its size was hard for Sheena to grasp. They could spend days here just exploring the innumerable branches off this canyon, or any of the other main canyons, which formed several parallel channels, broken intermittently by narrow perpendicular passageways. She wondered how they would ever find Ferir's tower in such a vast place.

Herin continued to lead them out into the main canyon. Seemingly in the middle of nowhere, he stopped and knelt at a large pile of rubble. "Here is what remains the obelisk. We almost overlooked it because of how crumbled it is. That piece you saw in our cottage came from this mound. Far as I can tell, being out here, exposed to the elements, it disintegrated much faster than the other features we have found."

Sheena nodded, and Neamin beamed. "I discovered this one myself!" Colleen smiled approvingly.

Creed bent and scooped up a handful of fine silt from the pile. He let it trickle through his fingers, and it caught in one of the occasional gusts of air that rolled down through the canyon. Herin watched him curiously, and then, not being able to restrain himself any longer, inquired, "What do you think, scholar Creed?"

Creed rose and studied the many parallel narrow canyons that formed the central one. "This was an outer perimeter post, and it was destroyed suddenly. The stones were reduced to powder abruptly, by force."

Neamin looked a little skeptical of Creed's conclusion, but spoke politely. "What makes you think that is what happened?"

Creed examined the dust on his hand soberly,

204

stating with great certainty, "Because this was a battlefield, and it is here that the defenders and the attackers clashed."

Herin inclined his head slightly, and Colleen searched for signs of battle. Creed scanned the area, and then pointed out several other rubble piles. "There, and there, and there are other parts of the defensive perimeter. That means that the main structure should be somewhere in the canyons over there."

Herin shook his head. "That's . . . kind of farfetched, don't you think?" He glanced at Sheena, but she simply shook her head. Creed would know better than anyone else, as far as she could tell. Herin seemed to take Creed's words under consideration. "Well, 'tis certainly an interesting idea. You know, the day is young, and that's not too far. Let's go and have a look, shall we?"

Colleen nodded, and Neamin muttered, "Okay, but it's just a blind guess."

As they moved toward the nearest opening to the maze-like set of canyons, Sheena asked in a low voice, "Creed, what you think happened here?"

Creed replied as they climbed over a pile of rubble. "Green mages shredded the defense matrix on this end of the tower complex. It was probably part of a coordinated attack by the rose league against the storm league."

Sheena felt a little crestfallen. "Don't tell me that means they ruined everything?"

Creed gave her a friendly smile as he said with confidence, "With the narrow structure of these canyons, I seriously doubt the sonic mages would have let them even touch Ferir's tower. The force of sound ricocheting off these walls could rip flesh from bone."

Sheena shuddered, and thought of another concern. "Please tell me there aren't any traps in those canyons?"

Creed shrugged, and she glowered at him. He merely laughed. "I am sure it's safe by now. Come on. How many other people have probably wandered around down here before us?"

She felt only mildly comforted. "I guess so." It was hard for her to know how serious he was being.

Herin seemed to show up out of nowhere. "What's the joke?"

Creed scowled ever so slightly, but Sheena responded politely. "Well, we were just hoping there aren't any kind of ancient traps out here."

Herin looked incredulous and chuckled. "Really? Out here? After years of being undisturbed, it seems like nothing of that sort would remain intact."

Sheena replied, "Right. I am just being silly, I guess." Creed shot her an annoyed look, but she wasn't sure why.

Reaching the main branching point of the many parallel canyons, Creed studied them cautiously. Sheena said what he was thinking. "Well, I suppose the question is which one do we search first?"

Neamin spoke up. "Maybe we should split up?"

Herin looked thoughtfully at the options, and then cautioned, "Well, I guess that's fine, as long as no one goes alone."

Neamin gestured to one of the farther ones as he said, "Scholar Sheena, would you care to accompany me this way?"

Sheena hesitated, but Creed replied briskly. "You should go with him. We will reconvene with the results of our explorations before we actually do anything."

Herin nodded firmly. "Yes, agreed."

Sheena overheard Creed and Herin talking as she walked with Neamin. Creed's voice came first. "I am

206

not technically on my own with the two groups of you in canyons on either side of me."

Herin sounded a little doubtful but conceded. "I am not so sure it's as safe as sticking together, scholar Creed, but I guess we should still be able to hear you if you call out loudly."

Sheena didn't entirely understand what Creed was up to, but she was suspicious that he was scheming something. Neamin seemed like a decent enough fellow, but she really would have preferred being with Creed over being with the slightly anxious researcher.

Chapter 19

Creed entered a central canyon, with Herin and Colleen entering the next one over. This put Sheena and Neamin on one side of him, and Herin and Colleen on the other. He poked around the rubble in the canyon for just moments, and then he left and walked to the crevasse farthest down. He knelt and traced an ancient, worn sigil in the ground. It was the path he needed.

He cared too much for Sheena to expose her to the hazards that the defense matrix posed to the unprepared. The rose league might have broken through the outer defenses, but that said nothing about the current status of the inner part of the defense matrix. That thing could cut down even a mage that was caught off guard.

Creed hoped that she wouldn't be too angry that he had sent her on a dead-end chase with the insufferable scholar boy. The guy was annoying, but Creed didn't really want to contemplate why that was the case. He liked to think it was because Neamin was ignorant but critical of the obvious, but the reality was that he wouldn't have cared one wit about him if Sheena had not been there.

Creed paced down the canyon, carrying the hope that he could enter the ruins and collect any valuable information for solving the cryptic nature of the third chronicler before it was dark. The canyon was narrow, but still some fifty paces wide.

He slowed as he came to one of the perpendicular cuts that crossed through the canyon. He was relieved to see that it only cut through the right side of the canyon he was in, revealing more canyons beyond. It would be embarrassing if it cut through enough canyons that the others could notice he was in a place they would not expect. Creed only glanced at it before pressing on.

Soon he caught sight of something a little odd. There was a rather well-preserved fragment of the inner defense system, scrawled with sigils, just sitting out in the open. Beyond, Creed could see a wall of rubble, conspicuously as high as the canyon itself, where the sides of the canyon had collapsed toward the center. The size of the boulders that comprised it suggested that it had been formed by something immensely powerful. Likely the last stage of defense, and an effective one, since it still stood.

Creed stopped just off to the side of the pristine artifact. As he studied it, he wondered what would have halted the rose league's advance if they were readily capable of shattering the defense matrix spires. What was a little rock wall compared to those?

An odd sound echoed down the canyon, and he jumped back sharply, reaching for his staff. He was fast, but not quite fast enough. Large rocks slammed into the ground around where he had been standing, and a hefty chunk of rock glanced off him, throwing him to the dirt. His head hit hard, and the world went black.

* * *

There was darkness, and a strange dank smell.

Creed felt his head aching, and he remained motionless where he lay in a heap on a dusty stone floor. He could tell that he bore shackles on his arms and legs. He wore just the simple clothes he traveled in. His cloak and outer coat were gone, as was his staff.

None of this was particularly concerning in light of his abilities. For now, though, his head hurt, and he was content to wait until the throbbing stopped before he did anything about his captivity. If they thought they were going to take a mage captive, then they were out of their minds. He lamented having let down his guard. Obviously the fragment had been a trap, designed for one of the scholars.

He was working on trying to ignore his head when he heard someone coming in with no shortage of ruckus. "I am telling you, I'm just from the sandhills gang!"

A man responded roughly to the plea. "Shut up, spy!"

A woman's voice protested further. "No, I am not a spy. I am just like you guys! Come on, what's a girl got to do to get respect around here?"

There was the sound of a lock turning, and a sudden change in brightness detectible even with his eyes closed. Another person was forcefully thrown into the room. A rough man's voice wafted in with a sickening tone. "You better hope that'un don't wake up before I gets back." The other person let out a frightened scream, and Creed came within a hair's width of defending himself, but through sheer willpower, he kept still.

The woman's voice had a genuine tremble. "W-what is that!? Y-you can't just leave me here with it! What kind of monster are you!"

The clearly undereducated brute chuckled darkly. "You're gonna get yours, spy, just you wait!" He slammed the door with a loud clang, and Creed scarcely managed not to flinch at the sound. The other captive took to a rather frantic pacing, and fiddled with the lock several times without success, muttering under her breath the whole while.

It wasn't long before the door opened and the woman backed away from it, but kept her distance from where Creed lay against the wall. A different man began to speak. "Are you ready to be cut apart alive, my dear?"

She sounded a little uncertain, but replied with surprising calm. "Come on, let's talk about this. Give me some task to prove my worth. Anything. Just tell me who needs dead."

The other person cackled in tune to the sound of a blade sliding free. "What? And give you an opportunity to worm your way into our operation? The kingdom obviously can't train its spies to be remotely believable. You're too eager, dear. You need to be far less simpering. But now we get to send them a message, one with lots of little meaty pieces."

It was time to interfere. Without moving, Creed spoke. "If you come any closer to her, you're a dead man."

Silence followed. Creed opened his eyes and rose slowly to the clinking of the chains that kept him close to the wall. A gaunt and pale man with an unnecessary number of weapons strapped to his body lifted a long, jagged, bloodstained blade in front of him. "Well, well, speaking of lousy spy, the monster pretending to be scholar speaks."

Creed glanced at the young woman, who wore what probably passed for adventurer's garb, with her back literally against the wall. The pale man waved his weapon tauntingly, while a couple of thugs near the door wore grim smiles. "So, you're a kind-hearted monster? What a pity. I was hoping for something a little more . . .

211

violent."

The pain in his head faded away, replaced by the heightened senses of the mage focus. "Not a problem," he told the man. "Only one sort of person can constrain a mage."

The pale fellow just laughed—or at least, he started to. It ended in a choking fit as yellow-green orbs appeared out of nowhere and swirled into a spiral, where they rapidly condensed into a vertical column immediately beside Creed. He reached out and grabbed it, and his skin glowed with the same light as Orion, his relic staff, came to full shape.

The pale man and his cronies backed away fearfully as several dozen pinpoint orbs of light effortlessly sliced the chains and shackles from Creed with narrow energy beams. Creed took a step forward and staggered, using his staff to steady himself. This time the pale man screamed and darted through the door, slamming it hard and turning the lock. Creed caught a glimpse of a small slit in the wall across from the room of his imprisonment. It gave a limited view of some treetops and the canyon wall of the earth scar.

Creed felt the throb in his head returning. He was pushing himself farther than he was ready for. The woman watched him with a mixture of awe and fear, and whispered, "W-what are you?"

Creed answered her while calmly estimating the level of power he would need to work his escape. "I am Empleheim's destruction mage. Like you, I don't belong here."

She glared at him, but only for a moment before asking, "Can you open the door?"

Creed raised his staff to a horizontal position in front of him, taking it in both hands. "And walk into another trap? No thanks." She shook her head, uncertain what other option existed.

Creed spoke sternly. "I need you to do two things for me." She looked at him blankly, but then nodded without a word. "When we get out, I am going to lose consciousness, too much, too early, so I need you to carry me out of here."

There was a moment of silence, and then she asked cautiously, "And . . . the other one?"

Creed felt the mage power swell within him. "Until then, don't move."

Two powerful beams of pure energy ripped through the bandit fortress from the outside, streaming past Creed and his fellow prisoner to coalesce somewhere in the wall behind him. With mesmerizing speed, the beams circled them, slicing an enormous cone-shaped plug out of the solid stone. They vanished as quickly as they had appeared, and Creed slumped and muttered, "Brace yourself."

He wasn't so capable of following his own instructions, and he tumbled forward as the core section slid free from the rest of the bandit stronghold and fell into the canyon below it. The distance was short enough that the sudden stop, though jarring, was not damaging. Creed, however, slipped back into unconsciousness prior to hitting the ground, and thus was not able to appreciate the accuracy of his calculations.

* * *

Creed woke to a crackling sound, the popping and spitting of damp wood on a warm fire. He could feel the heat of the fire, and the dull ache of his head. He sat up slowly and saw a brilliant sunset. Sheena would be terribly worried about him by now.

Looking past the fire, he noticed the young woman who sat nearby, her back against a boulder, her arms crossed, and a sword hanging from her side. She

213

stared at him rudely. Creed glanced at the ground next to him to see his staff lay close at hand.

The woman sounded hesitant, as though she weren't entirely sure what she saw was real. "I have been trained in a wide array of odd things, knowledge of the strange spheres of life, so that I might be prepared for anything. But nothing prepared me for what happened today. What are you, really?"

Creed flicked his tail emphatically as he replied. "My name is Creed. I am Fearian, a grand energy mage, and not from around here."

The woman did not appear satisfied. "Right. And old Empleheim is such a wonderful, dark, cursed ruin that it just makes perfect sense that you live there."

Creed shrugged. "It isn't like that anymore."

She eyed him for a moment longer, and then dropped her gaze to the fire. "I am Arnna, of the kingdom of Anidar's special knights."

Creed watched the flames himself. "A pleasure."

There was only a brief silence before she demanded, "Just what exactly is someone like you doing out here in a place like this?"

Creed answered softly. "I am trying to solve a mystery, here in the ruins of an ancient mage tower." He analyzed the area around him, hoping to get a sense of where he was. With how unremarkable the canyon looked in the fading daylight, it was somewhat of a mystery in itself.

Arnna snorted. "There isn't anything valuable here. If there had been, that scum would have sold it long ago."

Creed smiled slightly. "I don't think so. This isn't some old tomb with a few traps. It's protected, and if the watcher is still active, it's intelligent."

She looked at him with mild bemusement, and Creed decided not to pursue the matter further. She had no context to understand what he was talking about.

Instead, he turned the conversation to her. "What were you doing in that place?" Arnna tossed her head, sounding flustered. "Well, I was supposed to probe the strength of the bandits entrenched in the Bugillow, but they had some inside information about me. There was no other explanation for the speed with which they saw through my guise."

There was nothing for him to say about the matter, so he guessed, "You're some kind of spy then?"

She shrugged noncommittally. "Of a sort."

He decided to ask about something a little safer. "Where are we now?"

She looked at him pointedly as she replied. "Weeelllll . . . since I was weighed down, and those thugs are particularly dug in toward the front of the Bugillow, we are presently next to the reservoir in the north central region of this rather large death trap of geography."

Creed thought for a moment as he tried to picture their location. In his mind's eye, it seemed like he should be near the tower, only at a different point on the compass. He shivered and rubbed his arms. It was more than a little unfortunate that he was without his cloak or pack. It wasn't cold enough yet to be life threatening, but it was certainly unpleasant. He stood slowly, and Arnna asked, "What are you doing?"

Creed began to walk down the canyon. "We are close to the ruins, and we have to go this way to reach the lift at the southern end anyway."

She stood and shook her head. "Don't be so sure there is an exit there any longer. Those buggers were prattling on about fixing the 'leak' at the end of the Bugillow. I have no doubt it's those clueless archaeologists they were talking about. Fact is, we are just trapped here."

Creed continued down the canyon, looking for traces of the great mage tower. "There is another lift at the southern end of the canyon that they don't know about."

Arnna crossed her arms indignantly. "What?! That can't be. I have ALL the intel on this place. There isn't anything I don't know about the Bugillow!"

Creed gave her a sobering look, and then he knelt and traced the sigil that was cut into the ground. "Really? Then I supposed you can tell me what this is?"

Now that it was plain Creed wasn't going to stay put, she kicked dirt over the fire and came to stand beside him, frowning down at the finely etched symbol. She tossed her head and snapped, "Ah, yeah, that's just boring archaeological stuff."

Creed decided that this was not a profitable pursuit and kept walking. Arnna was, not surprisingly, interested in his nature as a mage, and she pelted him with questions about it. He gave her answers that were accurate, but likely well beyond her context to fully understand. He was on the edge of telling her to figure it out herself when he entered another dead-end canyon with a tall wall of enormous boulders. He stopped and stated, "It's behind there."

Arnna looked toward the end of the canyon, then laughed aloud. "Yeah, sure. That ain't happening."

Creed approached it, this time watching the rock ledges above him. He took his staff from his side and offered the explanation she hadn't asked for. "There are very few things that I can't simply cut through, but the challenge here is making an opening without creating a rockslide."

Arnna huffed sarcastically. "Oh, is that all? Well, just go blasting away then!"

Creed began to glow, and he tapped his staff on the ground sharply, causing a ring of yellow-green light

216

to appear around him. Numerous orbs of light rose from the ring, and with a flick of his hand, they rushed toward the rock wall. Brilliant beams shot through a particularly large boulder that sat at ground level. The stone popped and cracked with the sudden change in temperature along the edges that were cut.

Arnna started and jumped back cautiously. Creed waved his hand, dismissing the orbs in the blink of an eye, but continued to glow with his power. He didn't know what had halted the rose league, but it was likely beyond the wall. Being caught off guard once was bad enough, but a second time could be instantly fatal. Warring mages were substantially more dangerous than some thieving rabble.

Stone crumbled into coarse gravel, leaving a remarkably square rectangular passageway through the large boulder to the other side. Arnna remarked pensively, "You do realize people would kill to be able to do what you just did."

Holding his staff at the ready, Creed paused before entering the passageway. "They have, and they did. It's why this place is a ruin, and I am the last of my kind."

Arnna rolled her eyes at him. "You're such a ray of sunshine. You must be really popular back in Empleheim."

Creed ignored her. As he stepped cautiously from the narrow hole in the boulder, he marveled at the beauty he saw. While it was substantially overgrown, the brilliant white tower stood tall and almost complete. It reached to the sky gracefully, though the very top was broken off, which was why there was nothing visible from the upper edge of the earth scar. At one time, the tower base was surrounded by elaborate gardens and pools of crystal-clear water. Now it was a mess of vines, weeds, and dead leaves.

Creed sighed. There was something calming about seeing it so nearly intact. It reminded him of the days growing up around his grandfather's tower.

Arnna marveled at the sight. "This is incredible. How come I never heard about this?"

He replied as he examined their path cautiously for any kind of trap or guardian. "Because it's been this way for millennia. Which is also why I suspect that Ferir has some pretty nasty traps here."

Arnna glanced about suspiciously, but then shrugged as she said, "Uh, I don't think anything would last that long."

He regarded her with a little disdain as he pointed out what was obvious to him. "Mage traps don't require metal, wood, or cloth, so there is no reason they wouldn't still be active."

She sighed with exasperation. "Oh, of course they are magic traps! This is just all so sensible."

He glared at her, but then spoke calmly as he looked back at the overgrown forest. "You don't have to follow me. I can't promise that my reflexes are fast enough to protect you."

She tossed her head as she commented absently, "Eh, I will take my chances." Creed had been hoping that she might leave, but her persistence wasn't exactly surprising either.

They navigated rather slowly through the dense vegetation to the main entrance of the tower. Vines nearly completely obscured the large door. The door itself was sealed, and it lack any knobs or keyholes. Studying it closely, Arnna commented, "How can this thing still be shut so tightly? It's not even like a normal door. I hate to think what the windows look like."

Her words were strangely inspiring. Looking up, he could see one window along the side of the tower that was open. It was nearly three floors off the ground, but being that it was adjacent to a large old tree, his next course of action was obvious. Creed glanced about. It seemed suspiciously too easy, yet, aside from cutting his own entrance, which was sure to set off the defense matrix, there wasn't another option.

Arnna trailed behind him as he walked to the tree and started climbing. "Now what are you doing?"

He replied with the same kind of sarcasm that she had been using. "Do all spies ask so many questions?"

She scowled. "Hey, that has nothing to do with anything. It's not my fault you act so erratically that you're unpredictable." As he moved along a thick branch in the upper canopy of the tree, she began to climb as well, grumbling about how much easier things would be if he would just answer her questions.

Creed broke into a run along the branch and leapt from the end of it to land expertly on the ledge of the window. Arnna looked down, and then looked at him from where she stood on the same branch near the trunk of the tree. She demanded begrudgingly, "Okay, tiger boy, you care to tell me how you did that?"

Creed blinked and turned his head toward her, and then glanced at his tail. "My tail gives me far better balance than you humans possess."

She scrunched her face slightly as she warned, "Right. Then that means you're responsible for catching me."

Before Creed could entirely process what she had said, Arnna bolted down the branch, albeit a little more wobblingly than he had, and jumped toward him recklessly. Creed screamed as she slammed into his back with her full weight. They fell through the open window, crashing into a largely empty room.

Creed shouted with ire. "Get off me!"

An unreadable expression crossed her face, but

he merely glared at her. She got up, noting, "You're . . . soft . . . for someone who acts really tough."

Creed scrambled to his feet, quickly brushing himself off, complaining as he did. "You are just really weird."

Arnna laughed at his expense. "Oh, sure, all the people I know have such long, soft, luxurious tails."

Creed stalked toward the door with a snarl. "Don't touch my tail again."

Creed walked the short distance to the far wall of the room and stopped. Arnna spoke with mild annoyance. "Who has a room without a . . . ?"

While she was talking, he reached out and brushed his hand across the small citrine stone embedded in the wall. The stone, and its associated sigils, glowed, and the door shifted open. Arnna groaned. "Ugh. This is getting to be a little too much for me."

Creed coolly suggested, "Well then, maybe you should wait outside." Arnna crossed her arms but said nothing. He shook his head and continued into the corridor.

The moment he stepped into the darkened interior of Ferir's tower, lights seemed to spontaneously appear in parallel strips along the ceiling. Arnna flinched, and he sighed. So much for going unnoticed. Creed prepared for the worst, but he was surprised when the form of a young boy in a simple squire's robe materialized on the wall. Arnna jumped back sharply when the semi-translucent figure spoke. "Hello. I am the master's servant, Tonis. How may I assist you?"

Creed arched one eyebrow in suspicion. Watchers were not named. It was considered offensive to imply that the watcher had similar value to something alive. After a second's recovery, Creed replied calmly. "Tonis, I have a message for your master."

Tonis cast about as though confirming his suspicions, and then informed him, "My apologies, sir. The master is away right now. Can I take a message?"

Arnna whispered, "What IS that?"

As though her question were a normal one, Tonis responded. "I am the master's servant, Tonis."

Replying to the two of them in turn, Creed tried a different approach. "It's a watcher, part of the automated system that maintains and monitors the tower. Tonis, my message is too important to be told to anyone other than the master. Can I leave it somewhere that no one else will find it?"

Tonis tilted his head slightly, and then nodded. "Of course. You can leave it in the master's study. Please follow me."

Tonis flickered down the hallway, and Creed followed, with Arnna sticking unnecessarily close to his side. "Is he really just going to let us into his master's study? That seems too . . . convenient."

Not wanting to incite unnecessary concern, Creed told her, "Yeah, some watchers are more competent than others." There was something chilling about this one, though. Its tonal inflections were too realistic, its mannerisms too natural. He was no expert on watchers, but something about Tonis made him feel uncomfortable.

Creed attempted to keep his tone casual. "Tonis, when is your master supposed to be back?"

Tonis replied, "The master said that she would not be back for the length of time it takes to climb the sky."

Arnna was sufficiently in control of herself to give a snide comment. "Oh, then I guess she could be back at any moment."

He waved her to silence. "Tonis, is not your master Ferir Ruttoson?"

Tonis paused and looked down at the ground soberly. "The old master was Ferir." He looked up and smiled as he added, "But the new master is Seleen Kiusonna."

Creed stood still, trembling with restrained emotions, and a strong sense of uncertainty about what was going on. Tonis sought clarification. "For whom was your message?"

Arnna answered calmly for him. "For Seleen, of course."

Tonis's smile widened as he replied chipperly. "Of course!" He returned to moving along the wall.

Chapter 20

They followed Tonis through a series of
passageways and up several flights of stairs. Finally, the
illusionary form of Tonis, projected by complex sets of
sigils on the walls, came to a stop across from a large
ornate door. "Here is the master's study. Please leave
your message within."

There was a pulse of light through the beautiful
sigil pattern on the door, and then the door shifted into
the wall, revealing a generously sized library of sorts.
Creed spoke absently as he searched the room beyond
with his eyes while approaching with caution. "Thank
you, Tonis."

The figure smiled as he replied. "You are
welcome, sir."

Creed hesitated, but tried to dismiss his
uneasiness as he entered the study. The air was stale and
bore an odd sort of odor that reminded him of leather.
The study itself was impeccable. Rows and rows of
books filled floor-to-ceiling shelving, and a substantial
desk sat in the center of the room.

Around the edge of the room, the distance from
floor to ceiling was half again as tall as in the center, and
there was a short set of stairs that ran all the way around
the middle of the room to permit the half-level transition.

The walls were not entirely obscured by bound tomes, however, as there was a large area of the wall behind the desk devoted to finely painted portraits.

Creed carefully made his way to the desk. Arnna spoke with skepticism. "There is no way this is thousands of years old and still so clean! There should rodents everywhere, and dust, and moldy books!"

Creed assuaged her doubts, saying, "It's a great mage tower. The tower itself was built to be self-cleaning. It automatically excludes pests from entry, filters the air of mold and dust, and even defends itself against unwanted intruders. So . . . don't make it mad by doing something that puts us in that category."

Arnna glanced around nervously, giving Creed a sense of relief that she was at least taking him seriously. Walking to the other side of the desk, Creed glared angrily at it. "Of course she was here." A familiar metal stand on the desk was empty, save for a single silver shard. Creed finished with annoyance, "Not that the watcher wasn't a dead giveaway."

He picked up the shard and then tucked it into his belt for lack of having any pockets. Arnna spoke in a low but concerned voice. "Hey, tiger boy, are you trying to incur the wrath of the inanimate?"

Creed glowered at her before taking a seat at the desk. "This does not belong here anyway, and stop calling me that! Go look at books or something. I am here for a reason. You're here without one."

She tossed her head with indignation as she stated defensively, "I am pretty sure we are both here out of curiosity . . . tiger boy." She walked off, and Creed began to rummage through the desk. She did have a point; if he failed to leave some kind of message, it would be suspicious. Finding a piece of paper and a charcoal writing implement, he scribbled a vague note and folded the paper, indicating that it was for Seleen.

He figured that if it was supposed to be a your-eyes-only message, he should supply a formal seal. Searching through several drawers revealed nothing that he could use as a seal. One drawer was locked, and there was no key to be seen. A small beam of energy sliced through the locking mechanism at his command. He looked around casually to see if this provoked the defense matrix, and detecting no response, he opened the drawer.

Inside there was still no seal, but there was a well-worn, metal-bound volume. Creed removed it and turned it over in his hands. The metal was quite ordinary, and it bore no runes, or even any kind of lock. Opening it, he skimmed through some lines of text near the end.

"Our beloved Seleen has expressed her concern for the future. She fears that the gift will become the curse. The many others don't understand, nor do they know. Indeed, they cannot, for it would only bring about more trouble. Though my mind is murky these days, and my strength fades, I can tell that she is correct. So, with grief like the passing of a dear friend, I have given her my majestic stone. I retain the power that was awakened in me when we first met, but I can feel the wall that, without the stone, prevents me from reaching beyond the limits of my frail body. I have told no one of this loss, as the questions it would engender are unwanted. Certainly no one will notice. Few call on the aid of a rambling old chronicler mage when they have their own warped ambitions.

There are those who would do what is right, I suspect, but they have no one worth following. My life is at its end, and surely, I will follow many of the other great mages. Indeed, we all will. My young grandson Tonis could have been the next in line, a noble soul in an ignoble world. But, alas, my good friend Auriga is dead, and the boy suffers with a terrible physical problem that will certainly claim his life soon. I suppose I could have pressured Seleen to give the majestic opal to one of her prodigies, but I am certain this would disrupt Seleen's plans. Perhaps I am more sentimental than I ought to be, but I have often wept for her. She bears such harsh burdens, she works so hard, but it has been for naught. She is such a sweetheart, but she writes such poignant lines, and I read between those lines the great sorrow she carries with her. I know that any one of us, and really all of us, have tried to help her, but without lasting effect. I truly wonder what it is like to see life from her perspective? Surely we grew up together, and I was the first, but now, here, I reminisce over days long past, and consider my children, and my children's children, but she is alone, and neither the past nor the future holds anything but darkness for her. I hope fervently that she is not planning on throwing her life away. One should live life to the very last hour, not take it away prematurely, even by a day.

Or perhaps as the case may be, not
provoke others to take it away."

Creed tried to grasp what he was reading. It
wasn't the last entry in the journal, but it was the last one
that mentioned anything about Seleen. A later entry
seemed to indicate that Ferir had designated one of his
sons to carry on the work of chronicler. Yet there was
nothing about the third chronicler. There were several
entries that talked about Heket, and unrelated to those,
Creed also found some comments on rune sets that
might afford a way of deciphering the runes on Heket's
journal.

Forgetting about his quest for a seal to make the
note seem legitimate, Creed tucked the journal into his
belt and rose from the desk. The books in the study were
probably of great value from a historical perspective, but
very few of them would have anything to do with topics
related to the mages.

Aside from the chroniclers, none of the great
mages had written anything about their origins or
powers. Some of their descendants wrote things about
them, and certainly a number of their followers had. But
by the time the war was well underway, most written
works on the subject were either condemned by the
general populace or burned for fear that one league
might learn the secrets of another. Probably a few mages
hoarded books about their power, but it was doubtful any
of those would have survived so long outside of
unnatural conditions like those inside the great mage
tower.

He walked up to Arnna, who was staring intently
at a large painting of a group of people. Lost in his own
contemplations, he stated abruptly, "We should go."

Arnna flinched and gasped, then glared at him in
annoyance. "Why did you startle me?"

He brushed away her complaint with his hand. "It's not my fault you're jumpy."

Arnna looked displeased, but turned back to the painting and pointed to one of the figures. "Why did they include the watcher in their family painting?"

Creed shook his head. Trying to explain to her that what she was saying was impossible was not worth the time it would take, so he just denied it outright. "They didn't. No one would do such a thing."

As the words came out of his mouth, he actually looked at the painting, and was struck with a dilemma. Arnna unhelpfully replied, "I am sorry, but is it me, or are your eyes broken!"

Creed was torn between admitting that the young boy in the portrait seemed identical to the watcher and fabricating some other explanation. He gave her a smug look as he defended his pride. "Come on! Great mages often used family members as models for their watchers."

Arnna looked a little disappointed that he had an answer. Tipping his head toward the doorway, he said, "Let's go. We need to leave before we get into trouble with said watcher."

It was certainly the case that some watchers were modeled after the great mages themselves, but it was unheard of for one to be modeled after a family member, and then named with the same name as the family member. The physical form of the watcher was easily changed, so no doubt its appearance was different now than when it had first been constructed.

They exited the study as Creed mulled over the possibilities of what might have occurred. He stopped in the hallway and waited as the watcher flickered back into existence on the wall. Creed spoke calmly. "We have left our message for the master. Please show us out."

Nodding, the figure said, "As you wish, sir. This way, please."

Tonis led them through another series of hallways, and a couple more flights of stairs, before stopping before a large door. The sigils came to life of their own accord, and the door opened abruptly to the fully moonlit night. Creed took a step toward the door, but froze when a strange thought popped into his mind. Arnna reeled to avoid colliding with him, and then complained. "Hey, now, don't be so indecisive."

Ignoring her, he turned to the flickering form of Tonis on the wall. "Tonis, when were you born?" Tonis tilted his head slightly, looking curious about such a question, and then answered with a simple date and year. Arnna snapped her eyes toward Creed, and he explained. "He looks the age appropriate for his birth . . . and no watcher would ever respond to that question."

Turning back to the watcher, he asked, "Tonis, can you take us to the sigil control nexus?"

He nodded and moved back toward the main atrium. "Yes, this way, if you please."

Arnna glanced at the exit nervously, watching the door close. She nudged him, saying, "Okay, I thought we were about leave this creepy place. Can you give me one non-insane reason why we are going back inside of it?"

Creed answered evasively. "I am curious."

Arnna hissed in a low voice, as though she feared some maleficent force would overhear her. "That does not count!"

Tonis apologized as they descended more stairs. "The central lift has been damaged, and is no longer safe, so we will have to use this stairway."

Arnna muttered, "Is there anything else broken that we should know about?"

Tonis replied dutifully. "The defense matrix

along the periphery is also damaged, and the shield of the inner reach is down. However, the lifts at the edge of the spline mark are still functional."

Arnna looked displeased that her sarcasm was lost on Tonis, but Creed interrupted whatever derogatory comment she was forming with his own question. "Tonis, what is the spline mark?"

Tonis replied confidently. "The master informed me that the location where we currently are was created as a consequence of the removal of the spline."

Sighing, Arnna thought aloud, "Just how many names can one place have!"

Much to Arnna's chagrin, Tonis began what was likely to be some long-winded reply. "It varies according to culture, time, and the nature of the place in question. Generally speaking though, the number of designations that a single . . . ."

Creed interrupted him. "Tonis, what is the spline?"

Tonis stopped talking and turned back to Creed. "The master says it is the principle that once held the worlds together, and when it was removed, it left an indelible mark in the world itself."

They arrived before a rather mundane door. The sigils flickered, and the door opened. Tonis remained stationary on the wall. "I am sorry, but I cannot follow you beyond this doorway."

Creed paused. "Oh? Why is that?" Tonis met his gaze, but instead of saying anything, he merely shrugged. Creed didn't like the fact that not even Tonis knew why he was prevented from going into the sigil control nexus. He reassured himself that perhaps he was reading too much into things, since he wasn't sure if any watcher could enter its nexus. It was a little bit like entering one's own mind. Creed shook his head; what would that even mean?

Entering the enormous room, he immediately knew that he was utterly out of his element. Complex shapes seemed to rise randomly out of the floor. Like some large cylinder, it was many times deeper than he had anticipated. A large staircase spiraled down the outer wall to the bottom. The odd shapes were covered with a mind-numbing number of sigils. Traces of light flickered through the sigils at regular intervals.

Arnna spoke with reluctant wonder. "This is like nothing I have ever seen. And given today's events, that's saying something."

Creed descended the staircase, slowly looking around. He felt like he was just being silly now. The structure was bewilderingly complex, and he hadn't the slightest idea if what he saw was normal or out of place. He really needed Iekaruga, or better yet, Prinial. Though the older man was far more experienced, it was Prinial who was the prodigy. She had an innate sense of the sigils, and could understand sigil systems she had never seen before.

Creed paused and reached out toward one of the large, angular, irregular shapes that reached from the floor all the way to the ceiling. His hand stopped just short of touching the thing as it dawned on him there might be painful repercussions from doing so.

Coming up behind him, Arnna taunted, "I dare you to touch it."

He dropped his hand to his side and looked at her wryly. "You know, for an adult in your occupation, you sure have a weird personality. You must be really popular among your people."

Arnna looked oddly flustered, and despite the slow flush creeping up her cheeks, she insisted, "What?! You wouldn't believe how popular I am!" Creed rolled his eyes and turned back to descending the stairs.

As he neared the bottom, he admitted, "Okay,

so, I have no idea what most of this stuff is."

Arnna remarked sarcastically, "Oh, really? That's all right, tiger boy, neither do I!" He ignored her, but she was seriously starting to grate on his nerves.

Creed stepped off the last stair, feeling a little dumb. What was he even doing? It wasn't like he knew what he was looking for or what to expect. Arnna prodded him with her finger. "Annnnddddd, why are we here?"

Creed sighed as he turned from the bewildering array of angled shapes that formed an almost unpredictable network inside the nexus. "Nothing. Let's go."

Arnna looked beyond him and crossed her arms as she asked, "Oh? Then what is that?"

Creed didn't want to grant her any level of satisfaction, but he looked out at the room again. He clenched his teeth as he saw nothing that he had not seen before. He turned back toward her, stating humorlessly, "That's not even funny. I am trying to figure out something important here, for your information."

Arnna shoved past him anyway. "Come on, shorty. There is something over there that looks different."

Creed followed her, but felt the need to interject a reminder. "You do remember that my name is Creed, right?"

Arnna waved her hand in the air. "Sure, sure, like that is any better than tiger boy."

Creed snapped at her. "Hey, it's not a diminutive! I am not a boy!"

Arnna stopped and met his gaze with a surprisingly level of sincerity. "You most certainly are a boy. Maybe a serious gloomy one with scary amounts of power, but you can't change the fact that your years of experience have not yet produced a balanced, stable

232

perspective on life. Look at yourself for a minute. You're driven by little more than fancy and whim . . . tiger boy."

Creed wanted to give her a piece of his mind on the matter, but she returned to making her way carefully through the maze of columns and crossbeams. But he lost track of what he was going to say when he saw what she had caught a glimpse of from the stairs.

A perfectly symmetrical prism turned slowly, levitating in the air over a floor-level pedestal covered with dense, elaborate sigil patterns that regularly pulsed with light. The pedestal above the prism stretched up to the ceiling. It, too, was covered with pulsing sigils. Creed felt an odd mixture of emotions as he stared at it. Was it an aberration, or was there some more positive explanation? If what he read in Ferir's journal was correct, perhaps this was not like Hanni's situation.

Frozen in space and time, within the slowly moving prism, was Tonis. Not the projection that served as the watcher, but the actual young child. His arms hung limp and still at his sides. He was in an upright position, but unlike the prism, he remained motionless. His face was peaceful and calm, as though he slept.

Arnna blurted out, "That's really weird."

Creed was at a lost as to what it was. The prism was not of any material that he recognized. It was translucent, but surely it wasn't actually as solid as it appeared. Arnna looked at him, then back at the prism. With a shrug, she reached out and touched the edge of it as it turned past her. Creed scarcely managed a verbal squeak in protest before her hand made contact with the prism.

The entire thing inexplicably shattered into infinitesimally small pieces from the point of contact. Arnna pulled back at first, but then lunged forward to catch Tonis as his suspended animation ended as abruptly as the prism. The child took a slow, deep breath and let it out. He opened his eyes and looked around, his gaze stopping on Arnna's face. He spoke, his voice remarkably soft. "Are you here to help me?"

For once, Arnna appeared to be at a loss for words, so Creed answered. "Uh, well, sort of."

Arnna set Tonis down gently. He leaned to the side to look curiously at Creed for a moment, and then said, "You must be Creed, the black star."

Creed was bewildered that the child knew him, but more so about the title that he had never heard. Arnna offered her thoughts. "And here I thought your name was bad enough. What's this black star stuff?"

Tonis looked a little nervous. "Creed is a legend on the battlefield. His prowess as the lead assault mage of the star league is infamous. It is said that his form is like a dark star on the backdrop of the deadly light that he will cut you down with."

Tonis shivered as he cast his gaze around the room. He wore nothing but a simple white tunic fastened with a cord. His voice tremored slightly as well. "Have we lost then?"

Arnna studied him uneasily, but Creed knew what the boy faced from personal experience. "Tonis, it's pretty complicated, but I think we should get out of here before I explain everything to you."

Tonis stared at him wide-eyed. "How do you know my name? I am not famous like you are."

Creed badly wanted to correct the boy's use of the present tense, but Tonis had no context yet to understand why. Creed headed toward the stairs. "Let's go."

Chapter 21

Leaving the nexus room was easy, but Creed paused in the hallway. The watcher was gone, and the lights were out. Arnna moaned with frustration. "Oh, this is just great!"

Tonis called out. "Awaken!" He was answered by only silence and darkness. He wrinkled his forehead in confusion. "That's strange. It's always come at my call before."

Light flooded the hallway as Creed summoned his staff. Two spheres of light rose on either side of Creed and provided a measure of illumination. Creed turned to the young boy. "Do you remember what happened to you, Tonis?"

The child looked back at the doorway to the nexus and said, "I . . . I don't remember exactly. I am very sick, and the rose league attacked us while we were transitioning to another tower to consolidate our power. Everyone fled. They left me because we all knew that my time is short, but someone helped me hide, a friend of mine, and then . . ." Tonis put his hand to his head as he sighed and admitted sadly, ". . . I just can't remember."

Creed offered him a small comfort. "It's okay, Tonis. Let's just get out of here for now."

Arnna spoke in a low voice as they hurried back toward the exit. "Let me guess. This place is about to light up."

Creed nodded once. With the watcher system suddenly disrupted, it was only a matter of moments before the tower's logic entered emergency mode, and then it would activate its defenses. Creed hoped they could make it to the door before that happened, but he was prepared to fight whatever it threw at them.

They had only made it halfway to the stairs when a low red light lit the corridor, and a loud chiming sound began to reverberate through the tower. A solid barrier slammed down between them and the stairs. Creed turned sharply and ordered, "We have to run, fast! This whole place is coming down!"

Arnna jerked back, exclaiming, "What!"

Tonis appeared both fearful and resigned at the same time. "Leave me. I-I can't run."

Creed released his staff, and it vanished. He scooped Tonis up in his arms before dashing down the hall. "Arnna, RUN!"

She caught up with him and demanded, "Just exactly where are we running to?"

Creed had no idea, actually. No one mage tower had the same layout as another, and he had never seen a map of this one. He hedged slightly. "Away from the core of the tower!"

Tonis spoke firmly. "Turn here."

Creed veered down the hallway that Tonis had indicated, and Arnna asked, "And now where are we going?"

Tonis's voice was so soft that it was hard to hear him, but Creed gathered that not being able to run wasn't the only thing he could not do. "This leads to the evacuation tunnel."

At Tonis's directions, they made several other

turns, and Creed hoped that the boy knew where they were because it was a mystery to him. There really should have been some kind of clear markings on the floor or walls, he thought, but there was nothing obvious to him. The ground began to tremble, and Arnna shouted, "Look out!"

Creed narrowly dodged a falling stone ceiling tile and stumbled, rolling to his side to avoid crushing Tonis. Creed lay panting for a moment, and Tonis stated soberly, "I am sorry to say this, but you have to leave me. There isn't enough time to carry me out. I am . . . I am nearly dead already. What's a few extra weeks?"

Creed felt a spark of indignation. "Your grandfather would not approve of such logic, and I didn't save you just for you to be buried under rubble."

Arnna held her arms out, and Creed handed her Tonis. They continued their flight as the peripheral portions of the tower began to collapse. Approaching a room at the end of the corridor, Creed shouted, "Jump!"

There was a surge of energy behind them, and what looked like a lazy lightning bolt shot down the corridor toward them. Arnna, with Tonis clutched to her chest, dove through the doorway, sliding on her back across the floor. Creed vaulted into the room, slamming the door's sigil mechanism with his hand. The door shut an instant before the bolt crashed into it with a thunderous echo.

The sound and red light stopped abruptly, the remote room severed from the rest of the tower. The only illumination was the subtle glow of Creed's skin. He leaned against the door, trying to catch his breath. Arnna sighed with relief, setting Tonis down as she slumped down to the floor, gasping from the exertion of their mad dash.

Still a little breathless, Creed walked to the far wall, saying, "It isn't over yet, I'm afraid. The tower is

237

storing power for its implosion. We need to get above ground before the shock wave collapses this room."

Arnna groaned. "Wonderful. Next time I want some say in if we pursue your stupid curiosity."

Creed replied a little defensively. "Hey, I am not the one who touched the prism."

She crossed her arms and glared at him. "Oh, yeah? Well, you would have if I hadn't!"

Tonis interrupted both of them with a question. "Are you two married?"

Arnna laughed loudly, but Creed choked. Shaking his head vehemently, he answered as calmly as the situation permitted. "What? No way! We don't really even know each other." Tonis tilted his head slightly, looking a little intrigued at Creed's response. Creed frowned his annoyance at Arnna, but she merely shrugged with a humored smile.

As Creed placed his hand on the opposite wall from where they had entered, the sigils illuminated, and another door opened with a loud scratching sound. He leapt sharply to the side as rubble slid through the doorway. It was hard to see, but it looked like a long staircase, packed with broken rock. Arnna stood slowly, peering at it. "Oh, great! Of all the times to need a shovel."

Creed glanced over his shoulder nervously, and then stared at the rubble-filled stairwell. He wasn't sure how much time they had, or how far it was to the surface, but he remembered learning about the self-destruction system in his own tower. It was a last resort to prevent the enemy from obtaining an incredibly valuable stronghold. In theory, it wasn't supposed to be activated without the willful hand of the one in charge of the tower. Something about Tonis's integration into the watcher system, and sudden removal, must have triggered it accidentally. Regardless, it was leave or die.

Creed summoned his staff and took it in both hands. Holding it horizontally, he focused. Spheres of light rose from the ground, accelerating to a single point between himself and the stairwell. A wide beam of yellow-green energy blasted up the length of the stairwell. Creed jumped out of the way as hot gravel and sand, the remnants of the large chunks of stone that had been blocking the passageway, flowed down it and into the room.

Arnna stepped toward the cleared stairs, but Creed grabbed her arm. She jerked it out of his grasp with a scowl, though she did stop. Creed explained. "It's still pretty hot. If you touch anything with your bare skin, it will burn you."

Looking back at the stairwell, she spoke sarcastically. "You are such a genius, tiger boy. Here I thought you actually made our exit safer."

Creed shook his head as he walked past her. "Just don't touch the walls."

He looked at Tonis and manage not to sigh out loud. The boy was barefoot, which meant Creed, as the shorter of the two adults, would have to carry him. Creed picked him up, and Tonis said softly, "Thank you, Creed." Creed just nodded and started up the stairwell, being careful not to brush the edges of the walls.

It was scorching inside, and he sweated profusely as he ascended the surprisingly treacherous staircase. Sand and gravel slid around underfoot. The only thing that made it bearable was the circulation of cold air flowing down the stairwell and hot air rising along the ceiling. Creed accidentally grazed the searing wall while trying to catch himself from slipping on some loose grit. He clenched his teeth and pushed forward.

Finally reaching the top, he found himself in a peculiar canyon. Unlike the others, it was rather symmetrical, and it lacked any apparent exit. Creed looked up at the high walls and shuddered to think what would happen when the tower's shock wave struck. Arnna spoke what he was thinking. "Somehow I don't actually feel any safer."

For a moment he feared that he would have to cut through the canyon wall, which only made things more complicated than they already were. But then he caught a glimpse of a familiar sigil pattern on the wall. Of course the designers of Ferir's tower had built a means of leaving the canyon. What good was an emergency exit that didn't have a way out?

Creed continued to carry Tonis as he walked to the stone wall. He brushed the sigil pattern with his hand, and a passage opened that led out to a familiar place.

* * *

As Creed walked out into the canyon, the moonlight shining on its features, Arnna stepped up beside him and let out an exasperated sigh. "Oh, great. Forget a shovel. Now I need my sword!"

He saw a small cluster of people backed into a corner by a larger group. Creed whispered, "Sheena!"

He practically threw Tonis at Arnna and took off running. Arnna called after him. "Hey, where are you going?"

Creed called back. "My sister is in danger!"

Despite his fatigue from a long, hard day full of emotion, confusion, and no shortage of injury, Creed's mage focus overcame his weakness. He broke into a sprint, his dark complexion affording him concealment even in the light of the full moon. As he neared, he could see the same bandit group he had encountered before advancing on three frightened archaeologists.

Sheena stood in front of them, waving a hefty

240

stick menacingly. "Stay back, you, or you're going to have to deal with my brother!"

One of them scoffed at her. "Nice try, little girl. Now put down the stick, and we won't have to hurt you like the other one." Neamin clutched a nasty cut on his arm—not life threatening, but certainly debilitating.

The dim moonlight was suddenly supplemented by the brilliant flash of Creed's staff materializing from pure energy. He darted past the first row of bandits and leapt high into the air. The doubting bandit screamed as Creed brought the staff down hard on the man's head. He crumpled to the ground, and Creed rolled off him to come back up into a standing position.

There was a cracking noise as he popped the second nearest bandit with his tail. The man yelped in surprise, jumping back and clutching his hand. Creed smacked the butt of his staff against the ground. He began to glow brightly, and scores of yellow-green luminous orbs rose to form a glowing semicircle around him.

Creed spoke in a low voice that held the promise of retribution for anyone stupid enough to take him up on his offer. "All right, who wants to go next?"

Without warning, a bandit threw a dagger at him, and someone behind him called, "Look out!" The metal vaporized instantly with a loud sizzle when it was struck by a brilliant beam from an orb. Creed flicked his hand, and a dozen energy beams pelted the bandits, severing blades and incinerating cudgels.

Not a one of them held any kind of intact weapon following that. Several began to shake, and several more dropped their pointless hilts and fled. This resulted in general mayhem as they all broke and ran, slamming into each other in their desperation to escape the glowing form before them that represented a threat they could not comprehend.

Creed sighed as they dispersed, but then he was attacked from behind with a tearful shout. "CREED!"

He stopped glowing and staggered as Sheena grabbed him tightly, exclaiming, "Oh, Creed! I was so worried about you, and I missed you terribly, and . . . and . . . ."

Anything else she intended to say was lost as she burst into tears and buried her head into his shoulder. Creed leaned heavily on his staff and turned, taking her to his chest with his free arm as he spoke kindly. "I am sorry, Sheena. I should have told you what I was doing. I missed you, too."

Neamin's eyes were wide with his incredulity. "W-what are you?"

Creed said nothing, but Arnna emerged from the shadows, carrying Tonis, and replied for him. "He is a great mage, of a different people. Fearian, if I recall."

Neamin objected. "But—but that can't be. Mages are fictional, right?"

Tonis shook his head slowly while Arnna set him down. "Why would anyone think such a thing?"

Herin cleared his throat and asked the more relevant question. "Um, I don't believe we have met yet. I am Herin, Anidar's chief archaeologist of this region, and these are Colleen and Neamin, my associates."

Arnna put her fist to her shoulder in formal salute. "I am Arnna, an elite knight of the kingdom on special assignment."

Tonis spoke softly, and Creed realized that the boy had a stunningly beautiful voice for a child, or really anyone. "I am Tonis Ruttoson, the silent song."

Creed stared intensely at Tonis. There was a long-running, and slightly odd, proclivity of mages to grant titles to significant individuals of their kind. He thought the practice was dumb, but it did immediately signal that the person in question was regarded as special or remarkable for one reason or another.

Pleasantries and puzzles aside, Creed interrupted their introductions by stating the impending danger. "We have to get out of here. Preferably out of the Bugillow, but at least away from the canyon walls."

Herin looked dismayed as he shook his head. "I am afraid we aren't getting out of the Bugillow on this end. The bandits destroyed the lift."

Creed replied confidently. "There is another lift in the same place, the original one. We will use that." Herin looked confused, but didn't have time to ask about it before the ground started to tremble. Creed looked in the direction of the tower and informed them gravely, "It's too late. The implosion has already begun."

A bright light emanated from a point off in the distance. Tonis stood and spoke with an odd calmness. "The shock wave from an implosion can be very harmful. I will protect us." Several of them stared at him, stunned, but in his concentration, he didn't seem to notice. Tonis clapped his hands together sharply, but instead of producing the expected sound, the air between his hands distorted, and then took on a solid form. Creed blinked, not sure that he trusted his eyes.

The distortion condensed into a long, slender, black staff. Its shape went from a fine point at one end to taper smoothly to an open loop at the other. The loop, or perhaps hoop was more accurate, was perfectly circular. Suspended in the center was a dark red gemstone cut into a perfect cube. There was nothing obvious that held the gem in place, but visible distortions in the air bounced between the rim of the hoop and the cube.

Tonis took on a deep red glow, and he raised the staff momentarily before smacking it soundly on the ground. The ground's trembling became worse, and then a wall of destruction shot out from where the tower had been. The shock wave ripped through canyon walls, shattered house-sized boulders, and carried rocks as large as a man thousands of paces.

Arnna screamed in fear. Or rather, she opened her mouth. There was no sound, not from Arnna, not from anything. It was absolutely silent.

At some point down the canyon from them, the shock wave hit Tonis's mute invocation. The rapidly moving wall of sound advancing on them came to an instantaneous halt, and the debris it carried rolled to a stop a dozen paces beyond that. Tonis spoke softly, but his voice was the only noise that could be heard. "Allow me to return the kindness that you showed me."

Tonis brushed his hand through the air, dismissing the mute and his staff. He sighed as he slipped limply down to his knees. Arnna quickly caught his arm to prevent him from falling over as he muttered, "I am so tired."

Colleen expressed her wonder. "I-I-I can't believe this is happening! I never dreamed that mages were real, let alone so powerful."

Arnna glanced up and recoiled. "It isn't over yet! The reservoir must have been broken." Creed heard the rising roar of torrential amounts of water racing through the narrow passageways at high speed. Herin spoke for all of them. "Oh, no."

Creed looked down to where Sheena was still tightly clinging to him. "Sheena, I need your help. I don't have the strength to stop it alone, but with your power, I think I can."

Sheena smiled warmly at him from where she was nestled against his chest and whispered, "I am already yours, ciega. You don't even have to ask." Creed shook his head at her, yet couldn't prevent his smile.

She let go of him, and he held her hand as he focused. A massive wall of rushing water came crashing around the bend and cascaded toward them, reaching two-thirds of the height of the canyon. Sheena started to glow, as did Creed. He felt for the second time the bond form between them, and then he heard Sheena's voice in his mind. "Creed . . . um . . . about Arnna . . . ."

He could hardly believe that she was asking about such a thing under their current circumstance, but he also realized that he was no less skeptical of Neamin. Creed raised his staff sharply and fired a beam of energy down the canyon into the water. It flash-boiled a lot of water, but despite the continued beam, the flood advanced.

Creed replied in his mind as he began to glow more brightly, and wisps of yellow-green energy rose from his skin like infernal fire. "Don't worry, Sheena. Our meeting was incidental, and about the only thing we share in common is a disregard for the other person's self-respect."

Sheena sighed with relief as she apologized. "I am sorry, Creed. It's not that I doubt you. It's just that . . . well . . . I don't want to lose you."

The energy beam stretched to fill the width of the canyon. It ripped effortlessly through the water, producing so much vapor that clouds of steam blocked out the moon in the sky. Suddenly Creed noticed that the water was completely vaporized. He quickly lowered his staff, banishing the energy. Though the moon was now occluded, the angry red glow of molten rock could be seen for quite some distance. The light faded quickly from Creed and Sheena.

Arnna looked a little pale as she turned toward him and spoke wryly. "So, do you always rearrange geographical features?"

It was dark, but Creed had the sinking feeling that there was now a massive cylindrical trough that ran the length of the Bugillow. He muttered, "Oops."

Arnna rolled her eyes and looked down at Tonis.

"He must be really tired. He fell asleep."

Creed observed the boy, who rested limply in Arnna's arms, with a sense of sadness. "He has some sort of serious illness. It will claim his life if he doesn't get help."

Sheena spoke what Creed had already been thinking. "If anyone can help, I bet Father can."

Herin and his family were visibly shaken from the recent series of dramatic events, and by this point, Creed just wanted to go sleep, even somewhere out in the cold. He suggested, "Let's return to the lift for now. We can talk about what happened later."

There were nods all around, and Herin said, "Yes, I think that would be best. This way." They followed him in silence.

It took an hour to reach the lift, a very long hour. This was partially due to the need to navigate new rubble piles and shallow pools of water. When they reached the lift, it was plain that it had been burned with fire. Only the lower portion was damaged, but irreparably so.

The rest of them watched as Creed shifted through the dirt along the wall. For a moment he feared that he would make a fool of himself. He was greatly relieved to find a small citrine stone buried in the dirt. He blew the dust off it, and then replaced it in the center of the ancient lift's sigil control pattern. The sigils came alive with latent energy, and a narrow cylinder of stone rose out of the original lift.

Creed walked over to the control column and gestured for everyone to join him, and they did so, albeit some more reluctantly than others. Colleen mused, "So, they aren't just artistic expressions."

Creed placed his hand on the top of the column while he answered her. "No, sigils are not artistic in nature. They are complex systems of power and regulation that accomplish about any menial task if the designer is clever enough."

A pulse of light shot through the column, and then the entire vertical shaft was illuminated by sigil light sources. The lift rose smoothly and rapidly up into the large building. Though fire had not damaged the structure, the smell of smoke lingered. Despite the acrid odor in his outbuilding, Herin was marveling at the lift. "How can solid stone move with such fluidity?"

Colleen did not attempt an answer, but rather offered a practical suggestion. "I believe it would be best if you men sleep out here, while we women take our rest in the house. Neamin, please start up the main stove here in our workspace, and I will get some extra blankets."

Neamin nodded and began putting wood into the large metal stove that would heat the entire lift building. Herin joined his wife in retrieving blankets.

Creed sat down on the floor. He was hungry and tired. His head still ached faintly, and his mind swam with stray thoughts about Tonis, Ferir, and the mystery of the third chronicler. He hoped a solid night's sleep would provide some clarity on the morrow, but he wasn't holding out much confidence.

Chapter 22

Creed came slowly back to the land of the wakeful. He stretched, feeling every sore muscle from the previous day's escapades. Sitting up, he glanced about the lift building. Sunlight filtered through the windows, which suggested that it was well past dawn.

Neamin was the only other person there, and the young man busied himself with the large stove in the center of the room, adding pieces of split wood one at a time. Neamin closed the door of the stove and walked over to where Creed sat. "Breakfast is already on. You should join your sister."

Creed rose and idly brushed his clothes off. It was painfully obvious that Neamin wanted to say something, but was at a loss as to how to go about it. Creed took a stab in the dark. "We are not blood relatives. I am adopted." Neamin blinked with surprise. Creed continued. "Though she is also Fearian."

Neamin looked down. "Ah, okay." Creed walked toward the door to the cottage. As he reached it, Neamin called after him, "Thank you, Creed." He nodded and then opened the door.

It was much warmer in the cottage. People sat around the small table, chatting excitedly. They ate a simple pastry with fruit preserves spread on it. Sheena stood and smiled as he entered. She gestured to the only free chair, which was beside her. "Come on, sleepyhead. You've almost missed breakfast." He shrugged and took his seat.

Sheena touched his head gently, and he flinched as she scolded him. "Creed! You didn't tell me you were injured. You can't just let that go untreated." Sheena got up, and at Colleen's directions, retrieved a washcloth and a pail of hot water. To his mild embarrassment, she began to clean the wound on his head.

Tonis sat quietly, nibbling on a pastry. In the full light of the morning, it was apparent that not all was well with him. He was deathly pale, perhaps seeming even more so from the harsh contrast of his black hair and brown eyes. In health, his skin might have been slightly darker colored than, say, Sheena's fair complexion.

Creed jerked away as Sheena dabbed at his head. "Oww."

Her voice had a distinct lack of sympathy. "Now, don't be such a wimp, Mr. Lone-explorer."

Hein watched them momentarily before asking, "Did you ever find what you were looking for, scholar Creed?"

Arnna rolled her eyes at the label, but Creed opted to ignore her. "I don't really know. I found some information, but nothing that clarifies what I wanted to figure out. This tower was in far better condition than the others, but . . . ."

Creed trailed off as Tonis interrupted politely. "The others? What has happened to the other mage towers?"

Creed closed his eyes for a second; he had forgotten that Tonis had no idea he had been frozen in time. He coughed and looked at the boy as he tried to explain gently, and for the benefit of everyone else there. "So, you know that there arose twenty-four great mages,

249

twelve human, twelve Fearian, who ushered in an unprecedented age of peace and prosperity." Tonis nodded, but Herin, Colleen, and Arnna leaned forward to listen eagerly. "And after all but one of the great mages died, their power, sealed in precious stones, was stolen by their remaining member."

Tonis built on the story. "Yes, the great silver mage, Seleen, took them beyond the veil of time."

Creed nodded. "Right, and in so doing sparked a war among the mages. At least she got what she deserved for acting so recklessly."

Tonis shook his head soberly. "I-I never thought burning her at the stake was justified. She never had a chance to defend her actions."

Creed hesitated. Tonis's words made him wonder if the boy had met Seleen personally, and since there was no reason to remain uncertain, he asked, "Did you know her?"

Tonis sighed and put his hand to his head. "I think I did, but it's all foggy. I remember that she was sweet, and kind, someone who would care when no one else did. I remember . . . ."

Tonis flushed slightly and just stared at the table. Sheena broke from her ministrations to Creed and encouraged him. "What is it that you remember, Tonis?"

Tonis sounded embarrassed. "I remember crying, and she held me in her arms, and told me that it would be okay. But I don't remember anything else about her, or even when that happened. It's just all foggy."

Deciding not to state his opinion on the traitor of the great mages, Creed moved on with his story. "So, anyway, in the course of the war, many mages, and many more non-mages, lost their lives. Cities were flattened, and the general view of mages shifted sharply as a consequence. The sigil gates were destroyed or deactivated, severing any movement between Fearia and this world. The Fearians purged humans from their world, and in this one, being a mage eventually became something prohibited by law in most places. Mages were hunted, and mage power was outlawed. But that was a really long time ago."

Tonis tilted his head in curiosity. "How long?"

Creed took a deep breath, knowing what was coming. "Um, well, roughly three millennia."

Tonis jerked sharply in surprise. Herin did as well, and then demanded skeptically, "Wait a minute now. Are you telling us that you and Tonis are three thousand years old?!"

Creed spoke apologetically. "Look, I know it's hard to believe, but both Tonis and I were entrapped by one mechanism or another, and only recently released. I fought in the great mage war."

Tonis lamented, "I was never strong enough to fight in the war."

His brow furrowed, and he asked with terrible honesty, "Does this mean I am going to die soon?" Creed reassured him. "No, Tonis, you are not going to die soon if there is anything we can do about it."

Tonis looked back down at the pastry he held in his hands. "I was born sick, and I don't have much time left. After the majestic gems were stolen, there remained no way to restore my body. I suppose that is why I was where you found me, though I can't remember how I got there."

Sheena spoke passionately. "Don't worry, Tonis. Our father is none other than the White Lion of Empleheim, and he can heal anything!"

Creed cleared his throat loudly as he added quickly, "Yes. Regardless, you have nothing to worry about."

Tonis was not convinced, and he looked up at

Creed with a steady gaze. "Without the majestic gems, I have no hope of more than a couple months of life. Don't you think my family already called upon the greatest white mages of our time?"

Sheena opened her mouth to say something, but Creed nudged her into silence. "I understand, Tonis, but I can also tell you that our father is not like the white mages of the past." Tonis eyed him curiously but chose to not pursue the conversation.

Arnna exhibited her own curiosity. "You know, I think I have read about the White Lion of Empleheim, and I was pretty sure that he vanished along with all of Empleheim back when the curse fell on that place."

Colleen added, "Yes, isn't that whole story a myth? I mean, there isn't anything in the entire area at all. Neither ruins, nor any sign of human habitation."

Creed gave a succinct and vague response. "It would be difficult to explain, but Empleheim is now rising from its ruins, and it is indeed Adderil who leads us." Sheena nodded firmly in agreement. Retrospectively, Creed would think that perhaps he had exaggerated Empleheim's status as rising from ruins, given their minute size, but of course hindsight is always clearer.

* * *

After pleasant goodbyes, Creed, Sheena, and Tonis departed for Empleheim. Arnna also left, but she traveled in the opposite direction once they made it to the main road. Before departing back toward Anidar's capital, she quipped wryly, "I will be seeing you, tiger boy, but be good in the meantime."

Creed muttered flatly, "See you, Arnna." He really hoped that she was just speaking casually and not promising to come visit him.

Sheena turned toward him, echoing, "Tiger boy?"

Creed huffed with exasperation. "Some people just rub me the wrong way." Sheena chuckled at his discomfort.

Tonis, who was riding double with Sheena, changed the topic. "Sheena, are you also Fearian?"

She replied gently. "Yes, though my father is human." Tonis was silent for a while, and then stated, "I never met any Fearians personally, so I know very little about them, despite the fact that two-thirds of our league members were Fearian."

As the only one not from the distant past, Sheena inquired, "What are the leagues exactly?" Creed explained as they traveled down the road. "Well, when war broke out among the mages, it became very obvious that no one alone was going to overtake the others. So alliances were formed between groups of specific kinds of mages. Some were more tightly interwoven coalitions than others. The sylph league was formed more as a matter of survival than for conquest, whereas the vale league was all about conquest. Its members were summoner, black, and air mages. They were the principle opponents of my league, the star league."

Creed looked toward Tonis. "We never really engaged your league, the storm league, in battle, but that was mostly because you were busy fighting the rose league, right?"

Tonis nodded. "Yes, we were certainly preoccupied, and my grandfather's tower was the weakest part of our league."

Creed's curiosity was stirred. "Why was that?"

Tonis replied simply. "Grandfather had his tower built where it was for the purpose of studying the spline mark. He wanted to know more about the cause of the world disjunction. My father told me he would often speak of the secrets beyond, secrets that could only be discovered by understanding the event that splintered the world into pieces."

Sheena spoke with a sense of fearful wonder. "What kind of power could split reality into pieces?"

A chill ran down Creed's spine at the thought. "I don't know. It's nothing that even the great mages knew about. They built the sigil gates and joined two very different peoples into one for a generation, but understanding the cause of the separation of the worlds was not something anyone even talked about in my league."

Tonis reminisced, "Regrettably, my grandfather never discovered those secrets, and nobody after him was interested enough to drive his work forward."

Creed spoke mostly to himself. "Perhaps that is for the best, considering what most people did with the discovery of mage power."

It was a sobering reality that the power that brought about the golden age was the same power that, just a couple of generations later, brought all of life to its knees. What would become of this new resurgence of mages? Would they fall into the dissolution of their ancestors as well? Creed wasn't sure he wanted to think about it. Perhaps, at least as long as Achron led them, they would not turn on each other in a struggle for power.

Creed had a growing sense of respect for Achron's general approach to not unnecessarily encouraging his children to tap into the immense power within themselves. It was certainly different from his time, when anyone with the slightest talent was pushed to become as powerful as they could for the sake of their representative group. As Creed thought on his home in Hona Castle, he realized how much he now enjoyed the simple life they lived. He really did hope that it would remain so. He had no desire to ever return to a horrific life on the battlefield.

* * *

Their journey home was markedly uneventful, in part because Creed avoided the Cartise encampment this time. They were nice enough, but he was anxious to get home. The weather was shifting colder as winter enveloped the northlands. The cloak that Herin had given him, to replace the one he had lost, was pleasant, but not as thick as the previous one.

Their problems were compounded by the fact that he had lost not only his cloak but also his shoulder satchel. This meant they had less food than they had originally planned on for the journey. Of course, they also had one more person to feed, but then again, whatever the nature of his illness, Tonis ate very little. It took days, but they eventually reached the edge of Niado, weary, tired, but none the worse for wear.

Tonis gazed at the greatly overgrown ruins as their horses trotted by. "Is this where you live? It looks abandoned."

Creed chuckled under his breath. "Yeah, the current population isn't remotely close to what was originally here, but it's still home." Sheena smiled to herself, and Creed tried to pretend as though he had not noticed. It wasn't like it was odd for him to refer to Hona as his home, but for some reason it gave her great delight when he did.

They came within sight of the castle, and Creed glanced toward the sky expectantly. He was mildly disappointed that Harku made no appearance. Then again, Creed expected that their return was neither surprising nor sudden from either Achron's or Viwy's perspective. Keena had probably been aware of their location on a daily basis. Indeed, as they drew close to the castle, Achron stood casually near the stable, chatting with Viwy. Keena was with them. Her arms were crossed, and though she looked calm, she also looked stern.

Achron turned from his conversation to greet them as they stopped, and Creed dismounted. "Well, well, look who is home from adventures abroad."

Viwy shook his head with mock disapproval. "Tsk, tsk, such vagrant rebels. Did you find anything out about the other chronicler?"

Keena glared at Viwy, and the man quickly spun to take Creed's horse into the stable. Keena addressed, or rather, redressed, Creed. "I am glad to see that the two of you are safe, but later we are going to have a conversation about endangering your sister for the sake of your curiosity."

Creed looked away guiltily as he muttered, "Yeah, sure."

Achron only smiled as he stepped around them to grab the reins of Sheena's horse. He started slightly to see a slight, pale boy seated in front of his daughter. Sheena spoke gently. "Father, could you take him? He can't jump down."

Achron held his hands out, and Sheena set Tonis in his arms before dismounting herself.

Tonis looked at him seriously as he spoke in his melodic voice. "You must the white mage I have heard about. Can you help me?"

Achron studied him with growing concern, as he could see the boy was very sick, and he lacked the weight that would be expected of a child his age. "What afflicts you?"

Tonis cast about at his new surroundings while he replied. "I do not know. I was born dying, and have reached the end of what little strength I had. They said you could help me."

Achron stared at Creed with mild consternation, but Creed told him, "In your own power, I don't think you could do anything, but with the majestic opal, there shouldn't be a problem."

Tonis straightened in Achron's hold, his confusion very evident. "What? I thought the majestic gems were lost."

No one answered his question. Achron met Creed's eye, and Creed replied simply, "Dane."

Achron turned toward Keena. "Dear, please find Dane, and meet us in the library."

Achron carried Tonis into the castle, with Sheena and Creed following closely. "Tell me about yourself."

Tonis spoke softly, watching the scenery with great interest. "I am Tonis Ruttoson, grandson of the great mage Ferir Ruttoson. I was abandoned to my fate when the rose league attacked my grandfather's tower. Since I cannot run, nor can I fight, my compatriots did not deem me worth saving. A close friend of mine sealed me into the tower's systems, but I don't remember much about it. I gather this is a very different time than that to which I am accustomed."

Achron chuckled. "That is an understatement."

Entering the library, Achron asked, "Can you stand, Tonis?" The boy nodded, and Achron placed his feet on the floor. While Tonis steadied himself on a chair, Achron stepped aside and spoke to Creed in a low voice. "You do realize that white mages are normally not capable of healing inborn illness, right?"

Creed remained confident. "Yes, I know that, but I also know that Ferir was absolutely certain that with the power of the majestic opal, his grandson could be healed by a white mage, other than the great white mage herself."

Achron frowned slightly. "Also, I have no idea how to tap into that power."

Creed blinked. He had not thought about the fact that he was the only one who had thus far drawn upon the power of the majestic gems. "It's simple really. Take Dane's hand, and draw upon your own power. You will feel the power of the majestic gem in that context, and then you can harness that to restore Tonis."

Creed hesitated to share it, but he mentioned, "Tonis saved our lives back at Ferir's tower. He deserves a chance at another life."

Achron considered the boy thoughtfully, and then said, "I will do what I can to not make you a liar, Creed." Achron smirked at the annoyed expression that came across Creed's face.

"You needed me, Father?"

Looking up, they saw Dane standing in the doorway with Keena behind him. Achron gestured for his son to enter. "Yes, I need your help with . . . something."

Dane glanced uncertainly at Tonis, but nodded and came to stand near him. Dane bit his lip, and then blurted out spontaneously, "It wasn't my fault, Father. It was Ahnya who thought that I wasn't stirring fast enough!"

Achron met Keena's displeased gaze, and then shrugged with a sly smile, reassuring his son, "I am sure it was just an accident, but that's not why I need you." Dane let out a sigh of relief, but Keena cleared her throat loudly, and Achron added, "But that doesn't mean we won't talk about it after supper." Dane nodded, but kept his newfound calm.

Achron held out his left hand toward Dane. The young man took his father's hand, and Achron began to glow as he reached out with his right hand and grabbed his staff. The staff materialized in a pulse of light, and

Achron spoke to Tonis. "I am going to heal you, so don't be afraid if you feel strange for a couple moments."

Tonis smiled as he whispered, "I am not afraid."

His calm made Creed uncomfortable. Tonis seemed like such a nice person, but it was plain that years of living on the edge of death had warped his perspective greatly. He didn't seem particularly excited about anything, which was a stark contrast with how any male child his age should be. Oddly though, he was not gloomy either, something Creed still struggled with himself.

Dane began to glow as well, and Achron's own luminescence rose to such a level that wisps of white energy whirled about him, like tongues of fire caught in some invisible whirlwind. Achron, staff in hand, reached out and touched Tonis on the forehead with two fingers. A flicker of white light washed over him, and he gasped sharply, but he remained motionless.

Achron lowered and banished his staff as the light surrounding him and Dane faded. He informed the boy, "You had a kind of blood disease. I have healed you, but it will take a month or more before you really get your strength back. You may stay with us until such time as you are able to travel."

Keena stepped briskly to Tonis, stating emphatically, "He is just a child, dear. He can stay with us as long as he likes!"

Achron coughed as he spoke limply. "Err, right, of course, that's what I was trying to . . . um, shall we go eat?"

Keena took Tonis's hand and led him out of the library. "Come with me, Tonis. Don't listen to him. He tends to be a little stiff around new people. Let's go get you something to eat, shall we?"

Achron released Dane's hand and waved him toward the dining hall, muttering, "Of course it would be

259

that the only time I try not to sound like I am inviting random people to stay with us that Keena takes their side. What's up with that? I mean, I am accurately assessing that she typically scolds me for bringing homeless people to live with us every time I go somewhere, right?"

Rather than responding, Creed stared at the now empty doorway they had left through. "Something just doesn't add up." Achron looked at him with interest and waited for Creed to explain. "There is something about Tonis that doesn't make sense. His grandfather spoke of him in his diary, and then it seems like he was around and active for quite some time after his grandfather's passing, since he had heard about me. But he can't be more than eight years old. Yet, he acts like someone who is much older."

Achron rubbed his chin as he mused, "A child that isn't a child? Do you suppose we should be concerned?"

Creed shook his head slowly. "No, I don't think so. He doesn't seem like a malefactor, but more of a lonely and isolated personality."

Achron sounded smug. "Oh, yes, I am quite familiar with that type of person. If only they could take a hint from those around them, their lives would be so much happier."

Creed shot a vexed look at the older man before he walked toward the doorway. "Yeah, yeah, give me a break. I just got back." He could hear Achron suppressing a laugh. Creed successfully managed not to look at Sheena, who was no doubt smiling as she followed closely behind him.

Chapter 23

Tonis wasn't sure about this place. As promised, he felt rather strange. He didn't know if he was actually welcome, nor if he was actually physically whole for the first time in his life. His mind was still foggy. Some things he could remember very clearly, but other things were just a blur. Oddly, it was the more recent things that were a blur, and the more distant ones that were clearer.

The woman who led him toward the sound of friendly conversation, and the smell of good food, was Fearian. She was obviously Sheena's mother. She had the same blond hair with the curious brown streak running down the center of her head to flow down her back. He lamented his inexperience with Fearians. He knew, of course, that they were somewhat different from humans, but that was about the extent of his knowledge.

Tonis entered the large dining hall, and he marveled at the number of younger people there. He was hardly the only person his own age. Keena stopped at an empty space in the line of people who sat at a table, chatting and eating. "Okay, where did Shay go?"

A Fearian girl about his age with long auburn hair and bright hazel eyes replied with an innocent shrug, saying, "I don't know, Mother, but I am sure he had a good reason."

Keena turned to a similarly aged girl on the other side of the gap, and she responded while looking toward Tonis with an intense curiosity. "I do believe he wanted to go find frogs while it was still daylight, and I would rather not know why." Her hair was a beautiful dark red color, unlike anything he had seen before, highlighted by a blond streak that ran down the middle of her back.

Keena sighed and gestured to the chair. "Girls, this is Tonis. He will be joining us. Be nice to him. He is recovering from an illness."

Tonis stared at the empty chair that was surrounded by people he did not know. He wasn't often timid, but this seemed decidedly uncomfortable to him. The hazel-eyed girl smiled kindly at him. "It's okay. Shay rarely comes back to dinner from his adventures, and if he does, he can have my seat. I am Kayanna, by the way, and this is Kokkino."

Tonis spoke softly as he sat. "Thank you."

Kayanna looked surprised, and Kokkino masked a slight gasp with a question. "Where are you from, Tonis?"

Keena reappeared with a plate of food and set it in front of him, rebuking her daughter gently. "Kokkino, let the poor boy get something to eat."

Kokkino nodded dutifully, returning to her food as she said, "Yes, Mother." Keena left to join Achron at another table.

Tonis took a bite of the odd dish that seemed to be mostly fruit-based. He realized with some surprise that he was quite hungry. It had been a long time since he was last truly hungry. He often felt an apathy toward food, and eating more than a little typically made him feel sick.

He replied to the standing question without any

further provocation. "I am from the north reaches, the spline mark, or earth scar, as some call it." He took another bite of his food and then glanced at Kayanna, as he had expected there to be further questions, as opposed to the current level of quietness from the people next to him.

She had been watching him with a wide-eyed expression, and when he met her gaze, she quickly looked back at her food. He turned to Kokkino and received somewhat of a similar response, though she also spoke. "Well, you must have returned with Creed. Mother wasn't too happy that he snuck away with Sheena to search the ruins there."

Tonis scanned the faces around the table and inquired, "Who are all the people here?"

There was a long pause, and then Kokkino replied with a distracted tone. "Oh, um, mostly our family. There are several others who are our friends, but mostly we are just one big family."

Tonis ate some more of his dinner in awkward silence before he finally asked Kayanna, "Is everything okay?" She hunched her shoulders and stared down at the table with a great deal of embarrassment. Bewildered, Tonis looked to Kokkino for some answer.

The red-haired Fearian cleared her throat and spoke with about as much embarrassment as her sister seemed to feel. "It's nothing really, Tonis. It's . . . it's just your voice."

Tonis felt his face flush, and he stared at his food blankly. "I am sorry." He was not sure what else to say; he couldn't change his voice.

Kayanna elaborated. "No, Tonis, it's that your voice is so remarkably beautiful. It almost seems wrong to speak when you could be."

Tonis's face grew redder. "Um . . . . o-okay." It wasn't the first time someone had told him his voice was

263

pleasant, but he felt particularly self-conscious about it now.

Kayanna tried to ease his discomfort by redirecting their conversation. "Kokkino, what are you doing after supper?"

The other girl merely tossed her head. "Oh, I don't know. I was thinking I might go read in the library. It's pretty cold and wet out."

Tonis looked at his empty plate thoughtfully. This was the first time in, well, as long as he could remember, that he had eaten all the food that had been offered to him. Kayanna interrupted his ponderings. "What do you typically do after supper, Tonis?"

He glanced about the dining hall, seeing that the majority of people were done eating and were now talking idly. He replied calmly as he got up from his chair. "I often sing songs of the ancients." He walked slowly to a place where he could be seen by most, and without any hesitation began to sing a flowing, lilting song from a time long gone.

Though Tonis would never raise his voice in ordinary conversation, as it was detrimental to what little strength he had, when he sang, he could harness his power to supplement his lack of strength. And now as he sang, his voice flawless in tune, tone, and depth, the faintest red glow could be seen on his skin. His control over the sounds in the room allowed him to amplify his voice and reiterate it where fitting.

The song itself was not in a language that he understood, but its meaning was carried so strongly in its intonation and meter that it wasn't necessary to know the words. It was also substantially longer than most, but he had no difficulty completing it. While others fought battles or pursued grand discoveries, Tonis, as an ever-ill shut-in, had become a master of sound in song.

The room was hushed as he returned to his seat.

With a sense of wonder, Kayanna whispered into the silence, "Tonis! That was amazing!"

Kokkino pleaded, "Please tell me you are going to sing for your supper again?" Tonis was fatigued from his spontaneous serenade, and his speaking voice was soft. "Sure. It's what I normally do." His exhaustion told him that he probably wasn't as strong as he had felt. He was better, but not yet in possession the strength that would be normal for someone his age.

Conversation slowly returned to the dining hall. Keena came over to speak with him. "Tonis, I have never such a beautiful song, not even among my people, the Fearian forest caste. You look tired, though. Come, let me show you to your room."

Tonis nodded and attempted to slide off his chair. Instead, he slipped and fell. Kayanna gasped in concern, but Kokkino dropped to the ground quickly and managed to catch him.

He apologized with some shame. "I-I am sorry. I think I pushed myself too far."

Kokkino took him in her arms and stood up, assuring him, "It's all right." Turning to Keena, she asked, "Mother, where shall I carry him?"

Keena looked a tad skeptical about this, but then merely swept her hand toward the door. "This way. We will find him a room together." She glanced at her other daughter. "Kayanna, could you go retrieve some fresh linens and come join us in the east wing?" Kayanna bobbed her head enthusiastically and darted off on her quest.

Not many minutes later, Tonis was laid in a newly made, clean bed in a small bedroom off a long hallway. Keena calmly ordered, "Girls, please go help the others clean up from supper." They nodded obediently and departed. Keena placed her hand on his forehead reflexively, smoothing his hair as she would with one of her own sons. "You are incredibly skilled in music. Would it be too much to ask that you share this knowledge with my children?"

Tonis closed his eyes, but he replied simply. "It would be my pleasure to serve your family in such a way."

Keena pulled the blanket up over him and left. She paused at the door, and said, "Thank you, Tonis." He smiled slightly and let sleep overcome him.

* * *

Creed paced with agitated energy as he expressed his frustration. "It just doesn't fit together in any sensible way." Achron flipped idly through the journal as he nodded in agreement.

Viwy mused, "Maybe the third chronicler was not known to the other two?"

Creed contemplated this idea, but then let out a long breath. "Ah, who knows now. There isn't enough information to put together any kind of congruent story either way."

Achron felt like the whole thing had been a long shot anyway. He would like clarity on the matter as much as Creed, but he was content with what little interesting things they had already discovered. Something rather more interesting to him was the fact that Ferir's perspective of Seleen was so radically different from Creed's that it seemed impossible for the two to be referring to the same person. Out of curiosity, Achron commented absently, "You know, it seems like Ferir was absolutely infatuated with this Seleen mage. Are you sure that she didn't have some kind of intimate relationship with him?"

Creed wrinkled his brow at the notion, but replied with confidence. "I have no idea about her dalliances, but I can assure you that she taught no pupils, she had no children, and she died a traitor's death."

Viwy looked thoughtful. "So, you're saying that there was only ever one silver mage?"

Creed nodded. "Yes, that is correct. I never heard of anyone encountering another mage of that kind."

Achron reviewed the facts. "So, she never had any descendants, or trained any other mages. Did she have her own tower?"

Creed started a bit, admitting, "Uh, I don't really know."

Achron rubbed a finger over the book he held. "It would be interesting to know that. Regardless, it may be possible for Dorra to make some sense of the other journal with the runes referenced in this one."

Keena appeared in the doorway of Achron's study. Achron looked at her, arching one eyebrow. She seemed to be in a peculiar mood. Keena clutched her hands to her chest and let out a long, contented sigh. "He is just sooo adorable!"

Creed clearly wanted to interject a comment about this, but he wisely refrained from doing so.

Viwy coughed politely while making haste to leave. "Ah, well, I best turn in for the evening."

Achron nodded to Viwy as the man made his way out of the study, and then replied to his wife. "He certainly has a charming voice and gentle personality. Creed, did you say he was from the same timeframe as yourself?"

Creed affirmed Achron's understanding. "Yes, but he was never physically strong enough to serve as a battlefield combatant."

Keena spoke with enthusiasm as she turned toward the door. "Regardless, I hope he stays with us far longer than just to get his strength back."

267

She left, and Achron eyed Creed with a degree of perception. "Something about this doesn't sit well with you, does it?"

Creed sighed, staring absently at the floor. "He seems nice, but there are enough things that are off about him that I can't help but think there is something important missing. Tonis has a mage designation, and that means he was regarded as more than just a prodigy. He earned that title somehow, and most of us with mage titles earned them in battle."

Achron frowned with concern. "I sure hope this doesn't turn out for the worst." Creed had a point; Achron's own title had not been earned though his benevolence. However, he had something more important to worry about the unknown past of a mild-mannered young boy.

Achron tried to sound casual, but Creed's rapid shift in expression told him that he had failed. "So, how has this little adventure shaped your thoughts on Sheena?"

Creed narrowed his eyes and didn't say anything for a moment. "Where is Sheena?"

Rather than force his own question, Achron addressed Creed's. "Oh, well, I think she said she was going for a walk in the courtyard after supper."

Creed looked perplexed. "What? In this cold?"

Achron merely shrugged as he patted the journal, saying, "Anyway, I will pass this on to Dorra for analysis, if that's okay with you." Creed nodded and left the study without another word.

Achron couldn't stop the smile spreading across his face. Though Creed had failed to provide him with a direct answer, he felt like he had an answer regardless.

Chapter 24

The air was brisk in the castle's courtyard, supplemented by the occasional biting breeze. Winter would be here very soon, and it was already promising to be hard and long.

Creed felt the cold, but his mind was elsewhere. It was strange for Sheena not to be close at hand when she didn't have an obvious obligation. He was the one who sought solace away from others. Sheena was far more gregarious, and bold enough to insert herself into whatever group was available. But her odd behavior wasn't the only thing that brought him out looking for her. He really wanted to talk with her. Unresolved matters still remained between them.

She wasn't exactly hiding. Sheena sat with her back against one of the large trees in the courtyard, her arms wrapped around herself, staring blankly out toward the portico. Creed approached her. "Sheena? What are you doing out here in the dark and the cold?"

She looked up at him for a moment in silence. Her face was sad, not the sadness of sudden shock and loss, but that of a slowly settled sorrow. She responded quietly as she glanced away. "I am just . . . just thinking."

Creed glanced toward the portico, but he saw

nothing worthy of such intense thought. He took a seat and leaned against the tree next to her. "And what are you thinking about?"

Sheena explained without any of the humor he might have expected from his atypical tenacity to plumb her mind. "Not too much really." There was a pause, but then she added, "Did you know that Pyx asked Father for Addie's hand in marriage?"

Creed smirked slightly. "Well, that took long enough." The troublemaker among Achron and Keena's children was ever giving poor Pyx a hard time, and yet their attachment to one another was so inescapable that Creed was only surprised it had taken them this long to secure formal permission to be united.

Sheena barely smiled at his comment. Propriety was clearly hampering his communication, so he chose to simply ask. "Sheena, what's wrong?"

She sighed before beginning indirectly. "I remember that Addie was always telling Pyx she was going to marry him. She teased him mercilessly, and they often got into trouble for playing pranks on one another. But it was strangely fitting. Pyx has always been dutiful, and helpful, and willing to work hard without any clear reward, while Addie was one to be slacking, causing mischief, and generally unmotivated for most mundane tasks. They seem like such strange companions. But the more I think about it, the more I realize how suitable they really are. The superficial things that seem to conflict are just that: superficial. On another level they depend on each other, they trust each other, they genuinely need each other."

Sheena fell silent, but Creed could tell she wasn't done, so he waited mostly patiently. As he expected, she broke the silence again. This time her voice was thick with emotion, bordering on tearful.

"Creed, I see now that no matter how much I

want to help, no matter how much I want to be with you, I don't really complement you. You don't need me. I have no purpose in your life, and if anything, I merely interfere with your normal way of living. I am sorry I have bothered you so much. I-I thought I was helping you . . . but now I . . . I . . . ."

She trailed off, hanging her head in shame out of regret for being mistaken for so long. Even in the darkness, Creed could see tears running down her nose and falling to the cold courtyard ground. He put his arm around her shoulders, and for a moment said nothing. She neither leaned against him nor resisted his comfort.

Creed didn't want to say something that was false, nor did he want to be a simpering dolt. He stared out into the night as he made his reply. "I am not really good at things like this, Sheena. I wasn't taught finesse like Tonis, just how to fight. I don't understand you. You're a mystery to me. Every time I think I can figure you out, I just get confused. But . . . I think that is my problem. I try to figure out everything, but that can't apply to you. You're too wonderful to figure out. You became a part of my life by persistence, but not by accident.

"I don't really know what I need, to be honest, but I do know that you have become central to my life. Is there a day that I don't think about you? Or a moment that you have not brought some light into? Do we complement each other? I don't even know what that means. But you help me not make an idiot of myself most of the time."

Creed looked down at the ground himself, to avoid catching a glimpse of her face. He wanted to finish before he lost his nerve, and siting next the most beautiful woman he knew was certain to be paralyzing.

He continued in a soft but sober voice. "You see, Sheena, I love you, deeply, but I am really not sure how

271

to express that best. If I truly care about you, then is it love to subject you to someone as terrible as myself? Would it not be better to allow you to find some other, more wonderful person? I am just a battle mage out of place and time. All I know is how to hurt people, and—"

"NO!"

Sheena's shout of defiance startled him. Creed fell silent, turning toward her out of concern. Her eyes were wet, as was her face. The cold had brought about a rosy look to her cheeks and nose. She looked pained, or perhaps angry, as she stated in no uncertain terms, "Stop lying to yourself, Creed! You're not like that at all! I have seen you time and again care for others in the gentlest way. I have seen you spare the life of your enemies, and show tender kindness to the fearful and the destitute. I don't know what you were like in the past, but you're nothing like that now. So stop being so stubborn!"

Creed wasn't sure if he should reply, remain motionless, or take immediate evasive action. The second option occurred in lieu of his coming to a conclusion before Sheena threw her arms around him, embracing him and crying into his chest. Creed tried to reconcile her actions with her words. Opting to hold her close, rather than attempt to understand her emotional outburst, he wondered precisely what it was that had made her so sad.

After a moment, he heard her muffled voice. "I love you, Creed."

He reached out and tipped her face toward his own. "Even if I make you cry?"

She pressed herself tightly against him as she said, "Especially because you make me cry."

Creed sighed, partially with relief, and partially because it made so little sense to him that everything had to be normal as far as Sheena was concerned. There was another moment of silence, and then Sheena asked, "Creed?"

"Yes, Sheena?"

Her question didn't really sound like a question. "Does this mean that you are going to marry me instead of making me wait all my life?"

Creed cleared his throat as he replied. "Well, um, I g-guess so."

Sheena laughed warmly as she nestled against him, peering up at him from within the folds of his cloak. Her eyes were bright, and in the dim torchlight, her expression was unmistakably affectionate. Creed tried not to be overcome by the way her blond hair flowed smoothly around her lovely face, mingling with her soft brown mane in a transition not easily distinguished in the dark.

Creed made a neutral observation. "We aren't married yet, Sheena."

She grinned cheekily. "Yes, I know, but I am cold."

This did not clarify the matter for him. "Well, you aren't wearing your cloak, so . . . ."

Sheena gave him a sly smile and a candid explanation. "I was hoping someone would come out here and warm me up. And it's easier to feel sorry for yourself if you're cold."

He rolled his eyes at her. Sheena let out a surprised gasp when he stood quickly, lifting her off the ground and holding her to himself. Sheena scolded him lightly. "Now you're just being silly, ciega."

Creed merely smiled as he carried her to her room. He set her down, speaking softly so as not to wake anyone else. "Good night, Sheena."

Creed turned to leave, but she caught his arm, and then kissed him firmly on the cheek before she said, "Thank you, Creed! Good night!"

He pulled away slightly at her show of affection, and she giggled with delight before entering her room. Creed sighed as he whispered to himself, "I don't deserve you, Sheena, but if it makes you happy, then I who am I to deny you."

He returned to his own room for some much-needed rest from the journey of the previous days. Creed was not any closer to answering important questions about the past, but they seemed like nothing in light of his recent answers to questions about the future. His lingering doubts and concerns were but minor compared to the slowly dawning realization that he had just committed to Sheena in a life-changing relationship for them both.

* * *

A chilly autumn quickly gave way to a hard, cold winter that left multiple layers of snow on the ground. Unlike the bleak sky and perpetually white landscape, however, the inside of the castle was warm and cheery.

Deciphering the runes on Heket's journal using the rambling contents of Ferir's journal was turning out to be a painfully slow process, though Dorra worked diligently at it when she was not otherwise occupied with preparations for her baby's birth.

Tonis had adjusted rather well to living with the Windslo family. His skill in music only became even more obvious as he gained strength. He taught the other children the basics of singing, as well as concepts of sound and song. Eida, the young field caste girl from Fearia, had also adjusted to her place among them. She still seemed to struggle with what she had come from, to where she was now, but in general she was in good spirits.

274

This particular day, Achron was in a civil but vigorous discussion with Iekaruga. They sat at a small table on the second floor of the library. Others were on the first floor, reading, chatting, talking, and singing. It was quite homey, although the singers were not even close to being as pleasant as Tonis. At least they were not loud.

Iekaruga shook his head at his friend. "I disagree. Viwy's skills are not sufficient any longer to protect us from every threat. It is clear now that there are things that fall outside his ability to detect reliably. First there was Harku, and then Tonis, though I admit he could perhaps have been overshadowed by being with one of the majestic gems. We are fortunate that neither carried out sinister acts against our own."

Achron sighed and glanced out over the railing at the various goings-on below them before he replied. "I understand your concern, but I am not convinced it is safe enough to apply universally. I mean, what if there are dire consequences? It would be like sacrificing a child for the sake of the rest, and I am not at all comfortable with that notion."

Iekaruga gestured calmingly. "It hasn't hurt Prinial, or Ahnya . . . I think."

Achron wore a bemused smile. "Somehow I don't think her general approach to life is tied to the fertility rune, but it's the unknown consequences that I am talking about. We don't know if this will result in a loss in the ability to have children, a shortened lifespan, or perhaps something worse."

Iekaruga looked unconvinced. "Perhaps, but the reality is that I cannot complete what the ancients started without a mind mage, and without a fertility rune, Eida isn't coming into her power for at least another eight years. I am not so sure we can afford to wait that long."

Achron thought about it for a moment. They

recognized that Eida was very likely a prodigy, but, not being of age, could not access her power. The two mountain caste Fearians, Prinial and Ahnya, had stumbled upon a way to circumvent the odd tie that connected a Fearian girl's mage power to her physical maturity. The problem was that they had no information about what this might do to them in the long run, especially given the rather short period of fertility that Fearian women already experienced.

In Iekaruga's research of the sigil complex that ran beneath the city of Niado, he had discovered what appeared to be an elaborate system designed to protect the city, and thus the castle. Its nature was not understood, but Creed had admitted that it looked far more advanced than anything he had seen before. It was an addition that had occurred after his imprisonment in the tower.

Iekaruga believed that the system was completed, but never activated. However, to identify the central control system, and to make sure it was actually activated, they needed a mind mage to run some elaborate calculations not possible with pen and paper. Achron liked the idea of having automated defenses, but he was less eager about the notion of using one of their newcomers in such a potentially reckless way. The poor girl was still recovering from being rejected by her closest family member.

Viwy was generally reliable at detecting people approaching Niado, but of late he was having a series of lackluster performances. Tonis seemed like an atypical situation, and Harku was just sneaky. However, there might be other types of mages out there that would be invisible to their mist mage. There was also the possibility of Harku's clan deciding that they really did want their red gryphon back. Though they would be unlikely to be duped in that way again, and gryphons were kind of obvious compared to less dangerous things like domestic cats.

As if thinking about him had summoned him, Viwy popped up the stairs, announcing abruptly, "So, uh, we have some lone person coming from the north."

Achron raised an eyebrow. "Really? Just one person?"

Iekaruga added, "In the most inhospitable time of year?"

Viwy just shrugged. "It's not like I said it was a sane person. Some random human guy."

Achron scratched his head thoughtfully. "That's kind of odd. There isn't anything north of Empleheim but the Aeinor mountains, and those are mostly a desolate wasteland. Beyond that are the frozen straits, and only the desperate people live there."

Iekaruga looked amused at this assessment. "The 'desperate people'?"

Achron expounded on his statement. "Yes, there are several groups who subsist off fish and sea plants up along the cold coastline. They aren't exactly the most . . . normal people."

Viwy cleared his throat. "Ah, you don't say. I am guessing you have some kind of bias against them?"

Achron defended himself. "No, seriously, they have a lot of strange practices. I mean, you would have to be desperate to live out there, isolated from civilization, with long, cold winters, icy seas, and little food."

Iekaruga pointed out, "Many could accuse us of the same, so regardless of perceived desperation, we should probably greet our guest before he reaches Hona."

Achron let the matter drop. "Err, right. Come on, Viwy. Let's go do some greeting."

Viwy glanced about as though looking for a real reason while he excused himself. "Ya know, I have a whole lot of things I need to do, and I am sure Mekki will want some help with the children, and then there is the fact . . . that . . . it's really cold out."

Achron rolled his eyes before turning toward Iekaruga. The older man simply stroked his beard, gesturing an apology with his free hand. "I have more research to do on the defensive system. It is just one person. Surely you can deal with that on your own?"

Shaking his head slightly, Achron headed for the stairs. "I suppose that I can." He felt like they were both being wimps. It wasn't THAT cold out. Viwy had grown up in a tropical region along the sea, so he understood the man's aversion to the cold. However, Iekaruga's was less understandable. The man was mountain caste, after all. He was accustomed to higher altitudes and mountainous terrain. So it seemed that he should be used to cooler climates.

True, Iekaruga was several years older than Achron, at least physically. The millennium where he was stuck in the time loop made Achron substantially older from a technical perspective.

There was something a little strange to him about the accumulation of people in Castle Hona that were from the past: Creed, Hanni, and Tonis. They were all from a time so long gone few even knew that it had ever been. Only Creed retained a clarion memory of what was for him but a few years ago. Hanni remembered nothing, and Tonis had mentioned several times a sort of mental fog that made it hard for him to remember half of his past life. Some things were clear to the soft-spoken boy, but other things were as mysterious to him as they were to the rest of them.

Achron threw on his winter cloak. Emeril was walking down the main hallway toward him and asked,

"Where are you going, Father?"

Achron replied vaguely. "Oh, just out to check on something."

Emeril responded by grabbing her own cloak from the rack that ran along the wall. "Okay, then I will go with you."

He debated telling her to stay put, but then again, this could be an opportunity to prove her assertion wrong. Emeril had complained, several times, that she was the only one of his first litter who never got to go out on any kind of adventure. By a series of unintentional events, this was true. Yet Achron was loath to fabricate some bizarre excuse just for her to wander somewhere. She was a lone wolf in personality, and he worried about her taking on some initiative that might not end well.

As they strolled along the compacted snowy trail that led through the courtyard to the main gate, Pyx looked up from where he was supervising the youngest children, naturally with his now fiancée Addie. For consistency, Achron had subjected them to the same condition as Harku and Rin. His primary reason was one of practicality. It was easy to concede to the desires of another in a moment of weakness, so he wanted to watch and see if what was now a public declaration of ardor would stand scrutiny for a year. This was particularly true for Rin, his timid daughter. He did not expect Pyx and Addie to need such a span of time, as no one doubted how fond they had been of each other over the years.

Achron was a little uncertain about Creed's intentions toward his oldest daughter. Sheena adored the deeply introspective night caste Fearian, while Creed was still working through his own issues. However, since their unsanctioned journey to the earth scar, there had been a strange sort of reversal in their relationship. It was now Creed who often sought out Sheena. The young man seemed far more distracted than in times past, and noticeably nervous when he was around Achron. He suspected that he would soon receive another request for another daughter's hand in marriage.

This was not something that Emeril seemed to be in danger of. She wanted little to do with anything other than becoming like her father. Achron started the conversation, but knew what she would likely say. "Emeril, how have you been today?"

She glanced at him with mild humor, and responded with the candor that was part of her unduly honest character. "Oh, you know, just being bored out of my mind because it's winter."

Achron smiled as he said, "Come now, you could always read something."

She brushed away his suggestion with her hand. "You know as well as I that most of the books in the library are not particularly stimulating to read. And there is hardly anything that directly talks about mage power, or how to harness it."

Achron chided her gently. "You do remember that Creed said you cannot be a white mage no matter how much you try, because that is restricted to humans?"

Emeril held her head high and puffed out her chest as she declared, "Yes, I know, but ol' gloomy pants isn't always right. None of us born to you are normal. Just because you don't talk about it doesn't mean we haven't noticed the peculiarity that ties us to mage power in a way that is difficult to understand." Achron only nodded. It was genuinely impossible to hide everything from them, especially given Creed and Sheena's early display of the power she possessed and he wielded.

As they walked down the main street, or what used to be the main street, in front of the castle, they had to transition to wading through knee-deep snow. Emeril looked back toward the castle, noting their distance and direction, and then asked, "So, where are we going?"

Achron smiled. She was clever, and knew immediately that this wasn't just a random walk to get out of a stuffy castle. Achron replied nonchalantly. "Oh, it's nothing really, but we have a strange visitor that I intend to greet before he gets here."

Emeril sounded a little too gleeful as she pounded her fist into her palm. "All right. Do you think we are going to fight them?!"

Achron tried not to sound disparaging in his response. "Uhh . . . fighting is sort of a last resort for a white mage, so probably not."

Without hesitation she said, "Oh, of course. Unless it's something evil, and in that case—HA!" She punched enthusiastically at the air.

Achron sighed, wondering where she got these notions from. She had a really strong sense of justice, and right versus wrong, but thus far attempts to communicate things like compassion and mercy were not sticking. In some ways, it was a relief that she was not a mage. Creed had told him that Emeril was the majestic peridot, which meant she held within herself limitless power for an earth mage. However, that resident power had in no way caused her to be interested in their earth mage. Indeed, she had bluntly informed an overly hopeful Seifer that if he continued to bother her with stupid sentimentalism, she would plant her fist in his face . . . again.

Seifer was a pleasant fellow, even if he was a bit awkward. And fair enough, really; he was a Fearian who had thought he was a human most of his life. Harku had revealed the truth, that he merely looked human via the power of a metamorphic mage, and now he seemed uncertain about his identity at all. Creed had suggested something was out of the ordinary by revealing that humans could not be earth mages.

They had learned there was an impassable line that evenly split the mages into two halves. There were twelve kinds of human mages and twelve kinds of Fearian mages, with no overlap or redundancy. What Achron really wanted to understand was why this was true. Creed had no explanation for it, just knowing that there were no exceptions. In the present context, they were way outside even ancient knowledge, because the majestic gems were previously objects, not people. Half of his children possessed unfettered power for human mages, though they themselves were Fearian. It made him wonder if this pushed the limits of what was possible with mage power, particularly in the area of slipping beyond what was apparently some kind of inborn limitation that fixed a gulf between a category of mage and one's ethnic background.

Achron caught sight of a figure trudging through the snow towards them, and he forgot all thoughts about the mechanisms of mage power. Emeril clenched her fist and spoke in a low voice. "I am ready, Father. Just let me know when to strike."

Achron spoke with mild amusement. "Sure. Just promise me that you will only strike him AFTER I do." She nodded firmly, and he decided that pursuing her approach to strangers right now was not a profitable endeavor.

The man spotted them about the same time they spotted him. He waved in a friendly manner and hurried toward them. His clothes were simple, and repaired in a number of places with patches from other garments. He wore a thick winter cloak and ordinary leather boots. His stringy hair framed a face that appeared worn from travel. He greeted them, panting. "My friends! Please, tell me, is either one of you one of Empleheim's legendary white mages?"

Achron blinked, surprised and slightly on guard that the man was actually there to find a white mage, despite the clear evidence that no one had live in most of Empleheim for years. Nevertheless, he said, "Yes, I am a white mage. What is it you seek?"

The man fell to his knees and raised his hands in supplication, pleading, "Please, sir, my little Loral is sick, and nothing has helped her get better. Please don't let her die so young, I beg of you!"

Achron hesitated for a moment. It sounded a little too convenient, but he decided that if someone sought the help of Empleheim, it would be bad not to offer it if possible. "Rise, friend. There is no need for supplication of that kind. I will help you, but how far is it to your home?"

The man pointed back up the road. "Just a few days northward."

Nodding in acknowledgement, Achron turned to Emeril as he said, "Emeril, go inform your mother that I will be away for a couple days . . ."

Emeril put her hands on her hips and spoke with mild exasperation. "Father!"

Achron continued, putting his hand on her shoulder to calm her. ". . . and get a few days' worth of food for our journey. I will wait for you here." Emeril smiled brilliantly, and turned and darted back the way they had come. Achron gestured to the nearest house as he suggested, "Well, I guess there is no point in waiting out in the elements. Let's wait in there, shall we?" The man nodded, rubbing his arms to warm himself before turning toward the building.

Entering the house, they sat down on a stone bench, the only piece of furniture to survive years of neglect. Achron asked idly, "So, you're from the north, I presume?"

The man nodded. "Yes, I reside in a small farm just on the northern edge of Empleheim with Erna and of course my precious Loral."

Achron inquired further. "I see. How long has the girl been sick?"

The man shook his head with sincere concern. "It's been months, and I am afraid that we may be too late if she doesn't get help immediately."

Something felt off about the man. His reference to what Achron presumed to be his wife was odd, and he spoke like a scarcely cognizant person. His voice was slow and thick and lacked much in the way of expressiveness. It was mostly a monotone that was only vaguely supported by the expected facial expressions.

Achron asked a couple more questions. While he got answers, they were all brought back to the man's concern for what Achron presumed was his daughter, Loral. After several dead-end attempts at conversation, Achron gave up and waited in silence. He had learned that the man's name was Ike, but that was the extent of information to be gleaned from his attempts at being conversational. The man made no attempt to say more on his own, and they waited silently for Emeril's return.

The hush of the snow-strewn landscape, coupled with its monochromatic nature, was nearly to the point of making Achron uneasy when Emeril reappeared with a pack of supplies on either shoulder and a winsome exuberance of countenance that spoke volumes about her excitement for their coming adventure. He resisted the temptation to tell her that this was going to a dull adventure, all things told.

They set out down the main road, following the path that the man had already made in the snow. He said little to them, and led the way diligently enough that Achron struck up a casual conversation with Emeril. Achron tried hard to spend time with each of his children, to really understand them, their personalities, and what kind of future they desired. While he wasn't sold on what Emeril wanted for herself, he did want to understand her well enough to offer some acceptable compromise or alternative to her.

The conversation wandered, but it covered essentially the same things as before. Emeril wanted to be like her father, which was flattering, but very likely impossible. He mused about how they really need to find a man that appealed to her to keep her from focusing on her unobtainable dreams. It sounded terrible, or at least questionable, but Achron hadn't come up with another solution that had any weight behind it.

He imagined for a moment a casual invitation to some prospective male. *"Hey, how would you like to court my feisty-tailed daughter to distract her from wanting to be a mage?"*

He smiled involuntarily at the thought, and Emeril broke from her conversation to ask, "Um, what's so funny, Father?"

He attempted to suppress his smile and evade the question. "What? Oh, nothing really. You were saying?"

Emeril looked a little skeptical, but resumed her prior topic. "I was saying that I think Iekaruga's research on the sigil mechanism under the city seems to be coming to some kind of conclusion. He has been more excited about it in the last month than any time since he first began to study it." Achron nodded knowingly, and Emeril continued to talk excitedly herself about her own ideas for the mechanism.

The mention of the sigil mage made him think of an additional issue that would arise if they gave a fertility rune to Eida. Emeril would most certainly want one too. It would be tough to sell a convincing reason why it was okay for a young outsider to receive such a thing, and not his youngest daughter of Keena's first litter. He couldn't tell her that it was for her safety; that would just sound sinister. He supposed that he could try an argument about it being a matter of necessity, but that still wouldn't address why she couldn't have one, just why Eida could. It was a bad situation no matter which way he looked at things.

Their conversation wandered further, and Achron thought their travel to the northern border of Empleheim, which was arguably not a border since there was no nation to the north, was also wandering.

Chapter 25

Reaching the farmstead took a few days' cold walk. The place had certainly seen better days, and Achron was ever so slightly suspicious that it had been within the range of the time shift that had removed Empleheim from time for nearly a millennium. There were signs of repair on the old stone farmhouse, namely the thatched roof. There was freshly cut wood stacked along one wall, and even with the snow, it was plain that several of the small fields by the house had been worked in the last growing season.

They were still some distance from the mountains, but it was abundantly clear there wasn't anything else for miles around. For a moment, Achron wondered what kind of future there was for a young woman living this far out in the middle of nowhere.

He watched the column of smoke rise lazily from the chimney as they approached the door. The man stomped the caked snow off his boots before entering, as did they. The house was essentially one small room, with a dining area and fireplace in one end, and some mats on the floor at the other.

An old woman greeted them warmly with a crooked but friendly smile. "Hello. Welcome. Come in and warm yourselves by the fire."

She turned to Ike, asking, "Are these the people that will help our little Loral?" He nodded to her, and then pointed Achron toward one of the woven reed mats.

A young girl lay on her back, covered up to her neck with a thin blanket. A damp cloth was on her head, and she would have looked dead were it not for the subtle motion of her chest as she breathed. Achron walked over to where she lay and knelt beside her.

She was definitely one of the northern people. Her skin was tan, and her face bore her people's narrow features. Her hair was fine and ink-black. Expectations aside, all in all, she was a rather charming looking child of about nine. Achron studied her appearance briefly, then stole a glance at her parents. They looked only vaguely like northern people, which seemed odd, given how plainly Loral was.

He reached out and placed his hand on her head. She had no fever, but instead was slightly cool to the touch. He pulled the blanket back and inspected her thoughtfully. There was no sign of injury or disease on her neck, shoulders, or arms. She wore a piecemeal garment of furs and skins sewn into the traditional dress of her kinsmen. He held her wrist gently, feeling the pulse of blood through her body.

Achron was uncertain how to proceed. She was not obviously sick, but she was quite weak. Her heart rate was strangely slow, and her temperature far lower than normal. Her sleep was incredibly deep. Too deep.

Ike spoke with concern. "Can you—can you help her, sir mage?"

Achron answered calmly as he reached out and took hold of his staff. "I think so, but she faces something stranger than illness." Achron felt his power flow across him as his staff materialized, and he entered a focused state.

Ike responded uncertainly. "W-what else could it

be?"

Achron touched her forehead. There was a tie between her and something else that drew her strength from her. It was slow, but certainly the cause of her current condition. Achron began to glow. "She is under some kind of energy drain, but it's nothing I can't remove." Power flashed out from Achron, shredding the malignant force that bound the little girl.

Emeril, who stood beside him, let out a frightened gasp. Achron looked sharply at her, but she was staring toward the small kitchen. He turned in that direction, but saw nothing. He looked back at her, and she exclaimed with some shock, "T-they just d-disappeared!" Achron realized the fact there was no one else in the house was the thing that had surprised her.

Staring back at the kitchen himself, he muttered, "That . . . doesn't make any sense. They were the cause of her malady, but they sought us out to stop them?"

Emeril's gaze moved around the room nervously. "Of all the times to be without the power to defend myself."

Achron was a bit bemused by her response. "I seriously doubt that you are going need to defend yourself any time soon." Emeril looked a little sullen but managed not to pout.

Banishing his staff, Achron felt Loral's wrist again. Her heart rate seemed to be returning to something that was much closer to normal. Achron instructed his daughter, "You might as well get comfortable. I don't think she is going to wake up for a while." Emeril nodded and took her cloak off, hanging it by the mantel. Achron tucked the blanket around the girl's shoulders and followed his daughter's example.

He took a seat in one of the rickety chairs near the fireplace, and Emeril poked around in the kitchen, if the space qualified for that term. "There's not much here, Father. How could three people live off this?"

She showed him a reed basket that held maybe a dozen small tubers. Achron met her eyes with a solemn expression. "I don't think that three people have lived here in a really long time." Emeril gave him an odd look, but he chose to stare silently into the fireplace.

It was hard to know, but it seemed that Ike and Erna were entities constrained to operate for the benefit of Loral, but the food available did not afford sufficient physical strength to maintain the entities perpetually. What Achron didn't know was how the entities had come to be associated with her.

Emeril joined him at the fireplace in the only other chair. She sat down in it gingerly, as if uncertain whether it was worth trusting. "Father, we can't just leave her here by herself. There isn't enough here to get her through the winter."

Achron concurred with a nod. She was correct. Loral would not survive the winter in this remote location, not with the minute amount of food, and her limited strength hindering her from gathering more wood than what was in front of the house. Achron smiled slightly to himself. It simply wouldn't be right for him to wander from Niado and not return with some interesting person who needed someone to take care of them. There was something else going on, though.

The smile faded from his face as he realized that these incidences were not random. Something about his peculiar family drew those of note to his own. He wondered how long those drawn would be people that could be identified as friends. Surely this wouldn't last forever. Iekaruga's argument was valid; their decision about the fertility rune was not a minor one.

* * *

Shortly before nightfall, Loral stirred. Achron wasn't sure if this was because it took that long for her to wake, or because of the smell of the potato and meat soup that Emeril dutifully prepared for them. It smelled vaguely of garlic and onions from the few spices that could be found in the small house. The dried meat had come from the supplies they had brought with them.

Achron came quietly to her side. She sat up, sleepily rubbing her eyes as she yawned and asked, "Ike, what smells so good?"

He tried to speak softly. "So, Ike is not here."

She jerked away from him with fear, and fell over, trying to scramble to her feet. But she struggled to rise even to her knees, and Achron tried to reassure her. "It's okay. We aren't going to hurt you."

She whispered nervously, "W-w-we?" She looked toward where Emeril watched curiously from the other end of the farmhouse, and gasped, leaving her mouth hanging open.

Achron rebuked himself mentally for forgetting that the obvious differences between humans and Fearians that he was accustomed to were disturbing to those who didn't know that the other people existed. He attempted to compensate by saying gently, "Don't worry. My daughter Emeril is a Fearian, and that's normal for them. My name is Achron. What's yours?"

Her eyes darted back and forth between them, but then she finally spoke. Her accent, as he had expected, was fairly obvious, a strange softening of hard consonant sounds. "I-I am Loral, but what are you doing in my house? And where are Erna and Ike?"

Achron replied, "Your friends are gone. They were dependent on your strength, and I had to banish them to bring you back."

She sat up, folded her hands in her lap, and stared blankly at the floor, avoiding their gazes. "I-I

291

suppose that means . . . you know I am cursed?"

Achron tilted his head slightly as he queried, "Cursed? Could you explain?"

She drew a slow breath, and then looked longingly toward the kitchen. Emeril smiled and carried one of the cooling bowls of soup from the table to Loral. The girl turned away, but Emeril placed the soup in front of her. She glanced up at Achron with uncertainty, but he merely nodded toward the bowl. She sniffed at it cautiously and tasted it with a timidity that suggested she still wasn't so sure she wanted anything to do with them. This attitude didn't last long. After a bite or two, she consumed the rest of the soup with a voracious appetite.

She set the empty bowl down, her voice trembling slightly as she spoke. "I . . . I have always seen things that are not really there. Or, well, they are there when I see them, and then other people can see them, but then they are gone. I was expelled from my community because of it. Erna and Ike were like the others. Not really there, but yet there. They helped me survive alone out in the wilderness. But this winter has been especially hard."

Achron thought for a moment about what she said. It seemed to him that she must be some kind of mage prodigy, but he was at a loss as to what kind. Creed would know.

Emeril filled his silence with an offer of hospitality. "Loral, there isn't anything for you here. You should come back with us."

To their surprise, she shook her head vigorously. "No, I can't. I have to go to the land of Empleheim."

Before Emeril could say anything, Achron asked, "Why do you have to go to there?"

Loral explained. "My tribe historian taught us often of the cursed land of Empleheim, a place that was, then wasn't, then was again. I figured if I was cursed in the same way, then maybe I belonged in Empleheim. Once winter is over, I will go there, no matter how far it is!" She paused and looked intently at them. "And . . . where are you from?"

Achron replied with a smile. "I am from Niado, capital city of Empleheim."

Achron barely resisted raising his hands in defense as Loral threw herself at him, grabbing his arms and speaking much too close to his face for his comfort. "Y-you have to take me with you!" He remembered that her people didn't really understand the unspoken law of personal space common to most cultures. He nodded, and she continued breathlessly. "Can we leave soon? Is it far? Are there lots of other people there? Does it cost money to live there? Will you help me?"

He gently pushed her back into a sitting position. "Yes, it's not far, and we will leave in the morning. No, it does not cost money, but you will be expected to participate in things like cooking and cleaning."

She nodded emphatically, but then her face shifted to fear as a piercing howl could be heard uncomfortably close to the farmhouse. Achron glanced toward the door and noticed that it had a wood pole that sat in brackets. Emeril followed his gaze, and then quickly barred the door. Achron knew that there were plenty of wolves that ranged through the Aeinor mountains, but it was uncommon for them come down and harass the locals.

Loral whispered, as if she were afraid the wolves would hear her. "They just won't leave me alone. They have hunted me forever, it seems. Ike would chase them off with a torch."

Achron looked toward the door and considered this new information. "I think that it would be best to wait until morning." He wasn't eager to be out in the dark with a bunch of wolves about. What was more, if the winter had driven them to stalk Loral, then it was likely they were aggressive enough to challenge even someone with a torch.

Achron studied the young girl thoughtfully. There was a disconnect in his mind, and so he asked, "So, how long did you say these wolves have been following you?"

As though chilled by the dark memories, Loral shivered. "It wasn't long after I left my people that they appeared. A couple times they attacked me, but I managed to escape with the help of Erna and Ike."

Achron's eyes narrowed. Emeril wondered aloud, "What is it, Father?"

He shrugged, giving a stern glance back at the door. "Oh, it's nothing really, just a little unusual for wolves to be that persistent. They will be gone in the morning, so let's not worry about it now."

It was only partially true. The persistence of the creatures, presumably for months, suggested that they were driven by something much darker than animal instinct. It also meant that they were in very real danger, since they would have to camp out in the open at least once, as there weren't many ruins between them and what had been the better populated regions of north Empleheim.

To distract Loral from her fear of the wolves, Achron started a casual conversation with her. He learned that she was an only child, and that at the age of eight she began to experience strange things. Her village chose to force her to leave the frozen coasts for the Aeinor mountains because she was viewed as cursed. It grieved her parents, but they complied with their village on her expulsion. She had been on her own ever since. The entities that were bound to her were the main reason she had not died in the mountains. Somehow they had made it this far, but she was out of strength, and they had stopped in the summer at the farmstead to recuperate.

Loral paused after sharing her background and hunched her shoulders in shame. "Will I . . . will I be driven from Empleheim for being cursed?"

Achron shook his head firmly. "No, Loral, you will not." Glancing at his daughter, he could see that she looked more than a little moved by Loral's story of rejection and persistence against the elements. He announced, "I think it's best if we all get some sleep now. We're going to have a long walk back."

Emeril nodded, and Loral returned to her mat on the floor. Almost unconsciously, Achron tucked the blanket around her. She reached up abruptly and put her hand on his cheek as she spoke with sincere gratitude. "Thank you, sir!"

He gave her a fatherly smile. "You're welcome, Loral. Now get some rest."

He moved back to the fireplace and added some more wood before setting down in the chair. Emeril sat next to him. They remained in silence for an extended time. Emeril watched the sleeping form of Loral before she asked, "Father, what kind of mage is she?"

Achron shrugged. "I don't know, but it doesn't matter. She needs a home, and I see no reason why we can't give her one."

Emeril pursed her lips. "Mother may not think positive thoughts about your bringing home another orphan."

Achron merely chuckled. "Yes, well, I think we are just going to need to restructure how we do things at Hona. We have too many children who need supervision, and not enough supervisors."

Emeril looked curious. "And what will you do about that?"

Thinking out loud, Achron mulled through the possibilities. "Hmm, we are going to have to divide up the supervision among more people. We need someone mature and reliable to assist Pyx. Mekki is too busy with her own little ones, and Dorra's child will be born soon. Iekaruga is vital in teaching the older ones, so that really leaves someone among those your age to take over watching the youngest children."

He could read the growing nervousness on Emeril's face. He knew that it wasn't a lack of interest in helping her siblings, but being so committed would leave her no opportunity for adventures, or for pursuing her goal of becoming a mage. Achron confided in her, "You know, I was thinking it would give Creed something useful to do."

Emeril sighed her relief audibly, and then they both laughed. It was a long and somewhat uncomfortable night in the meager dwelling, but there was a sense of peace that came from knowing they would be returning to friends and family, and the warm, cozy community that was growing in Castle Hona.

Chapter 26

Achron woke early. He restoked the fire and began heating a pot of water to which he added a mixture of dried fruits. In its essence, it was like the porridges that were common in Empleheim back when he was growing up, only made strictly from coarsely ground dried fruit. It cooked down to what looked like a thick applesauce. Unlike its cereal counterpart, it was far sweeter.

He couldn't deny the convenience of the fact that Keena's upbringing involved extensive and diverse culinary uses of fruit, and now fruit formed the largest portion of their diet in Empleheim. Achron wasn't opposed to such a dietary staple, but he did hope to find a more reliable source of red meat. Fish was plentiful, but not something he wanted every day. At least they had the simple cured and dried meats that he had purchased on a supplies run to Wythwood. He supposed they had far more than many, but still, he missed the more substantial amounts of meat available back during Empleheim's glory days.

Emeril yawned loudly and got up from where she had been resting on one of the mats near Loral. She shook the sleep from herself as she walked to the kitchen, took a wooden bowl off the mantel, and held it out toward Achron. He ladled some of the hot fruit mixture into it, and she continued on to the table, sitting down and blowing on her breakfast.

Achron grabbed a chunk of bread from his shoulder bag and tossed it to her. She caught it and used it in lieu of any tableware. He was grateful for Iekaruga's sigil work that made it possible for them to grow their own wheat for flour. He removed the pot from the fire and poured two more bowls. They had enough food to get home, but not much more than that.

Loral stirred slightly, and then sat up with a start, looking around wild-eyed. She blinked at them and then sighed with relief. Rising and coming to the table, she stared at the bowl of unidentifiable stuff for a moment before she looked up and saw them watching her with concern. Loral blushed a little as she admitted, "S-sorry, I thought that you . . . might have left without me, o-or maybe you were just a dream."

Emeril gave her a hesitant smile, not sure what to say, but Achron laughed lightheartedly. "We wouldn't leave without you. After all, we did come all this way to help you." She nodded, and watching Emeril for a moment, took her bread and scooped some of the fruit porridge with it as Emeril had. As soon as it touched her tongue, a confused expression flitted over her face. Achron asked, "What is it?"

She spoke a little oddly, as though she wanted to say something else, but instead said what she knew to say. "Oh, um, it's sweeter than I expected. Thank you for something to eat." She ate the rest of it without further comment, but not as voraciously as she had eaten their soup from the day before. Achron recalled that her people rarely had access to sweet foods, and their palates were based on salty and bitter tastes. She was going to have a substantial adjustment to make.

After they finished breakfast, Achron smothered

the fire and ensured they were not leaving anything important. He had no intention of coming back to this place if he could help it. Achron stepped out into the sunny winter morning, grateful for the absence of biting winds or falling snow. He was relieved to observe that even without a winter cloak, Loral was bundled warmly enough for traveling through the snow.

As they began walking toward home, Loral asked, "Sir, where in Niado do you live?"

He smiled at her. "Please, call me Achron. We live in the center of the city, in a castle called Hona."

The girl's jaw dropped. "What?! A castle? My lord, forgive me for not offering you the respect you deserve."

Achron coughed loudly as he hurried to correct her. "Hang on there. I am not a king, or lord, or even a nobleman. We live in the castle because it's convenient."

She looked perplexed as she tried to get clarity on the issue. "B-but . . . doesn't the king object?"

Emeril snorted slightly at her question, and Achron restrained his own amusement. "Well, you see, Empleheim returned, but its people left the place when it disappeared. Basically, we are the only ones who live in Empleheim now."

Loral made the obvious connection with her youthful logic. "But if you're the only ones who live there, doesn't that make you the king?"

Achron frowned at Emeril as she burst into laughter, and then attempted to dissuade Loral of her conclusion. "Uh, not exactly. I am more like the leader of my family among several families that live within the walls of Hona Castle." Achron wasn't formally any kind of leader, but informally he did seem to have the final authority over Hona, and for some reason, all of Empleheim by extension.

Loral went on to say something else, but Achron

didn't hear it. He caught a sharp motion out of the corner of his eye and responded at full speed. His hand snapped out and took hold of his staff. In a glimmer of brilliant light, Tianna burst into existence, and the Aegeis ripped out from its top instantly.

The wolf that had leapt at them was already airborne when it was hit by the Aegeis. It was repelled by the translucent shield with a great deal of force, and it tumbled through the snow for more than a hundred paces. It made no effort to rise, but a dozen or more other wolves could be seen emerging from the scrub, trees, and snow drifts. Even in the bright morning sun, Achron's skin glowed with a pale light.

Stepping back from him, shock written on her face, Loral stuttered, "I-uh . . . w-what are y-you?"

Emeril answered for him, and he wasn't sure if he wanted to laugh or groan. "It's okay, Loral. We are like you—mages! My father is a white mage, a great healer, and a demon slayer!"

Achron scanned the area carefully. Wolves didn't normally attack in the daylight. He caught sight of one gray wolf that was easily twice the size of the others. Its eyes glowed an infernal blue. It wasn't circling with the others, but watched from a distance. It reminded him of the various demon creatures he had faced in Fearia.

Another wolf challenged the Aegeis, but bounced off without effect. Achron was concerned that while a human opponent might not figure out that the Aegeis yielded to non-violence, an animal would likely alter its approach after a few failed attempts.

He took his staff in both hands and pointed it toward the larger wolf. By the time the creature had determined Achron's intent, it was far too late. A blinding beam of light lanced out from the staff, nearly instantaneously covering the distance between him and the creature. It pulled back, as if to dodge, but it failed miserably. The beam cut completely through it. It slumped to the ground and faded. It was as he had suspected, an unnatural creature from another place. The wolves, no longer subjected to its control, scattered in fear.

He tapped the staff on the ground, and the Aegeis returned. There was a moment of silence, and then came Loral's quivering voice. "What is a mage?"

Achron spoke softly, still assessing the area. He had no desire to be surprised by a second creature. "Don't worry. You will learn more about it at Castle Hona. We will teach you how to use your 'curse' as a tool to help others." She nodded, and they resumed their travels.

When they camped that night, Achron and Emeril took turns keeping watch. Their precaution was probably unnecessary, but it was better than being surprised by something dark. The rest of the journey back to Hona was without incident, though they returned cold, wet, and tired.

* * *

Viwy and Keena met them at Hona's main gate. She glanced from him to Loral and back, merely shaking her head. Despite her gesture, she wore a delighted smile. Viwy asked with mild interest, "So, uh, what happened to the guy that needed your help healing his daughter?"

Achron shrugged as he replied cryptically. "He wasn't actually real."

Viwy folded his arms and mused, "Oh, huh, here I thought there was something a little odd about him."

Keena kissed Achron tenderly, and then knelt before Loral. "Hello, there. I am Keena. What's your name?"

Loral spoke a little shyly. "L-Loral."

Keena smiled kindly at her. "Welcome to Hona, Loral. I will show you to your new room. I hope you don't mind sharing it with a couple other girls." Loral merely shook her head.

Achron and the others formed a line behind them as they entered the castle. Loral's eyes were wide, trying to absorb everything she passed. The little group moved through the dining hall, where Creed and Sheena were setting the tables in anticipation of the mid-day meal. Creed glanced at them curiously, and then tensed, the flicker of a glow on his skin as he became focused. Achron stopped beside him, as did Viwy and Emeril. Keena continued with Loral, both oblivious to Creed and his sharp reaction.

Achron stated, "I am guessing you can tell us a little more about the north girl's power?"

Creed didn't relax as he warily watched them disappear down the hallway, answering with distracted detachment. "She is a summoner, and the summoners formed part of the vale league, sworn enemies of the star league."

With a hand to the Fearian's shoulder, Achron brought him back to the present. "She is not a member of any league, just an outcast little girl without a home."

Creed seemed to release his apprehension, at least partially, and he turned back to his work. "I guess it's hard to let get of old prejudices. Where did she come from?"

Achron explained the circumstances of their encounter with Loral. Sheena contemplated the sad tale. "Is it the fate of all mages to suffer at the hands of their own?"

Sighing a little, Achron noted, "Many fear the inexplicable, and many more fear what is beyond their own abilities. It isn't really fate that drives people to

302

treat even their family members with disdain. Rather, it's the darkness within that taints every motive and every thought. Not everyone experiences that level of rejection. Regardless, I need to talk to you, Creed." Achron headed for the library, adding, "You, too, Viwy."

Soon they were gathered on the main floor of the library, around the large table that served as a teaching space and a conference area. Iekaruga entered, followed by Keena. Achron quietly asked his wife, "Where is Loral now?"

Keena answered with a chuckle. "Receiving a professional tour from her roommates Kokkino and Kayanna." Achron smiled to himself. If anyone could introduce her to the slightly eclectic life at Hona Castle, it was those two.

Scanning the faces of his expectant audience, Achron explained their purpose in gathering. "All right, my friends, we have a problem. As you know, Emeril and I have just returned from a brief journey to the northern reaches of Empleheim. There we encountered a young girl who is a mage prodigy."

Viwy snorted with a mixture of sarcasm and humor. "The more, the merrier?" Achron shot him a disapproving look. The mist mage gave an apologetic shrug, and Achron continued.

"That isn't the problem. What is the problem is that the girl had been hunted by a large wolflike creature, of exactly the sort I encountered in Fearia. So, either there is a demon gate somewhere in the Aeinor mountains, or there is another sigil gate that is active."

Iekaruga observed, "It seems like a low risk if the only thing that has showed up from the place in all this time is a single creature that was hunting a mage."

Achron shook his head. "We can't rely on that. We don't know if this recent happening is a longstanding pattern, or the appearance of a new one."

He asked Creed, "What was in the Aeinor mountain range during the mage war?"

Creed furrowed his brow as he filtered through his memories. "Oh, nothing really. Rocks, pine trees, a little wildlife, and lots and lots of ice." Achron felt some relief in knowing that if anyone would know what was there, it was Creed. The next step was to ask Viwy to scan the area for people.

"Oh!"

Everyone whipped around to stare at Creed after his exclamation. Creed quickly modified his previous statement. "So, on the human side there isn't anything to note, but on the Fearian side, that's where Kurri Fea'sol's tower was, the great dark blue mage." They all looked at him blankly, and he added, "That's ice."

Viwy muttered sarcastically, "Oh, of course, I already knew that."

Achron inquired, "Was there also a sigil gate there?"

Creed nodded. "Y-yes, there was one there."

Iekaruga expressed his doubts about the matter. "It seems unlikely that my people would have left even a remote gate intact when they expelled the humans from Fearia."

Achron considered both comments. "Whatever the circumstances, it is plain that those dark creatures from Fearia are passing through it to Aeinor mountains on the human side. This is not a problem we can afford to ignore."

Keena interrupted with a level of practicality that had not yet existed in the conversation. "It's the dead of winter. The mountains are treacherous enough without being covered in ice and snow. If it must be dealt with, then it must be dealt with in the summer."

Achron opened his mouth with a ready reply

304

about risk versus benefit, but then he sighed and conceded. "Uh, yes, you are correct. We just can't afford to investigate it now. Not with there being so much snow on the ground that horses would have no food, and going on foot would be long and dangerous."

Achron caught and held Viwy's gaze. "Be vigilant, my friend."

Viwy gave a nod as serious as his tone. "Always."

Achron turned back to the rest of the group. "All right, that's all I have. Back to life as we know it." There was a general murmured agreement, and as people dispersed, Achron addressed Creed before he could escape. "One moment more, Creed. I need to speak with you."

Creed froze. His nerves were clear on his face, but he managed a stable reply. "Sure."

The room had emptied by the time Achron pulled out a chair from the table and took a seat, indicating Creed should do the same. The young Fearian lowered himself into a neighboring seat. Achron didn't keep him in apprehension.

"With the addition of Loral, another child just old enough not to need constant attention, but young enough to get into substantial amounts of trouble, it has become obvious that the way we have been operating isn't going to work any longer. Pyx is arguably the only person whose time is strictly dedicated to watching the children, and he can't watch the younger ones and the older ones at the same time. Dorra is having her own child soon, Mekki has her hands full now that her little ones are running about, and most of the others have various things to keep them busy. So, that said, I would like you to help watch the youngest children. At times this will be just mine, but other times it will include Mekki's and probably others."

Creed turned a relieved sigh into an expression of acknowledgement. "Oh, uh, that's something I can do if you need me to."

Achron replied calmly, "Yes, it is. If you'd like, I can have Sheena help you."

Creed blinked innocently but shifted his position in his chair uncomfortably. "That would be best, I think, probably."

Achron nodded, casually glancing around the library. "Thank you, Creed. That's all I had to say. Was there anything you wanted to ask me?"

Creed responded far too hastily. "NO! Uh, I mean yes, or maybe . . . ." He cleared his throat loudly and stared intently at the doorway. "I am sure something will occur to me that I need to ask you eventually."

Achron hid a smile, saying, "Okay. Don't be shy if you have a question, and if I am not around, you can always ask Keena."

Creed merely shook his head in the affirmative, still avoiding Achron's direct gaze. Achron rose and left him sitting alone in the library.

As he rounded the corner, he found Keena waiting by the door. She slipped her hand into his and fell in step beside him. After they passed out of hearing range, she commented with feigned rebuke, "Achron, dear, that wasn't very nice. The poor boy is already frightened enough about the situation."

His face broke into a slight smile. "What's this? Since when were you so supportive of Creed's positive outlook toward our wonderful little Sheena?"

She returned his smile and then looked down the hall as they walked together, her gaze steady and reflective. "Since I saw clearly how he makes her so very happy. Sheena isn't really afraid of anything, other than losing Creed, of course. Since they got back from their 'adventure,' there has been a distinct change between them. Have you noticed that he no longer spends his time alone brooding?"

Achron laughed. "You mean he still spends time alone?"

Keena chuckled as she added, "Okay, so what little time he can't be with her, he is highly distracted with something other than dour thoughts of the past."

It was true. Creed could no longer convince himself that Sheena as a lifelong companion was an unobtainable goal. Now he was in the awkward circumstance of working up the courage to ask for her hand in marriage. He was not practically family like Pyx, nor was he used to operating as an independent leader like Harku. Achron hoped that Creed wouldn't wait too long, for Sheena's sake if nothing else, but it wasn't a rush either. There were at least three more years before his eldest girls experienced the trials of coming of age as Fearian females.

Emeril still worried him, given her complete lack of interest in anything other than becoming a mage. He was not so worried about the Quirieyo sisters, since they were not his own children, and since there were obvious relationships developing between Ahnya and Kraysin and between Prinial and Dane. Clearly they were not as far along as the other three pairings, but that was likely only a matter of time. So, other than Emeril, his oldest children seemed to have bright and secure futures.

Yet this relief also brought to light the reality that they were just the beginning. Achron felt like an unfortunate pattern was forming. Thiesa, his only daughter of Keena's second litter, while young yet, was without a prospect, and this time there was no obvious reason. Thiesa was energetic and took joy in the simple company of others. But Tonis was probably too young to join in her company, and Seifer was too old for her to identify with. Either was certainly possible, but given their current routines, it was unlikely unless one of them made a concerted effort, and neither appeared to be interested in doing so.

Chapter 27

The sun was high in the sky, and a warm summer breeze played through the trees. Arru felt all the excitement of the season. Not only because the warm days meant they could play freely in the river, but also because of the double wedding that would be taking place at summer's end. Harku was to be married to Rin, and she couldn't be happier for the two of them.

She paused in the bright sunlight, just delighting in the feel of it on her skin. She swore to herself that she would never take the sun's light for granted, not after having spent her childhood without it. But the past was past, and she no longer had to fear the sunlight making her deathly ill. In a similar degree of relief, she no longer had to marry her brother either. She wondered that her people had not tried to capture her, but she was thankful that they had not.

Arru was less sure about what to do with herself at Castle Hona. There was no shortage of things to help with, in light of the number of people who lived there. For the moment, that number was a little smaller, as there was some pressing matter to the north that took Achron and a couple of the others on a journey. It was much farther than their normal excursions, and they were not expected to return for a while.

The timing of it was quite poor, in her opinion, but she understood enough to know that it was also a fairly important task that they pursued. She had come to trust their impromptu leader Achron. He was very wise, and in her experience, there wasn't a situation he could not figure out if he needed to.

Arru brushed her vividly red hair out of her face, glancing toward the Fearian girl who walked beside her. Eida, who looked like any other girl their age, other than her long cat-like tail and slightly pointed ears, also knew past familial difficulties. They had both lost their mothers at a young age, and similarly they had both been regarded as without value by their fathers. Despite their very different geographic origins, they knew a special bond through shared hardships.

Eida commented casually, "Do you think the boys will be able to resist dunking us this time?"

Arru grinned at her friend. "Oh, you know, it's probably as likely as our resisting dunking them." Eida laughed good-naturedly.

The girls were on their way down to the river. It was the hottest part of day, and they had just finishing scrubbing the floors in the dining hall. Others had cleaned elsewhere in the castle, and they were all going to cool off in the river, ostensibly wading in water up to their knees. The clothes they wore for splashing were simple, sleeveless, linen garments that ran from shoulder to knee like a tunic. They would dry quickly in the sun.

As they came down the hill toward the river, they met up with Thiesa and the Whiels girls, Brea and Cilla. Arru suddenly realized the sisters had also experienced the loss of their father, though in their case, it was a tragic loss when they were very young, and now they had Iekaruga as their stepfather. That blessing made her glad for them, but provoked a slight jealousy in her heart.

Thiesa turned toward them, and Arru marveled for the umpteenth time at the girl's intense violet eyes. Her long brown hair was tied up on her head in preparation for play in the river, but her lighter colored mane still flowed beautifully down her back. Arru was at times tempted to alter her form to match her Fearian friends—she was a metamorphic mage, after all—but she decided that that would reflect poorly on her sense of self.

Thiesa greeted them with a warm smile and an energetic wave. "Hey! Come on! The guys are already down there having fun without us."

Eida responded a little smugly. "Oh really? I seriously doubt they could be having fun without us."

Arru giggled, Brea and Cilla grinned, and Thiesa mused, "I suppose their lives are substantially duller when we're not around." Laughing together, they made their way down to the river.

At ten years old, Cilla was the youngest among them, and Thiesa, along with her brothers, was the oldest at thirteen. Arru was still amazed at the very idea of Fearian litters. She couldn't imagine having that many children at one time. She flushed a little, as she felt like it was probably inappropriate for someone her age to be thinking about such things.

As they crossed the road and the riverbank came into full view, Arru could see Pyx sitting on the bank, a fairly safe distance from the water. He was not participating, of course, just making sure no one got hurt. Normally he would be accompanied closely by Addie, but she was back at the castle working on her wedding dress, a garment which would have to be made by hand. Pyx looked rather distracted, but who could blame him, with his wedding fast approaching.

Arru thought it rather funny that he was the one who watched out for them, given that some of them were starting to get taller than he was. She had learned that Pyx was a type of Fearian referred to as sea caste, and his people were often very short. His tail was like that of a fox, and there was a suspicious reddish cast to his hair, mane, and tail. Despite his somewhat cuddly appearance, Pyx could be stern when he needed to be.

As they joined Marral, Harto, Byrn, and Zollen, Thiesa cupped her hands around her mouth and shouted, "Okay, you guys, how did you possibly finish your chores first?"

Marral laughed as he tossed her a head-sized wooden ball, wrapped tightly with animal skins to prevent a direct hit from being too painful. He spoke with an exaggerated wink. "Well, we were dusting, and that never takes us long!"

Thiesa regarded Zollen with suspicion, but he just shrugged as he replied cryptically, "All for the greater good, my sister."

Eida crossed her arms, replying less cryptically. "Good? Sounds more like laziness to me."

Zollen glared at her, his annoyance evident, but then looked away without further response. The two of them had a strange, unspoken rivalry going on. Arru couldn't really figure out if it was just a friendly competitive thing, or something far more serious. Either way, they were often at odds, though mostly ones of logic, not so much anything close to physical fighting.

Thiesa spoke in a commanding voice. "All right, it's girls versus boys!"

Byrn's face immediately darkened. "Um, can we just choose up sides at random? No offense, but you girls are taller than we are, which makes things kind of unfair."

Arru smiled. Byrn was the explorer among them. His dark red hair was not vastly different from her own, but of course she didn't have a long ringed tail like he did, nor a mane, which in Byrn's case was about the same color as his hair. Of course, at his age, his mane was shaved from the neck down, per Fearian cultural precedent. He was not as deep a thinker as Zollen, or the voice of reason that Harto was, but he was always interested in pursuing new and interesting ventures.

Zollen asserted, "Don't worry, Byrn. We can compensate in other ways."

But the game only partially confirmed his statement. It was close, but this time the girls won. Zollen sighed as he looked toward the sky and said, "I guess we don't have time for a rematch." It was more of a resignation than an actual question.

Eida tried to sound encouraging. "It's all right. I am sure you will win the next one."

Cilla and Brea giggled, and Harto echoed Byrn as he lamented, "We aren't ever going to win such a mis-weighted contest. How am I supposed to pass the ball when all the opponents are taller than I am?"

Cilla spoke up a tad too tauntingly as she corrected him. "I am not taller than you are, Harto."

He rolled his eyes. "Yeah, but you're faster than I am, so you might as well be."

She scrunched up her face and stated bluntly, "That doesn't even make any sense."

Marral broke in with a discreet lack of levity. "Oh, but it made sense to me. Maybe it's just beyond you."

Brea eyed him skeptically as she replied in her sister's defense. "Yeah, somehow I don't think that's the case here."

They all strolled to the old retaining wall that sat below the street. It had once held the river at bay when it was in flood stages. Now it held nine dripping children, who warmed themselves in the summer sun.

Thiesa thought aloud, "What do you think

Father and the rest of them are doing right now?"

Byrn sounded vaguely disappointed as he answered. "I wish I could go on adventures with Father."

Marral gave an exaggerated sigh. "I am sure they are viewing breathtaking vistas without us."

Zollen's gaze was distant, and he spoke with a measure of maturity that belied his age. "I doubt it's as wonderful as you suspect. The climb will be difficult, and I overheard Father say that there were dark things in those mountains. Things not from this world."

Arru shivered unconsciously, but Eida stated firmly, "Maybe there are, but I have seen how Creed can fight, and I have confidence that they can face anything there and still return safely."

There was something to be said for Eida's experience. No one else there had really seen their father, or those he took with him, engaged in the art of the mage other than Eida. Brea and Cilla had been saved by Achron and Hanni, but they weren't clear on the details due to the nature of the event and what they had gone through at the time. Arru hadn't actually seen them do much of anything in her own rescue, aside from Hanni's immolation, and Achron's breaking of the cursed bracelet she wore. She wondered just exactly what they were like in action, real action.

* * *

A brilliant beam of light sliced three of the creatures in half. A rapid spray of white fireballs reduced two more of the strange black lizard-like things to ash. Hanni remained calm, nearly motionless, her staff raised slightly in preparation for striking at the next threat that dared to raise its head. The remains of the creatures they had slain faded away before them.

Iekaruga muttered, "Very curious. They must be

made out of pure mage power to leave no trace when they are vanquished."

Creed sighed, relaxing his arm and letting it drop to his side. "I think that is the last of them."

Achron stood behind them, and with him Viwy and Sheena. Viwy touched the end of his staff thoughtfully, and then confirmed Creed's suspicions. "Yes, that appears to be true . . . for now."

Creed had mixed feelings about Sheena's participation in the endeavor of investigating the Aeinor mountains. It was a delight not being separated from her, but the reality was that they faced potentially great danger. Achron had insisted on it out of concern that they might indeed find that danger. Sheena was critical to his being able to fight more difficult enemies. Creed wasn't sold on the idea personally; between Hanni and himself, it seemed like they should have sufficient strength to deal with anything that showed up. However, he wasn't in charge. Achron was.

Iekaruga was there to shut the sigil gate down, and Viwy was there to make sure nothing vile sneaked up on them. Creed had been surprised at Iekaruga's willingness to come, what with his son Fennis being only a few months old. But Dorra had assured him she could care for the baby herself, and that he would regret not going to see some new sigil structure.

They moved on through a narrow pass and down into a valley strewn with ancient ruins. As they descended, Creed pointed and said, "There!"

Achron looked where he had gestured and nodded. "Yes, that's it."

Among the ruins was a stone platform covered in intricate sigils. A glimmering sheet of distorted air hung over the platform, affording a view into the other world. It was a bright, if cool, day in the Aeinor mountains. The valley was filled with a tall, soft grass and the occasional wildflower, but aside from the buildings and the gate, there wasn't anything else to be seen. Through the gate, however, there filtered a strange bluish light that contrasted strongly with the pleasant summer day.

As they approached the gate, Sheena brushed her hands through the grass and murmured so that only Creed could hear. "You know, it's really rather romantic here."

He tried not to groan. It was true, and it was also true that his asking her father for her hand in marriage was long overdue. However, right now didn't feel like the best time to be considering something that made him nervous by just thinking about it.

Iekaruga began to investigate the sigils, musing, "Ah, good, this is similar to the others. It shouldn't be any trouble to deactivate it."

Achron looked steadily at the place on the other side of the gate and raised his hand abruptly. "Wait." Every set of eyes swung toward him in curiosity.

Achron spoke slowly, as he seemed to be thinking out loud. "With those creatures coming through the sigil gate at a high rate, then there must be a demon gate not far from it. We would be in the wrong to just close this gate without first dealing with the real problem."

Viwy instantly stated his concern. "I don't know, Achron. There are a fair number of Fearians who are not so fond of us humans. I wouldn't want to be banished back to this world separated from the protection offered by Creed and Hanni."

Achron acknowledged Viwy's concern with a nod. "Yes, if we are separated, we should meet here at the gate. So long as we destroy the demon gate, we shouldn't be in any real danger here in this valley."

He met the gaze of each one, and Hanni spoke

softly. "Let us end this aberration."

Iekaruga assented, and Creed spoke as Sheena took his hand. "I am up for it."

Creed felt a little bad that his league had been planning to assault the mage tower that lay somewhere on the other side of the gate. Obviously, having another league's tower just north of one of their own was viewed as a risk they could not take. The sylph league hadn't technically been an enemy of theirs, but Kurri's tower was a liability, at risk of being captured by one of their enemies.

He had been taken out of duty before the plans for a siege of the tower were completed, so he wasn't sure what they would find on the other side of the gate. Would it be obvious if his own league had destroyed the tower? Or would he find that another league got there first? Creed supposed he would know shortly, but he didn't know if he wanted to know.

They slipped through the gate to the Fearian side of the world, and were immediately arrested by what they saw on the other side. Despite the diverse experiences represented by the members of their group, it was like nothing any of them had seen.

* * *

Creed stood just a step within the portal, staring in awe. It was vaguely the same mountain valley, but the entire thing was surrounded by an enormous shell of ice. Long, spindly columns ran from the height of the dome to the ground. Water fell from the ceiling in a slow but steady dripping. The air was quite cold, but completely still.

Then the horrid stench of decay stuck him full in the face, and Creed grimaced at what it probably meant. The place had a gloomy atmosphere, as the sunlight that penetrated the thick ice shell was minimal.

Creed caught motion out of the corner of his eye, and responded with a blinding beam of energy from the tip of his staff. The large creature, like those they had slain on the way to the gate, slumped lifelessly to the ground before fading away. Sheena came up behind him and covered her nose with her hand. "What is that terrible smell?"

Creed took in the sight of the various brown and black lumps scattered across the muddy scape before them. "You really don't want to know."

Unlike the other valley, this one, deprived of light for an indeterminate length of time, was nothing but mud, rocks, and slow-moving water flows. Also, corpses, lots of corpses in various states of decay. Some were cloth and bones, while others still retained some semblance of their form. Viwy shuddered. "Rats. Of all the times I should have stayed home."

Iekaruga pointed with his staff as he said, "Over there!"

Following his direction, they looked and saw a gigantic column of thick, translucent ice, and within that column a structure was just barely visible. Creed could hardly believe his eyes. It was undoubtedly Kurri's tower, trapped in solid ice. Despite the size and height of the tower, it was completely embedded in ice that rose all the way to the dome far above it.

Achron cautioned in a low voice, "This entire area seems to be sealed in ice, which means the demon gate is under here somewhere."

Creed turned toward Hanni. "The whole place is melting. Be careful what you do, or it might come down on our heads." She nodded, but remained with her staff at the ready. Hanni was incredibly powerful, even for a prodigy, and for a moment Creed wondered if she could simply melt it all in a single act.

Creed halted sharply. It reminded him of something, something he had not thought of in a long time. Achron must have noticed his sudden hesitation, and asked him, "What is it, Creed?"

He shook his head as he dismissed the notion. "Oh, uh, nothing really." Achron appeared to suspect that was not the whole story, but he left it stand.

They advanced slowly, avoiding the mud, muck, and decay as much as possible. A strange scraping noise came from the direction of the tower that grew louder as they moved that way. As they circled one of the columns, the source of the noise became apparent. One of the dark lizard creatures was protruding half a body length out of the ice, clawing and wriggling in an attempt to free itself. Apparently, the ice around it was still hard enough that it was incapable of escaping.

Iekaruga expressed his thoughts on the matter. "I see. This entire area was once a single frozen sphere of ice." He swept his hand at the scene around them. "These were caught in the ice, and fell out of it as it thawed, but under these conditions they have not decayed as much as one would suspect. Presumably, this has been in thaw since the mage war then."

Viwy shook his head in disbelief as he murmured, "Surely not even a mage could make this much ice?"

Creed looked down at the ground as he spoke somberly. "It's . . . it's a mage burst." He didn't have to look at his friends to know what they were thinking. He gazed up again toward the tower. "Occasionally, a mage can release all their power in a single burst. It's not something most people are able to do, not even many prodigies." Creed looked at Achron with a blank gaze as he finished. "It's also invariably fatal, because it costs the wielder the normal reserve power that protects them from their own abilities."

Eyeing the struggling creature, Creed summoned an energy orb from the ground. A beam of light severed the freed part of the creature from the stuck part. It twitched in the mud for a moment before it faded from reality.

Achron examined the ice dome far overhead. "It's difficult to know how stable this thing is. While the Aegeis can protect us, it can't protect both us and the sigil gate. I would hate to think of where the next nearest route home is."

Viwy noted whimsically, "We really need to get our own gold mage." Achron chuckled lightly, but Creed was more concerned about their safety than Achron's humor.

Sheena provided her own insight into the situation. "I guess this explains why the appearance of these creatures in the Aeinor mountains is a recent phenomenon."

Creed smiled at her astute observation, and then continued advancing toward the tower as he spoke. "That makes sense. Now we need to find that gate as quickly as possible. This place is unnerving."

Maneuvering around an ice column, Viwy stepped gingerly past a bloated corpse. "Just what happened here anyway?" Creed glanced about the slowly decaying carnage as he posited an explanation. "It looks like the vale league attacked this tower. Apparently they were winning, and some sylph league mage decided that it would be better to lose their life than lose their pride."

Sheena questioned hesitantly, "Are you sure it was a matter of pride, and not a matter of saving those they cared about?"

Creed considered that for a moment before responding. "A mage's tower is an irreplaceable mark of their power and authority. Only the great mages had the abilities to construct such magnificent structures. To lose it to the enemy would be the height of shame. Since a mage burst would ensure the end of nearly every mage caught in the blast, I am pretty sure it wasn't about saving anyone."

They came shortly upon the black gate. It was still partly covered in ice, not far from the frozen wall that encased the tower. Creed breathed a sigh of relief to see that the gate was not part of a supporting pillar, or when the gate was destroyed it would take everything with it.

Iekaruga murmured, "It's fortunate for us that it hasn't fully thawed, or we would have faced a much greater opposition than we did."

Achron began to glow as he took his staff in both hands. "Stand back." The rest of them stepped away, and a burst of white light reduced the gate, and the surrounding ice, into powder. A loud cracking sound reverberated throughout the valley, and water fell heavily from far above them. Everyone held their breath as they waited for the echoes to fade.

Chapter 28

After several strained moments of waiting to find out if the whole ice shell was going to come cascading down on them, Achron gestured toward the sigil gate, and the group turned to make their way back as quickly as possible. Hanni's voice stopped them. "Wait! Is that . . . a person?"

In the direction she indicated, the faint outline of some figure near the entrance of the tower was barely discernable in the dim light. Viwy whispered nervously, his eyes darting back and forth. "We should really get going about now."

Hanni ignored him and started carefully toward the tower. Achron looked a little nervous himself, glancing at the ceiling, but he followed her anyway. Viwy muttered mostly to himself, "Oh, for the love of . . . we are all going to get stuck in ice, aren't we?"

Iekaruga walked past him with a shrug. "Well, except for the furthest person from Achron. That person will just be crushed to death."

Viwy's eyes widened substantially, and he hurried after them with a desperate cry. "W-wait up, guys!"

Creed seriously doubted that the Aegeis was so short-ranged, and he took his time, hand in hand with

Sheena, picking his way through the muck after Hanni and the others.

Hanni seemed deep in thought. Upon reaching the sheer wall of ice, which rose to breathtaking heights before it blossomed into a massive fluted shape that held the ice dome up, she placed her palm on its hard, smooth surface.

Just an arm's length beyond her was a figure, frozen solid in the ice. He appeared quite young. His face was contorted in concentration, his eyes closed. He was suspended above the step that led into the tower, his dark blue robes frozen in place, as though some invisible wind had riled them. In both hands he grasped a long, clear, crystal staff whose shaft meshed flawlessly with a fist-sized aquamarine. The oval-shaped gem was flattened and symmetrically faceted on both of its broad surfaces.

Viwy made the tactless observation, "Wow, boy, is he dead."

Achron seemed far more thoughtful as he peered intently at the figure. "Well, not necessarily. Cold maintains things. If he froze quickly enough, he might be revivable if he thawed equally quickly."

That sounded farfetched in Creed's opinion. Freezing had obviously been the demise of the rest of the natural entities they had encountered.

Hanni began to glow with a red light, stating, "Uncertainty in life is better than leaving him to certainty in death."

Creed appreciated her sentiment, but seriously doubted what she would do could work. Sheena backed away slightly, concern written on her face. "That's a nice thought, Hanni, but what if it brings the whole place down?"

Hanni hesitated and looked to Achron for guidance. "Father?" Achron studied the figure a moment longer, and then nodded.

Without any further warning, Hanni stepped to the side and pressed her staff to the ice. Instantly, a large sphere around the boy became water, and the melted ice rushed out onto the ground. Iekaruga pulled back quickly to avoid getting wet, and Viwy let out a yelp as he half-danced, half-splashed away from the sudden flow of surprisingly warm water. His success in the matter was partial at best.

Achron bent and plucked the previously frozen mage out of the water as it flowed by, and, his own skin glowing faintly, touched the boy's forehead gently. The boy breathed out sharply, expelling water, and coughed a few times before he muttered something incomprehensible. He did not open his eyes or stir beyond that.

A sudden, loud snap rang out. For a moment, a terrible silence prevailed as everyone stared nervously, at the ice and at each other, afraid that any sound might escalate their precarious situation. Their caution was clearly insufficient, as the steady crackling noise continued. Spidery fissures in the main ice column radiated outward and upward from the point where Hanni had freed the mage. Achron's soft but stern command set them into motion. "To the gate, quickly!"

Viwy scooped up the crystal staff, and they all ran for the sigil gate. Creed narrowly evaded slipping on the muddy terrain twice, and caught Sheena when she stumbled. An enormous cracking sound filled the air, and the gigantic central ice column snapped about halfway up and fell toward them. Creed slid to a stop as he whirled to face this new threat. It felt mildly inappropriate, but he slammed the butt of his staff into the mud abruptly before throwing his hand forward. Dozens of orbs of yellow-green light flew out of the ground, and focused beams of energy sliced the column into hundreds of smaller pieces. Creed flipped his staff horizontally, and holding it with both hands, fired a single large beam of energy in a short burst. The sudden heat vaporized the middle of the column, and the subsequent explosion hurled the fragments, which were still the size of a horse, out of trajectories that intersected with him and his friends.

Creed wheeled about and grabbed Sheena's hand, continuing their flight. Many of the large ice shards he had produced crashed through other, smaller supporting columns. A particularly loud snapping sound nearby caused him to turn just in time to see a log-sized chunk of ice come crashing down above his head. It instantly became a rather hot shower. He looked gratefully at Hanni, who stood resolute, her right hand extended, her left hand holding her staff. The air around her was distorted by an intense heat, and she glowed faintly with a fiery light.

A massive piece of the dome's ceiling slid free with a deafening boom, and it fell directly over the ice-encased tower. Creed caught just a glimpse of it tearing through the tower as though it were made of paper. More of the ceiling rapidly collapsed outward from the gap the first piece had left.

A second later he was standing in a much more serene valley on the human side of the world. The sigil gate portal flickered and vanished. Creed sighed with relief. They were safe once again.

Viwy scowled with disgust at the mud that caked his clothes all the way up to his waist, vehemently informing no one, "Great! Okay, so next time, I get to pick the destination for our little adventures. And it won't involve mud, ice, or those demon things!"

* * *

Everyone watched as Achron set the boy he had revived on the ground in the soft grass. Creed was a little apprehensive about this person's response to the sudden change in circumstances. It had been hard enough for him to make the transition when he was brought back, and this would probably be worse. Creed took a couple of steps back, pulling Sheena's hand so she would do the same. She did so just in time, for the boy jerked sharply and clambered to his feet.

He shook his head and rubbed at his eyes, blinking in the bright sunlight and swinging his arm around frantically. "You won't have it! Not even if I am the last one standing . . . you shall never . . . never . . . ."

He stumbled, taking a step backward, but caught himself, staggering sideways as he glared at Hanni, and then Creed. "Not the vale league, nor the star league, nor anyone!" He raised his arm in a sharp, but slightly erratic arc, and the faintest poof of snowflakes formed in a trail after his hand.

Viwy rolled his eyes as he muttered, "Oh, but you are the last one standing."

The snowflakes promptly melted and blew away in the breeze as a mist. The boy stared in shock, and tried again with no greater success.

Creed informed them, "His power is depleted, and it will probably take days to return."

The blue-robed mage teetered slightly, and Achron caught his arm. He demanded, "What is the meaning of this!" He glanced around for the first time, and his expression darkened. "A-and why am I on this side! Where is the gate? Where is Kurri's tower!?"

Sheena tried to answer him gently. "The tower is gone. You were trapped there, in ice, but now it's . . . ." She looked down soberly.

The young mage shook his head, ripping his arm free from Achron, his eyes wide as he shouted, "NO! I-it can't be!" He stepped back and put one hand to his head. "W-what was I doing? I can't . . . can't . . . ." He continued to back away from them. He repeated his previous snow-inducing gesture with no more effect than before. There was a sudden shocked recognition on his face, and he gasped and sank slowly down to his knees.

Hanni walked up to him and held out her hand. "Come on, we have to go home."

He scowled at her. "I would never go anywhere with a star league member. You might as well just kill me now!"

Hanni was not the least bit perturbed by his animosity, and she replied coolly, "The star league no longer exists, and don't be stupid."

He flinched slightly at her comment and stared at her hand, which was still extended toward him. He looked skeptically at her and then turned away. "I-I can't trust you."

It was unfortunate that the rune-shaped scars that marred her face were uncorrectable. Not even Harku, a prodigy metamorphic mage, had been able to correct the problem. It apparently ran far deeper than the surface. It didn't really seem to bother Hanni, but Creed felt like it reflected in a single instance everything that was wrong with the mages of his time.

Hanni remained motionless. Achron sighed and walked past her to grab the mage again and pull him to his feet, stating with an obvious lack of humor, "My daughter means you no harm. I am Achron. What is your name?"

The boy yanked his arm from Achron's grasp once more, and wobbled a little but stayed upright as he fixated on Achron's staff. "Y-you're a white mage, are you not?" Achron nodded, and he demanded, "Tell me if this wretched star leaguer speaks anything true."

Achron grimaced and looked toward the sky as

327

he explained. "Nearly three millennia ago, the great mage war claimed the lives of most of the mages. The leagues vanished, and the great mage towers remain desolate to this day. Nearly all of the ones we have seen have been little more than ruins. The two sides of the world are now mostly isolated, with little intermixing of Fearians and humans. I suppose you must have been trapped there in that massive ice sphere since that time."

The young mage studied each of them in turn, as if he were searching for verification of this story, then dropped his gaze to the ground. "It must be . . . the mage burst."

His face hardened as he shouted at Achron, "Why did you save me! I died a noble death!"

Achron tipped his head at Hanni. "I didn't save you. Hanni did. I merely revived you."

Viwy, who was busy trying to remove as much mud from his clothes as possible by scraping the fabric with a brick, looked up from his endeavor to state in a demeaning manner, "So, this is the part where you take her hand and thank her for saving your frozen posterior."

The blue-robed mage recoiled, and would have crossed his arms indignantly, but instead flailed them slightly to keep himself from falling over. "I have nothing to say to the likes of her!"

Iekaruga spoke for them all. "Let's go home, friends. The demon gate has been closed, and I can only assume the sigil gate was destroyed on the other side. We should be on our way."

Hanni dropped her hand to her side and headed toward where they had left their horses just beyond the rim of the valley. She seemed stoic, but Creed wondered what was going on inside. It was hard for him to tell, as this Hanni was a strange mixture of the cousin he knew growing up, and yet an entirely another person following her complete memory loss. He and the rest of them walked back toward the edge of the mountain-sheltered grassy oasis.

Only Achron remained. The ice mage watched them silently for a moment, and then, looking a little embarrassed, he spoke with resignation. "I-I am Leen. I should probably travel with you until we reach some semblance of civilization."

Achron shrugged as he turned, hiding a smile. "Sure, if that's what you want."

Creed doubted that the guy was worth taking with them, but he didn't really have any say in the matter. Leen looked to be about ten years old. His hair was a dusty blond color and cut quite short. His green eyes gave him a rather penetrating stare, but he was clearly still recovering from the shock of being frozen.

When they reached the horses, Achron addressed Creed first, before speaking to Leen. "Sheena is going to have to ride with you, Creed. Leen, you can take this horse."

Leen's eyes bespoke his dismay as he approached the animal, but Creed was too distracted to notice if the ice mage actually said anything. Sheena was standing almost unbearably close to him. He gave her a wry expression, but she merely grinned. It was obvious that riding double up with him was not a burden on her.

Viwy helped Leen on his horse and offered him some cursory instructions before handing the young mage back his staff. Leen looked at the staff thoughtfully for a moment, and then frantically tried to prevent his horse from walking off in a random direction. Creed groaned internally. It was going to be a long journey home.

* * *

Creed stood in front of the modest wooden door. He could have been intensely admiring the subtly but pleasantly carved inlay that reminded him of vines on a trellis. Or maybe it was the silver-trimmed metalwork of the hinges and the handle that could have held his rapt attention.

The only other person in the hallway nudged him gently, whispering, "Come on, ciega. It's not like he bites."

Creed muttered, "Don't rush me. I am trying to be ready for anything. I mean, what if he says no, huh?"

Sheena chuckled lightly. "Don't be ridiculous. He thinks very highly of you. Why would he say no?"

Creed wiped his hands on his tunic before staring at them in displeasure. "Yeah, tell that to my excessively sweating palms."

Heaving a sigh, Sheena reached past him and rapped loudly on the door. Creed glared at her, but jerked his gaze back to the door as it swung open. Achron loomed before him, holding the door ajar. "Creed? Did you need something?"

Creed noticed that Sheena was suddenly and conspicuously absent from the hallway, and he swallowed as he started a little awkwardly. "Uh, yes. I need to talk to you . . ." Achron arched one eyebrow and made himself comfortable against the doorframe. Creed finished hastily, ". . . in private."

Achron opened the door wide, stepping out of the way and gesturing for him to enter. "Sure. Come on in."

Achron's study was always in a mild state of disarray. Half-read books were piled on his desk, several documents stacked haphazardly on one corner, and some map lay crumpled in the middle of what would have otherwise been a clear space.

Achron nodded toward a chair in front of his desk, but Creed shook his head, swallowing again unnecessarily. "Ah, no, I think I should stand."

Achron tilted his head slightly and gave him a skeptical look, but only said, "Okay. So what do you need to talk about?"

Creed took a deep breath and tried to calm his pounding pulse. "I shouldn't have put this off so long, but Achron, I have to ask for your blessing concerning . . . ."

To his shock, Achron cut him off. "Absolutely not."

Creed flinched and stammered, "B-b-but why?"

Achron swept his hand through the air, his tone completely pragmatic. "Keena and I have already talked about this, and for your sake, to say nothing of Sheena's, we cannot allow this. Whether you like it or not."

Creed clenched his fists, feeling the nails dig into his palms, which were no longer so sweaty, and objected. "What! Achron, I love her!"

Achron blinked rapidly, his arms dropping to his sides. "You lost me there. Aren't you talking about leaving?"

Creed spoke with some exasperation. "No, I am talking about marrying Sheena!"

A sheepish expression spread over Achron's face. "Oh . . . uh . . . so, Keena and I have talked about that, too, and we think that would be best sooner rather than later."

There was a moment of awkward silence, and then Achron asked, "So, you are sure you're not planning on leaving then?"

Creed felt like he was talking to a wall, but he restrained his annoyance as much as he could. "I am not leaving, but reasons for doing so are popping in the most unlikely places."

Achron raised his hands defensively. "Sorry, just trying to clear the air." He glanced at the door as he

331

added, "And you had better let me talk with Keena before you broadcast your intentions for Sheena." He put his hand to his mouth, musing, "Though, at this point it would hardly be a surprise to anyone who isn't overtly blind and deaf."

Creed felt heat rise in his face as he crossed his arms and stated, "Hey, it wasn't that obvious."

The corners of Achron's mouth turned upward. "Sheena wasn't even pretending to be subtle, you know."

Creed sighed as he turned and walked to the door, commenting ruefully, "I don't think she knows how to be subtle." He stopped at the door as his expression grew serious. "She wouldn't have gotten past my defenses if she had been subtle." Achron nodded soberly.

Creed knew that his love for Sheena had been a hard-won battle that Sheena had fought alone for years without faltering. He didn't understand what she saw in him, but he was certain that he was the one to gain from their union.

Back in the hallway, he had scarcely closed the door behind him before Sheena tackled him, almost knocking him to the floor. "See! That was painless!"

Creed replied flatly as he gently tried to shift her off him to no effect. "Then why does it feel like I nearly died?" She laughed, leaning close to him with a fervent light in her eyes.

He failed again to pull away from her. "Hey, we aren't married yet. For all you know, he said, 'not a chance.'"

A sly grin played across her face. "Like Father would say no to you, and if you weren't so hesitant, we could have been married a while ago." Creed rolled his eyes, but as he looked down at the radiant smile of his wife-to-be, he found it hard not to be caught up in her contagious excitement.

* * *

"I just don't like him, Achron."

Keena spoke with a reserved distaste as the two of them strolled along the riverbank. They had taken to evening walks together to have some measure of privacy in sharing their concerns, opinions, and perspectives. Hona Castle had become a rather busy place, and there wasn't much room for private conversation within the walls. Achron, for his part, listened to her complaint thoughtfully.

It had been several weeks since he had returned with yet another hapless mage connected to a less than ideal past, but this time the young man in question was haughty, and treated some of the others with contempt. What bothered Keena in particular was how he seemed to despise Tonis, who, in her mind, was a truly precious person to have among them. Leen, on the other hand, was not someone she was remotely impressed with.

Achron replied soothingly. "I know he is a little rough around the edges, but maybe he just needs some positive examples to learn from? I can't say that I was a star model of gentility when I was his age."

Keena hedged around his dismissal of the problem. "He isn't our child, and that makes correcting him more awkward. I just don't like the way he acts toward the other children. If he is going to stay with us, then you must lay down the rules to him. Otherwise, I have to strongly insist that he leave."

Achron nodded but asked, "Okay, but where would he go? And do we really want a powerful but naïve mage running around out there, waiting to be picked up by the first crazed noble or warmonger who realizes they can

333

use such a person to their own advantage?"

Keena sighed, flicking her tail with consternation. "I guess not, but it isn't fair that the others have to deal with him." Achron chuckled. She gave him a reproving glare, but then smiled as she sighed whimsically. "Maybe I am just worried about this too much."

Silence fell between them as she wondered what would become of their family. Hona Castle and its surrounding area were still largely desolate, the city of Niado an inhospitable ruin. For now, they had sufficient means, but concern rose in her mind about where they would continue to get enough food as the children got older and began to form their own families. They were not equipped to perpetually meet the needs of a growing population. With three of their daughters on the verge of marriage, they were undoubtedly going to have more people to care for soon enough.

Thinking on that did cause her to remember her own initial hesitation about Creed. He had proved to be an asset, and more, a friend to her oldest daughter. Painful as it was to admit that she had judged him wrongly based on his lack of Fearian culture, now he was part of their inner circle as it were, though she still held his adventuresome abduction of Sheena against him. It gave her pause to reconsider her opposition to Leen.

Keena returned to her concerns about their future needs. The wealth of Empleheim was not endless, and they were steadily consuming the reserves in the treasury, as substantial as they were. Clothing was wearing out, and surely the aged trees in the orchard would eventually expire.

Aside from the immediate challenges of providing for such a large family, there was also their rising presence among their neighbors. Fear and dread of the "curse" of Empleheim seemed a sufficient deterrent to the average person, preventing them from having unwanted guests, but that could not last indefinitely. With every foray they took beyond their home, there was an apparent increase in the awareness of their existence.

While Keena could envision a perfect scenario where everyone stayed in Empleheim through the foreseeable future, she doubted that could be realized, or was even desirable for everyone, especially not Leen.

She watched the river water ripple over and around the edges of the bank. Inexorably flowing along its path, unwilling to be halted by any barrier. Its course was set, and it would flow down that course regardless of what came in its way. Yet, ironically, its course was set precisely by barriers, the banks, that forced it to have such a linear and certain destination.

Achron interrupted her musings. "What's on your mind, my love?"

She smiled fondly at him. "I don't want you to go out and about on superfluous quests about ancient history, but at the same time, I recognize the necessity of reaching out beyond ourselves to ensure that we can continue peaceably."

Achron pursed his lips and returned to gazing out over the river. "Sometimes I think you take things way too seriously. I would have been satisfied with, 'Oh, nothing really.'"

Keena stopped at the edge of the bank, eyeing him with mild annoyance. Achron cleared his throat a little uneasily, stepping to the edge himself and commenting, "That water sure is flowing quickly at this part of the river." She wrinkled her nose at his infuriatingly weak attempt to transition the conversation.

There was a loud splash and a spluttering noise. Achron found himself sitting in the water following the firm shove Keena had given him. The river might have been swift, but it was hardly deep by the bank. Achron spat and coughed as he expressed his displeasure at his inundating. "Hey! What did you do that for?"

Keena tossed her head with feigned aloofness. "You're not taking me seriously, so I thought it wouldn't hurt to freshen up your perspective a little."

Achron smirked. "My beloved Keena, of course I am taking you seriously. Just not your objections." Keena sighed a little, but offered him her hand. He took it, and she immediately knew from the look in his eyes that her reflex probably hadn't been the wisest one.

With a sharp tug, Keena joined Achron in the river, albeit a little more gracefully than his entry into the water had been. She glared at her husband. "Did you HAVE to do that?!"

He smiled slyly. "Well, I figured it would allow us to both reach a unity of position, serious or otherwise." Keena snorted contemptuously, but it failed to prevent her from laughing, and the combined sound was far more comic than if she had tried to be funny. Achron erupted into laughter, and she promptly shared in his mirth.

He pulled her into a soggy embrace, the river still steadily tugging at them, as though it wanted them to come with it on its certain course. His gaze was filled with warm affection. "I do love you, Keena, sodden, serious, or . . . ."

She interrupted him with a suggestion. "Sweet?"

Achron smiled and with a tender hand brushed her dripping hair back from her face. "Well, that's nearly always true."

She returned his loving smile and whispered, "Nearly?"

Achron merely winked at her before giving her a passionate kiss.

MAGUS INDEXIUM
A Condensed Guide to the World

Achron *(AY-kron)* **Windslo**

Biography

A thousand years ago, Adderil Windslo was the leader of the kingdom of Empleheim's Order of White Mages, which renamed itself the Order of the White Lion following Adderil's defeat of a neighboring kingdom's black mages. After Fearian casters on the other side of space attempted to curse him, he and Empleheim were forced out of time for a millennium, during which time he took the name Achron. With Keena's help, he restored Empleheim to time's flow, and they, their twenty-four children, and their friends are building a home in the old city of Niado.

Mage Power

Achron is a grand white mage with powerful healing capabilities. Following the Empleheim event, he possesses the ability to move in and out of time and to slow time around himself at will. He wields the relic staff Tianna, the silver star. He holds the honorary title the White Lion of Empleheim.

Aegeis *(ah-JEE-us)*

The Aegeis is a shield that rests atop the relic staff Tianna, the silver star, and is cast into a large, translucent sphere when the staff is tapped on a surface. It resists even the most powerful of attacks, but it permits one with a gentle touch to pass through unhindered.

Ahnya *(AHN-yah)* **Quirieyo**

Biography
With her sister Prinial, the mountain caste Fearian Ahyna is one of the first female Fearian prodigies, due to the accidental influence of a fertility rune pendant she was given as a child. She is a powerful mage, and apprentice and protector to the sigil mage Iekaruga. Others know her as distracted and wild, but she is developing a close friendship with Kraysin.

Mage Power
Ahnya is a prodigy grand water mage. She is highly proficient at controlling water from a variety of sources and using it in both defense and attack. She holds the relic staff Leviathan, the raging sea.

Arru *(AH-roo)* **Loon**

Biography
Arru, sister of Harku, is the only living red gryphon of the gryphon clan. Due to a cursed charm she was forced to wear, she was confined to the darkness of the clan's cave until Achron released her from its curse. Her father intended to have her marry her brother according to clan traditions that a golden gryphon must wed a red

gryphon. But when Harku brought Rin to the clan cave, he sneaked Arru out in the form of a mouse. She now lives at Hona Castle and spends much time with the other children her age.

Mage Power
Arru is a metamorphic mage, but she does not often use her power, deferring to her brother's greater abilities as a prodigy.

Aspect (or mage aspect)

Definition
All people, both Fearian and human, are born with an innate mage aspect. In most individuals, the aspect is too weak to be utilized as mage ability, but in some, the aspect is strong enough to be grasped and refined. With the exception of prodigies, the mage aspect remains dormant until the person reaches physical maturity. Prodigies, however, are able to access their powers at unusually early ages, and are exceptionally powerful mages because of this. Aspects are divided into two exclusive groups, with twelve aspects belonging to humans and twelve belonging to Fearians.

A mage is normally protected from their own aspect by a measure of power held in reserve; however, occasionally a mage possesses sufficient strength to deplete even this reserve and release a pulse of mage power that encompasses a large area surrounding the mage. Most often, a mage burst is fatal, since the reserve power is no longer present to protect the mage.

When circumstances dictate that a mage needs to employ capabilities beyond normal physical capacities, the mage may invoke focus, a state in which they experience heightened senses and strength, together with decreased interference from emotions and distractions.

Air mage aspect

The manipulation of air is the domain of the air aspect. Despite the seeming similarity of a shared medium, the sonic aspect is very different (see Sonic mage aspect). Air mages can compress, accelerate, and expand air in both narrow and broad applications. Nearly any inanimate object can be turned into a high-speed projectile, and an intensely focused pulse of air can cut cleanly through an armored soldier. The air aspect is limited to Fearians.

Black mage aspect

While wielders of the aspect of decay, known as black mages, have a long and sordid history, the aspect itself is not intrinsically evil. Decay is a natural process necessary for the continuance of ordinary life, and its creative use can be benevolent, though it is the opinion of most that animation of the deceased is perhaps less benign. The black aspect is a human aspect.

Earth mage aspect

The aspect of earth is easy to understand, but difficult to perfect. Earth mages can alter the principle components of substances from one thing to another. Transmutation by any other name, it is extremely versatile as an ability, but mostly one of utility. Substances with greater numbers of components require more skill and power to make a conversion, while pure substances are the easiest. For practical reasons, the earth aspect is limited to the inert, stationary, and non-living. The earth aspect is a Fearian aspect.

Energy mage aspect

Energy mages are capable of manipulating focused energy. More akin to concentrated beams of light than lightning, the energy mages are typically constrained to direct combat. They can also engage, in limited applications, in cutting things with unerring precision. Only Fearians possess the energy aspect.

Fire (red) mage aspect
The fire aspect is most noted for its destructive power, but it also carries the idea of purification and utility. Because of the highly limited imaginations of most, it is often simply weaponized as a mechanism of destruction. With both the power to invoke open flame, as well as the ability to dramatically raise the temperature of anything, fire mages are capable of a wide array of feats, assuming they possess the skill to control what they are doing. The fire aspect is a human aspect.

Ice (dark blue) mage aspect
The ice aspect is the corollary to fire, and it involves not just the generation of low temperature, but also of ice itself. Because cold cannot be readily identified by the eye, ice is a difficult aspect to manipulate with skill. Ice formed too quickly is dense and sinks in water; it can also be substantially colder than freezing, requiring an extensive amount of time to thaw. Though not as obviously destructive as fire, it can be no less deadly. This aspect is limited to humans.

Metamorphic mage aspect
The ability to transition one's physical form into that of other forms is the purview of the metamorphic aspect. The forms taken are limited to those living things that are real or can be imagined. The transformation need not be complete, such as the addition of wings, nor even more than taking on the appearance of another person. Because the mind is the basis for the transition,

the mind of the mage retains its full functionality regardless of the form taken. Metamorphosis is temporary for all but those most skilled with the aspect. This transformative power can be applied to others, though dramatic or long-term changes are difficult. Because of the nature of the aspect, a metamorphic mage can only change into a form of the same gender. Only humans can have the metamorphic aspect.

Mind mage aspect

The mind aspect involves numerical, rational, and logical contemplation. It permits those who harness it to think through multiple things in parallel, like having several, or even hundreds, of minds subservient to their own. It also provides an incredibly precise estimation of common physical parameters like velocity, mass, and distance. While seemingly not applicable in most contexts, many who master this aspect are a force to be reckoned with, as they can predict most material outcomes with a high degree of confidence. This makes them good strategists and excellent card players. Their main weakness lies in the fact that their predictions are predicated on what they believe to be true, whether or not those beliefs are actually true. Only Fearians can harness this aspect.

Mist mage aspect

Illusionary mage power can manipulate visual perception, making it eclectic in its applications. The mist itself is not fog; rather, it is a dispersed, occluding cloud of mage power. So long as the mist mage remains in contact with the mist, they can accomplish a diverse array of things relating to the senses, altering others' perception of vision, hearing, and even touch. A mist mage can also translocate instantly over short distances. Mist mages cannot themselves be deceived by the effects of the mist, or anything related to mage power, and are able to perceive things related to mage aspects over even great distances. The aspect of the mist only occurs among humans.

Rune mage aspect

Runes are inscriptions of mage power on objects, from clothes to weapons to books. The rune mage must practice his or her skills in both mage power and literacy of the runic language. Runes are sharp, angular symbols sharing geometries with triangles and squares, and the rune mage imparts power to them as they cut into or draw upon an object. Most rune work revolves around adding useful properties to practical objects, with more complex properties requiring more complex runes. During the mage war, however, some rune mages turned their power toward darker purposes.

Much knowledge of runic spelling, grammar, and syntax has been lost since the golden age. Only humans can become rune mages.

Sigil mage aspect

For a sigil mage, there are no small projects. Sigils are formed out of arcing lines reminiscent of circles. In a practical sense, sigils can be thought of as runes used on a massive scale. In a few cases, sigils can project similar effects to runes, but sigils only function when cut into stone or stone-like materials and require an external power source. Sigils work as arrays of complex patterns that, arguably, only sigil mages understand. The mage imparts power to the sigils through the initial design and through properly shaped citrine gemstones that store power. Sigils work in an either, or both, vector scalar fashion, and can be arranged three-dimensionally. After the golden age, most understanding of specific sigil function was lost, though many sigil-embedded structures created from that time remain. Sigil work is found only in the hands of Fearians.

Sonic (dark red) mage aspect

The sonic mage aspect is more complicated than it first appears. Ultimately, it deals with waveforms. The sonic aspect can induce, and halt, sounds in any amplitude and wave form. With the correct modulation, this can result in a gelling of the air itself as a consequence of constant even wave oscillation. In the right hands, a whisper can carry for miles, and a thunderclap cannot be heard at point-blank range. Because the aspect deals with waveforms, there is some application in other areas where waveforms occur, such as in a lake, or even in the mind. This aspect is restricted to humans.

Summoner mage aspect

While many of the aspects manipulate what is present, it is the summoner aspect that forms what is pure mage power. The entities created are endued with loyalty to the one who summoned them, and with intelligence in semblance to how the summoner perceives them. Summoned entities require a nearly constant level of mental effort from the summoner. Those skilled in the aspect can push this effort to the back of the mind, but its physical toll can be severely taxing. Summoned entities can operate much like their real-world counterparts, though they lack any will to oppose the one who summoned them into existence; neither are they introspective at any meaningful level. Though they can seem very real, they are truly only automatons. Mage tower watchers are essentially sigil-driven summoned entities. Only humans can invoke the summoner aspect.

Water mage aspect

The water mage is among the most versatile of mages, in part because of the high frequency of occurrence of their subject matter: water. Though a water mage can spontaneously generate and control massive amounts of water in an instant, this water is not created de novo, but rather drawn instantly and evenly from across all the available water in the world. Water mages are less immediately lethal than their fire mage counterparts. The water aspect is restricted to Fearians.

White mage aspect

The white mage aspect is the corollary to the black mage aspect. It is not health and healing as much as it is pre-generation. Living things are returned to their pre-damaged state, reversing injury and, in the most dramatic cases, death. The degree of power required is proportional to both the time since the injury or disease, and the degree of reversal needed. White mages excel as healers of injuries and disease, but are not so effective against birth defects or longstanding illnesses. Most white mages are also knowledgeable scholars of the human body, a knowledge that helps avoid false hope for those whose illnesses cannot be resolved by the mage's power.

From a pessimistic perspective, the white aspect merely delays the inevitable, while the black aspect merely accelerates it. Because it returns things to their former state, the white aspect is uniquely positioned to break rune-emblazoned objects by nullifying their runic state. The aspect itself is immutable, which is to say that it cannot exist in an accelerated decay (black aspect) or forced altered state (rune aspect). This aspect is only found among humans.

Creed *(khreed)* **Eastark**

Biography

Creed, the night caste Fearian grandson of the great
energy mage Grypni, fought in the great mage war three
thousand years ago. After being hit by a forbidden art
and possessed by a dark entity, he was locked in his
grandfather's mage tower until he was discovered and
rescued by Achron, who took him in as his adopted son.
Creed knows more of mage power and the golden age
than any other resident of Hona. Because of his difficult
past, he often focuses on negative events and emotions,
though his friendship with Sheena has greatly aided him
in joining in normal life at Castle Hona. His concern for
Sheena's best caused him to spend extensive time and
thought working through the ramifications of their
relationship, but the two are now engaged to be married.

Mage Power

Creed is a prodigy grand energy mage, capable of
powerful shows of the cutting forces of his mage aspect.
He carries the relic staff Orion, the power core. He holds
the mage title "the black star."

Dorra *(DOR-rah)* **Whiels Xis**

Biography

Widowed mother of Brea and Cilla, Dorra came to
live at Castle Hona after the townspeople of Wythwood
tried to kill her, suspicious of her rune-inscribed jewelry.
She was taken as an apprentice by Iekaruga to learn
more of mage power in written form. The two are now
married and have an infant son, Fennis.

Mage Power

Dorra is a master rune mage, and a frequent advisor in understanding rune-enhanced artifacts. She has utilized her runic abilities in her jewelry business as well. She possesses the relic staff Ferrilin, the etcher's point.

Eida *(EYE-dah)* Ostar

Biography

First encountered by Creed during a trip to Fearia to investigate the great mind mage Heket's tower, Eida is a young field caste Fearian girl who was strongly influenced by the anti-human Fearian contingent, particularly her own father. Meeting Achron and Viwy convinced her that humans were not the evil force she had assumed, but for her change in philosophy, she was banished from her home and from Fearia. She is slowly adjusting to life at Hona Castle. Eida is a direct descendant of Heket.

Mage Power

Eida is a prodigy mind mage, but as a female Fearian not of age, she cannot yet use her power. Achron and Iekaruga are discussing the possibility of giving her a fertility rune to accelerate her access to her mage abilities. She is the current holder of the relic staff Yindil, the infinite sum.

Empleheim *(EHM-pul-hiem)*

Geography

Empleheim is located in the northern woods, south of the Aeinor mountains. It experiences four seasons, but due to its overall cooler climate, its agriculture is predominated by winter crops. The mountains provide granite and metal mining opportunities.

History

A wealthy and influential kingdom on the human side of space, Empleheim lost everything in one bizarre moment. As the curse from the Fearian side reacted with Achron's white mage power just at the time he was experimenting with time reversal, a strange catalyzation ripped Achron and every structure and object in Empleheim from the plane of time. Its people were left standing in an empty country. Having lost their national identity, their possessions, and their livelihoods, the Empleheimians dispersed into surrounding nations.

Places

The grandest and most significant city in Empleheim was its capital Niado, which straddles the banks of the river Rylet. After being returned to time, most of Niado sits as a decaying ruin. But Hona Castle, once the center of the kingdom's government and home to the royal family, is now the lively home of the Windslo family and their friends. The land around Hona Castle is slowly being reclaimed and repurposed to support the needs of the new residents of Niado.

People

The kingdom of Empleheim is the birthplace of Achron. It was also the home of his fiancée Emeril, who waited there for him after the Empleheim event, in hopes that he would return to her one day. Her grave is located outside the city of Niado. Its current population is contained at Castle Hona.

Current Status

Due to its sudden disappearance a thousand years ago, Empleheim has a reputation as a cursed land, and it has been largely left alone by the surrounding countries. Within its former capital city, a small but growing group of Fearians and humans are restoring it to life.

Fearia *(FEER-ee-ah)*

History

Fearia is one of the two mirrored sides of space. Its population is entirely made of the Fearian people, whose pointed ears, manes, and tails visibly distinguish them from humans. There are only two ways to travel between the Fearian and human sides: through sigil gates, which have been shut down since the great mage war, or by the mage power of certain Fearians trained in spatial translocation (gold mage aspect). Fearia has been troubled by the presence of evil forces, monstrous creatures that seem to exist solely for murder and mayhem, for as long as anyone can remember.

Places

Fearia's capital city is Ravenloc, a gleaming white city built on an island in the middle of a large lake. The land is divided among the various castes (see Caste System, below), and each major caste has its own capital as well, including Frinwood, the capital of Keena's forest caste.

People

Keena, Iekaruga, Ahnya, Prinial, and Eida are all natives of Fearia. Keena's mother, the Fearian High Queen Yanna, lives in Ravenloc.

Caste System

Fearian culture contains a number of complex and, to a human, confusing elements, including a caste system. Land usage is divided by caste, and each caste has an overall purpose that contributes to Fearian society. While there is room for individual variability, each caste can be distinguished in appearance by mane length, mane color, tail length, tail pattern, tail shape, and other features.

Golden Chronicle

The golden chronicle is a substantial tome that records Fearian history dating to before the great mage war. Its metal covers are sealed with a powerful blessing and can be opened by few. Its history is organized into three distinct columns, each speaking from a different point of view. Two copies of the golden chronicle exist, the original in Fearia and a reserve copy on the human side. Keena serves as guardian of the reserve copy, which is currently in the library at Castle Hona.

Great mages

Auriga

Auriga was the great mage of the white aspect. She possessed the majestic opal. Ferir was hopeful that a powerful white mage working in tandem with the majestic opal could heal his grandson Tonis of his inborn illness, but Auriga had already passed away by that time.

Ferir

Ferir was the great mage of the sonic (dark red) aspect. He possessed the majestic spinel. His mage tower was located in the canyon called the earth scar or spline mark, and was in nearly perfect condition before Creed removed Tonis from its watcher system. He was the grandfather of Tonis and the human chronicler of the golden chronicle.

Grypni

Grypni was the great mage of the energy aspect. He possessed the majestic idocrase. His mage tower, now in ruins, was located just outside the city of Niado. He was the grandfather of Creed and Hanni.

Heket

Heket was the great mage of the mind aspect. She possessed the majestic chrysoprase. Her mage tower was located in the field caste region of Fearia, and its ruins served as Eida's refuge from her difficult life. She was an ancestor of Eida and the Fearian chronicler of the golden chronicle.

Kurri

Kurri was the great mage of the ice (dark blue) aspect. She possessed the majestic aquamarine. Her mage tower, located on the Fearian side of the Aeinor mountains, was encased in an enormous ice shell by Leen's mage burst during the great mage war, and subsequently destroyed by collapsing ice.

Seleen

Seleen was the great mage of the silver aspect. She possessed the majestic diamond. During the great mage war, she stole the majestic gems from the other great mages and took them outside of time.

Hanni *(HAH-nee)* Innohan

Biography

The granddaughter of the great mage Grypni and cousin to Creed, Hanni was subjected to a rune mage's enslavement via a runic curse engraved on her skin. Integrated into Grypni's tower's defense system since the time of the mage war, she was rescued by Achron from the curse that robbed her of her memories, her personality, and her will. She has regained her ability to speak and function normally, though she cannot remember anything of her past. Taken in by Achron and Keena, she has grown particularly close to her adopted sister Rin.

Mage Power

Hanni is a prodigy grand fire (red) mage. She is unaffected by fire and can produce, control, and extinguish it with great finesse. She wields the relic staff Behemoth, the terrible flame.

Harku *(HAHR-koo)* Loon ("Fishy")

Biography

While he sneaked into Castle Hona disguised as a cat, Harku is, in reality, a metamorphic mage from the gryphon clan sequestered in the Dagger Peaks. He is the current golden gryphon, intended to be the next clan leader. However, when he was ordered to marry his own sister to take his rightful headship, he fled, seeking another red-haired girl to substitute in Arru's place. Although he discovered Rin and brought her back to the clan, he was refused and banished by his father. He now lives at Hona Castle and is engaged to be married to Rin.

Mage Power

Harku is a prodigy grand metamorphic mage, capable of turning himself and others into a variety of forms and altering appearances. He holds the relic staff Ribble, the shapeless form.

Iekaruga *(EE-kah-RU-gah)* Xis

Biography

A mountain caste Fearian, Iekaruga is married to Dorra, with whom he has an infant son named Fennis, and stepfather to Dorra's daughters Brea and Cilla. He spends most of his time studying the sigil system that runs under Niado or tutoring his apprentices and the Windslo children in the mage arts.

Mage Power

Iekaruga is a sigil mage dedicated to recovering the lost sigil arts from the golden age of the great mages. He carries the relic staff Monicle, the inscriber's quill.

Keena *(KEE-nah)* Mirestial Windslo

Biography

Keena first met Achron when she begged him to kill her, to prevent the Blue Serpent mages from forcing her to open the golden chronicle, of which she is the keeper. Achron rescued her by taking them both out of time, an act that accidentally bound them in space and time. In place of paying her life debt to Achron with servitude or equal measure, she gave him the free gift of her love by marrying him. They have twenty-four children, all forest caste Fearian like their mother. Keena manages the castle life and is often a voice of reason to her husband and others.

Leen Fea'sol

Biography

Like Creed, Hanni, and Tonis, Leen hails from the time of the great mage war. When Achron sought to close the sigil gate in the Aeinor mountains, the ice mage prodigy was discovered frozen alive in the gigantic ice dome formed by his own mage burst at the great mage Kurri's tower. After Hanni released him from his icy enclosure, he agreed to come live at Castle Hona, for lack of anywhere else to go. Leen generally acts in an arrogant and forceful way toward others. He is a direct descendant of the great ice mage Kurri Fea'sol.

Mage Power

Leen is a prodigy ice (dark blue) mage, though he had depleted his power via a mage burst when he was first found. He is the current wielder of Creiallis, the frozen tear.

Loral *(LOH-rahl)* **Elushia**

Biography

Loral comes from the people group that lives along the cold coastlines to the north of Empleheim. When she began to see and create inexplicable things at age eight, she was banished from her village as "cursed." The entities she had unintentionally summoned helped her survive, but also drained her energy to the point she could barely function when Achron and Emeril found her. After Achron freed her from her bond to the entities, he brought her back to live at Hona Castle, where she could learn to control her power.

Mage Power

Loral is a prodigy summoner mage, though neither she nor her village were previously aware of mage power. She can create entities from pure mage power.

Mage Classes

Apprentice mage

An apprentice mage is the first level at which someone can be objectively recognized as a mage. The apprentice knows how to access their mage aspect but has little to no control over it. At this level, they lack sufficient power to be a danger to anyone; however, prodigies are an important exception.

Novice mage

A novice mage is distinguished from an apprentice by the ability to hold consistent control over their aspect with the aid of a staff. Without a staff, they are not able to control it.

Master mage

A master mage exceeds a novice by having "mastered" the ability to control their mage aspect even without a staff. However, as with all but the great mages, a master mage sans staff has substantially reduced power.

Higher mage

A higher mage is set apart from a master mage in that they have refined their channeling of their aspect to the point that it flows freely through them while they manipulate it. As a result, their skin glows in a color corresponding to their mage aspect and to the amount of power being drawn for the task at hand.

Grand mage

A grand mage is no longer limited to carrying their staff with them, but can instead draw it into existence out of their aspect. The staff is reduced to the immaterial part of their aspect when not in use, meaning that they, so long as they are conscious, cannot be separated from their staff, and hence their power. The caveat to this is that only the relic staves created by the great mages of old are capable of persisting in this condition.

Great mage

The great mages ushered in the golden age. Their power was unparalleled, and they accomplished a wide array of feats that seem impossible in the current time. It was great mages who created the relics (staves and otherwise) and built the mage towers. Their power is believed to have been nearly limitless, and they had no need of staves at all. Their legacy is left in ruins, and their power sequestered in the majestic gems of yore. It is not currently known how one becomes a great mage, but since they appeared in a previously mage-less existence, it is thought that one cannot reach this level of capacity apart from some outside influence.

Mekki *(MEH-kee)* **Ousnum Teekin**

Biography

The sea caste Fearian Mekki, along with her brother Pyx, was sent by the Fearian high queen to aid Keena and Achron when their second litter was to be born. Although Mekki initially despised humans, she eventually came to respect Achron and to love Viwy, to whom she is now married. Mekki and Viwy have six children of their own, and she also helps with many of the more mundane aspects of castle life.

Prinial *(PRIHN-ee-ahl)* **Quirieyo**

Biography
The most promising of Iekaruga's apprentices, Prinial came to Castle Hona, along with her master Iekaruga and her sister Ahnya, in pursuit of understanding the sigils left behind from the golden age. She is steady, calm, and thoughtful—in essence, the complete opposite of her sister in personality, though the Fearian mountain caste girls look much alike. Prinial has come to enjoy spending much of her time with Achron and Keena's son Dane.

Mage Power
Prinial is a prodigy higher sigil mage with a strong aptitude for writing and interpreting the swirly-lined marks. Her staff is a simple wooden one, topped with a citrine stone and inlayed with sigil-etched granite.

Pyx *(piks)* **Ousnum**

Biography
From the time he and his sister Mekki came to Castle Hona, Pyx's primary task has been helping to watch and care for Achron and Keena's many children. He has been pursued by Addie since she was quite young, and after an unfortunate practical joke nearly separated them permanently, the two often share Pyx's duties and are now engaged to be married. As a sea caste Fearian, Pyx is shorter than many of the older children he is responsible for.

Relic Staves

Each of the twenty-four great mages created a potent staff aligned with his or her mage aspect. In the current age, these are known as the relic staves.

Arbik, the yellow eye

Arbik is the relic staff of the mist aspect. It is currently held by Viwy. Made of ebony wood, its narrow height is topped by a latticework sphere that contains a cymophane stone. Arbik can produce a shrouding mist and can reveal hidden objects. Viwy uses its power in seeing beyond sight.

Behemoth, the terrible flame

Behemoth is the relic staff of the fire (red) aspect. It is currently held by Hanni. Its metal shaft is decorated by six large rubies, set in pairs on the upper part of the staff. Hanni can summon her staff from pure fire.

Creiallis, the frozen tear

Creiallis is the relic staff of the ice (dark blue) aspect. It is currently held by Leen. Formed out of pure crystal, the shaft of the staff flows smoothly into the large, oval aquamarine gemstone at its top. The gemstone is flattened laterally and covered in symmetrical facets on both faces.

Ferrilin, the etcher's point

Ferrilin is the relic staff of the rune aspect. It is currently held by Dorra. Ferrilin's shaft is metal, separating into two tines at the top that support a large piece of amber between them. The shaft is also engraved with repeated bands of angular shapes.

Leviathan, the raging sea

Leviathan is the relic staff of the water aspect. It is currently held by Ahnya. Leviathan's metal shaft is shaped like a tuning fork, with a large emerald-cut blue zoisite suspended between its tines. Ahnya summons it from water she draws from the ground.

Monicle, the inscriber's quill

Monicle is the relic staff of the sigil aspect. It is currently held by Iekaruga. A cylinder of stone flanked by lengths of an off-white wood, Monicle is capped by a large square-cut citrine stone. With Monicle's power, Iekaruga is able to trace sigil power back to its source, even over great distances.

Ontomana, the deafening silence

Ontomana is the relic staff of the sonic (dark red) aspect. It is currently held by Tonis. The black wooden staff forms a narrow point at one end and an open, circular hoop at the other. Within the hoop is suspended a cube of deep red spinel, held in place only by sonic waves.

Orion, the power core

Orion is the relic staff of the energy aspect. It is currently held by Creed. The top of the metallic staff is an idocrase cut into an octahedron, held in place by four tines that meet at its crest. By sigil enhancement via a citrine stone, Orion can be shortened and extended.

Ribble, the shapeless form

Ribble is the relic staff of the metamorphic aspect. It is currently held by Harku. This staff is made of a fine-grained, soft yellow wood that is cut in a fern-like spiral at the top. In the center of the spiral is a diamond-cut imperial topaz.

Tianna, the silver star

Tianna is the relic staff of the white aspect. It is
currently held by Achron. Tianna's haft is made of silver
and is lined with semispherical opals patterned in swirls
along the whole length of the staff. At its base, Tianna's
shaft forms a triangular point, and at its top, a fluted, six-
point sconce. The sconce serves as the resting place for
the Aegeis.

Yindil, the infinite sum

Yindil is the relic staff of the mind aspect. It is
currently held by Eida. Yindil is simple in appearance,
with a shaft of ribbed brown wood crowned by a fist-
sized cabochon chrysoprase.

Seifer *(SEE-fur)* Jihue

Biography

Orphaned at a young age and left to fend for
himself, Seifer came to Hona Castle by hiding in the
wagon Achron and Hanni brought back from their first
supplies run to the human city of Wythwood. He knew
nothing of mage power, only that he had always been
able to change objects to stone, although inconsistently.
Creed was instantly concerned, since the earth aspect
belongs only to Fearians, but in time it was revealed by
Harku that Seifer was actually a metamorphosed
Fearian, and not human at all. Seifer has attempted to act
on his interest in Emeril, but she has refused him in no
uncertain terms.

Mage Power

Seifer is a novice earth mage, capable of turning

items to stone and reverting them again. Under the instruction of Iekaruga, he is gaining knowledge and aptitude in the use of mage power.

Tonis *(TOE-nihs)* Ruttoson

Biography

While he was born a prodigy in the era of the great mage war, Tonis was also born with a serious illness that prevented him from taking active part in the conflict. To preserve his life, he was integrated into the watcher system in the tower of his grandfather, the great mage Ferir Ruttoson. There he was discovered and rescued by Creed and Arnna. Upon their arrival at Hona Castle, Achron cured him by calling on the power of the majestic opal. Tonis is noted for his exceptionally beautiful voice and his gift for music, which he is now trying to share with the children of Hona.

Mage Power

Tonis is a prodigy grand sonic mage, highly skilled at the manipulation of sounds and other waveforms. He is the wielder of Ontomana, the deafening silence. He holds the mage title "the silent song."

Viwy *(vwee)* Teekin

Biography

Viwy stumbled across Hona while he was searching for the source of mage power he detected near Niado (which was Grypni's tower). After some initial confusion about Fearians, he settled into the Windslo family life as the castle's watcher. He is married to Mekki, and they have six children from one litter. Viwy often accompanies Achron on missions away from

Niado due to his sight beyond sight and his abilities with concealment.

Mage Power

Viwy is a higher mist mage. He can translocate himself and others close to him via mist; produce vividly lifelike illusions; and detect people and items associated with mage power. He wields the relic staff Arbik, the yellow eye.

The Windslo Children

Sheena

The firstborn child of Achron and Keena, with blond hair, a brown mane, and green eyes. She is the majestic idocrase. She is engaged to Creed.

Rin

The second child of the first litter, with red hair, a dark red mane, and brown eyes. She is the majestic ruby. She is engaged to Harku.

Kraysin

The third child of the first litter, with brown hair, a dark brown mane, and blue eyes. He is the majestic sapphire.

Dane

The fourth child of the first litter, with blond hair, a blond mane, and blue-green eyes. He is the majestic opal.

Addie

The fifth child of the first litter, with reddish blond hair, a reddish blond mane, and light brown eyes. She is the majestic amber. She is engaged to Pyx.

Emeril

The sixth child of the first litter, with light brown hair, a brown mane, and light green eyes. She is the majestic peridot.

Thiesa

The first child of the second litter (seventh overall), with dark brown hair, a brown mane, and purple eyes. She is the majestic amethyst.

Marral

The second child of the second litter (eighth overall), with orange-blond hair, an auburn mane, and purple eyes. He is the majestic ametrine.

Harto

The third child of the second litter (ninth overall), with brown hair, a dark brown mane, and green-blue eyes. He is the majestic aquamarine.

Byrn

The fourth child of the second litter (tenth overall), with dark red hair, a dark red mane, and brown eyes. He is the majestic spinel.

Zollen

The fifth child of the second litter (eleventh overall), with blond hair, a dark blond mane, and dark blue eyes. He is the majestic zoisite.

Shay

The first child of the third litter (twelfth overall), with light brown hair, a blond mane, and hazel eyes. He is the majestic topaz.

Kayanna

The second child of the third litter (thirteenth overall), with auburn hair, an auburn mane, and hazel eyes. She is the majestic citrine.

Kokkino

The third child of the third litter (fourteenth overall), with dark red hair, a blond mane, and brown eyes. She is the majestic garnet.

Niia

The fourth child of the third litter (fifteenth overall), with pink hair, a blond mane, and green eyes. Along with her identical twin sister Norra, she is the majestic tourmaline.

Norra

The fifth child of the third litter (sixteenth overall), with pink hair, a blond mane, and green eyes. Along with her identical twin sister Niia, she is the majestic tourmaline.

Gray

The first child of the fourth litter (seventeenth overall), with blond hair, a white mane, and gray eyes. He is the majestic diamond.

Weth

The second child of the fourth litter (eighteenth overall), with dark brown hair, a dark brown mane, and green eyes. He is the majestic emerald.

Krysi

The third child of the fourth litter (nineteenth overall), with white blond hair, a white blond mane, and dark blue eyes. She is the majestic cymophane.

Yirrum

The fourth child of the fourth litter (twentieth overall), with blond hair, a dark blond mane, and amber eyes. He is the majestic sphene.

Rhesa

The fifth child of the fourth litter (twenty-first overall), with pink hair, a red mane, and blue eyes. She is the majestic morganite.

Onni

The sixth child of the fourth litter (twenty-second overall), with black hair, a black mane, a green left eye and blue right eye. He is the majestic onyx.

Inno

The seventh child of the fourth litter (twenty-third overall), with black hair, a black mane, a blue left eye and green right eye. She is the majestic obsidian.

Adderil

The eight child of the fourth litter (twenty-fourth overall), with blond hair, a brown mane, and green eyes. He is the majestic chrysophrase.

Thank you for reading our book!
We hope you enjoyed it.

If you would like to contact us, or to find out more about
our other books and latest news,
visit us at dartkaymckinney.com.

9 781087 974248